ALSO BY TILLIE COLE

A Thousand Boy Kisses

a thousand broken

Pieces

a novel

Tillie Cole

Bloom *books*

Published by Bloom Books, an imprint of Sourcebooks
P.O. Box 4410, Naperville, Illinois 60567-4410
(630) 961-3900
sourcebooks.com

Cataloging-in-Publication data is on file with the Library of Congress.

Printed and bound in the United States of America.
LSC 10 9 8 7 6 5 4 3 2 1

For those who have lost a loved one, I walk with you.
For those who have lost a piece of their heart, I hold your hand.
For those who don't know how to move on,
I pray this book gives you solace.

For Dad.
I will miss you forever.
Until we see each other again.
"Endure Fort"

"I have come to understand that death, for the sick, is not so hard to endure. For us, eventually our pain ends, we go to a better place. But for those left behind, their pain only magnifies."

—POPPY, *A THOUSAND BOY KISSES*

Prologue

Savannah
Age thirteen
Blossom Grove, Georgia

I COULDN'T HEAR ANYTHING BUT THE DEAFENING BEATING OF MY HEART. Too fast in rhythm, thundering like the destructive summer storms that ripped through Georgia when the heat soared.

My breathing grew labored as my lungs began to slowly cease to function. The air that was in my chest hardened into granite boulders, pushing down on me so hard that I was frozen in place. Frozen looking at Poppy fading away in the bed. Seeing my parents clutching on to one another like they were dying too. Their baby, their first daughter losing her fight with cancer before our very eyes, death hovering beside her like an ominous shadow, readying to take her away. Aunt DeeDee stood with her arms wrapped around her waist as though it was the only thing keeping her standing.

I felt Ida squeezing my hand so hard she could have broken bones. I felt my younger sister's slight body trembling, no doubt with fear or pain or complete disbelief that this could actually be real.

That this was *actually* happening.

My face was soaked with the tears that fell in rapids from my eyes.

"Savannah? Ida?" my mama said softly. I blinked through the watery haze until I saw my mama before us. I began to shake my head, my body seeming to jerk back to life from its numbed, catatonic state.

"No…" I whispered, feeling Ida's terrified gaze fix onto me. "Please…" I added, my near silent plea drifting into vapor in the stagnant air around us.

Mama bent down and ran her trembling hand down my cheek. "You need to say goodbye, baby." Her voice wobbled—hoarse and exhausted. She looked over her shoulder, to where Rune was sitting on the bed, laying kiss after kiss on my older sister's hands, her fingers, her face, looking at his Poppymin like he always had—like she had been designed solely for him. A choked cry escaped my lips as I watched them.

It wasn't real. This *couldn't* be real. She couldn't leave him. She couldn't leave *us*…

"Girls," Mama pushed again, urgency in her tone. My heart fractured when Mama's bottom lip began to tremble. "She…" Mama closed her eyes, trying to gather some kind of composure, cutting off whatever she was going to say. I didn't know how she did it. I couldn't. I couldn't face this. I couldn't *do* this.

"Sav," Ida said from beside me. I turned to look at my little sister. At her dark hair, green eyes, and deep-set dimples, her skin, which was red from crying. At her sweet, heartbroken face. "We have to." Her voice was shaking. But she nodded her head at me in encouragement. Right now, Ida had more strength than I could muster.

Ida stood, never loosening her iron-tight grip on my hand as she guided me up. When I was on my feet, I glanced down at our clasped hands. Soon, this is how it would forever be. Just our two hands, no third to hold, to guide us.

I followed behind Ida, each step feeling like I was wading through molasses as we approached the bed. It was positioned to look out of the window. So Poppy could see outside. Falling pink and white cherry blossom petals drifted by on the breeze, scattering onto the ground as they dropped from the trees. Rune looked up as we approached, but I couldn't meet his eyes. I wasn't strong enough to see him at that moment. The moment we had all been dreading. The one, deep down, I never really believed would arrive.

As I took as deep a breath as I could, Ida and I rounded the bed. The first thing I heard was Poppy's breathing. It had changed. It was deep and rattly, and I could see the exhaustion, the struggle on her pretty face…

The effort it was taking her to simply hold on for just a few minutes more. To remain with us for as long as she could. Yet, despite it all, she widened her smile when she saw us. Her sisters. Her best friends.

Our Poppy…the best person I had ever known.

Lifting her thin, frail hands, Poppy held one out for each of us to hold. I closed my eyes when I felt how cold she was, how weak her grip was now.

"I love you, Poppy," Ida whispered. I opened my eyes and fought not to fall to the floor as Ida laid her head on Poppy's chest and held her tightly. Poppy closed her eyes and pressed the ghost of a kiss on Ida's head.

"I love…you too…Ida," she replied, holding on to our younger sister like she would never let her go. Ida was Poppy's double in every way—her personality, her looks, her always-positive outlook on life. Poppy's fingers ran through Ida's dark hair. "Never change," she murmured as Ida lifted her head. Poppy placed her weakening hand on Ida's cheek.

"I won't," Ida said, her voice breaking as she stood back, reluctantly letting her hand fall from Poppy's. I focused on that release. I didn't know why, but I wanted Ida to hold on to our sister. Maybe if we just held on to her, together, Poppy wouldn't have to go, maybe we could keep her here where she was safe…

"Sav…" Poppy whispered, her eyes shining as I met her gaze.

I crumbled, my face falling as I began to sob. "Poppy…" I said, taking hold of her hand and holding it to me. I was shaking my head, over and over, silently begging God, the universe, *anyone* to stop this, to bless us with a miracle and keep her here with us, even if it was for just a bit longer.

"I'm…okay…" Poppy said, cutting through my silent pleas. Her hand was trembling, I brought it to my lips, to press a kiss to her cold skin. But when I did, I saw that Poppy's hand was steady and the trembling was mine. Tears tumbled down my cheeks. "Savannah," Poppy said, "I am…ready…to go…"

"No," I said, shaking my head. I felt a hand land on my back and an arm thread around my waist. I knew it was Mama and Ida keeping me upright. "I'm not ready… I need you… You're my older sister… I need you, Poppy."

My chest ached to the point of pain, and I knew it was my heart splintering into tiny fragmented pieces.

"I'll…always be…with…you," Poppy said, and I noticed a sallowness to her skin, heard the terrifying rattle in her breathing deepen and grow more erratic. *No…no, no, no…* "We will…" Poppy sucked in a faint breath, a *fading* gasp of air, "meet again…"

"Poppy…" I managed to say, before racking sobs took hold of me. I lowered my head to Poppy's chest and felt her weak arms encase me. She may have been losing strength, but that hold felt like a secure blanket around me. I didn't want to let go.

"I …love you…Savannah. So…much," Poppy said, fighting her slowing breath to speak. I squeezed my eyes shut, trying in vain to hold on. Poppy pressed a kiss to my hair.

"Savannah." Mama's voice sailed into my ears. "Baby…" she murmured. I lifted my head and met Poppy's weak smile.

"I love you, Pops," I said. "You've been the best big sister I could ever ask for." Poppy swallowed and her eyes shimmered with tears. I studied her face. She was so close to leaving us. I memorized the green of her eyes, the natural streaks of warmth in her dark hair. She was pale now, but I held on to the memory of the peach tone of her soft skin. I held on to the memory of her sweet scent wrapping around me, to her face full of laughter and life.

I didn't want to let go of her hand, I didn't know if I ever would be able to, but as Mama squeezed my shoulders, I did, refusing to disconnect from her gaze until Mama and Daddy moved beside the bed and blocked her from my view.

I stumbled back, shock settling in. Ida gripped my hand and curled into my chest. I watched, almost dissociated, as Mama and Daddy kissed and held Poppy and said their goodbyes. White noise filled my ears as Mama and Daddy moved back and Rune approached the bed. I stayed, transfixed, Ida breaking down against my chest, Aunt DeeDee, Mama, and Daddy falling apart to the side of the room as Rune said something to Poppy, then leaned down and kissed her on her lips…

I held my breath as, seconds later, he slowly reared back. And I watched it. I watched Rune's face and saw in his shattered expression that she had gone. That Poppy had left us…

Rune's head was shaking as my heart was impossibly, cracking even more. Then he bolted from the room, and as he did, I slammed back into the here and now with a deafening crash. The sound of agonized crying was the first thing that greeted me, the devastating noises slicing my soul in half. I looked at Mama, then Daddy. Mama had fallen to the floor, Daddy trying to keep her in his arms. Aunt DeeDee was turned against the wall that was propping her up, sobbing uncontrollably.

"Sav," Ida cried, gripping tighter on to my waist. I held Ida close. Held her as I stared at the bed. Stared at Poppy's hand. Her hand that lay unmoving on the bed. Her *empty*, still hand. Everything seemed to be happening in slow motion, like some camera trick used in the movies.

But this was real life. This was *our* house. And that was *my* beloved sister on the bed. On the bed with no one beside her.

Mama reached for Ida. My little sister fell into our parents' embrace, but I was moving forward like a magnet was drawing me close to Poppy. Like some invisible force, some transparent thread, was beckoning me to where she lay.

On a stuttered breath, I rounded the bed. And I stilled. I stilled as I stared down at Poppy. No breath came from her mouth. There was no rise of her chest, no flush to her cheeks. Yet, she was as beautiful in death as she was in life. Then my gaze dropped to her empty hand again. It was upturned, like it wanted to be held, just one last time.

So I sat on the edge of the bed and wrapped my hand in hers. And as I sat there, I felt something in me change. In that moment, I lost something in my soul that I knew I would never get back. I brought Poppy's cooling fingers to my lips and pressed a kiss to her soft skin. Then I lowered our entwined hands to my lap. And I didn't let go. I *wouldn't* let go.

I wasn't sure I ever could.

Lost Breaths and Moving Clouds

Savannah
Age seventeen
Blossom Grove, Georgia

THERE WERE PRECISELY FORTY-TWO CRACKS ON THE LINOLEUM FLOOR. Rob, the therapy leader, was talking, but all I heard was the tinny drone from the heating system whirring above us. My gaze was unfocused, catching only spears of daylight slicing through the high windows and the blurred outlines of the others in the circle around me.

"Savannah?" I blinked my eyes into focus, glancing up at Rob. He was smiling at me, body language open and an encouraging smile on his face. I shifted nervously on my seat. I wasn't blessed with the skill of talking out loud. I struggled to put words to the turbulent feelings stirring inside me. I was better on my own. Being around people for too long drained me; too many of them made me close in on myself. I was nothing like my sister, Ida, whose personality was infectious and gregarious.

Just like Poppy...

I swallowed the instant lump that sprouted in my throat. It had been almost four years. Four long, excruciating years without her, and I still couldn't think of her name or picture her pretty face without feeling my heart collapse on me like a mountain caving in. Without feeling the shadow of death's unyielding fingers wrap around my lungs and starve them of air.

The knowing pangs of anxiety immediately began clawing their way up from the depths of where they slumbered. Sinking their teeth into my veins and sending their poison flooding through my body until it had captured me as its unwilling hostage.

My palms grew damp and my breathing became heavy. "Savannah." Rob's voice had changed; even though it echoed in my ears as everything around me tunneled into a narrow void, I heard its worried inflection. Feeling the weight of everyone's stares on me, I jumped up from my seat and bolted for the door. My footsteps were an arrhythmic drumbeat as I followed the stream of light in the hallway toward the open air. I burst through the door to the outside and sucked in the wintery Georgia air.

Dancing spotlights invaded my vision, and I stumbled to the tree that sat in the grounds of the therapy center. I leaned on the heavy trunk, but my legs gave way and I dropped to the hard soil. I closed my eyes and laid my head against the wood, the rough bark scratching the back of my scalp. I focused on breathing, on trying to remember every lesson I had ever been taught about coping with an anxiety attack. But it never seemed to help. The attacks always held me hostage until they were finally willing to release me.

I was utterly exhausted.

My body trembled for what felt like an age, heart sputtering and lurching until I felt my lungs begin to loosen, my windpipe finally granting my body the oxygen it so badly craved. I inhaled through my nose and out through my mouth until I sagged farther into the tree, the smell of grass and earth breaking through anxiety's sensory-blocking fog.

I opened my eyes and looked up at the bright blue sky, watched the white clouds traveling up ahead, trying to find shapes in their structures. I watched them appear, then leave, and wondered what it looked like from up there, what they saw when they looked down upon us all, loving and losing and falling apart.

A droplet of water landed on the back of my hand. I glanced down, only to catch another drop fall on my ring finger's knuckle—they were coming from my cheeks. Exhaustion rippled over me, consuming all my strength. I couldn't even lift my hands to wipe away the tears. So I focused on watching the journeying clouds again, wishing I could be like them, constantly moving, never having time to stop to process and think.

Thinking gave me space to break.

I didn't even realize someone had sat down beside me until I felt a subtle shift in the air around me. The clouds still held my attention.

"Anxiety attack again?" Rob said. I nodded, my hair rubbing against the loose bark that was scarcely holding on to its home. Rob was only in his thirties. He was kind and was exceptional at what he did. He helped so many people. Over the past four years I'd seen a myriad of teenagers come through the therapy center's door and leave, changed, empowered, and able to function once more in the world.

I was simply broken.

I didn't know how to heal, how to put myself back together again. The truth was, when Poppy died, all light vanished from my world, and I'd been stumbling around in the dark ever since.

Rob didn't speak for a while but finally said, "We have to change tactics, Savannah." The edge of my lips lifted as I saw what looked like a daisy form in a cloud. Ida loved daisies. They were her favorite flower. Rob leaned back against the tree beside me, sharing the wide trunk. "We've received some funding." His words trickled into my ears one syllable at a time as the world, painstakingly slowly, began to stitch itself back together. "There's a trip," he said, letting that hang in the air between us. I blinked, the sun's afterimage dancing in the darkness when I squeezed my eyes shut to banish its blinding glow.

"I want you to go on it," Rob said. I froze and eventually turned my head to face him. Rob had short red hair, freckles, and piercing green eyes. He was a walking autumnal color palette. He was also a survivor. To say I admired him was an understatement. Punished as a teen for his sexuality by those who were meant to love him, he had fought his way through hell to reach freedom and happiness, now helping others who struggled in their own ways too.

"There's a trip... I want you to go on it..."

Those delayed words filtered into my brain and my old friend anxiety began to reemerge.

"A small group from all over the States is going on a five-country journey. One of healing." He rolled his head to look up at the clouds that had previously captured my attention. "Teens dealing with grief."

I shook my head, every second making it more and more pronounced.

"I can't," I whispered, instant fear wrapping around my voice.

Rob's smile was sympathetic, but he said, "I've already spoken to your parents, Savannah. They've agreed it would be good for you. We've already secured your place."

"No!"

"You've already finished high school. And you've gotten into Harvard. *Harvard*, Savannah. That's incredible." Rob briefly paused to think but then added, "That's Boston. Far, far away from here."

I understood the subtext. I couldn't function at home, so how on earth would I function in another state at college?

When Poppy died, I threw myself into my studies. I had to occupy my mind at all times. It was how I stayed above water. I had always been studious. I had always been the smart one. The bookworm. The one who talked of physics and equations and molecular structures. Ida was the loud one, the dramatic sister, the funny one, capturing all the attention—in all the best ways. And Poppy…Poppy had been the dreamer. She had been the believer, the creative one, the one with music and never-ending happiness and hope in her heart.

The one who would have changed the world.

When Pops died, I couldn't face school anymore—people's stares, the sorrowful glances, the spotlight that followed me around, broadcasting me as the girl who had watched her older sister die. So I homeschooled, and I graduated early. Harvard accepted me; I'd done enough to get in. But with all my schoolwork complete, my newly found time became my enemy. Idle hours spent reliving Poppy fading, her slowly dying before us. Endless minutes that gave my anxiety breathing room to strike, to draw out its advances like mercenaries toying with an easy target. I felt Poppy's absence like a noose pulling tighter around my neck day by day.

"I know it might seem frightening. I know it's something you might not believe you can do," Rob said, his voice gentle and encouraging. "But you *can*, Savannah. I believe in you." I felt my bottom lip tremble as I met his eyes. "I'm not giving up." A gentle smile. "We're going to get you through this. We're going to get you to Harvard this fall. And you're going to thrive."

I wanted to smile back, to show my appreciation for him even thinking of me, for never quitting on me, but nerves held me back. New people. New places. Unknown lands—it was utterly terrifying. But I had no fight left in me to contest it. And Lord, nothing else had worked for me. Four long years of individual and group therapy hadn't been able to lift me back up or put me back together again. I was too tired to argue. So I turned my head again and stared back up at the sky. A large cloud rolled in, and I stilled.

It looked exactly like a cello.

I entered Blossom Grove to the symphonic soundtrack of singing birds. No matter the time of year, there was always something unearthly about this place. A slice of heaven placed down on Earth, a glimpse of the celestial, of peace. Or maybe it was just whose spirit rested here that made it so special. Protecting the place that she adored so much.

The trees were bare, the buds of the blossoms not yet ready to show us their beauty, winter keeping them at bay for just a little while longer. But it didn't make the grove any less beautiful. I breathed in the fresh air that whistled through the brown branches until my feet led me to the tree that protected my best friend.

The white marble headstone shone like an angel in the lowering sun, dusk blanketing the grave in idyllic golden hues. Poppy Litchfield stood out in golden writing, Forever Always etched underneath.

I wiped some fallen leaves from the top of the headstone and sat down before it. "Hello, Poppy," I said, already feeling my throat grow tight. I knew that for many, four years after the death of a loved one was enough for them to find their way back to some kind of life. To move on in whatever way they could. Yet for me, four years may have well been four minutes. It felt like only yesterday that Poppy left us—left Ida and me. Left Mama and Daddy and

Aunt DeeDee. Left Rune. The fractures that splintered through my heart were still open and unhealed.

Those four years had not changed a thing. A pause button had been pressed that day. And I hadn't been able to press play since.

I pressed a kiss to my fingers, then placed them on the headstone. It was warm under my hand from the sun that always spotlighted in this grove, letting the world know that someone truly beautiful resided here.

I peered down and saw a photograph stuck to the bottom of the headstone. Tears pricked my eyes as I stared in awe at the stunning scene it boasted. The northern lights were captured perfectly in the picture, greens and blues soaring across a star-spattered black sky.

Rune.

Rune had been here. He always did this. Every time he came home, he would spend hours at Poppy's grave, under their favorite tree. Spend the day talking to his only love, his soulmate, telling her about his life at NYU. About the apprenticeship he had secured with a Pulitzer Prize–winning photographer. About his travels around the world, visiting far off countries and sights—like the northern lights—that he would always capture on film and then bring home for Poppy to see.

"So she won't miss out on new adventures," he would tell me.

Then there were the days when he would visit Poppy, and I would sit behind a nearby tree, unnoticed and hidden, and listen to him speak to her. When tears would cascade from my eyes at the unfairness of the world. At us losing the brightest star in our skies, at Rune losing half of his heart. As far as I knew, he had never dated anyone else. He told me once that he would never feel about anyone else the way he felt about Poppy and that although their time together was short, it had been enough to last him a lifetime.

I had never experienced a love like theirs. I wasn't sure many did. Where Ida searched and prayed for a Rune-and-Poppy-type love, I feared it would only cause me more pain. What if I lost them too? How would I ever cope? I didn't know how Rune survived each day. I didn't know how he opened his eyes every sunrise and simply *breathed*. I'd never asked him. I'd never found the courage.

"I had another attack today," I told Poppy, leaning against her headstone.

I rested my head against the warm marble. Drank in the soothing birdsong that always kept her company. After several silent minutes, I pulled out the notebook from my bag. The one I had never dared open. I traced the words *For Savannah* written on the cover in Poppy's handwritten script.

The notebook she had left to me. The one I had never read or even opened. I didn't know why. Perhaps it was because I was too scared to read what Poppy had to say, or perhaps it was because it was the final piece I had left of her, and once it was opened, once I'd finished the very last word, then she was truly gone.

I hugged the notebook to my chest. "They're sending me away, Pops," I said, my quiet voice carrying around the near-silent grove. "To try to make me better." I sighed, the heaviness in my chest almost bruising my ribs. "I just don't know how to let you go."

The truth was, if Poppy could talk to me, I knew she'd be heartbroken at how her death had paralyzed me, wounded me irreparably. Yet, I couldn't shake it. Rob told me that grief never left us. Instead we adapted, like it was a new appendage we had to learn to use. That at any moment, pain and heartache could strike and break us. But eventually we would develop the tools to cope with it and find a way to move on.

I was still waiting for that day.

I watched the setting sun disappear through the trees, the waxing crescent moon rising to take its place. The golden blanket adorning us turned to a silvery blue as night arrived and I stood to leave. "I love you, Pops," I said and reluctantly walked through the grove to our home. Our home, that these days, missed its heartbeat.

Because she was buried in the ground behind me. Eternally seventeen. The age I was now. Never to grow old. Never to shine her light. Never to share her music.

A travesty the world would forever be deprived of.

Abandoned Dreams and Frozen Ponds

Cael
Age Eighteen
Massachusetts

"It isn't happening," I said, staring down at my mom and dad on the couch. I stood in the center of the living room, seething, body live-wired with anger as I listened to what they were saying.

A morsel of guilt tried to carve its way into my heart as I watched my mom's tears spill over her eyes and track down her cheeks, but the fire flooding my veins burned that flicker of remorse to vapor.

"Cael, please..." Mom whispered, hands held out, placating. She shifted to the edge of the couch, like she would come to me, to offer me some kind of comfort. I shook my head, taking three steps back until I was almost on top of the unlit fireplace. I didn't want her comfort. I didn't want *any* of this. What were they even *thinking* right now?

My dad sat on our ancient brown couch, stoic, like the upstanding lawman he was. He was still dressed in his uniform, Massachusetts's Finest glaring at me, face reddened as Mom cried over me *again*.

My jaw clenched so hard I felt my bones might crack. My hands curled into tight fists, and I fought the urge to plow them into the brick of the fireplace my back now brushed up against. But that was my every day in this hellhole. In this house full of memories I no longer wanted to have lodged in my brain. My dad was sick and tired of patching up holes I'd made in the walls with my fist. Just as sick as I was of my constant stream of anger. But that anger never left me. So I guess we both weren't getting what we wanted.

"You're going, kid," Dad said, authority lacing each of his words. He was a man of few words. Succinct, and expected his orders to be obeyed. Everything inside of me screamed to tell him where the hell to go. His hard tone was fuel to the flames inside of me. I tried. I really tried to keep calm. But I was losing it. Like a ticking time bomb, I could feel I was about to blow.

"Cael, we have to try something," Mom said, a subtle plea in her broken voice. Once upon a time, my mom upset would break me. Now? Nothing. "We've talked to your newest therapist. You graduated from high school last year. You refused to start college. This trip can help you. Give you back some purpose. Now, you just exist. No job, no direction, no school, no hockey. We've talked to the coach at Harvard. He checks in on you all the time. He still wants you. He wants you on next year's roster. You can do this. You can still go—"

"I DON'T FUCKING CARE ABOUT COLLEGE!" I screamed, cutting off what she was about to say. I *had* cared about college once. It was all I thought about. All I *dreamed* about. So I could join *him*, so that we could play side by side, like we'd always planned…

My eyes involuntarily went to the mass of pictures on the wall above my parents on the couch. Shot after shot of me and him throughout the years. Playing in stadiums, arms around one another, smiles on our faces and sticks in our hands, Team USA written across my chest. I wasn't even sure how to smile anymore. It felt foreign for my facial muscles to function that way. I averted my gaze from those pictures—now a goddamn shrine to what could have been. I couldn't even look at them. They were all a lie. Told a story of a life that was fictitious.

Nothing about those days was real.

"I'm not going," I said, a dark warning in my tone. But my dad remained unfazed. He got to his feet. His broad and tall frame had once towered over me, but my six-foot-four height put me three inches above him now, my broad shoulders and athletic body matching his in strength and power. "I'll never forgive you for this," I spat, my mom's quiet cries in the background ricocheting off the constant shield I held around me. Nothing seemed to penetrate these days.

Dad put his hands in his pockets. "Then that's something I'm just gonna have to live with, kid."

I knew there was no changing his mind.

I vibrated on the spot, searing heat rushing through me like I was made of lava. Without glancing at my mom, I fled for the door, slamming it on my way out of the house. I threw myself into my Jeep. My breath turned to white mist as it met the frigid cold. Snow lay deep on the surrounding fields, and my boots were soaked through just from the walk from my house to the drive. Winter held New England firmly in its clenched fist.

I put my hands on the steering wheel, squeezing the leather. Like it did every time I got behind the wheel, that night came crashing back into my mind. My hands shook just by sitting in the Jeep. My breath grew labored, and I felt weak, so goddamn weak at how the memories took me down, at how just sitting in a car could ruin me, that I gave myself over to the anger inside. I let it flood my body, hot and livid, until I shook from it. My muscles grew so tight in my chest that they ached. I gritted my teeth, letting the boiling-hot flames inside of me sear any trace of who I was before. I let it build and build, from my toes to my scalp until it was all I was made of. Then I let it take over. I handed over the reins and roared out into the night, full of all the fury that was trying to escape. I slammed my hands on the steering wheel, kicked out my leg until my foot collided with the stereo system, knocking it out of the dashboard until it hung, suspended before me.

When my voice grew hoarse and all my breath was expelled, I stayed tense in the seat and glared at the rural white farm-style house that was once my sanctuary. I *hated* this place now. My gaze flickered to the top right window, and a slice of pain managed to sneak through, stabbing at my heart. "No," I hissed, and I averted my eyes from that bedroom. *Not now.* I wasn't letting that pain in now.

I tried to move the car. But for a moment, I was paralyzed. Caught in the Purgatory I'd been thrust into a year ago. When everything had flipped on a dime and the cookie-cutter mask that had disguised our idyllic family life was firmly yanked off—

I closed my eyes and let the fire take over. Slamming the key into the ignition, I opened my eyes and skidded out of the drive, the tires scrambling to find purchase on the black ice that coated our dirt driveway. I smelled rubber burning as I pushed the accelerator to its max. The fear of driving was there, like a low-grade fever threatening to spike. But I held it down. Just let myself burn and eviscerate any of the emotion that tried to edge through.

It had to be this way. I couldn't sink back to that place where everything was empty and lacking—a sinkhole that was impossible to climb out of. Instead, I leaned into this visceral rage that now controlled me. I gave myself over to hate—of the world, of people, of everything that stood to expose what I'd buried down deep.

But mostly, I focused on hating *him*. The hatred and fury I had toward him were a roaring pyre doused with gasoline.

I blinked, coming back into myself. I had driven without direction, without thought, lost in my head, and found myself approaching the one place I tried to stay away from.

We have to try something…

My mom's words ran on a loop inside my brain. *No*, they wanted me gone. They wanted to get rid of the son who was causing them strife. Me! No talk of the *other* son. But me, the one who remained. The one *he* had left behind. The one he hadn't even cared about when did what he did…

The first sign of my chest collapsing began to needle into my sternum. Frantically, I pulled into a parking bay and threw the driver's door open. The chill from Massachusetts's harsh winter slapped against my skin. My black Henley, beanie, and ripped jeans did nothing to stave off the cold. But I let it sink into my bones. I *wanted* to hurt. It was the only time I was reminded that I was still alive. That and the anger that had tunneled into my soul a year ago and had only grown in strength ever since.

Before I knew it, my feet were moving. I passed car after car, recognizing each one as I did. What was I even doing here? I didn't *want* to be here, yet my feet kept propelling me forward. They took me in through the side door, where the sounds that were once like home to me now felt distant and no longer part of my life. Low voices shouting calls, sticks slapping against ice, and pucks and blades cutting through glass.

Yet, I felt nothing.

Climbing the stairs higher and higher, I didn't stop until I was in the nosebleeds, well out of sight. I sat down on the hard plastic seat and threaded my hands together. Every muscle in my body was tight as my eyes focused on the ice. As I watched my former friends and teammates practicing. Making runs, breakaways, and dekes. Firing shot after shot at Timpson, the goalie who rarely let anything pass. His nickname wasn't Shut Out for nothing.

"Here!" the most familiar voice called, cutting through the arena, and I felt a sharp stab in my stomach.

Eriksson powered forward, taking the puck, and soared up the ice. With a perfectly aimed shot, it sailed into the net, lighting up the lamp.

I used to be *right there* beside him.

My leg bounced in agitation, and I fought to not inhale the freshness of the ice, to feel the sharpness of the cold air filling the arena. I pulled off my beanie and ran my hand through my dark hair. The tattoos on the backs of my hands stood out against my paler skin. Tattoos. So many tattoos and piercings now covered my body, just about erasing any sign of the person I was before.

I closed my eyes when the sounds of warring hockey sticks and boards being slammed into began to instigate a migraine from hell. Jumping to my feet, I pounded down the stairs toward the side door. I had just made it to the hallway when I heard, "Woods?"

I froze mid-step. Heard the sound of Eriksson leaving the ice, bladed feet awkwardly running on the hard surface behind me. But I kept moving, I kept going, avoiding my former best friend until a framed jersey mounted on the arena wall stopped me dead in my tracks. Woods 33 stood proudly in the hallway. In Memoriam was written on a bronze plaque above it, an individual team picture with his smiling face beaming back at me.

It was a punch right to my gut. I hadn't been prepared for it. It had sneaked through. It had struck unannounced—

"*Cael!*" Eriksson's voice was closer now. I turned my head and saw him approaching, and my heart started to slam against my ribs. The look of hope and excitement on his face almost made my legs give out. "Cael! You should have told me you were coming." Stephan Eriksson was breathless from trying to catch me. He still held his stick from the practice he'd just run out on, and pulled off his helmet, placing it on the floor by his bladed feet. I just stared at him. I couldn't make myself move.

He'd been there with me. He'd seen it all *with* me.

Eriksson's attention flickered to the framed jersey before me, sadness engulfing his expression. "Coach had it put up a couple of months back. Said some really nice things about him. You were invited, but..."

Shivers ran up my spine, causing every inch of skin on my body to break out in goose bumps. I could see Stephan studying how I looked now. See him looking at my tattooed hands and chest and neck. See him tracking my pierced nose and bottom lip, the black gauges in my ears.

"I've been trying to get a hold of you, man," he said, trying to edge closer. He gestured to the direction of the ice. "For months. We miss you." He took a deep breath. "*I* miss you. It's not the same without you, brother."

Brother...

That word was like a machete slicing my chest, splitting me where I stood. Feeling the familiar fire melt the ice that had built in me the minute I stepped into this arena, I spat, "I'm not your brother." Then, looking at the framed jersey that hovered like an omen beside me, I slammed my fist right into the center of the navy-blue number 33. I felt the broken glass dig into my knuckles and the warmth of my blood hit my skin as it began to drip down to my wrist.

"*Jesus*, Woods! Stop!" Stephan shouted, but I was already pushing out of the exit door and into the darkening winter evening. I ran across the lot, lungs burning, and jumped into my car, ignoring Stephan trying to signal me down from the side door.

What the hell had I been thinking, coming here?

I skidded out of the parking lot, trying to stop my hands from shaking. That frame. That framed jersey. *Why did they have to do that? Why did I have to see that?*

I drove and drove, pushing the speed limit, but couldn't stop my hands from shaking. Was this what he'd felt like when he'd roared down the road?

When he'd done what he did? My blood trickled down my arm. My knuckles were split open, wounds raw.

But worse, I could smell my blood.

Blood...

The coppery scent immediately yanked me back to the moment I prayed I could forget. The one that was as tattooed onto my brain as deeply as the black and red ink on my neck. I felt my breathing stutter, the white puffs of smoke bursting into misty staccato balls before me. My stomach swirled, the fire I held on to like a crutch extinguishing by the second as that night came tumbling back.

I made a harsh right turn onto the dirt road that led to home but slammed my foot on my brakes halfway up, at the pond. I was panting like I'd just run a marathon. I couldn't be in the car. It was too enclosed, too stifling, reminded me too much of that night...

Jumping from the driver's seat, I ran to the pond, inky thick ice coating its surface. I stopped at the edge, head tilted back as I stared at the darkening sky.

In memoriam...

A choked, strangled sound wrenched from my throat. I bent down, palms flattening on the ice. Anything to ground me. *Christ.* How did we even get here? How had it all gone so wrong?

Why hadn't he said anything? Why hadn't he just *talked* to me—

Throwing my head back, I screamed into the night sky, hearing sleeping birds fleeing from the surrounding trees. I slowly stood, throat raw, body jumping with adrenaline, and moved to the shed that I hadn't opened in I didn't know how long.

Placing my bloodied hand on the handle, I wrenched it open and found my old skates staring back at me. I ignored the punch to the gut I received when I saw the second pair leaning beside them.

Grabbing mine, I kicked off my boots, not caring if my socks were soaked through as they slapped on the snow. I slipped them on and felt nauseous as that familiar rush of *rightness* took me in its hold. I glanced up at the sticks that stared back at me like they had a soul, like they had memories that lay trapped in the layers of wood.

Before I could overthink it, I grabbed for the one with black and gold tape—Bruins colors. As I held it, it felt sacrilegious. I never believed I deserved to hold this stick. How could I when it belonged to my hero? The one who'd taught me everything I knew. The one I'd looked up to, emulated, laughed with and run to. The one who'd shone so bright he lit up the whole friggin' sky.

Now, I was permanently stuck under his eclipse.

Instinctively moving to the pond, I placed my right blade on the ice and pushed off until I was gliding along the surface. The harsh wind slapped at my face. My lungs, which felt like they'd forgotten how to function, drank in a long gasp of air. The tip of the stick in my hands dragged across the pond's frozen surface. I tapped it back and forth like I was passing a puck in between. It came as natural to me as breathing. *This*. Ice. Hockey.

I closed my eyes as I circled the pond. And like I had slipped into another plane, I heard the distant echo of two kids laughing…

"You think you can take me, kid?" Cillian's deep voice rang out over the snow and wind as I ran toward him, stealing the puck from under him. "Hey!" he laughed and chased me down the pond at what felt like a million miles an hour. These days, he couldn't catch me. When I slipped it through the two branches that made up our makeshift goal, he wrapped his arms around me, swooping me off the ice. "You're better than me now, kid. How the hell did that happen?"

The smile on my face was so wide my cheeks ached. I shrugged.

"You know that, right?" Cillian said, releasing me and circling where I stood. "You're gonna go all the way. Everyone sees it. All eyes are on you."

I didn't see it. Cill was the best hockey player I'd ever seen. I was pretty sure I would never measure up. He was older than me and was the star of every team he'd ever been on. Ever since I could remember, I'd wanted to be just like him.

"It's in the stars, kid," he said, roughing at my messy hair with his gloved hand. "We'll play at Harvard together, then hit the big time. NHL, All Stars. Olympics." He smiled and pressed a kiss to my head. "Together, yeah?"

"Together," I replied, feeling like the luckiest kid in the world. Me and Cillian. Together, the two of us could conquer the world…

A sinking feeling pressed onto my shoulders, a ten-ton weight pushing me down into the ground. I opened my eyes, only to find myself standing in the dark, in the middle of our neglected and abandoned pond. Alone. No future we'd dreamed of waiting before us. No *Woods Brothers* conquering the world. Just me, and the specter of my brother hovering over me like a vacuum, sucking anything good and light into its ravenous void.

The wood of the hockey stick groaned in my hands as my fingers wrapped around it like a vice. The longer I stood there, immobile, fury filled the emptiness in my soul and built and built until I lifted that stick high and slammed it down into the ice with every bit of strength I could obtain, shattering and splintering it into a thousand broken pieces.

Our dreams were shattered now too, so what was one more casualty in this shit show of a situation? Pushing back off the ice, I shucked off my skates, kicking them into the mass of overgrown, leafless trees surrounding me, and slumped back to the ground.

You're going, kid...

Dad may have well been behind me as for how loud his voice was in my head. I was eighteen. And about to go on a trip around the world with others apparently "like me." I was eighteen and should be working toward the future I'd dreamed of. But the one I had been promised had been stolen from me by the one I loved most, the one I *trusted* most in this world. Nothing else mattered anymore. I was completely alone.

And for such a long time now, I hadn't even found it within myself to care.

Timid Hearts and First Sights

Savannah
New York

"ARE YOU ALL PACKED?"

I looked up from where I was sitting on the edge of the hotel bed, lost in thought.

Ida stood before me, her long, dark hair down in soft waves and a dimpled smile on her pretty face. Mama and Daddy had brought me to New York to catch the flight to our first stop on the therapy trip. We were to meet in the airport, where I would meet the rest of the kids going, and our two therapists, of course. I had video-called with the therapists a few times and they seemed nice. It didn't take my nerves away though.

Ida had refused to stay behind in Georgia, insisting on coming to see me off.

I pressed my hand over my closed suitcase. "I think so." Ida had shared a room with me last night. She'd regaled me with stories from school and the latest gossip from the cheer squad she was part of.

If sunshine was personified, it was Ida Litchfield.

Ida dropped beside me on the bed and threaded her hand through mine. I stared at our intertwined fingers, her bright pink polish next to my clear. Ida placed her head on my shoulder, and just that simple act of sisterly affection brought a lump to my throat.

"I don't want to go," I confessed on a whisper, feeling the fluttering in my heart that ignited the anxiety I knew was preparing to strike.

Ida squeezed my hand. "I know…" She trailed off, and I knew she had stopped herself from saying more. I waited, unsure if I wanted to hear it. But then, with a shaky inhale she said, "But I need you to." The sudden sadness in her tone was a knife straight through the heart.

I stilled at her confession and turned my head to look at her. She kept her face down, head tucked into the curve of my neck.

"Ida—"

"Please…" she said, quietly begging, then slowly raised her head. It gutted me to see her usually happy eyes crushed with sadness. A sheen of tears washed over her green irises. My heart began to race. Ida glanced at the window showcasing JFK Airport, then looked back to me. "I need my sister back," she finally said, and I felt that knife slice even deeper. I wanted to say something, but guilt infused my cells, making it impossible.

"Losing Pops…" Ida trailed off, a lone tear spilling over her left cheek. I dusted it away with my thumb. Ida gave me an echo of a grateful smile.

She took a deep breath. "Losing Pops was the hardest thing I've ever gone through in my life." I placed my free hand on her knee. "But seeing Mama and Daddy in the aftermath…seeing *you*…" Ida paused, and I knew she was back there, reliving those first few months after Poppy's death. The darkest days we had ever endured. The aftermath, the *knowing* that nothing would ever be the same again. "Seeing what it did to you all…that hurt most of all. My family. My perfect, beautiful family was irreparably hurt, and I couldn't do anything to make it better. Mama and Daddy were crumbling. Poppy, *our* perfect Poppy had gone, and I missed her so much I couldn't breathe, but…" Ida cut herself off.

I tugged her closer. "What? Please, tell me."

Ida shifted and looked me in the eyes. "But I knew I had you. I wanted to cling to you, Savannah. To be sure you didn't leave me too."

My breathing stuttered. Ida was so young when it all happened. Old enough to remember it all but too young that it must have been almost impossible to process her grief.

"I used to sneak into your room at night, just to be sure you were breathing."

I didn't know.

"Ida—"

"I held on to the fact that although Poppy was gone, I knew she was in a better place. I could just feel it, in my heart. After all those years in pain. Fighting to live…" She shook her head. "I can't explain how; I just knew she was watching over us. Whenever I thought of her, I felt a subtle kind of warmth wrap around me that I can't even describe. At times, in our house, I felt her presence, like she was walking right beside me, sitting on the couch next to me." She laughed in a self-deprecating way. "It brought me so much comfort. Still does. It probably sounds silly—"

"It doesn't," I said reassuringly. In fact, in the beginning, I'd prayed for that too. I had asked Poppy for a sign so many times and nothing had ever come. I'd just wanted to know she was okay. That her life hadn't truly ended. That she was somewhere better than this world, laughing and loving, maybe reunited with our Mamaw, who she adored so much. That she still loved us and was around us, helping us cope with her irreparable loss.

"But the thing I've found hardest since we lost Poppy…" I held my breath, waiting for what she would say. Ida's shoulders dropped and she whispered, "Was that awful day… I lost you too."

Whatever had been left of my heart was obliterated, Ida's words having the effect of a grenade. Ida's hand became a death grip around mine. "I watched you fade, Sav. I watched you turn so into yourself that you became impenetrable. You built walls around your heart so high that no one could breach them." Two more tears fell down her face. "Not even me. You locked us all out." Ida exhaled a long, slow breath. "Just under four years ago, I lost two sisters, and…" Her voice caught and it destroyed me. She cleared her throat and rasped, "I just really, really want you back."

The pain in her voice made me feel nauseous. Because she was right, wasn't she? I had pushed everyone out. I'd let my little sister suffer and I'd done nothing to help her. But it wasn't on purpose. The walls had built themselves without my direction and trapped me deep inside. And I'd let them.

I was still there now, but hearing what it was doing to Ida…

It took me too many minutes to speak, but on a deep breath, I confided,

"I don't know *how* to come back." This time Ida wiped the tears from my cheeks. "I've been trying, Ida, I promise…"

"I know you have." Ida wrapped her arms around me. The moment she did, my racing heart calmed a touch. "I'm so proud of you for how much you've tried, but I need you to go on this trip. Not just for me, and not just for Poppy, but for *you*." Ida pulled back and cupped my cheeks. There was so much love and encouragement in her eyes. "You deserve to live, Sav. You are so loved and so special, so smart and beautiful and kind, and you *deserve* to be happy." Ida's throat became clogged again. "That's all I want for you. Happiness. Pops would want that for you too."

I stared at my sister and fought against the voice inside my head telling me to resist, that I didn't need to go. That I was fine. That I just needed more time, more therapy with Rob back at home. Therapy that I had been having for years…that hadn't worked…because nothing was working…

"Okay," I said, betraying the fear inside of me, and held on to my sister tighter. Poppy had always been my older sister, the one I went to for everything. But I was Ida's older sister now. The one she should be able to go to, to confide and trust in. So I had to try. For her, I would try.

A sudden knock on the door startled us. Ida laughed at how hard we jumped, and I found myself smiling too. "Girls, it's time to go," our daddy said from the hallway.

Ida ducked her head to meet my lowered gaze. "Are you okay?" I could see the worry in her eyes. The fear that she had said too much, pushed me too hard.

I felt raw and rung out, but I held her tighter. "I'm okay." It was a lie. We both knew it. And we both ignored that fact.

"Who knows," Ida said, smirking. "Maybe there'll be some cute boys going too. To make the trip just that little bit more bearable."

I rolled my eyes at her bright smile. "Ida, I'm sure I won't care."

Ida grasped my hands. "Or *foreign* boys. Ones with accents and romance running through their veins."

I shook my head at my little sister as we got up from the bed and grabbed my jacket and luggage. I ignored the trembling of my hands and the butterflies swooping in my stomach. Ida threaded her arm through mine, and we headed out into the hallway. Mama and Daddy were waiting. Mama stepped forward, worry etched on her face. I'm sure it looked like we had been crying.

"We're okay," I said, before she could ask. I squeezed Ida's arm. "We're… we're going to be okay."

I just hoped if I told myself that enough, I could somehow make it true.

JFK airport was as loud and bustling as I had expected. My daddy led us in the direction of a bunch of people who were grouped together to the side, away from the lines and harried clusters of travelers frantically checking arrival and departure boards. I immediately recognized our therapists, Leo and Mia, from our video calls. Ida still linked my arm, my steady support, but seeing new, curious faces turn to look at me had my nerves skyrocketing and me wishing I was anywhere but here right now. I counted four other teens around my age with their families too. They all looked over when my daddy reached out to Mia and shook her hand.

"Savannah!" Mia said and held out her hand to me next. She had short, blond hair and kind blue eyes. She looked to be in her mid-forties and had a warm smile. Leo introduced himself next. He was a taller man in his fifties, with ebony skin and beautiful dark eyes. Leo and Mia had told us on a video call that they were psychologists who specialized in grief.

My daddy took my bags from me. "Savannah, let me introduce you to the others who are going on the trip," Mia said. Ida released her arm from mine, and for a moment I almost refused to let her go. Ida met my eyes and nodded in encouragement. Tucking my shaking hands around my waist, I took a deep breath to stave off my burgeoning panic and followed Mia, leaving Leo talking to my parents and sister.

First was a girl with tan skin and dark eyes. "Savannah, this is Jade."

"Hi," she said, greeting me shyly and waving her hand. She seemed to be with her father and her grandparents.

"Then we have Lili and Travis." Lili had curly brown hair and blue eyes; Travis had red hair and black-rimmed glasses. They both waved unenthusiastically. It seemed like no one was excited about this trip.

26

"And this is Dylan." Dylan stepped forward and gave me a hug. I froze, unused to being around people so tactile, but then I awkwardly hugged him back. He gave me a wide smile when he pulled away. Dylan had dark skin and the most beautiful caramel eyes I'd ever seen. He was tall and slender with a gentle and welcoming smile.

"That's almost all of you; we're just waiting for one more—" Mia stopped mid-sentence. "Ah, here he is now."

I turned and momentarily stopped breathing when I saw a tall boy approaching us. He had dark brown hair—short on the sides but longer on top—that fell over his forehead messily in thick waves, and a myriad of tattoos and piercings. He was broad framed and clearly worked out—physically fit, maybe a sportsman? He was dressed in all black and kept his gaze to the floor as he followed who I assumed were his parents. I found myself watching him as he got closer. He seemed to be just as closed off as me, and for a moment, there was a flicker of camaraderie in my chest toward him.

"Hello, Cael," Leo said, and the boy finally raised his eyes. They were stunning. Crystal blue—almost silver in tone. They were the most striking eyes I'd ever seen. As if feeling my stare, he brushed off Leo's greeting and turned my way. My heart stuttered as he blinked, his long, dark lashes brushing over his cheeks. "Come. I'll introduce you to everyone."

Cael and Leo stepped toward us. I dropped my gaze but still felt Cael's eyes on me. Leo introduced Cael to the rest of the group, then finally reached me. "And this is Savannah," Leo said, and on a deep breath, I lifted my head. Cael stood right before me, and I had to tilt my head to look him in the eyes.

"Hi," I said, and Cael nodded in greeting. He tipped his head to the side, as if observing me more. His jaw clenched and he wore a stormy expression on his handsome face.

I felt heat rise to my cheeks but was saved when Leo announced, "Okay, that's everyone." He smiled. "It's time to say goodbye to your loved ones, guys." Any warmth that had built in my face drained as I faced my parents and Ida. My heart immediately kicked into a sprint, so much so it made me lightheaded. I tried to focus on my breathing, on not breaking at the first challenge I faced.

Mama came straight forward and wrapped me in her arms, I hoped she didn't feel me shaking. I could hear a hitch in her breathing and felt a few stray tears fall on my shoulder. I gripped on to her tighter and had to battle with myself to let go. "You are going to do amazing," she said and ran her hand up and down my back in reassuring strokes.

I nodded, unable to find my voice. Mama stepped back and Daddy wrapped me up next. "You call us at any time, okay? We're only a phone call away." I nodded, and he reared back, meeting my eyes. My bottom lip trembled, and by the sadness engulfing his face, I knew he had seen it. "I'm so proud of you, sweetie. This will be so good for you. I just know it." He coughed and pointed upward. It took him a few moments to speak. "And she'll be watching you. She'll be with you every step of the way, carrying you through." His words, although kind, were a sucker punch to the chest.

"Yeah," I whispered, holding myself together. I wouldn't fall apart. I had to do this. I *had* to.

"My turn!" A single laugh broke through the darkness of my anxiety as Ida wrapped her arms around me in an almost-suffocating hug. "I love you," she said simply. I felt those words down to my bones. I was doing this for her. I was doing this for *all* of my family.

"I love you too," I replied, sounding much more confident than I felt. When Ida withdrew, she was smiling at me, dimples popping. "I'm so proud of you." I nodded, unable to speak. "Call and text me. I want to know everything, every single step of the way. And photos! Lots of photos please!"

"I will." I stepped back, and each footstep felt like my feet were made from granite. I really didn't want to go. Everything within me was screaming for me to refuse, to board the flight back to Georgia and return to my normal life. But I knew my normal existence wasn't good for me. And as I took one last glance at my mama and daddy, at my sister, and the tears building in their eyes, I knew I had to be better for them.

I had to be better for *me*.

Picking up my carry-on, I joined Mia and Leo. Most of the others had already said goodbye to their families. When I looked up, Cael shrugged off his father's hand on his shoulder rather aggressively and walked away from his parents, a severe look on his face, not even giving them a goodbye. He came to a stop next to me, body stiff and mood dark. But I felt his body warmth like I was beside a furnace. On my other side was Dylan.

"You ready, Savannah?" Dylan asked.

I shrugged, and Dylan nudged me affectionately, trying to be a comfort. "Let's see if they can help us, huh?" Despite his playful tone, I caught the flicker of despair in his voice, and his infectious smile lost some of its splendor.

As I glanced at my family once more, my heart began to race, and the anxiety I had fought back barreled into me at full force, knocking the air from my lungs. My body jerked, and my hand immediately went to my chest. I gasped, trying to find some much-needed oxygen. My hands shook terribly, and I felt a bead of sweat build on my forehead.

"Savannah?" Mia came to stand before me, and I saw Mama and Ida step forward in my periphery. I breathed in through my nose. I turned to my sister and Mama, caught the worry on their faces, but held out my hand to halt them. They immediately stopped, and I cast them a watery smile.

I had to do this on my own.

"Savannah, can you talk?" Mia pushed, gentle concern lacing her question. Ringing had begun in my ears, keeping me locked in my panic, but after a few measured breaths, the ringing slowly faded, and the overwhelming sound of the airport came crashing in like a sensorial tidal wave.

I faced Mia and nodded. My body felt weak, and exhaustion quickly set in—as it did with every anxiety attack I'd ever had. My nerves were wrought.

"I'm okay," I said shakily, and Mia placed a reassuring hand on my shoulder, a flash of what looked like pride flickering on her face. I cast a glance at my family. I saw the deep worry on Mama's and Daddy's faces. Ida's eyes were glossy, but she smiled and blew me a kiss. I smiled at my little sister and fought to gather a modicum of composure.

"Okay, let's go," Leo said, and Dylan stepped closer to me.

"You good, Savannah?" he asked.

"Yes, thank you," I replied. I appreciated his concern.

Then I felt someone close in on my left, the scent of sea salt and snow-laced fresh air wrapping around me. I stilled when I realized it was Cael. He towered beside me. I had to glance up at him. He was facing forward, a dark void remaining in his light stare, but then he blinked and looked down at me.

He stepped a fraction closer still, and a sense of warmth grew within me. His arms were crossed over his chest, closed off. No words were said. I didn't even know him, yet strangely, it was as though he was protecting me.

As we began walking, Cael and Dylan stood on either side of me like protective sentinels. Checking that I had my carry-on bag, I reached inside and brushed my fingers over the notebook I carried everywhere. I hoped Daddy was right. I hoped that Poppy would be with me on this trip, walking by my side, hand on my back for strength. And I prayed that, no matter what happened on this trip, maybe this would be the time I could open the first page of my notebook and hear from my sister once more.

I just needed to find the courage.

As we passed through security and waited in the airport lounge, I wondered if this trip would be able to help any of us. I supposed we would see. As much as I wanted this to work, I still felt numb inside. And I was sure, as I looked around at the six teens selected, the ones Leo and Mia were trying to save from the permanent black hole of grief, I could feel the clogging sadness leaking from our souls. In each face, I recognized the masks of normalcy we all wore, disguising the person screaming in pain underneath.

I felt an uphill battle awaited.

With a long breath, I sent a silent plea to my sister.

Poppy, please, if you can hear me. Help me. Please, just one last time. Help me get through this.

Help me learn how to live without you.

Help me be okay.

Jet Planes and Rainy Skies

Cael

I DIDN'T KNOW WHAT TO EXPECT FROM THE OTHER PEOPLE GOING ON THIS trip. Everyone was from different places within the United States, accents varying. We were from a range of backgrounds. But watching everyone wait in the lounge, hardly anyone speaking, it was clear we were all lost in the same stinking cesspit of loss—Mia and Leo seemed to have chosen their six hopeless cases well.

My eyes tracked to the seat opposite me. Savannah. I couldn't deny that the minute I'd clocked my eyes on her, she had stopped me in my tracks. Surprising, seeing as though I hadn't remotely noticed anyone that way in a year. She was point blank the most beautiful person I'd ever seen. I gripped tightly on to the arms of the chair when my first thought was to tell Cill about her...

I shifted in my seat, that pull in my stomach turning to nausea at the thought of him. I tightened my jaw so much, I felt my teeth ache. What the hell was I doing here?

Reaching for my bag, I went to take out my headphones, but the string that pulled them closed had become tangled. I pulled and pulled at the string, but the more and more I yanked at it, the more it became knotted.

"Argh!" I bit out in frustration, when the string snapped in my hand and ripped the side of my bag. I kicked my bag away from my seat and clutched my hands in my hair, gripping at the strands, just trying to breathe. I gritted my teeth together and tried to force myself to calm down. But it was no good.

My feet shuffled on the ground, legs bouncing in agitation. I couldn't sit here. Couldn't just *burn* in this seat. I reached forward and dragged my bag to me. Then, just as I was about to jump to my feet, to try to shake off this impossible weight around my neck, I lifted my head and immediately caught Savannah smiling at something Jade, one of the other girls, was saying to her. The minute I saw that smile, something inside of me calmed. A wave of peace crashed over me. And for second—a single euphoric *free* moment— everything stilled. Not numbed. *Never* numbed. But seeing that smile... I didn't understand why it affected me so much. She was just a girl. And it was just a smile. But, for a split second, there was a cease-fire within me.

Lili, the third girl on the trip, leaned over her seat and joined the conversation. Savannah politely smiled as Jade and Lili laughed. Savannah didn't laugh. Her arms were locked around her waist, and I noticed the sleeves of her shirt pulled down over her palms as if it gave her some kind of comfort, protected her somehow.

I tipped my head to the side as I studied her. I'd never seen anyone have a panic attack before. Never seen something so emotionally disabling come over someone so suddenly. Savannah had blanched, then begun to shake, body jumping as she fought for breath. Her blue eyes had widened with fear, and her lips had paled.

Usually I didn't feel anything but pissed. Hadn't in so long. Wasn't affected by movies, books, or personal stories—no matter how tragic. Hell, even my mom crying daily and my dad trying to comfort her still didn't break through the impenetrable walls that now encased my heart. But seeing the petite dark blond with wide blue eyes fighting for breath in the middle of JFK was the first time some kind of emotion had snuck in.

For a moment, a brief moment, I had actually *felt* something.

As if feeling my stare, Savannah took her gaze from the planes taking off outside and turned my way. Red immediately burst onto her cheeks under my attention, and that same pull inside of my chest yanked again. Then Dylan returned from wherever he'd been, and he dropped down beside her. He passed her a bag of chips. The small smile she gave him, this time, made me tense. Savannah…she was stunning. There were no bones about it. She was beautiful, but if it was even possible, she seemed more closed off than me. The quietest of the group by far, and that was saying something. Dylan leaned in and said something to her I couldn't hear, and she huffed out an amused laugh.

I felt another pull in my heart. And I didn't like it. I didn't want to feel again. I had grown used to the fire. Preferred it to those agonizing early days after Cill…

Travis sat down beside me, breaking me from the spiral I was about to go down. I looked over to the redhead, thick, black-framed glasses sitting on a pale face full of freckles. "You want one?" he said and held out a box of Twizzlers.

"No," I said sharply and looked back to Savannah again. Dylan was still talking to her. She simply replied with nods and kind smiles.

I couldn't take my eyes off her.

Travis cleared his throat. "So, no hockey this year?" I froze, his question as effective as a bucket of kerosene being thrown over my head. I turned to the boy about my age and felt fire swarm through my veins, hot and potent. It took me a moment to realize that everyone in our group was looking our way. I saw Savannah and Dylan watching us, Lili and Jade beside them, waiting for my answer.

"I don't talk about hockey," I replied, even more sharply this time. I glared at Travis, making damn sure he didn't continue with this line of questioning, but he just nodded like my answer wasn't laced with a threat to not continue down this road. In fact, he didn't seem affected by my shitty attitude at all. And he was clearly a hockey fan.

Great. Just what I needed. Someone who knew my past.

Travis took another bite of his Twizzlers and casually said, "I like data." He pointed at himself. "Math nerd." He ignored my dark expression. "Sports makes for some of the best data." He shrugged. "I watched some of your junior hockey games while gathering it. I recognized your face the minute I saw you, and your name, of course." A flicker of sympathy filled his brown eyes and I saw it—he knew why I was here. If he followed hockey, if he followed my stats, maybe Harvard's stats too, then he would *know*.

That was the part I could never escape from now. What happened to Cill…it had been huge news in the sports world. In the hockey world, it was the biggest shock in recent years. The biggest tragedy.

But in my personal world…it was Armageddon.

I jumped up from my seat, cutting him off before he could say anything else. I felt the group's eyes on me as I did, could feel the same pity directed at me, the same way they had looked toward Savannah earlier. Spotting a coffee shop, I beelined for the long line. My fists were clenched at my side and I fought not to plow my fist through the nearest wall.

An addictive scent of almonds and cherries suddenly swarmed around me. When I turned to look behind me, Savannah was there, *right* behind me. Her wide blue eyes were focused on me. She had a blush to her cheeks again. My chest tightened, threatening to feel something, but I pushed it away. I couldn't deal with feeling *anything* right now. Not after being reminded of my bro—

"*What?*" I snapped, my voice laced with venom.

Savannah looked shocked by my attitude. "A-are you okay?" Her nervous, sweet voice sailed into my ears and hit me like a freight train. She was southern. Bible Belt, I'd guess. Her country accent wrapped around the vowels of her question like silk, soft and melodic. The opposite to my harsh Massachusetts brogue which cut like glass.

"What do you care?" I bit out, voice hard. "Just go back to the group and leave me alone." I turned back to the line, feeling my stomach turn for some inexplicable reason. I didn't care that I'd snapped at her. I *didn't*. I felt her presence behind me like that of an angel—comforting, caring, calming. But I didn't want that. I *wanted* to sear, wanted to stay incinerated. I waited a few seconds, then couldn't help but look behind me. I caught her retreating to the lounge where the others waited, head slightly bowed.

She'd clearly gotten the message.

Ordering a coffee, I had barely made it back to the lounge when the announcement to board the plane came through. Mia handed us each a ticket and we fell into line. I held on to my coffee and broken bag and ignored everyone else. I saw Savannah with Dylan two spots in front of me and tried not to let guilt creep into my heart. She'd only been checking on me. I couldn't remember anyone in a long time even caring anymore. I'd successfully pushed everyone I loved away. But she had tried...

It didn't matter. I didn't need her or anyone in my life.

Like cattle, we were led to the plane, and I huffed a disbelieving laugh when I arrived at my seat. It was one of the plane's middle seats, in a row of four. My three companions were already seated—the free seat was between Savannah and Travis, Dylan next to Savannah on the aisle.

Perfect.

I sat down, stowed my bag under the seat in front of me, and went to put on my headphones. Before I could, an elbow nudged me. Travis. "I'm sorry," he said and pointed to his mouth. "Sometimes I forget how to keep this shut. I need to learn how to not say everything that comes to my head out loud. I shouldn't have mentioned anything." The guy looked so guilty that I couldn't stop some of my irritation from falling away.

"I don't *ever* talk about hockey," I said again, making sure to hammer that point home, then put on my headphones, my music immediately drowning out all noise. I closed my eyes and didn't intend to open them again until we landed. But as the scent of almonds and cherries sailed past me again, I cracked an eye open and caught Savannah nervously looking my way. And I didn't know what propelled me, but I found myself answering her question from the coffee shop line. "I—" I took a deep breath, then said, "I'm fine..." In a break between songs, I caught her hitch of shocked breath. "Thanks," I tacked on awkwardly.

A flicker of what seemed like relief passed in Savannah's gaze, and she nodded, focusing back on the paperback in her hands. I didn't pay attention to what it was; I was too busy trying to keep my eyes closed and not picture her pretty face and the way she'd just looked at me.

Like she cared.

The Lake District, England

Frost clung like white lace to the many gray walls we passed, walls made up by layers and layers of ancient brick. Tiny, windy roads tested the driving skills of the bus driver, fat drops of rain pelting against the windows as we swayed side to side on uneven asphalt roads littered with potholes, trying to reach our destination. Small, old buildings sat dotted around fields that stretched for miles and miles, only a mass of sheep and cattle in residence. I gripped on to the edge of the seat, counting down the minutes until we got to the accommodation. I hated being in any kind of car or bus for too long.

I stayed transfixed at England spread out before me, trying to take my mind off everything. I'd never been here before. And I'd only ever heard people talk of London and other major cities when it came to the UK. Apparently, we were going to be far, far away from any of them. Good. I didn't want to be near masses of people.

Out here in the rural countryside, the skies were moody and overcast, no sun in sight. The air was frigid, and in only the short walk from the airport to the bus, that cold wind cut deep to my bones. But I had a fondness for that sensation—for a moment, it reminded me of how it felt when I stood out on the ice. Warm breath turning into white mist with every measured exhale, the bitter and brutal chill slapping against your skin like a whip made of a thousand blades.

After ten more minutes, the bus that was taking us to England's Lake District came to a slow stop. I'd sat at the back of the bus so was the last to depart. But as I stepped off the bus's steps, the sight of the lake before me made me still. It was huge, as far as the eye could see, mist hovering over its surface like a fallen dark cloud. It was like something from an old-fashioned Gothic movie. Boats bobbed in the distance, dressed in the gray fog. Small islands looked haunted with their spindly trees and camouflaged birds calling from within the mist. Mountains surrounded the lake like stark castle walls, and tourists milled about in small rows of shops on the other side of the lake, wrapped in warm winter coats, hats, gloves, and scarves.

I hadn't held out much hope for this trip. But this…this was something to see. No big stores, no high-rises, no heavy traffic. Just the sound of the lake and the whistling frigid wind whipping around the trees.

"Welcome to Windermere!" Mia said as the driver collected all our luggage from the bus's compartment, placing it on the pavement where we stood. Standing behind us was a large hostel-type building, made of the same gray brick everything else seemed to be made from in this place. Outside, the hostel had benches and a fire pit with logs surrounding it. It was dark and eerie. And it was completely on its own.

I imagined that was why it had been chosen.

"This is home for the next couple of weeks," Leo said and gestured for us all to grab our bags and follow him up the path to the front entrance. Wooden rowing boats were docked on the stony shore that surrounded the house, and makeshift wooden swings hung from the branches of the surrounding trees.

As we followed Mia and Leo into the house, we were led into a hallway, then to a large room that was furnished with couches and a TV. "We have sole use of this hostel for the duration of our stay," Mia explained. Leo began handing us each a key. "The boys will be sharing a dorm room, and so will the girls," Mia continued. I took a deep, exasperated breath. I was sharing with Dylan and Travis. The last thing I wanted to do was share a room with other people. I wasn't unused to it; in hockey we roomed with others all the time.

But that was then. That was *before*. Now, I needed solitude.

"We'll each be in the supervisor rooms next to your dorms." Leo pointed to the stairs. "In case you need us for anything. How about you get settled, and then we'll meet back here in about an hour to discuss what will happen on this leg of the trip." Leo smiled. "I know jet lag must be kicking in, but believe me, from experience, it's best to push through as long as you can to help switch to this time zone."

I rarely slept anymore anyway. I didn't think my body knew what time zone it even lived in.

Lili led the way to the stairs. The girls started up to the top floor, when Dylan grabbed Savannah's luggage and began climbing to the top.

"Oh, you don't need to do that," she said, her southern accent trickling over me again. It sounded like she was singing.

"No problem," Dylan said and dropped it off outside her room.

Travis nudged me as we reached our room. He wagged his eyebrows in suggestion, then tipped his head toward Dylan and Savannah. I stepped away from him. But I got what he was insinuating. And I tried. I really friggin' tried to not let it bother me, but no matter how much I fought to repel the thought of them together, the twist in my gut told me I'd been unsuccessful.

Ignoring the boulder that was forming in my chest, I followed Travis into the room. There were two sets of bunk beds. I took in the size of them, and then the size of me, and just accepted that I'd be getting no sleep even if I could manage it.

I threw my rucksack on the bottom bunk of one of the beds against the far side of the wall. No way was I even attempting to get on a top bunk. The walls of the room were a generic cream, the bed sheets a rusty red color. Travis followed me, throwing his bag on the top bunk above mine. I gritted my teeth. I was hoping he would have bunked with Dylan. I'd never known a person so oblivious to someone not wanting to speak to him.

Just as I thought of Dylan, he walked in. He looked at me on the bottom bunk and Travis up on the top and walked to the spare bunk. "Just like the Four Seasons, huh?" he said, cracking a joke. I just lay back on the bed, ignoring them. It wasn't uncomfortable, but as predicted, my feet hung over the edge. I was agitated and tired and just wanted to stay here and not deal with whatever Mia and Leo had in store for us.

I slipped on my headphones and turned up the music just in time to block out Travis and Dylan talking. I closed my eyes and just tried to think of nothing until a hand shook my shoulder.

I yanked my arm away and opened my eyes. "What?"

Dylan motioned for me to remove my headphones, seemingly unfazed. "It's time for the meeting," he said when I slipped them off. I must have fallen asleep, which was surprising. Sleep didn't come easily to me these days.

I sat up, trying to inject some energy into my body. Dylan gestured to the bed. "I just about fit. Not great for you though, huh?" Dylan was fairly tall. About six feet on the nose. Travis was more around five ten. At six four, I was used to being the biggest in the room of most people my age. In hockey, I was just one of many.

Silently, I followed them out of the room, down the stairs, and into the main living room. A fire was roaring in the open fireplace. A large red rug covered the stone floor. Framed paintings covered the walls, landscapes from what I assumed were the many lakes and mountains in this region.

The girls were already seated, taking up one of the three-seater sofas. Despite myself, I immediately sought out Savannah. She looked tired. Her blue eyes were red, her peach skin pale. She was drowning in a thick cream sweater that she held tightly to her by the arms wrapped around her torso. She had pulled her long hair up onto a messy bun on the top of her head, and I couldn't stop looking at the curve of her neck and her pretty profile when she turned her face.

I sat beside Dylan and Travis on the second three-seater sofa. Mia and Leo entered a few minutes later, and each sat in an armchair beside the fire. They were holding a bunch of what looked like notebooks in their laps.

"So, what are your impressions of our first stop?" Mia said, smiling.

As far as therapists went, Mia and Leo seemed okay. But I didn't want or need therapists trying to dig into my psyche and help me. I just wanted to be left alone.

At least Mia and Leo didn't seem pushy—not yet. In the past year, I'd been through four therapists. None had ever gotten me to "open up." I barely spoke in the sessions, clock-watching until our time was up. None of them had ever been able to smash through the walls that had built themselves around me after Cill died. I didn't hold out much hope that Leo and Mia would be any more successful than their predecessors.

"It's beautiful," Jade said, her voice boasting an accented English.

Mia nodded when no one else offered an answer. Leo cleared his throat. "We have designed this trip to help you. Each country we visit is to aid you in overcoming the challenges you have been facing." Leo met each of our eyes. "Mia and I have an open-door policy. You're free to come and talk to us anytime. But you'll also have one-on-one time with us too. We understand, for some of you, conventional therapy has not been successful." The hairs on the back of my neck stood on end when I saw Leo's eyes momentarily flit over to me. Maybe I'd just imagined that. "But we hope this new approach will make you more comfortable about helping you through your individual grief journeys.

"You have all lost someone or more than one person of significance in your life. We won't push you to share with the group who those people are. We do, however, encourage you to bond, to share your personal pain, but how much you confide is up to you. You are all in the same boat, and peer support can be life-changing in terms of your own path to healing. But please know, we are here for you."

Mia smiled, and I caught Savannah's shoulders relax. Seemed she liked to talk about whoever she'd lost about as much as I did.

"Now," Mia said and got to her feet. One by one, she handed us what I saw was a journal and a pen attached to it. "As well as sessions with us, we will have a group session each day. These will be focused on anything from techniques to help you deal with feelings, or an open space for us to talk and answer any questions you may have. Or, of course, if you ever want to share your story with everyone else here." She held up a spare journal. "But one thing we require as a must is for you to start keeping a journal."

Mia sat back down, the flames from the large open fire casting shadows across her face. "These journals will be for your eyes only and can be used in several ways." The journal lay in my lap like it was laced with poison oak. "You could write about your time here—the experiences you have. The sights you see."

"It could be a place for you to write your feelings. Help you process your grief as we work our way through it," Leo tacked on. "It could be a place for poetry, if you so wish. If you draw, it could be where you sketch out whatever inspires you."

"Or, something we have found has worked exceptionally well for previous groups," Mia said, "is the journal could be where you get to express whatever you didn't get to say to the one or ones you have lost." The mood in the room went from neutral to downright clogging. Mia seemed to feel this, and her voice grew gentler. "We know, for many of you, you didn't get closure." An invisible hand gripped on to the front of my throat and began to squeeze. "You didn't get to say goodbye." She gave that sentence a moment to breathe, which was the last thing I needed. "When that happens, there are lots of things left unsaid." I shifted on the couch and felt people's eyes fix on me. Or maybe they didn't. I just felt like I was under a huge friggin' spotlight. I forced myself to still, feeling that hand around my neck squeeze tighter and tighter as unwanted images of that night began flashing through my head. The loud screeching of tires, the sound of metal crunching…the smell of blood—so much blood—the horn…the continuous, never-ending sound of the horn…

"And for others, it may be somewhere you tell your loved one how you're feeling, how life without them has been. Your dreams and fears. Your aspirations and your apprehensions. Everything and anything you want. No one will be reading them but you. These are for your eyes only," Leo said.

"You could use it as a place to talk to them again, no matter how trivial. Like a conversation," Mia said. My eyes began flickering around the room. Most of the others were nodding, seeming to readily accept our task. I wanted to get up and leave, my hands itching and my feet bouncing on the floor. I wanted to catch the first flight back to the States and get the hell out of this place and away from this group.

But then I caught sight of Savannah.

She was clutching the journal in her hands, her knuckles turning bone white. She wasn't nodding in agreement. She didn't seem sold on the idea like everyone else. Instead, she was staring at the plain blue color of the journal with such a devastated expression that I felt my stomach drop. Her breathing had grown quicker, and I was sure she was about to fall headfirst into another anxiety attack.

So, I watched her, just to make sure she didn't slip. And I began to wonder who had left her life and ripped it wide open. Had it been an illness that her loved one had had, or was their death quick and unexpected? Was it the other person's choice, like it had been—

"It's not happening," I suddenly bellowed, my harsh voice filling up the room. Those thoughts…I'd hit my limit. Couldn't take thinking of it anymore. I waved my journal in the air. "This is useless. And I have nothing to say to *him* anyway."

"We understand you think that way, Cael, we do," Leo said. I looked around the room, needing to find a way out of here. I felt caged. Trapped. I needed to *leave.*

"But we want you to hold on to it. Our hope is that, after some time with us, on this trip, you may feel differently. Maybe learn to open up. To explore your feelings."

I scoffed a laugh, then got up and walked to the fire. I threw the journal straight into the roaring hearth. "*That's* what I think of the journal," I said, feeling deep satisfaction at watching the blank pages begin to burn. "I'm not writing in it. What's the point? What's the point in *any* of this? He's dead, and he's not coming back."

There was total silence in the room, but my inner rebellion cheered me on. I would never talk to Cill again. Not in any form. Especially not in some journal where the entries to our lost ones were nothing more than a pathetic fantasy, a way to trick us into feeling better.

The crackling of the burning logs sounded like a thousand thunderbolts crashing as it devoured every inch of the journal. It felt like hours as I watched it. Then, I looked up and caught Savannah's gaze. Her face wore an expression of shock, but there was also something else... Understanding? Sympathy? I didn't know. But I didn't like how it made my chest ache, made my heart beat in double time. I didn't like how her big blue eyes were locked on me like she could see right through me.

I couldn't stand being in this room. I turned to walk away, to get the hell out, when Leo stood in my path. "Please, Cael," he said. I stared at the door. It was my escape to freedom, to get away from this woeful attempt at healing us. I felt the others' eyes fixed on me. How were they just sitting there accepting this? How did they *want* this?

Leo took a step closer. "Cael, please sit down." His voice was firmer now.

I fought with the need to disobey, but when I found myself looking over my shoulder at Savannah again, the expression of worry on her face made guilt or something like it run through me. Did she want me to leave or stay? Did she understand why I didn't want to be here? Was she scared of me? My stomach pulled tightly at that thought.

I didn't want her to be afraid of me.

I turned to face Leo. His hands were held up like he was handling a rabid dog. "We're just going to talk about the trip now and what we'll be doing. That's all." I smelled the journal burning in the fire, the paper singeing. It comforted me.

I turned back to Savannah again. Her eyes were filled with tears. It friggin' cut me. She met my gaze and then looked at the journal I'd thrown in the fire. I didn't know what she was thinking. Did she think what I'd done was wrong?

"Cael?" Leo pushed.

"Whatever," I said, then sat back down. I wasn't sure why I didn't leave. I decided not to think about it too much. Leo sat back down too, and I stared at that journal melting and merging with the burning logs. It reminded me of my now-ruined heart. That had burned to ashes too.

Mia's soft but steady voice cut through the weighted silence that followed my outburst. "Tomorrow, we climb." I blinked, turning my attention away from the hearth. I'd zoned out without realizing it. I felt the soft, velvety material of the couch brush under my palm, and the sound of Travis blowing his nose beside me hurtled me back to the here and now. When I looked over to him, his glasses were resting on the top of his head, and he was wiping at his eyes. He looked over at me too, and I saw the raw pain he was harboring glaring back at me.

Had I done that? Had my outburst done this? Or was it the idea of writing in the journal?

As I looked around the group, there wasn't one person spared. The way they all clutched the journals, it had to be that. The thought of the person you lost…expressing how it felt to miss them…it was brutal.

Losing someone you loved—the club no one ever wanted to be in, but one we would all be forced to join at some point in our lives. No one would escape it. It was simply a matter of when.

I found myself nodding at Travis, a subtle nudge of support, and he gave a small self-deprecating smile in return. I found myself wanting to know his story too.

One thing was for sure—we were all completely messed up.

"The Lake District is known for many things," Leo said, moving past how troubled we had all become. "Mountain climbing and walking being two of the most popular. And that's why we're here," he said and inched forward in his seat. "We're going to climb. We're going to walk. And we're going to explore this beautiful landscape on foot. Three of the region's biggest peaks."

My brows furrowed. We were here to walk? I could see the outlines of the misty mountains from the window in the living room.

"We have everything you will need for hiking," Mia said. "So we are giving you the rest of this evening to yourself. Dinner is at seven. Then it's an early start tomorrow. For now, get settled. Unpack. Hang out, get to know each other. And we'll see you soon."

Mia and Leo left the room, Leo's concerned gaze fixed on me as he did so.

"Well, that was heavy," Dylan said, earning a few awkward laughs from the others. I stared down at the journal in the fire. I had nothing to say to my brother, no feelings or life updates to share with him. He'd neglected to inform me of his, so I'm sure he would recognize the sentiment.

He'd given me, his little brother and best friend, no consideration when he'd made his choice. No communication. No signs. Just the seven scribbled words he'd rushed to write on the back of an old hockey ticket before he blew our world apart.

Instinctively, I reached down to my pocket and checked for my wallet. It was still there. And in the back zipped compartment was that goddamn ticket. And those words. Words I hadn't looked at in months, burning my skin like they had been written in an eternal open flame. Impossible to extinguish, forever seared into being.

That ticket hidden in my wallet felt like it weighed a hundred tons. But I couldn't bring myself to throw it away. It was the thing I hated most in the world, yet my most treasured object.

Getting to my feet, I didn't even look back at the others as I ran for the front door. I rushed straight into a sheet of ice-cold rain. The wind slapped at my face, a thousand palms across my cheeks. I didn't have my jacket, but right now, the elements attacking my body felt good. The stinging of my cheeks reminded me I was still here, alive, even if I wasn't really living.

Just thinking of that room filled with broken kids like me, Savannah clutching the journal to her chest like it was her biggest fear made flesh, made me furious. Travis crying just at the thought of writing something down.

It was bullshit. All of it.

Reaching down, I picked up a rock and launched it into the lake with all my strength. Before it had even hit the surface, I had another in my hand, bigger this time, pushing my forearm to its breaking point. Allowing the pent-up rage to race up my throat, I roared into the quiet night as I threw more rocks into the lake.

A broken branch came next. Then more rocks. One after the other until my muscles burned and my voice grew hoarse.

When I was exhausted, the questions came. Questions I knew would never be answered. One in particular—*why? Why* did he have to do it? *Why* did he have to leave me here like this? This wasn't who I used to be. But now…I didn't know how to be anything else.

Breathless and tired, I was left with only the self-hatred that always came after an outburst. Hatred with myself for not seeing the signs. For not seeing he was struggling. Tears built in my eyes. I tipped my head back to the heavy flow of rain, letting my tears meld with the heavy droplets, disguising the pain.

On a deep breath, I blinked open my eyes. I always felt a brief spell of numbness after an emotional outburst. It gave me a few moments of peace. Just a few precious moments to not sear. To just feel nothing.

I shuffled to the very edge of the lake, my boots an inch deep in the freezing water, and stared out over it. It seemed endless. Still and ancient. Like it would have seen a million people just like me, lost and alone and here for some kind of redemption arc. Some last-ditch attempt to save them from themselves and the shit hand the world had dealt them.

The gray clouds and moody weather reflected my dark inner thoughts. Then I cast my attention to the peaks, and for the first time in a while, I actually looked forward to something. There was a flicker of a spark. Some heat from a long-forgotten ember, deep down in my subconscious.

I liked exercise. I was physically fit. For a long time, sport was going to be my life. I was going to go professional. I lived for the dopamine rush that came with playing with my team, with the addictiveness of competition. Of playing the game I once loved more than breathing. I thrived in the coldness—the ice rink being my best friend. The idea of being trapped in hostel rooms and forced to talk about my past and feelings sounded like hell. Being outside in nature and walking, just…walking…, *that* I could do.

I stood out on the lake's edge until I was drenched and shivering, and the chill of the harsh wind began to rattle my bones. I turned to go back to the house, taking the long, winding path that skirted around the back of the garden. Just as I was about to leave the surrounding forest's tree line, I caught sight of someone sitting on the elevated rocky ledge that looked over another part of the huge lake.

Savannah.

I recognized her blond hair and petite frame. She was alone, huddled underneath a large umbrella, and she was holding something to her chest. For a moment, I thought it was the journal we'd just been given. But the notebook she held was larger and different in color.

I wondered what it was. For a second, I debated going over to her. I didn't know for what. I had the sudden urge to just sit with her. She'd met my eyes in the living room. For a few minutes, it was like I'd ripped my chest open and she was seeing all my jagged scars.

Maybe she'd understand. Maybe she would be the one person who wouldn't need to ask me probing questions because she knew what this living nightmare felt like. To have someone understand...to not have to explain what it felt like to be shattered so thoroughly, to understand that no words existed that could possibly ever explain this level of soul destruction. And to understand what it felt like to be alone with such devastating pain that, maybe, sometimes, made you wonder if it would be easy if you just ceased to exist too...

But then something inside stopped me, and the controlling, consuming darkness that kept me from doing so many things these days wrapped its arms around me, and I headed past where she sat and went straight into the house.

It reminded me I wasn't here to make friends. I just had to get through this trip. Then I could go home. And as to anything that happened after that?

I didn't even care.

Rolling Hills and Bobbing Boats

Savannah

It seemed impossible.

I stood at the bottom of Helvellyn Fell, surveying its massive size with my eyes. It stretched higher and higher up until its peaks disappeared in the low-hanging clouds. I couldn't even see the top, and they expected us to climb this? The day was—thankfully—dry, but the ground was crisp underfoot as the winter frost kissed the blades of grass that blanketed the uneven ground.

As I exhaled, my breath turned to white smoke and my lungs burned as I inhaled the frigid English air. A man named Gordon was our guide. An ex–British Army sergeant who would lead us over the next several days up and down the Lake District's three famed peaks.

I wasn't exactly athletic. Nothing about this appealed to me. But I was here, and I was introverted enough that I wouldn't put up a fight.

Ida's face popped into my head when I felt like backing down, and I took a deep breath and tried to psych myself up for the task ahead.

I *had* to try. For her, I would.

That was fast becoming my mantra.

I was wrapped up in layer upon layer of thermal clothes, with gloves, a hat, and a scarf that also covered half my face. It was freezing, but so far, I was warm enough to cope.

"Everyone ready?" Gordon asked.

I nodded like everyone else, and then we began our ascent up a steep set of jagged stone steps. After I climbed just a few, my thighs began to burn. Gordon raced up them like he had been here a million times—he probably had. Mia headed up the group, Leo pulling up the rear. Dylan walked next to me, seeming to find this walking in the moors easier than I was. Travis and Cael were behind us, with Lili and Jade up ahead with Mia.

Halfway up, I glanced behind me. Cael was climbing the steps with ease, not even a flush of exertion on his face. I had no idea why he hadn't passed Dylan and me to take his obvious place at the front. Travis was clearly finding it hard, but Cael stayed beside him, eyes focused on the top of the steps. Until he looked at me, and I quickly faced forward again. Just by looking at him, I couldn't help but replay yesterday in my head. In the living room. When he had jumped from his seat and thrown his journal into the fire, when he had challenged Leo and Mia. He was so angry. It seemed to pour from his every cell. Yet there were moments. Short, barely there moments where he caught my eye and his hostility disappeared and left the ghost of a sad and vulnerable boy in its wake. Only for it to capture him once again and bury him beneath high flames.

And yesterday… Cael had met my eyes in my moment of sadness. When that journal was placed in my lap and I began to break. He had seen me begin to fall apart, and the understanding I saw in his silver-blue depths reached out to me. Like for a moment, he just…*got* me.

The journal was designed to give me a place to talk to Poppy. To tell her how I'd been since she'd been gone…

My heart twisted just recalling the sheer terror that had sent through me. Because I could only tell her how I had failed. How I had crumbled. How life without her seemed pointless. How, after she died, something within me had collapsed, shattered my heart and soul into so many pieces it was impossible to ever glue them back together. That when she took her last breath, all my joy for life left too. That I had held her hand so long after she died that her fingers had been molded into a clutching position when I was finally forced to let her go.

And I would have to tell her that I had let her down. That I had failed her so badly that it had impacted everyone's life around me. Ida, Mama, Daddy…I had no friends, no life, and I was scared.

I was *petrified* that I would never be able to let her go. That this would forever be my lot—

Suddenly, my ankle overturned, and I stumbled on one of the many cracked and uneven stones. I felt myself begin to fall back. Dylan turned just as my heart dropped, but he was too far away to catch me. Then, just as I feared I was about to crash to the ground, strong arms took me in their hold and kept me standing. I scrambled to grip on to the black sleeves of a jacket, and I knew exactly who had caught me the moment I smelled that familiar scent of sea salt and fresh snow.

"I've got you," Cael said quietly, when my boot slipped once more on the icy ground, and I tried to find my balance. His voice sent shivers down my spine, ones that had nothing to do with the freezing temperatures and everything to do with the closed-off boy from Massachusetts who held me tightly in his arms.

And I felt he *did* have me. In his arms, I felt safe.

My racing heart began to slow as Cael righted my feet and steadied me on the step above him. I closed my eyes and managed to ward off my panic, then turned to face Cael. It took me a moment to realize that his hands were still on my waist. I swallowed deeply when I met his eyes. I was a large step up from where he stood, and he was still considerably taller than me. He was wearing a black beanie, but a few strands of his dark, messy waves escaped to fall over his striking silver-blue eyes.

"Thank you," I said, and Cael searched my face. I didn't know what he was looking for, but I felt my cheeks begin to burn under his attention. This time, my heart was racing for an entirely different reason. A feeling I wasn't used to.

He cleared his throat. "Are you hurt?" he asked. His New England accent was strong—thick enough to rival my Georgian. I was so struck by him talking to me softly that I didn't answer him.

But then he pushed. "Savannah?" Cael speaking my name brought me back from my wayward thoughts and grounded me again.

"Savannah? Are you okay?" Leo rushed to us and stopped beside Cael. Cael never took his eyes off me.

Dylan rushed to my side, and I caught everyone watching. I felt Cael's hands on my waist tighten slightly as the others pulled my focus.

Feeling my face burn from all the attention, I said, "I'm fine."

Cael began to bend down, and I swallowed as a strand of his dark hair brushed over my cheek. It smelled of mint. He checked my ankle, his large hands wrapping around my boot, testing the flexibility. There was no pain.

Embarrassment seemed to be my only injury.

"That okay?" he asked gruffly as he bent it left and right, making slow, careful circles.

"Yes," I said, voice hoarse.

"You sure?" Leo asked, concern on his face. I wouldn't be the reason the group couldn't carry on.

"I promise," I said. It was true. I had been too caught up thinking of Poppy and lost my footing. Thoughts of Poppy often made me lose concentration.

"Okay, then let's keep going," Leo said.

Cael released my ankle, and I felt a cold breeze wrap around me at his absence. He stood again then, rocking on his feet, like he was debating something in his head. Then he offered me his arm. "Do...do you need help the rest of the way up?"

I didn't answer with words. They escaped me at that moment. Instead, I carefully threaded my arm through his and let him walk beside me as we caught up to the others, who were waiting for us at the top. I tried to ignore the light fluttering of wings in my chest that his offer brought.

Dylan flanked my other side. When I felt his stare burning into me, I turned, only for him to subtly nudge his head in Cael's direction and gave me a bewildered expression. I knew Dylan only liked me as a friend; he'd given me zero romantic vibes. And he clearly found Cael helping me as surprising as I did.

I hadn't had many friends in my life. My sisters were always my everything. But I had felt an instant connection with Dylan. He was sweet. And funny. And I was pretty sure he was a complete lost soul, just like me. Only his bubbly personality awarded him a better facade, and his suffering was successfully disguised.

Cael's arm was strong under mine. He didn't say anything as we climbed.

But our shared silence didn't feel strained. It was…*nice*. Peaceful. I'd always been quieter in nature. I didn't need noise to fill any kind of void.

But this, to be serenely silent with another person, was a blessing I wasn't expecting on this trip. People always wanted to talk. It seemed Cael shared my preference for silence.

When we reached the top step, any cold I had been feeling from the harsh wind and low temperatures had vanished, and a sheen of sweat covered my forehead.

I fought to cool down, to catch my breath, my thighs screaming in exertion.

"Are you okay?" Lili asked me. Jade and Mia listened in too.

"Yeah, I promise. I just slipped."

My head was lowered in embarrassment. But then I felt Cael's arm tense underneath mine, a sharp breath escaping his lips. I looked up. I exhaled a quick breath too at the sight before me—the view that had captured Cael's attention. A green patchwork quilt of English countryside stretched before us. Trees of all shades of green and browns, stone walls, and snow-covered bare branches made an oil painting from the view. A mist roiled over the ground, like the sky had lowered to join with the earth for a few sacred hours.

It was utterly beautiful.

"Everyone grab a drink of water, and let's keep going," Gordon said, breaking through my admiration. As I went to take off my backpack, I realized my arm was still threaded through Cael's, holding on like he was my lifeline.

"I'm so sorry," I said, flustered, as I quickly withdrew my arm. I busied myself with my water. When I glanced up, I caught Cael's intense gaze locked onto me, but I quickly ducked my head. My cheeks felt set ablaze. My first thought was that Ida would be screaming in excitement right now, making suggestive comments and egging me on.

She had texted me last night, and Cael had ended up being the subject.

IDA: How's England?

ME: Cold and wet, spooky and Gothic. It's beautiful.

IDA: And what are the others on the trip like?

ME: Lovely. Hurt. Some quiet and reserved. Others not so much.

IDA: And what about the tall, dark hottie with the tattoos?

Her question gave me permission to reflect on Cael. I'd heard him outside at the lake. Screaming as he threw things into the water. And then I'd heard his silence. When his fury must have ebbed and another emotion took over. It made me sad.

ME: Angry

I sent that message but then remembered when he'd turned to me in the room and only desolation remained in his pained eyes. Just for a second, but it had been there. A second of his tattered, exposed soul.

IDA: It happens. Remember Daddy was real angry for a while

I recalled Daddy after Poppy had passed. He was so mad at the world for taking his baby away. It was awful seeing him that way, but I knew the man who lay underneath. I knew that hotheaded man wasn't who he was in his soul and that he would return to us again. Maybe…maybe the Cael who'd met my eyes in the living room was a short glimpse of the lost boy beneath.

IDA: He may need a friend. Someone to be there for him while he gets through it. Someone who understands

I stared at Ida's message. My pulse raced at that obvious suggestion.

ME: Maybe

IDA: Keep me informed on the climb! I can't believe they have you scaling mountains!

I smiled at the memory of Ida's messages as I drank in the idyllic view before me. She was such a romantic. Always seeing the good in people. Then I immediately thought of Poppy. She would have said the same about Cael too. Poppy was a helper. She would have taken one look at Cael and would have made it her mission to help him, help him through the pain he was so clearly feeling. She did that for me so many times growing up.

For a moment, that thought filled me with a heady kind of lightness, remembering her that way. How much she'd adored her family. How intensely she'd loved us all, loved the world. How much she'd loved Rune—right until her very last breath. But like on most days over the past four years, that happy thought soon turned into the gut-wrenching memory of seeing her on that bed, looking out of the window, broken and frail, death looming over her, breathing labored.

Any heat the climb had brought to me was quickly washed away by a spear of ice chasing down my spine. With shaking hands, I pushed my water bottle away and closed my eyes.

Just once...just *once*, I wanted to think of her and not feel beaten, not feel bruised. I wanted to remember her as she used to be—perfect, joyful, full of life. Not sick or sad or fighting to remain positive when there was nothing but tragedy awaiting at the end of her story.

Remembering her on her deathbed haunted me. It would wake me up in the middle of night. And every time I awoke, for a split moment, I would always believe I'd only had a nightmare and that Poppy was in her room, safely tucked up in bed.

Then I'd remember, and I'd lose her all over again. I lost her repeatedly, each morning when I woke and had to be reminded that she was gone. Every significant moment that happened to me, I would want to tell her. Every song I knew she'd like, and she wasn't here to hear it. Every piece of classical music I heard, and picturing her with her cello, eyes closed, head swaying, completely lost to the melody.

For four years, I hadn't watched an orchestra live. That was Poppy's stolen dream, and it felt like it would be a betrayal to watch one. I could barely listen to classical music without crumbling.

It was one of the worst things, I thought, when you lost someone. Having good news to share, and for a second—just one borrowed second of peace—being excited to tell them. Before reality inevitably crashed down, and you were reminded that you would never tell them anything again. And the good news you wanted to share suddenly didn't seem so exciting anymore. In fact, it felt like a stab in the chest, and you no longer looked forward to anything significant happening to you ever again.

A loved one's death wasn't a onetime thing that you had to endure. It was an endless cycle. A cruel Groundhog Day that burned away at your heart and soul until there was nothing left but scorched flesh where they once had been.

I shook off my hands when they began to tremble. I inhaled slowly, deeply, the cold air reminding me of where I was. The uneven earth beneath my feet crunched on the icy mud. I needed to walk. To move. To cast off this gutting feeling that was closing in. I almost fell to my knees in relief when Gordon began to lead us on.

For the first time in my life, I wanted to walk. I wanted to walk and walk until I couldn't think. Until my muscles were so sore and exhausted that I would fall into a restful sleep.

Just for one night.

"Slow down, ranger," Dylan said, jogging to catch up with me. I didn't. I pushed on, chest tight from how fast I was breathing. I kept my attention focused on the route before us. Everything around me was still and calm, my rapid breathing the only thing I could hear, until, "Jose would have loved this." Dylan's words were barely above a whisper, but I heard it, the whistling wind carrying it straight to my ears.

I slowed down and looked over at my friend. His eyes were downcast, and his hands were in his pockets. He flickered a nervous gaze to me, then said, "My best friend." He shrugged, like whatever he was going to say was trivial. "He's who I've lost. Why I'm here." It wasn't trivial at all. It was monumental. The *most* important thing.

"I'm so sorry," I said and saw that he had paled, his beautiful face crumpled in sorrow. Dylan forced his infectious smile, smothering the inner sadness that I could see was screaming to be released.

Silence stretched between us. Dylan's shoulders curled inward, and I felt a distance growing between us. I was terrible at this. At comforting others. At saying the right things. My heart tore apart for him. But I didn't know how to make it better.

Poppy was a helper… be *a helper…*

Dylan cast his gaze around us, at the lake down below that now appeared minute from this far away. I knew he was thinking of Jose. His eyes shimmered, and I couldn't take it anymore. Reaching out, I threaded my arm through his and pulled him close. Catching a hitch in his breath, and an extinguished sob, I laid my head against his shoulder and tried to show without words that I was there for him.

The wind caught a falling tear from my eye and carried it into the air. I didn't know Jose. But I was beginning to know Dylan and how special he was. So I knew Jose must have been special too.

"As special as special can be…" I heard Poppy's voice whisper into my ear, and that memory wrapped around me like a warm blanket. She'd want me to be there for others. To open myself up to them too.

I wasn't a tactile person, but Dylan's breathing seemed to come easier as I held him. Somehow, it made me feel better too. Sharing in one another's pain.

"He loved being outside," Dylan said. He laughed, and it was so pure it took my breath away. "He was always dragging me from my house and outside with him. Basketball, baseball, hiking, football. You name it, he wanted to do it, watch it, experience it." I squeezed him tighter so he knew he could continue if he wanted to. I was a good listener.

Dylan laughed, then said, "There was one time, we—" His laughter abruptly faded, and I heard that heart-wrenching sound that told me his throat had clogged, taking away his voice from the slam of a memory. A surprise attack from grief so strong it could drop you to your knees. I knew that good memory of Jose had been hijacked by one that was tormented. Dylan lowered his head, and he gave himself over to his agony.

Unsure what to do, I almost stopped and told Mia and Leo that we needed to turn back. That Dylan was hurting and needed some rest. But then Cael passed by us, and only for our ears he said commandingly, "Keep walking." He nudged his chin in the direction of Gordon, and I saw a flicker of sympathy for Dylan cross his handsome face. Cael stayed just a hairs-breadth in front of us. He glanced over his shoulder, like he was trying to not speak to us, to not engage. But then his shoulders sagged in defeat, and he said, "It helps. Just…keep walking. Push through. Exhaust the pain. Don't give it room to breathe."

Cael's eyes were haunted, and like me, I knew he'd been here before too. I imagined we all had. The triggers were awful. How a seemingly okay day could turn into a nightmare just by a familiar scent passing by, a memory resurfacing, or a million other things that made you remember your loved one was gone.

Grief was walking through a minefield with no protection or guide.

So we walked. With my arm through Dylan's, and Cael staying close by, we walked. We scrambled up gravel paths and carefully navigated a treacherous route called Striding Edge. We ate our lunch overlooking breathtaking views, then descended what had originally felt like an impossible climb.

When we reached the bottom, red faced, chill-slapped, and breathless, Leo said, "Turn around, guys." We did, seeing Helvellyn lording above us once more, looking both majestic and domineering. "Look what you've just accomplished," he said, and his words penetrated deep. "You climbed this. Even when I'm sure you didn't think you could." I exhaled a long breath and felt a bloom of pride burst in my heart. We had done it. *I* had. "Now, let's get back to the hostel and warm up."

I sat beside Dylan on the bus home, my arm again linked through his, hands held tightly. He didn't talk again that evening, but he held my hand in his like a vice. Cael sat on the seat across the aisle, his headphones firmly in place. But like he felt my gaze, he turned my way. *"Thank you,"* I mouthed. Cael's nostrils flared, and he curtly nodded his head in acknowledgement. Then he turned away, posture once again rigid and sealed off.

As night fell, I stared out of the window. We had done it. We were broken, and exhausted, and emotionally drained. But when we returned to the hostel, something inside of me had calmed. The oxygen that gave my grief life, like it was some living thing that existed inside of me, had been extinguished…for a little while, at least.

And I fell asleep. No nightmares. No insomnia. Just sleep.

I'd never been more thankful for a night of complete and utter silence.

"How did you all find yesterday?" Mia asked. Leo and Mia had gathered us in the living room for a group session. I wrung my hands together. I understood the premise of group sessions, but I never felt they worked for me.

"It was good," Travis said.

"I enjoyed it," Lili tacked on.

Mia smiled. "Good. Soon, we take on peak two: Scafell Pike."

Leo leaned forward in his seat. "But today we have our group sessions, and soon we'll start some one-on-ones. The rest of the day is yours. Maybe, for some of you, a chance to start your journals." Leo carefully regarded Cael, who was sitting, arms crossed and staring outside of the window. I was pretty sure he hadn't been given another one. It was obvious it wouldn't be welcome.

I blanched at the thought of the journal. I was still unsure if *I* actually could do it.

"Right now, we want to do some breathing techniques," Mia said. "For many, when going through grief, bouts of anxiety can be a common experience." I stared at my fingers, at the clear nail polish that was now starting to chip. "Anger can also be a heady emotion to deal with," Mia continued. "So we want to equip you with some tools to help cope if and when those times arise."

"They are also good for mindfulness," Leo added. "So, please, sit up straight in your seat and close your eyes." I did as they said, straightening my spine. "I want you to inhale through your nose for eight seconds," Leo instructed and counted out loud. "Now, hold that breath for four seconds. Listen to your heart beat. Hear its rhythm in your ears. Then, breathe out for four seconds." My shoulders relaxed a little. "When you panic or are stressed, this can be a great tool to help refocus and control what you feel is uncontrollable."

I placed my hand over my heart and felt it beating underneath my palm. "Sometimes," Leo said. I kept my eyes shut. "When we think of the ones we lost, we can feel powerless, out of control. This exercise can help you feel grounded." At his words, I automatically saw Poppy on her deathbed. Saw her in her casket, laid out in the front room of our house, Mama and Daddy rarely leaving her side, Rune sleeping on the floor beside where she lay. Refusing to leave her until she was lowered to the ground…where he just took up residence instead.

My heart fired off into a sprint at that memory. I could feel anxiety's talons begin to stretch inside of me, ready to take me in their hold, but then I breathed in for eight and held my breath for four. A ghost of a smile pulled on my lips when I heard the pace of my heart and felt it begin to slow, my panic subsiding until I could exhale a normal four-second breath. I had been taught this technique before, of course. But here, it was *working*. Maybe it was distance from Georgia where I lost Poppy or the peaceful ambiance of the Lakes that made this time help. Maybe I was subconsciously opening myself up to healing. I wanted so badly for that to be true.

"Good," Leo said, and I didn't open my eyes but wondered if he was talking directly to me.

"Another aspect that can be difficult," Mia said gently as she reminded us to keep breathing, "is for those who were there at the time of their loved one's death. Or shortly in the aftermath. Those memories can be disabling. They—"

A loud crash made me snap my eyes open, only to see Cael darting from the room. He had overturned a side table, the water it was holding spilled on the floor. I heard the front door slam, and silence engulfed the room.

Leo and Mia made no move to clean up the water. "Should we go after him?" Travis asked, concern clear on his face.

"We'll give him time to calm down," Mia said. "This will be hard for you all," she added. "You will feel every emotion possible. The stages of grief are not linear. They are cyclical. Anger, denial, bargaining, depression, and acceptance. They don't have to follow a particular order. You may not experience them all. And for some, one of the stages will have the biggest hold. You may experience all five, then begin them all over again."

"Grief," Leo said, "is a lifelong emotion. People who are forty years into their loss will still experience moments where they are utterly undone. What we aim to do on this trip is help you cope. I'm afraid grief is incurable. But we *can* learn to live with it. We can learn to find happiness again. To smile and laugh. And there will come a time where memories of our loved ones are more positive than negative. Where we will be able to talk of them again with happiness, not sadness, and remember the good times." He gave a wan smile. "That may feel a ways off right now. But it's achievable. We must let you all get there at your own pace and express your pain in whichever way you need to."

"There are no rights or wrongs here," Mia said.

"Now, let's try that again," Leo said, and he continued the class.

An hour passed and we were given free time. I grabbed the paperback I was reading and headed outside. It was a crisp, freezing day, but the sun was shining and the lake was glass still.

I bundled myself up in my coat, hat, and scarf. I heard the sound of voices coming from the living room but wanted some time alone. I walked around the back of the house, heading for the ledge that I had come to like reading on, when I heard wood scraping on the ground.

As I cut through the tree line to the lake's shore, I saw Cael untying one of the rowing boats from its tether. He hadn't come back inside since he'd left the group session. I knew Mia and Leo had checked on him. But I'd been… worried. Yes. I'd been worried for him. Maybe a part of me had wanted to come outside and read, just to make sure he was okay. He had been there for me a couple of times now. I wanted to return the favor.

Cael was dressed in his black coat and beanie, his messy hair escaping under the hem. His face was flushed, and his body was tense.

I stepped farther forward, and Cael's head whipped up. His jaw clenched as he watched me stand here, but he continued untying the boat.

"What?" he growled, barely looking at me.

"Are you okay?" I asked, heart in my throat. I hated seeing him this way. Seeing anyone this way. Drowning in such obvious pain.

Cael yanked the boat free and tossed the tether to the shore. His boots were in the lake, the water shallow and not yet wetting his jeans. I didn't think he was going to answer me, until he said, "You coming?"

I reared my head back in shock and stared at the boat. He was asking *me* to go with him? It was a traditional wooden rowing boat. Two oars attached on either side. I stared at the boat like it was an open flame. I opened my mouth, not knowing what to say, yet found myself uttering, "I…I'm not sure we're supposed to use them."

A disbelieving, almost cruel laugh fell from Cael's mouth before it was swallowed by a severe look of ire…and maybe a hint of despondence. "Just when I thought you might be *different*…" He shook his head, face reddening. "Of course you're not. Why would anyone here be able to understand—" His clogged throat seemed to steal his words before he leveled me with a look so laced with disappointment it physically hurt me. "Just go back to the others inside."

I watched the water cover his legs up to his knees as he trudged the boat out to a deeper part of the lake. He went to jump into the boat, when I found myself saying, "Wait!"

Cael stilled, then turned around. I felt my pulse race, blood rushing through my veins. And I caught what looked like a hopeful expression on Cael's handsome face. It was so raw, so open, so sincere…so *vulnerable* that it shattered my heart. "I…" I cut myself off, clutching my paperback to my chest. The wind picked up, tossing my hair over my face. *"He may need a friend…"* Ida's words circled my head. Cael shook his head in frustration and made a move to leave again, when my feet propelled me forward and I said, "I'll come with you."

Cael exhaled a long, deep breath, and in that moment, I understood. He didn't want to be alone. As standoffish as he was, as cloaked in darkness as he was, he was lonely and didn't know how to ask for company.

Cael's eyes narrowed as he observed me. For a moment, I thought he had changed his mind; then he slowly stretched out his hand. Nerves accosted me, but I took a breath, just like Mia and Leo had taught us, and I placed my hand in Cael's. His smothered my own, but his grip was firm, and as he gently drew me closer, he rasped, "Can I?" I didn't understand what he meant, until he placed his hands on my waist, and I realized he wanted to lift me onto the boat.

"Yes," I whispered, his hands on me causing those butterflies to flutter in my chest again. Cael picked me up like I weighed nothing at all. I gripped on to his biceps. He was muscled and lithe beneath my fingers. Travis had mentioned something about ice hockey in the airport. It hadn't gone down well with Cael at all, but that must have been where he got his fitness and athletic physique from.

"Thank you," I said and sat on one of the wooden plinths. Effortlessly, Cael climbed inside. "Your jeans," I said, seeing they were soaked to the knee.

It was freezing outside. A flare of panic cut through me. He could get sick. The thought of anyone getting sick these days sent me into a blind panic.

"I'm used to the cold," he said in response, then sat down and picked up the oars. He began rowing, the boat quickly taking us from the hostel's short shore to the wider depths of the vast lake. Other boats milled in the background, tourist cruisers lapping around the perimeter in the distance.

Cael was focused, pushing himself as hard as he physically could. The boat cut through the lake like a hot knife through butter. I held on to the side, the wind picking up in conjunction with Cael's speed. His face was flushed, and his breathing began to quicken. Minutes passed and sweat began to pour down his face. But Cael kept going, kept exorcizing the anger that seemed to live in a limitless stream inside of him.

It made me think of what Mia and Leo had told us about the stages of grief. That for some, one stage held them captive longer. I wasn't sure where I sat. I seemed to feel any of them on a given day.

The farther into the lake we got, the more the beauty of the place became apparent. From this new perspective, the lake looked completely different. Snow-capped mountains surrounded us; bare-branched trees housing thousands of birds stood proudly on small, isolated islands. I closed my eyes and felt the ice-cold wind hit my face. It stirred something inside of me. It made me feel somewhat...*alive.*

I didn't realize Cael had stopped rowing until the breeze on my face died and I opened my eyes. I swallowed back nerves when I saw Cael was watching me. The anger he was holding on to seemed to have dimmed, and that deep kind of desolation returned to his silver-blue eyes. Seeing me watching him back, Cael removed his beanie and ran his hand through his messy hair. He was rarely without it, and the sight of him hat-free...he was beautiful.

Cael looked out at the people on the other side of the lake. The tourists. Eating ice cream, feeding ducks, booking lake tours. I followed his line of sight. They seemed so carefree. So unburdened.

"What are you reading?" Cael's graveled voice sounded exhausted. I wasn't surprised. He had rowed at a breakneck speed until he clearly couldn't go anymore. But I also knew it wasn't just physical exhaustion that had brought him to this place. Life was exhausting too.

I had been clutching the book to my chest. When I pulled it away, I said, "It's about the Lake poets."

Cael's brow furrowed in confusion. "Who?"

"The Lake poets." I gestured around us. "Famous English poets who came to the Lake District to get away from the hustle and bustle of city living in the nineteenth century. They wanted to live among nature and rest and live a slower-paced life. They wanted a place to be in touch with their feelings."

Cael looked out over the lake again, oars stowed and his arms resting on his legs. He appeared lost in thought, until he said, "I can see that."

I tipped my head to the side, taking advantage of his preoccupation with the lake to study him. Tattoos seemed to cover every inch of him, small gauges in his ears, a lip ring in his bottom lip. I'd only seen him wearing black clothes. Yet even without color, he was stunningly beautiful. One of if not *the* most beautiful boys I'd ever seen.

"What did they write about?"

I blinked, too lost in studying Cael to process his question. When I didn't say anything in response, he turned to me, resting his chin on his crossed arms.

"Pardon?" I asked, cheeks blazing at being caught studying him.

Cael's eyes seemed to flash with annoyance. "The poets. What did they write about?" It was like he needed something to quickly occupy his mind. Something to take him away from whatever hell kept him trapped.

I could do that for him. "They were the English Romantics. Wrote of beauty, thoughts, and feelings—a bit out there for the time. Some of the most famous poets were Wordsworth, Coleridge, and Southey." I shrugged. "I guess they were seen as rebels. Shaping what they wanted poetry to be, disregarding the old rules. Using it to express their feelings."

"Do they have any of their poems in that book?"

"They do," I said and turned to one of my favorites by Wordsworth.

I went to hand it to him to read, when he said, "Can you read it?" My heart beat like a drum and heat infused my face. I went to shake my head, to refuse, when he said, "I like your accent." And my thundering heart just about stopped.

"I like your accent..."

I could feel my skin burning with embarrassment, but Cael still wore that devastated look in his eyes, and I yearned to make it better.

So I read.

"I wandered lonely as a cloud..." I read each beautiful line about skies full of stars, daffodils, and waves and marveling at these remarkable sights when pensive and still. And I felt every line. Reciting this poem in the place that was its muse was surreal and beyond a blessing.

When I finished, Cael's attention was fixed on me. He didn't say anything immediately, then rasped, "It sounds just like here."

I smiled and nodded. It was my sentiment exactly. "I'm nearly done, if you want to read it when I'm finished."

Cael stared at me again. And I felt like he was looking for something in my face. I had no idea what. "Thanks," he said.

I shifted in my seat and watched a small motorboat pass us by. A young family was on board. A mama, daddy, and two little kids wearing little red life vests. They seemed so happy and carefree. I remembered those days.

"Do you feel any better yet?" I dared ask Cael.

Cael inhaled a long breath and slowly exhaled. "I never feel better," he confessed, and his voice sounded as splintered as shattered glass. His expression was guarded, and I wondered what it had cost him to reveal that to me. Cael was so formidable, so tall and domineering, intimidating. Yet right at this moment, he seemed so fragile, so broken down by life I wanted to hold him tightly until he felt okay.

My heart fell. Because Cael's simple confession was as raw as my own feelings. I flexed my hand, wanting to reach out and hold his hand, but I didn't know if he'd want that—I didn't think I had it in me to be that bold.

A few silent minutes passed before he asked, "Where are you from?"

The boat swayed soothingly as a larger tourist boat sailed by, causing small ripples to flutter across the lake. "Georgia. A small country town called Blossom Grove."

Cael smiled the smallest and briefest smile, but it was enough to lift some of the gray from the day and let in a little sun. "A real Georgia peach, huh?"

I couldn't stop myself blushing if I tried. He had smiled. He was talking to me and it felt like a blessing.

"He may need a friend..." I decided Ida was right.

"Yeah. I suppose. You're from New England?" I asked in return.

Cael's smile evaporated, his walls building back up. He nodded curtly. "Small town outside of Boston."

I fiddled with the edges of the paperback I was holding. "I'm meant to go to Harvard this fall." I surprised myself with that admission. I didn't know why, but Cael suddenly tensed, and his eyes that had been so open and vulnerable quickly frosted over and took away any vulnerability he was exposing. I watched his body language change from open to defensive, and his usual high walls quickly rebuilt.

"Time to go," he said coldly and took hold of the oars.

Confused, I said, "Did I say something—"

"I said we're going *back*. I'm done here," he bit out harshly, voice brokering no argument. Chills sank into my bones, and I tried to think of what had just happened. What had set him off.

We didn't speak again as he steered us back. The same edge of frustration had returned to him, and he powered his way to the hostel's shore, just as harshly as we'd rowed out, his demons reattached to him.

When we approached the shore, I saw Dylan sitting on the ledge I liked to occupy. He gave us a wave, and only a couple of minutes later, we docked. Cael jumped out of the boat first, then yanked it all the way in so we were back on the stone-laced sand.

I went to climb out, only to feel Cael's hand fasten tightly around mine. "Can I?" he asked distantly and slid his hands to my waist when I nodded. He carried me from the boat, then placed me softly on the shore. The way he cared for me physically was in direct opposition to the way he was speaking to me. He caught my concerned stare for a couple of seconds, opening his mouth like he might say something, explain, but he then left for the hostel without another word. I watched him walk away, heart in my throat.

"Hey, Sav," Dylan said, jumping down from the edge of the ledge to head my way. I was still staring after Cael. Dylan followed my gaze. "Went rowing?"

I nodded, not wanting to share anything from the past hour. I didn't know why, but our time in the boat felt like it was personal, just mine and Cael's. I'd seen a glimpse of another side to him. He'd…he'd shown me the broken boy beneath the anger, had lowered his shield of fire.

I wanted to help him.

"Seems like a tough guy to get to know," Dylan said, pointing to the door Cael had just walked through. "Can be pretty scary at times."

I looked to my friend. "I don't believe he's dangerous. He's…" I sighed, still feeling confused. "He's hurting," I said and heard the defensive tone in my own voice. I understood that he seemed aggressive and unapproachable—he even did to me. But the way he had been on the boat…so quiet, defeated…it was obvious he was in so much agony it felt visceral.

"I know," Dylan said, a hint of guilt in his voice. He shuffled his feet. "Travis said Cael played hockey." I knew that. But Dylan said, "Like, high level hockey. As in, he was about to go pro, or at least he could have. At the very least he'd have been going to college to play, then on to the NHL. Played Junior Hockey for Team USA. He was their superstar." Pieces of Cael's scattered jigsaw began to fit together.

"I'm used to the cold…"

A wave of protectiveness washed over me. "I'm not sure Travis should be sharing Cael's story." Dylan seemed taken aback by the harsh edge to my words. I was too. But I meant them. Our stories were ours to share when we were ready.

"I think Trav's just a bit starstruck," Dylan said, carefully. "Travis is harmless, Sav. Chatty and has no filter, but harmless." Dylan tipped his head in the direction Cael had just gone in. "When Travis said Cael was good, I think that was an understatement. Apparently, he smashed every known record for his age group and even some beyond. By the sound of it, he was the most promising hockey star the junior league had seen in years. Then he just…stopped playing."

A knowing edge hung on Dylan's last word, and it became clear to me that Travis knew exactly why Cael had stopped playing, knowledge he'd relayed to Dylan. But I didn't want to know. If Cael ever wanted to tell me why he was here, why he'd stopped playing hockey, I wanted him to decide that.

"I'm going inside to read," I said, changing the subject. Dylan seemed frozen and unsure if he had upset me. He hadn't. But I was feeling...*protective* of Cael. I didn't think too much about why. "Are you coming?"

Dylan smiled in relief and threw his arm around my shoulders, then led us inside, chatting about anything and everything. We settled in the living room. I read about the poets by the roaring fire, Dylan, Travis, Jade, and Lili watching and rating British sitcoms on TV.

Night drew down, stars spattering across the sky, and I closed my now-finished book. I got up to head to bed, when I spotted Cael in the hallway's alcove, sitting in the cushioned window seat, arms crossed over his chest, headphones on and staring out of the window.

I walked over to him and carefully placed my hand on his arm. Cael turned and abruptly pulled his arm away. He glared at me for a second, before I saw his gaze soften a bit when he realized it was me.

He pulled his headphones back and said, "What?" He wasn't being harsh to me. Rather, he sounded exhausted, gloomy.

I handed him the book. "I've finished," I said. "It's really good."

He stared at the offered book like it was a live grenade. I saw the battle play out on his face on whether to accept it or not. It was clear he fought some kind of war within himself. But then he met my eyes and his shoulders lost all tension. He held out his hand and carefully took the book from me. "Thanks," he whispered and turned back to the window. I took that as my cue to leave.

I was almost at the door when I heard, "Night, Peaches." The surprise that unexpected nickname brought to my chest was so strong it felt like it had left a mark. I turned to see a haunted yet kind expression on Cael's face; then it quickly disappeared.

"A real Georgia peach, huh..." he'd said that on the boat.

"Night, Cael," I said, voice a little bolder, and drifted up the stairs, for once letting my heart race. Because this time, its too-fast beat actually felt...nice.

Heartfelt Words and Warm Embraces

Savannah

THE CHILL FROM CLIMBING SCAFELL PIKE STILL CLUNG TO ME LIKE A cloak. The weather today had not been like that of the Helvellyn climb. It was wet and stormy, the rain so heavy and cold that it seemed to sink into our skin and ice the marrow of our bones.

I had taken a scalding-hot shower to chase off the chill when we'd returned. But there was just something about today that had made me feel *off*. The gray clouds were oppressive, and the exhaustion from our hiking mixed with that of the jet lag was weighing down on me. I felt weary. And I yearned to go home. I wanted to feel the comfort of Ida's tight hugs, and I wanted to curl up on the couch with Mama and Daddy and just hear them talk about their day.

More than that, I wanted to see my Poppy in her Blossom Grove.

"It's been four years since your sister passed?" Mia asked, and I stared at the fire roaring in the small office that was acting as Mia and Leo's counseling room. I tensed at Mia's words. "How old was she when she died?"

I swallowed the lump that had risen to my throat. My throat always tightened when I was asked about Poppy. Like my body was defending itself from talking about my sister, from further ripping into an already open wound.

"Seventeen," I replied, forcing myself to comply. I wanted to be anywhere but here right now. But I had promised I would try. So, I clasped my hands together in my lap and kept my gaze downcast. I pulled the end of my sweater's sleeves down until they covered my palms. A nervous habit I'd always had in the moments I felt uncomfortable.

"Seventeen...the age you are now," Mia said, and she had clearly connected the dots. I nodded and stared back at the flames. The logs crackled and it reminded me of summers at the beach growing up.

"Was it quick? Her illness?"

I inhaled a fortifying breath and shook my head. "No," I whispered. "It stretched out over a couple of years." Tears brimmed in my eyes, and my mind took me back to those early days when Poppy was diagnosed. I could still remember Mama and Daddy sitting us down and telling me and Ida. I didn't think either of us had really understood the gravity of Poppy's illness. Well, not until we'd moved away to Atlanta for her treatment. Not until her appearance had changed, Mama and Daddy's smiles had become strained, and I'd realized that things weren't going the way we'd wanted.

I couldn't fight the memory that pushed into my mind...

I walked into Poppy's hospital room and stopped in my tracks. Ida's hand was wrapped in my own. She squeezed it to the point of pain when we saw Poppy looking so small in the middle of her hospital bed.

But that wasn't what had stopped us. Wasn't what had made tears spill over my eyes and track like twin waterfalls down my cheeks. "Your hair," Ida said, speaking for us both.

Poppy smiled and ran her hand over her bald head. "Has gone," she said, seeming just as upbeat as she always was. She tipped her head to the side. "Do I suit it?"

She did. She absolutely did. But then, she always looked beautiful. She was sixteen. Had been fighting cancer for a while. Had been getting lots of treatments...but I wasn't sure they were working. Ida and I were kept away a lot. I hated being away from Poppy. Something was missing in me when she wasn't around.

"You're perfect," I said and meant it.

"Then come here," she said and ushered us to the bed. "I missed you both so

much." As we climbed on, we were careful not to sit on the wires that were stuck in her arm.

Poppy wrapped her arms around us both. But I didn't feel comfort from that hug. I only felt terror. Because Poppy always gave the tightest hugs. But as she held us, squeezing us close like she would never let us go, I felt her weakness. Ida laughed and kissed Poppy on the cheek, oblivious. But I felt a change in my older sister. Some hidden sixth sense made the hairs on the back of my neck stand on end and a pit of dread burrow in my stomach. When I looked at Poppy, I saw the reason for it in her green eyes.

She wasn't getting better.

I could tell by her faltering expression that she knew I knew it too. "I love you, Sav," she whispered, voice choked. Poppy was always strong, but in that moment, she couldn't stop her voice breaking, and it told me what I feared most. She was going to leave us.

On a choked sob, I couldn't help but fall back into her arms. I vowed to never let go…

"She didn't deserve to die," I found myself saying, too tired to even be shocked at my willing participation. A low buzz of irritation began to build inside of me. I was tired and lonely, and I was so mad at the world.

"Most people don't deserve to die, Savannah. But sadly, it's also an inevitability in life." My hands curled into my palms, my nails digging into my skin. Mia leaned forward. "Some people are only in our lives for a short time, but the mark they leave on us is a cherished tattoo."

My bitterness fell away at those words and devastation quickly swept in, a flood of sorrow dousing the anger that had built in my veins. A cherished tattoo… She had been.

"I miss her," I whispered and felt that cold ache in my bones grow stronger. The exhaustion I felt was an anchor keeping me from moving, from sheltering myself from all these thoughts that I didn't want in my head, memories that I didn't want to relive. The exertion of the past several days was enough to make me powerless to resist them.

"I know you do," Mia said and passed me a tissue from the box on the table. I hadn't even realized I was crying. I wiped at my tears and stilled when Mia asked, "It's good to remember those we have lost. Is there something you can do that Poppy liked to do? A way to feel closer to her?"

My breathing became as choppy as Windermere Lake earlier today, because there was.

I was depleted from the hiking. But what made me the most tired was the constant running from my sister. I didn't know if it was because all my fight had been burned away along with my energy over the past several days, but I was sick and tired of avoiding the message Poppy had wanted to give me.

Above all that, I just plain *missed* her. I missed Poppy so much that at times I thought that how intensely I mourned her would kill me too. "I have a notebook," I said, never taking my eyes from the fire. I felt the heat on my face, the burning wood scent clinging to my freshly washed hair. "Poppy... she left me a notebook. One that she had written in." I shifted on my seat. "One I've never been able to open."

"And what do you feel about that now?" Mia gently pushed.

My shoulders dropped in defeat. "That I'm tired of fighting it."

"Do you feel like reading it now or at some point soon? In private, of course," Mia said. An oil painting of another part of the Lake District caught my eye. It was hung on the wall, and it immediately made me think of the Lake poets. They came here to escape, to get away from the world that was changing too much and robbing them of their happiness.

They came here to spend their final days in peace.

Maybe I was meant to be here too. Away from everything I knew in a place of calm and peace. Maybe this was where I was meant to hear from Poppy again. Here, on a trip to help me move on from her death and hold on to some semblance of life. To remember her lovingly, how she deserved, and not a memory I should be afraid of.

"I think so," I said and felt my breathing come a little easier. Though I'd be lying if I said there wasn't a pit in my stomach at the thought of finally opening the first page. What would Poppy have wanted to say to me? I couldn't imagine.

"I think that's a good place to leave it for today, Savannah," Mia said. I moved my aching legs and had to stifle a groan. There was no part of me that wasn't sore. I didn't really understand the purpose of this part of the trip; all I felt like we'd done was push our bodies to the breaking point. All of us were ground down and depleted of strength. It hadn't been the uplifting experience I'd hoped it would be.

I rose from the chair, and Mia smiled at me. "You did really well today, Savannah. I'm proud of you."

"Thank you," I said and gingerly made my way from the room. I climbed the stairs to my dorm and, with every step, felt nerves accost my body. I was climbing toward the notebook.

I was finally going to do it.

Luckily, Lili and Jade weren't in the room when I entered. For a few minutes, I simply sat on the edge of the bed and stared at my suitcase that was across the room. It was empty but for the notebook in the zipped pocket.

Suddenly, an arrow of light darted through the window, casting a refracted rainbow onto the wooden floor—one that ended just where my suitcase was placed.

I shiver raced up my spine. I was never religious like Poppy, and when she left us, any belief in a greater power seemed to drain from my soul. To me, we were all made of stardust. And when we passed, we'd take our place back amongst the stars where we were created. But, I froze and stared at that celestial strip of colored light. The hairs on my arms and the back of my neck raised like static was flowing around me.

Eyes closed, I tipped my head up toward the ceiling, in the direction of the stars, and wondered if this truly was Poppy telling me she was here as I embarked on reading her final words to me.

I stood and peered out of the window. The sun had burst through the overcast gray sky, its blinding reflection shimmering on the water like a golden halo. The rain had stopped, and the distant snowcapped peaks were illuminated like they were under a spotlight, casting them into a brilliant white glow.

It was...surreal.

Feeling the heat on my face from the winter sun's rays, I crossed the room and retrieved the notebook from the suitcase. My hands trembled slightly as my fingers met the paper, but it didn't deter me from what I had to do.

I went downstairs and took my coat and a blanket from the hook. As always, I made my way to the rocky ledge that overlooked the lake. And before I sat down, I stopped and just stared at the sight before me.

I wasn't sure I'd ever seen anything more majestic than this view. Windermere's water was calming, the wind was cold, but the sun on my face brought a glint of something that I had missed for so long—hope.

Sitting down, I wrapped my coat around me and crossed my legs. Poppy's notebook lay in my lap. I lost track of time just admiring Poppy's handwritten script. *For Savannah.*

My eyes shimmered as tears built within them. I wiped them away quickly, not wanting anything to harm or mar the final piece of my sister.

I closed my eyes and breathed in deeply. Then, on a measured exhale, I opened my eyes and finally turned the page. And I began to read:

My Dearest Savannah,

If you are reading this, I am gone. I have returned home. And I am no longer in pain.

I am free.

One of the greatest joys of my life was being your older sister. I adore you, in every possible way. My quiet and reserved sister with the kindest heart and the warmest smile. My sister who is happiest curled up in front of the fire with a book, low music playing in the background. The one who loves her family—especially her sisters—with breathtaking fierceness.

But Savannah, you are the sister I know is struggling most with my passing. I know you, just as you knew me. We had no secrets between us. We were the best of friends. And I know that my leaving has affected you the most. I know that you will not speak of it. I know that you will keep your pain trapped deep inside your big heart, and that breaks MY heart. I have faced my fate. I embrace death and what comes next with my eyes wide open and joy in my soul.

But I ache at the thought of leaving you and Ida. I can scarcely think of the life that should have stretched before us. The memories that we would have made. The three of us against the world.

The Litchfield sisters…as close as close can be.

But I also know that life still awaits you. And I want you to embrace it. I want, with all my heart, for you to take on the future with as much love as you showed me. Take Ida under your wing and LIVE. Live for us all.

You are so smart, Savannah. All my life I have been in awe of just how clever you are. How you view the world with a quiet intensity. How you miss nothing, studying the whole world around you. But the best is how much you love those you allow into your heart.

I adore my family. I love my Rune with everything I am. Yet the way you loved me and Ida... Lord, it is one of the best memories I will take with me. And I know that even in heaven, I will still feel that love transcending through the clouds. Not even death could take you away from me. I want you to know that.

I know because of my illness you have doubted the world. I know you struggle with my fate and feel it's unfair. But I've never felt that way. Plenty of bad things happen to good people. But I believe that a better place awaits us. That my passing, for us as sisters, will only be a temporary thing. A few minutes in the vastness that is eternity. And that before we know it, I will have you back in my arms and in my heart, where you always have been.

But for you, that is a way off. And what plagues me most, as I write this to you, is that I fear you will stop living. You may be quiet, and observe in silence, but that doesn't mean that you don't FEEL on an unprecedented scale.

And Savannah, I cannot bear the thought that my passing has hurt you. I fear you will let it limit you, and that is not what I want for you. I want you to live. I want you to thrive, and I want you to change the world with how smart you are, how lovely you are. So, I decided to write this journal to you. I know I'll be watching over you. I could never stay away from you too long. And even though I'm not standing there before you, I want to help you move on.

I need you to know that I am good, Savannah. I am at peace. I'm no longer in pain. And I am happy. I already miss you. Just the thought of not walking beside you in life is enough to crack my stern resolve. But my faith makes me believe that I WILL be beside you. In spirit.

I need you to believe that you are never alone.

I'm going to fill this journal with messages for you. And I'm going to convince you just how special you are. I'm going to help you cope with my loss. And I'm going to love and support you through the pages, when I can't be there in life. Because, my beautiful sister, I love you more than life itself and will never be truly gone. You will always have me. I just need to convince you of that fact.

I love you, Savannah. Never forget that, because love will always carry you through.

Your devoted sister,
Poppy

A shuddering cry ripped from my throat, so loud that birds from the surrounding trees scattered into the sky. I ran my hand over the page as tears fell in deep rivers from my eyes. My shoulders shook with how badly I was crying, and I was defenseless in stopping this gut-wrenching sorrow from spilling out. Poppy…my Poppy… I shook my head and tipped my head up to the sky. I wanted to believe she was watching me. I wanted to believe she was there for me, walking beside me like she'd said, but—

The sound of a branch snapping behind me made me whip my head around. Cael stepped out of the tree line and held out his hand. "Sav—" he tried to say. His permanent scowl was gone and worry etched into his handsome face, but the gutting sadness, the tears and the cavern of loss this letter had buried inside of me, turned into anger, so swift and quick that it left me out of control.

Closing the journal, I jumped to my feet, ignoring my screaming muscles and snapped, "What are you doing here?" Cael held up his hands, trying to show he meant no harm. But it didn't matter. I felt wired with fury. The ache of loss was so potent it was like fuel to an already roaring fire. "Why did you sneak up on me? Were you watching me?" My voice was rising higher and higher and I couldn't control it.

Cael didn't move, like I was a horse that could be easily spooked. "I was out walking, and I heard you. You seemed upset. I wanted to make sure you were okay." His voice was gentler than I'd ever heard it, reassuring, but it ricocheted off me like Teflon.

"I DON'T NEED YOU!" I screamed, my loud outburst echoing around the quiet lake. "I don't need this place!" I said, gesturing to the hostel and the surrounding peaks. Then like someone had pulled out a plug, I felt the raging anger inside of me begin to drain away, taking all my fight and strength with me in mere seconds. My shoulders sagged and rolled inward—utterly depleted.

"I just need her," I whispered. I covered my face with my hands, and I broke. I broke so badly I feared I would drop to the ground, but before I could, strong arms wrapped around me and helped me keep standing.

And I cried. I cried and cried against Cael's chest. I threaded my arms around his waist and just held on. It was so nice just to hold someone and not pretend for one more minute that I was okay. Nice to not get up each day and put on a mask that I was sick and tired of wearing.

"She died," I said, all my imprisoned sadness storming to the door to freedom. "My sister. My perfect older sister *died*. She died and left me here to exist in this world without her, and I can't... God, Cael, I just don't know how to live without her here. How do I ever feel whole again?" I buried my head into Cael's chest, wrapping my fists into his thick coat. He just held me tighter. Held me against him and kept me sheltered in his embrace.

I cried again until I felt dehydrated and worn. My chest was raw from exertion, but I still held on tightly to Cael, so tight that I wasn't sure I could ever let go.

Cael removed one of his hands from my back and began running it through my hair, soft and soothing. My breathing was hitched in the aftermath, my body flinching as it tried to piece itself together again after so thoroughly breaking apart.

I breathed in Cael's fresh scent. Let the smell of snow and sea salt infuse my body. I focused on trying to keep breathing, but I felt my heart kick into an arrhythmic sprint, the familiar panic that attacked me daily rising to the surface.

Cael's hand stopped on my hair, and he slowly leaned me backward. He read my face with his careful, moon-shimmer eyes and instructed, "Breathe in for eight, Peaches." I stared into his eyes and did exactly what he said. I didn't have any fight left within me to resist. He breathed with me, and I mirrored his actions.

"Now hold for four," he said and the hand that was on my hair dropped to run up and down my spine. Goose bumps followed in his wake, but the rhythm of his hand became my guide. Like Mia and Leo had taught us, I listened to the echo of my heartbeat, and I listened to it begin to slow. "Exhale, Sav," Cael said, and I did. I repeated the exercise a few more times. My panic slowly subsided, as did my sobs until only I remained. I was numb, but there was a new feeling within my soul. A glimmer of lightness that I couldn't recall feeling since before Poppy was diagnosed.

Cael's hands slid up my arms, running over my coat, until they cupped my face. Crackling embers ran down my spine, and I glanced up at his face. He was searching my eyes, every part of my face. Then he pressed his forehead to mine. No words were spoken, but that skin-on-skin contact brought kisses of warmth to my cold body.

"Are you okay?" he asked after several suspended seconds.

"I think so," I said. Then stopped myself from finishing that sentence. I was so *sick* of the placating. So, I shook my head, revealing my truth, feeling his soft hair kiss my cheek. "No," I finally confessed. "I'm not. I'm not okay. Not at all."

Cael didn't immediately say anything. Didn't comfort or offer me anything about him in return. It made me uneasy. Feeling too raw and exposed, I made a move to step away, embarrassed at being so vulnerable, when he rasped out, "I'm not okay either."

My gaze darted up and collided with his. His eyes glistened, and I got the sense that that was the first time Cael had admitted that to anyone... maybe even to himself. My arms were still wrapped into his coat, so I freed them and lifted one hand to place on his cheek too.

His skin was rough from the short stubble under my palm. I swallowed. I'd never touched a boy this closely before. Cael held his breath, but when my finger ghosted over his cheekbones and down his tattooed neck, he exhaled and closed his eyes. This moment was a respite. We were breathing the same air, and we were sharing our pent-up pain. Sharing our secrets in the safety of the cocoon we had created.

I could have stayed this way forever.

Then, a drop of rain hit my cheek, followed by another in quick succession. Remembering my journal, I broke from Cael and quickly grabbed hold of it. I brought it to my chest, just as the heavens opened and the rain began to pour. "This way," Cael said and grabbed hold of my arm. We didn't run toward the house; instead, we raced toward the shore and a roofed jetty that sat beside the rowboats.

I ran after Cael, and the surge of energy it took to bolt from the torrential shower made a heady, unexpected burst of laughter spill from my lips. Cael's hand gripped me tighter as the foreign sound sailed into the air and seemed to explode like a firework above us.

As we reached the jetty and ducked underneath the pitched roof, I leaned over and fought to find my breath. White puffs of smoke created a cloud around me, until my lungs calmed and my pulse slowed to a steady beat.

The rain pattered on the wooden roof, but inside the jetty was dry. I lifted my head and saw the lake spread before us, the pitched roof making a picture frame of the famous stretch of water. "Beautiful," I whispered, overcome by the sight. Ducks swam joyfully in the torrent, raindrops causing thousands of ripples to flutter over the lake's surface.

I tore my attention from the view and brought it to Cael, and my heart sank. Guilt quickly took me in its hold. "Cael," I said, hearing the shame in my own voice. He was staring at the view too. But his spine was straight, and his jaw was tight. I feared he'd shut down again. "I'm so sorry."

I didn't think he was going to answer me, or even acknowledge my apology, back to the distant Cael he'd been since we arrived. I wouldn't blame him. I had never spoken to anyone so badly in my entire life. He was only trying to help me, and I threw that act of care right back in his face.

I left my apology floating in the stagnant air around us, allowing the sound of the rain to fill the uncomfortable, awkward silence. Without taking his eyes off the lake, he said, "You sound beautiful when you laugh."

My sunken heart jumped back into my chest and began to pound at the unexpected utterance of those six words. Cael moved to the edge of the jetty, and sat down, letting the cold breeze kiss his face. It didn't go unnoticed that he had left a spot for me beside him, an unspoken invitation for me to sit down too.

Clutching my journal, I did just that.

"Cael—" I went to apologize again, when he said, "I'm sorry about your sister."

Just the mention of Poppy closed my throat. "Thank you," I rasped out. I wondered if he would push anymore. But he didn't. I traced Poppy's handwriting on the cover of the notebook. I could just picture her in her window seat in her bedroom writing this. Even with all that she had been fighting, she had still thought of me.

"She was called Poppy," I found myself sharing. I thought I'd be shocked that I'd spoken her name out loud. But I'd found that when it came to Cael, some deep part of me knew he was safe. Cael sighed and crossed his legs, resting his elbows on his knees. He was giving me the space and time I needed to speak.

I blinked away tears. "She had cancer." I held the journal to my chest. I tried to fool myself that it was like receiving a hug of support from my sister herself. "She died just under four years ago after a long and tiring battle."

Cael's head bowed, almost like he was in prayer. I cleared my throat of its tightness and said, "She was my rock. My ship's anchor, and I've been unmoored ever since."

Minutes passed in complete stillness. I stared at the snow on the distant peaks. I'd never seen snow fall. I'd hoped I would see it here, but the English winter had only graced us with gray skies and endless rain. The notebook slipped from my lap as I adjusted my legs and landed in front of Cael. I realized that the rain had begun to slow, and then a large cloud cleared, and the sun came back out to cast its golden rays all around us.

A familiar halo over the lake.

I went to reach for the notebook, but Cael was already holding it out for me. A slither of sunlight had escaped through the wooden panels in the jetty walls and was spotlighting Cael's outstretched hand...like Poppy was reaching out to him too.

I placed my hand on his and lowered it back to his knee. Cael frowned in confusion. "Poppy left this notebook for me," I explained. "Today was the first time in almost four years that I've been able to open it." His eyes widened. "I've only read the first page. That's what I had just read when you found me." Sympathy engulfed his face.

"Here," he rasped, and held out the notebook again, like it was made from glass, and he was afraid it would break in his hands. That sunbeam landed on his hand again. And I felt it. Felt Poppy guiding me to share this... to share my pain.

"Read it," I said, and Cael's face paled. He began to shake his head no. I placed my hand on his again and turned the cover to reveal Poppy's first entry to me. "Please," I said, then added, "It would be nice for someone here to know her too."

I saw stark fear in Cael's expression at my request. But whatever he saw in mine made him look down and begin to read. I closed my eyes, and tipped my head back, letting the cool breeze run through my rain-dampened hair. I let a small smile grace my lips when I smelled a familiar hint of snow and sea salt...then what appeared to be vanilla.

There was only one person I knew who smelled like that.

The feeling of a hand covering my own broke me from my peace. I opened my eyes and looked down at those hands, only for Cael to turn them over. He threaded his fingers through mine, grasping hard. He had placed the notebook down on the ground.

Butterfly wings fluttered in my chest. More so when I saw his free hand protectively covering Poppy's beautifully handwritten script. "He killed himself," Cael said, barely loud enough for my ears to detect. But I heard it. I heard it, and although it was an almost silent confession, it was as effective as a scream in a large cave, echoing off the walls and slicing through my heart.

Cael's grip tightened even more in mine.

"Cael—"

"My big brother. Cillian. He...I—" He shook his head, cutting off his shaking voice, unable to carry on. "I'm sorry, Sav. I can't—I can't talk—"

My soul ached at that news. My heart screamed in pain. I couldn't imagine that. I couldn't imagine losing Poppy or Ida in such a tragic way. I wouldn't be able to bear it. How did you ever move on from a loss like that?

Cael... No wonder he was so lost and alone.

I brought our joined hands to my lips and kissed the back of his hand. Kissed the opaque broken-heart tattoo that was etched into his skin in thick black ink. He couldn't finish what he was trying to say. Couldn't bring himself to say those words aloud.

"I'm sorry," I said in return, my words not capturing the level of sympathy I felt for him. Expelling any shyness into the open air, I inched closer to Cael and placed my head on his broad shoulder. His body was taut and tense as I did so. But then he exhaled a long, labored breath and laid his head against mine.

We sat, joined, watching in silence as the sunlight glittered off the lake. I had never had this. Had someone share in my pain and be so open about theirs with me. But my stomach fell when I thought of what he'd told me. His older brother had taken his life. That's why Cael was so angry. So broken inside. That's why—

"She loved you," Cael said, interrupting my racing mind. His minty breath dusted over my cheek. He moved his head a fraction, and his lips ghosted over my hair. I closed my eyes and let the feel of his intimate comfort embrace me. "She loved you so much."

"She did," I whispered, not wanting to pierce the fragile bubble of peace we had created. I opened my eyes and watched a bird of prey circle above one of the lake's many small islands. "I miss her more than I can say."

"I miss him too," Cael finally said, and I felt just how much that was by the way he melted into my side, like he was seeking any form of human contact, a safety net from a great fall that admission had caused. I wondered how long he had been walking alone, shunning any support from the world. I moved closer to him again, so close there wasn't even an inch of air between us.

Two broken pieces searching for a way to feel whole.

"She left you an entire notebook," Cael said. He paused, then quietly confided, "I was left seven rushed words on an old, discarded hockey game ticket."

My soul shattered for him. Poppy's passing had destroyed me. But I had answers as to why she had died. I was under no doubt that she adored me; she'd made sure to tell me often enough. I had gotten to say my goodbye, even if that goodbye had ultimately been my undoing.

Cael... He had been robbed of that vital moment.

I heard his breathing starting to hitch, and I was sure I felt a tear fall from his cheek and hit the side of my face. But I didn't want to disturb this moment. I knew it was poignant to him.

It was for me too.

Sitting in silence, we watched the winter sun begin to ebb and darkness cloak the top of the peaks, chasing down the hills and spreading out onto the lake before us. Stars tried to peek through the overcast sky, and the moon hid its glow behind thick unrelenting clouds.

I shivered, the lowering sun taking away any heat from the winter's day and plunging the night into bitter coldness. Cael must have noticed, because he turned his head, lips grazing my ear and said, "We'd better get inside."

I nodded but didn't move for a few moments, not wanting to break from this pleasant numbness we had slipped into. But when a gust of arctic wind found its way into the jetty, we had no choice.

Straightening, I reluctantly released Cael's hand and got to my feet. Cael followed suit, picked up Poppy's notebook then handed it back to me. I met his eyes then. The first time since we had sat down and spilled our mutual heartaches.

There was something new in his stare. Like he was seeing me differently. I certainly was him. Gone was the unapproachable boy from just outside of Boston. And in his place was Cael Woods, a broken boy who was mourning the tragic death of his big brother. Despite how different we were on the surface, underneath it all, we were kindred souls.

Cael slipped his hand through mine again, and the chill that had taken us under siege was fought back by a striking sword of warmth. Cael led the way from the jetty and toward the hostel. The frosty ground crisped underfoot. I looked up to the sky and the dark clouds that impeded the view of the stars.

I walked as lonely as a cloud… Wordsworth's poem came to my head. As we entered the hostel and separated reluctantly at the top of stairs to go to our respective rooms, I realized that maybe I wasn't as lonely as I believed I was.

And neither was he.

I couldn't help but recall how he'd been when I'd shouted at him. My fury…it hadn't offended him—it had called to him. In that moment, I'd been a living reflection of how he felt inside. I'd burned with grief like he'd burned.

He'd seen me, and in depths of my despair, I had understood him too. And he had calmed. He'd confided in me.

Cael… He was suffering so badly…

After I showered, I climbed into bed. Curiosity won out; I took hold of my cell phone and searched the internet for Cael's name. Hundreds and hundreds of hits appeared. The first picture shown was from a couple of years ago, and I couldn't believe my eyes. He was dressed in hockey gear. But he was free of tattoos, free of piercings…free of grief. His wide, infectious smile was breathtaking. But what made my chest tighten to the point of snapping was the person beside him, the one with his arm wrapped proudly around him.

Cillian.

I ran my finger over Cael's boyish, carefree face. Then I froze when I read the caption. *The Future of Hockey. Harvard's star center, Cillian Woods, with younger brother Cael.*

Harvard.

The next story made my heart fall further. *Cael Woods heading for Harvard! The Woods Brothers go Crimson!*

The article explained that Cillian had gone to Harvard. Cael had signed on to go too. Cael was a year older than me. *Harvard…* That was why he'd brought us in from the lake that day. I'd told him I was going too…but he'd clearly *not* gone. It didn't take a genius to understand why.

A sense of something bigger than me danced above my head. I wasn't one to believe in something unworldly, but I couldn't deny the serendipitous nature of our meeting. There was something about Cael Woods that had called to me from the moment I saw him. Drew me to him like a moth to a flame.

Made me want to protect him and help carry the weight of his broken heart.

With an aching soul, I turned off my cell phone, already feeling guilty about encroaching on his life this way. I shouldn't have done it. But I couldn't shed the image of his carefree smile from his face. Couldn't stop thinking of Cillian with his arm around Cael, smiling at his younger brother like the proudest sibling in the world. I couldn't help but wonder what had happened to him to believe that death was his only way out of whatever plagued him. I wondered if Cael even knew.

I brought the phone to my chest, like I could embrace young Cael through the screen. Hold him before his world was blown apart. My head was a tornado of thoughts, haphazardly lapping around one another. Poppy's face came to my mind. Right now, I would have talked to her. She would have known what to say.

Then I felt my hands itch with the need to tell her somehow. I placed my phone on the table beside me and picked up the journal we had been given by Mia and Leo. Opening the page, I did just that—I let myself confide in my big sister like I always had...

My Dearest Poppy, I began, and for once I didn't fight back the grief that I had been holding off for way too long. *I read your first entry today.* I blinked away tears but held strong. *I miss you so much. Hearing from you after so long was like visiting heaven itself, only to be told I had been there too long, and it was time to go home.* I thought of my day. Then thought of Cael and me on the jetty. *I'm not doing well, Pops. I've been sent on a trip to help me cope with your loss. I didn't think it would help.* I brought the bottom of the pen to my lips while I thought of what to say next, then began writing again. *But I have met a boy. His name is Cael...*

And I wrote to my sister. Wrote to her like no time had passed. Like she was simply in another place in the world, remote and unable to answer my calls. Alive and well and waiting for my letters to reach her.

And when I put down the pen, there was a new ease to my breathing. The weight I constantly carried on my sternum was a fraction lighter. Placing my head on the pillow, I closed my eyes and tried to chase sleep. But then Cael's face came into my head and my heart squeezed again as I replayed his confession. Cillian. His brother was named Cillian Woods. I wanted to make sure I never forgot it. He deserved to be remembered.

I thought about Cael's cracked voice, the kiss to my hair, his cheek against my head. And I ran my fingers over the hand that he had held so tightly while shedding his deepest trauma.

It still felt warm.

Shared Secrets and Farewell Skies

Cael

STEPHAN: Your mom said you're away. Just checking in. Miss you, man.

I STARED AT STEPHAN'S MESSAGE, THEN LEFT IT ON READ AND MUTED MY cell. His unanswered messages were now in their hundreds, and I had ignored every one of them. The truth was, I couldn't face my best friend. I couldn't face my parents. They'd texted me constantly since being here, and I had ignored every single one. Their calls too. I left it to Mia and Leo to tell them I was safe.

I couldn't face anyone from home. Especially now. I was split open from yesterday with Savannah. I couldn't stop thinking about finding her out on the ledge, sobbing and falling apart. How she'd been shaking with fury, the same destructive emotion that lived in my veins. How she'd screamed at me, her pretty face contorted with pain. And I couldn't stop thinking about the jetty. Her vulnerability, her honesty. How when I held her hand, it felt easier to breathe. Why? What had it meant? Being beside her, holding her…it had given me a moment of peace I never got. And it only grew deeper with what she'd told me.

What *I'd* told her.

Cillian.

I hadn't even meant to. It just...*tore* from me, like the confession was clawing to get out and just be heard by *somebody* else.

I'd told somebody about Cill. I'd told *Savannah* about Cill... I didn't know how to feel about it. I felt different this morning. I was completely shaken. The darkness was still there, lying low in my veins, but...*shit*, I'd told someone about Cillian. And the bitterness within me wasn't quite so strong. It wasn't consuming my every waking minute. I'd forgotten what this even felt like.

What was happening?

"You ready?" Travis said as I packed the last of my clothes in my case, lost to my thoughts. Today was our last climb. Tomorrow, we left for Norway. Unaware of how rattled and confused I was, Travis waited for me in the doorway as I grabbed my coat and hiking boots. He was always trying to reach out his hand for friendship. I'd shunned him at every point.

He was kicking the floor with his toe. "Sorry if I'm a lot," he said out of nowhere. It shocked me still. I met his eyes. "I don't have many friends, especially not after..." He shook his head and started for the stairs, leaving what he was saying unfinished.

I didn't know if it was Savannah's influence or if it was that I wasn't feeling myself, but I called out, "Trav." Travis turned, freckled face red from embarrassment. "We're cool."

A long exhale left his chest and made me feel like a total prick. Truth was, I hadn't gotten to know anyone on this trip. Ignored them all and hadn't cared who'd been caught in my cross fire.

Except for Savannah. But she was different. Had *been* different since I'd first laid eyes on her. And more so now.

"Really?" he said, expression brightening. I nodded and pointed to the front door and the bus that awaited us. I saw most of the group was on the bus already. My nerves made my hands shake when I thought about seeing Savannah again. How did I face someone I'd just told about my brother?

Everyone was talking amongst themselves when Travis and I climbed on, and I took a seat a few rows in front of where everyone else sat, not looking anyone in the eye. I wasn't trying to ignore them this time; I just needed space.

I stared out of the window at the lake. The rain had finally stopped. The clouds had cleared, and the sun was high in the sky. It was still freezing…but it wasn't as dark and depressing as yesterday.

Maybe, after speaking to Savannah, inside of me wasn't as dark and depressing either. Even just a sliver of some internal light was progress.

Running my fingertip along my bottom lip, I could still feel the softness of Savannah's hair against my mouth as I'd kissed her head and inhaled her cherry and almond scent. I still felt her soft palm against my calloused one, battered and rough from years and years of hockey. I'd needed to hold her. I didn't know if it was for her or for me, but in that moment of vulnerability, I'd had to hold her hand.

I hadn't wanted to leave that jetty. Our problems had seemed so much smaller as we huddled in that wooden hut. Our sadness was freed, just for a couple of hours, and we just…*were*.

The seat beside me dipped. I turned my head and my stomach flipped. Savannah. Savannah looked up at me under her long, fair lashes, blue eyes seeking permission that this was okay. That her being beside me was okay.

Her presence immediately set me at ease. No more shaking hands. And strangely, there was no regret for telling her about Cillian.

"Hey, Peaches," I said, voice strained. I felt bare and open to her gaze. Vulnerable. I wasn't used to being vulnerable to anyone. Never had been in my life. But I had been to this pretty girl from Georgia, in the rawest possible way.

Savannah dug into her backpack and brought out a sandwich bag filled with pastries and fruit. "You didn't come down to breakfast." She shrugged, that blush of hers I loved so much bursting on the skin of her cheeks. "I thought you might be hungry." I stared at this girl in wonder. This Georgia peach who had managed to climb over my high walls.

"Thanks," I said and took the bag from her. The truth was, I'd been a coward that morning. I bailed on breakfast because I didn't know what I would say to Savannah when I saw her. I didn't know how to be around someone who had seen all my hidden scars, so open and exposed like that.

I should have known she wouldn't make it awkward.

Quite the opposite…she'd made it okay.

Savannah settled into her seat. The bus began to move. I tried to not let the usual discomfort of being in a vehicle unnerve me. So, I stared out at the views that had cemented themselves inside my brain. I would never forget this place.

"Last day," Savannah said. I knew she was pushing herself to talk to me. She was even more reserved than me. I understood that it wasn't natural for her to make idle conversation. But I also understood she was trying.

For me.

"Yeah," I said and reached into the sandwich bag, bringing out a choco-late croissant. I sighed after taking a bite. I was starving.

"One more climb," I said, wanting to try to say something, to engage. To make last night not feel so *big*.

Savannah nodded, and then a small smile graced her pink lips. I paused mid-bite just to witness it. I didn't know how she did it, but this girl could just cut through whatever dark fog surrounded me like she wielded a sword forged of pure light.

No one on this trip smiled much. Some had smiled a little bit more here in Windermere. But, as bad as it sounded, I didn't care about anyone else's smile. Only hers. Because Savannah's smile lit up the sky when she did. Her smiles were as shy as she was, but just that small upward curl at the corner of her lip tugged like a freight train at my heart.

"I think my legs are thankful it's the last one." I felt myself smirking back, and Savannah stared at me too. Maybe in the same way I stared at her. I searched inside for any discomfort. But around her…there was only peace. I couldn't wrap my head around it.

Savannah pressed her head to the back of the seat, seeming content; then Dylan and Travis came and sat on the seats in front of us.

They leaned over the back of the chairs. "Hey, you two," Dylan said, and I caught Savannah shaking her head in humor at the boy she seemed close to. "What're you talking about?"

I wore no sign of a smirk now, and when I looked at Savannah, her smile had disappeared too. It didn't take a genius to know we were both still raw and thrown from our talk yesterday, so I said, "How annoying you both are." I surprised myself that I'd even cracked a joke. It felt strange coming from my lips.

Dylan's mouth dropped open in mock offense. "Cael. You talk! And you have a sense of humor!" Travis laughed. I used to be humorous. *Before*. I supposed it was the first time on this trip that I'd ever really let anyone but Savannah see an echo of the real me. Savannah's shoulders shook in quiet laughter, and when I briefly glanced at her, I saw the relief on her face. And maybe a hint of pride.

Our secret talk in the jetty was still safe. And it would only ever be ours.

"So, are we excited for Norway?" Travis asked. I shrugged. I wasn't really excited for any of the countries on this trip. But I liked this place. I was kind of sad to be leaving it. There was just something about being out here in the Lakes, away from the rest of the world, that calmed me.

"I can't wait," Dylan said. "I just hope it's not more hiking." Travis nodded in agreement.

I didn't think Savannah was going to speak, but she said, "I know people from Norway. I'm excited to see their homeland." Dylan and Travis listened for more information. But Savannah stopped there, and I noticed a slight strain to her mouth. I wondered who she knew from there and who they were to her.

Savannah didn't speak for the rest of the journey. Neither did I. But that was okay, as Dylan and Travis talked for us all. For once, their incessant chatter was kind of nice. When the bus stopped and we found ourselves at the bottom of Skiddaw, I looked up at the mountain and the ice that capped the high peaks.

One more climb.

I buckled my rucksack straps around my waist, when someone stood beside me. I looked down to see a pink beanie covering dark blond hair. Savannah peered up at me, and then she walked beside me. We climbed up hill after hill, scrambled up rocky paths, and Savannah never once left my side. When we reached the top, we stared down at the view—at the green and white quilt that the fields made, and the water that sparkled like it was made of pure glitter.

Being up this high made me feel so small. It made the world and beyond feel so infinite. So vast. It was as unsettling as it was comforting.

We climbed down and reached the bottom, breathless and tired. But we had done it. Dylan and Travis came to stand beside us, Jade and Lili flanking us too. And we all peered up at the peak we had just climbed and a surprise shot of emotion clawed up my throat. I coughed, trying to chase it away, but it only sank back down to my chest and into my stomach, pulling the muscles tight.

"You might be wondering why we brought you here, to the Lakes," Leo said and cut through the silence. He came to stand before the six of us, Mia moving next to him. His face grew somber. "You've all been through so much. I know we've barely scratched the surface on that, but this five-country trip has been designed to help you cope with your grief."

Mia stepped forward. "Resilience," she said and let that word hang in the air around us. "To cope with grief, you need *resilience*."

"We brought you here to get away from the hustle and bustle of life," Leo said. "Where else more perfect than this little heaven on Earth." He gestured to the Lake District around us. "What better place than a region brimming with peaks to climb, and breathtaking views to become lost in. But a place that would also push you to your very limits."

"And you did it," Mia said, pride lacing her voice. "Jet-lagged and cold and body worn, you did it. You took what felt like an impossible task and you faced it head-on. One foot in front of the other, one step at a time, you climbed these mountains, scrambling and breathless, exhausted and depleted. You *did* it. You made it to the other side. You. Did. It."

"If we had told you when we first got here, my guess is that you would never have believed you could do this..." Leo trailed off, and shards of ice cut down my spine. Savannah edged closer to me, the side of her hand brushing against mine. I wondered if Mia's and Leo's words were hitting her with the same impact. "But you did." Leo met each of our eyes. "Just like we will get you through your grief."

My knees felt weak, because I didn't see how I would make it through this hell I was in. I understood the metaphor. The peaks represented our grief, obstacles in our way to happiness. But I would have backed myself to climb these peaks. I was physically fit. Had a sportsman's determination. Coping with my grief? I didn't back myself at all. I worried more than anything that I could never defeat it.

Feeling myself start to spiral, I rocked on my feet, only to feel Savannah's hand brush against mine again. And I didn't know why I did it. I didn't try to overthink it, but I reached out with my little finger and I wrapped it around hers.

Her hand was trembling, and it immediately made me focus on her and shake off the panic that had settled within me. Savannah was in hell with me too. *Everyone* who was here was in the fire with me too.

We weren't alone.

I inhaled a deep breath. *Resilience.* I wasn't sure I had any when it came to coming to terms with what Cillian did. I wasn't sure Savannah did either when it came to her Poppy. But if this trip didn't help us? What then?

"Resilience," Mia repeated. "You *are* resilient. Each and every one of you. And you are all stronger than you know." She smiled. "*We* see it in you, shining as brightly as the sun. We see hope. We see bravery. We see strength."

"We're proud of you," Leo added and then left us all on the spot, to let their words soar above our heads. The long sleeves of our coats hid Savannah's and my joined fingers—still clinging on, finding strength through one another. It was our secret—how much we were keeping each other standing. I absently watched other people on the peak climbing and striving to complete the difficult route.

The sound of boots crunching on the frozen ground pulled my attention. When I looked behind me, Dylan, Travis, Jade, and Lili were heading back to Mia and Leo who were waiting at the bus.

But Savannah remained beside me, suspended in the moment.

"We did it," she said, giving a sliver of hope echoing what Mia and Leo had said. I wondered if she believed she could get through her grief too, that this trip was going to heal her, help her move on.

"We did," I said and watched an older couple reach the bottom of the peak. The woman threw herself into her husband's arms in celebration. I curled my finger tighter around Savannah's. To experience that level of happiness again seemed so out of reach.

It seemed *impossible.*

Savannah broke through my inner despair by quietly whispering, "I…I think Poppy would be proud of me." A slight tremble returned to her hand as she said it, and a sorrowful rasp laced her voice. This time I had to look at her. Savannah's gaze was facing the peak, so I lifted my free hand and brought my finger to her chin. Her skin was freezing to the touch. I slowly guided her face toward me. Her eyes were lowered. I waited until she lifted her blue gaze to meet mine. There were tears in her eyes, but when one fell down her cheek, it was met with a wisp of a smile.

My heart fired off into a sprint. Savannah gripped my finger tighter, and I allowed a single, fleeting moment to think of my brother away from how I last saw him. How he had been *before*. My eyes closed and I could just see him now, cheering for me as he had when I was on the ice, huge grin plastered on his face and his fists in the air. I could picture him here too, waiting at the bottom of the peak, shouting *"That's my brother!"*

A choked sound ripped from my throat at the visual, and my tortured mind tried to quickly slam the door on that thought, tried to prevent the damage it could do. But I held on to that image regardless; it was better than the other one that haunted me every minute of every day.

When I opened my eyes, the view was hazy, until a tear fell down my cheek, clearing my sight. I focused on Savannah, taking solace and fortitude in her touch, and managed to find the courage to say, "He would be proud of me too."

Savannah gave my finger two soft squeezes. I noticed she did this when she wanted to give me comfort but clearly lacked the words. And as simple as a gesture it was, it was a healing balm over an open wound. It stopped the pain for enough time to help me catch my breath.

After holding each other together for several more minutes with our understanding stare, we turned back to the bus, but never let go of one another. Not even when we sat back on the bus.

As we rolled away, I wondered if somewhere, somehow, Cillian really was cheering me on. If he was helping me move on from his loss. I rarely let myself wonder if he had somehow lived on. If he'd made it to an afterlife where there was no more pain and only peace and freedom surrounded him. We weren't religious. Never talked about what we thought came next. I didn't really have any strong beliefs. But I wondered if he ever saw me here, left behind, crumbling without him, and wanted to reach out and tell me it was going to be okay. That I would see him again someday. And that although life on this Earth couldn't hold him like he needed, he was free now.

Sadness clawed up my throat trying to rob me of the need for that to be true, but two soft squeezes of Savannah's hand helped me fight those claws back down and clutch on to that morsel of hope.

I rolled my head to Savannah. She squeezed my hand again and sent my pulse soaring. *Resilience*, I thought as we took to the winding roads back home.

I prayed like hell it could get me through.

The fire was blazing, England's clouds still giving us a break and awarding us with a star-filled sky for our final night, like it was saying its farewell too. Around the lake was pitch black, but for Bowness, the tourist area, was still filled with people. I imagined it looked like this all year round, no matter the weather. I would live here if I could.

We had eaten dinner and were now all gathered around the campfire outside on folding camping chairs. I'd forced myself to be here tonight. Not to escape to my room or the window seat that had become my sanctuary here. My emotions were all over the place. It made me feel shaky, and, for once, I didn't want to face that alone.

Mia and Leo had gone inside, leaving the six of us to ourselves. As much as I liked Leo and Mia, it was nice to be out from under their microscope. Leo had watched me like a hawk. I knew he'd seen a change in me. He had yet to broach it with me yet, clearly letting me sit in this new state for a while.

But I knew he'd pull me aside at some point.

Dylan, Jade, and Lili were using long sticks to roast marshmallows in the flames. Savannah was right where I wanted her—beside me. She had an amused expression on her face as she watched Dylan and the others laugh and joke around.

"I got the goods!" Travis shouted, coming from inside of the hostel, cans of soda in his hands. I huffed a laugh as he handed out the cans like they were beer. I took a Coke from him and sipped at the sugary drink.

Soon, Dylan, Jade, and Lili sat around the fire, and we all descended into silence, until Dylan said, "So, do we think any of this is working?"

The mood of the group immediately shifted from somewhat happy to morose, and like so many times on this trip, we couldn't escape from the truth of why we were here. Grief was like that, forever reminding you it was close by.

Jade shifted in her seat and said, "I think it's helped a little." She cast her wide, brown eyes around the group and nervously said, "It was a car accident." I froze in my seat when those words fell from her mouth. She stared into the fire and said, "My mama and little brother. One random Tuesday morning." My heart fell. Savannah was lock still beside me. "It was instant; they didn't feel a thing. I at least know they didn't suffer." Jade began to break. Lili and Travis sat on either side of her and placed a supportive hand on her back. "There's just me and my papa now. And my grandparents." She wiped at her eyes. "It's…it's been difficult to move on. Impossible to live without them most days."

I played with my hands, picking at my nails just for some way to expel this nervous energy that was swarming around me. When Cillian died, I'd shut down completely, kept everything inside. I wasn't used to talking about death so freely. Wasn't sure I could yet. The few times I wanted to scream how I was feeling from the rooftops, to finally just let the dam of grief break, my protective wall would close everything down.

I felt a tug on my coat sleeve. I glanced to my left. Savannah was offering her hand. My heart's too-fast rhythm immediately slowed when I took hold of it. She gave me two familiar squeezes and we stayed linked in the space between our chairs. I stayed transfixed at her perfect profile. How did she always know when I was breaking?

Maybe it was because she was breaking too. I gave her two squeezes right back. A flush bloomed on her pale cheeks.

"Being here. Away from Texas—my home," Jade said. "It's given me time to breathe." She gave a watery smile. "I think it's helping. It's helping me sort some things out in my mind."

Lili laid her head on Jade's shoulder. They had grown close since landing in England. So close that Lili offered her support by saying, "I lost both my parents." Savannah flinched, her hand pulling slightly in mine, like that thought was a dagger to her heart. I held her tighter, giving her an anchor, and found myself thinking of my mom and dad. My gut twisted when I thought of how I was when they saw me off at JFK. I hadn't even said goodbye. I'd still had zero communication with them. I didn't even know how I'd begin…

"They were recreational sailors. Loved the water." She smiled, and I saw the love she had for them shining through her sadness, even in the dark. "One day they went out to sea and a storm blew in unexpectedly." Her bottom lip trembled. Jade wrapped her arm around her. "The boat was found, wrecked. But they never were."

"I'm sorry," Dylan said, and I wanted to say the same. But I couldn't speak. I didn't know how they were able to.

Lili smiled at Dylan and wiped her tears from her cheeks. "I think this trip is helping me too." She looked to Jade. "Having others who are going through the same thing…it helps. Makes me feel less lonely." She sat up straighter. "I'm an only child. I live with my grandparents now, who are great, but I feel like I've been going through this alone…and…yeah…" she trailed off with a tired sigh. *It's not the same,* I finished off for her in my head.

It wasn't. I loved my mom and dad. They had lost their eldest son. I had lost my brother and best friend. We couldn't understand each other's grief because it was different. An ache set in my chest when it hit me—I was an only child now too. And that was the worst thing…that he'd left me all alone. For the rest of my days.

I caught Jade and Lili's curious eyes landing on me, Savannah, Travis, and Dylan, obviously wondering if we would share our stories too. But I wasn't going to speak about Cill. I couldn't. I'd barely told Savannah anything, and what I did confide in her felt like I was ripping out my heart as I did so. By the stiffness in Savannah's body, and the way her pretty eyes were downcast, I think she felt the same.

Travis cleared his throat and sat on the edge of his chair. His eyes were darting nervously around the group. "You don't have to share if you're not ready," Dylan said, voice supportive. He and Travis had grown closer of late too. It seemed we were all pairing off. I looked down at my hand in Savannah's.

I was glad she was with me…more than glad.

"No," Travis said, and "I can talk," he said but closed his eyes, like it was easier to say this out loud if he couldn't see everyone before him. "I was the only survivor in my class from a school shooting." The blood ran from my face when he revealed that. I couldn't imagine… I didn't even know how to react to that.

"Travis…" Dylan said and immediately crossed the fire to where he sat. He kneeled beside him. Travis opened his eyes and smiled, but it was strained, and his lips trembled. His trauma was exposed for us all to see.

"It's the guilt that's the worst, you know?" Travis said and wrung his hands together. "Like, why me? Why was I the only one he didn't hit? Out of a class of twelve, I was the only one who dodged a bullet." Travis shook his head and his chin wobbled as he fought to fight back his tears. "That's what I can't get over. I see parents of my friends looking at me sometimes and I know they're wondering why it was me and not their child that was spared." He let out a humorless laugh. "I ask myself that too. But mainly…" He took a deep breath. "They were my *friends*. I'm from a small town in rural Vermont. I'd known these kids since kindergarten, some even before that. They were my only friends, and now they are all gone. And I witnessed them—"

Dylan wrapped Travis up in a hug before he could finish that sentence. Some things didn't need to be said out loud to be understood. Savannah sniffed beside me, and when I turned to her, tears streamed down her face. They looked orange in the light of the fire. I couldn't bear seeing her this way, the sight splitting me apart. So, I shifted my chair until it was right next to her.

"I want this to work," Travis said and pointed to us all. "I want this trip to work so badly, because I can't keep living with this darkness I carry inside, with this weight on my chest. Some days I can't get out of bed because the grief is so tiring. It feels like I can't breathe."

"You miss being happy, *feeling* happiness," Dylan said in understanding, and Travis nodded. "Me too," Dylan confessed.

"Me too," Jade said, followed by Lili.

"Me too," Savannah said, almost inaudibly. My heart was beating so fast at how much we were all sharing that I thought it would burst right out of my chest. But I allowed myself to think of my life before. Because there *was* a before and after when it came to grief.

I allowed myself to think back to winters on the pond playing hockey, Christmas mornings and game days...simple memories from when we were truly happy.

I *knew* happiness then. And I had taken it for granted. But it made me think that if I'd felt it once, maybe, just *maybe*, I could perhaps feel it again.

"Me too," I finally whispered, the wood from the fire crackling loudly as I did so, drowning out that wish that took so much energy for me to cast out. But Savannah had heard me. And she leaned against me and put her head on my shoulder, two squeezes to my hand.

I was starting to crave this feeling. Because Savannah, from Blossom Grove, Georgia, made me *feel*. After a year of drowning in darkness, Savannah made me feel something I thought was forever lost to me—hope.

She made me hopeful that there was more to my life than *this*. I didn't know what was happening between us. I refused to let myself overthink whatever was binding us together. For once, I wanted to just let the universe take the reins and guide me.

I cast my eyes over the lake and the peaks one last time before we went to bed. I would forever remember the English Lake District as the place where Savannah entered my life. I had no idea what would happen on the rest of the trip, what would happen to me. No idea what Savannah and I would become. I didn't know if what Mia and Leo had planned for us would truly drag me out of this infinite darkness I was stuck inside. But one of the many bricks that had built a wall around my heart had fallen because of this girl. Just one solitary brick, but it was a start.

It was a *start*.

And that had to count for something.

8

Resurfaced Dreams and Frozen Smiles

Savannah,

As I sit here writing in this journal, I am watching you outside in our yard. You are sitting under the apple tree and reading. Ida is practicing her dancing to the side of you. And I am smiling so wide just watching my two best friends. One loud, one quiet, but both perfect in my eyes.

When I am gone, I will keep this memory playing on a loop inside my head. And when I look down and glance down upon you, I will still cherish the bond we all share.

I want you to cherish one another for the rest of your lives. Never lose that bond that we held so tightly in life. And when you hold one another, know that my spirit will be holding you both too. I will always be beside you. Whatever journey your life takes you on, have courage and confidence, as I will always be there beside you. You will never be alone again. Just like I have never been alone in this life. How could I be with you in my life and heart?

Say yes to new adventures, Savannah. They may just lead you to happiness.

Always Forever,
Poppy

———————

Savannah
Oslo, Norway

ME: Can you guess where I am?

I took a picture of the view before me and pressed send. It was only seconds later when a message came back.

RUNE: I recognize that place.

Then he added: How is it going?

I watched the people milling about below in the square, a large ice rink taking up most of my view. There were already people skating. It was beautiful here. We had only landed in Oslo last night, but I was already in love with the place. I could imagine the Kristiansens living here. At that thought, a wave of sadness crashed over me.

ME: She would have loved to see this. Your home country. It's so beautiful.

Poppy often talked of visiting Oslo with Rune…but life had other plans for her before she could.

It took a few minutes for Rune to reply. I wondered if he was busy or whether my words had made him sad.

RUNE: She would have.

Three dots appeared underneath, and he added: I believe she's with you now. I blinked away the sheen of tears that built in my eyes.

ME: I'd like to believe that too.

Those three dots appeared again, then: Your sister will never leave you. And she would be so proud of you.

My chest tightened, and I stared back down at the busy square, the smell of the food trucks drifting up to the hotel's window I was sitting at. Rune was right. Poppy would be proud of me. She always was. Any little achievement I made in school, she acted like I'd just changed the world. In sixth grade, when I won the science fair, Poppy celebrated like I'd won the Nobel Peace Prize.

ME: I know

I didn't have any other words to say.

RUNE: You can do this, Sav. I believe in you too.

I smiled as Rune sent that final message. Since Poppy died, Rune had grown even closer to my family. He had become the big brother to me and Ida that he was always destined to be. It would always be unfair that he had lost his soulmate. She was so young…they hadn't even been given a real chance to make it.

I felt the rumblings of despair stir within me. It only lessened when a knock sounded on the door. I opened it to find Jade and Lili on the other side. "Come on," Lili said, taking my hand. Jade grabbed my coat off the coat stand in my room. "You're coming skating with us."

"Oh, I can't skate…" I tried to say, but as they tugged me down the hall and down the three flights of stairs to the chilly square, I understood they weren't giving me a choice. It felt familiar, three girls running through the city to have fun. I'd spoken to Mama, Daddy and Ida this morning too. I missed them more than breathing. But I was okay. I was pushing through.

Jade led us to the skate-rental cabin. As Jade and Lili handed in their shoes in exchange for their skates, I said, "I have never been skating before." They looked at me like I'd grown an extra head. My face flamed under their disbelieving scrutiny.

"We'll help you," Lili said and gestured to my boots. "Hand them in and get some skates."

I did as she said, feeling nerves accost me. I sat on the bench and laced the skates on my feet. I tried to stand, and almost fell to the ground. "Woah!" Jade said and linked my arm. "Let's take this slow."

Lili linked my other arm and we headed for the ice. The cold breeze from the ice kissed my face, causing chills to race down my body. It smelled fresh, and clean…it smelled like Cael.

I roved my gaze over the rink, wondering where he was. I hadn't seen him yet today. Hadn't seen Dylan or Travis either. Maybe they were all together. Lately, he'd been a little better at mixing with the rest of us. And he didn't seem so shut down. I hoped that remained that way. I…the way I was feeling toward Cael was…all-encompassing. He gave me butterflies, and my heart thundered in my chest when he was near, when he held my hand or clutched my finger with his. But it was hard to be around someone who was so consumed by anger, hard to truly let them in.

But since the night in the jetty, he seemed a little softer. I believed that was because he'd spoken of his brother's death, said aloud what had happened.

He had freed the words that had been so hard for him to say, that had festered inside of him until they had turned blood into fire.

I hoped more than anything that speaking to me had set him on the right path.

"One step forward," Lili said, taking me from my thoughts, and I placed my blade on the ice. I immediately slipped and released my hold on Jade and Lili to grip the boards on the side of the rink. I expelled a nervous laugh. Lili and Jade stood before me. "You go. I think I need to stay here for a while," I said. Lili opened her mouth to protest, but I nodded. "Honestly. I just need to get my bearings."

"You sure?" Jade asked.

"I'm sure," I said and watched them skate off. They were a little wobbly at first, but within minutes they were circling the rink, waving to me as they passed. I inhaled the frigid air, that fresh scent wrapping around me again. A hand landed on my shoulder, and then Dylan and Travis were pushing onto the ice in front of me.

Dylan held out his hand. "Let's go, Sav." Travis slipped and grabbed on to Dylan, bringing them both crashing to the ground. The sound of their loud laughter, so free and easy, made me smile. After what Dylan had told me about his best friend, after the horror that Travis had revealed to us last night…their unburdened laughter sounded like the bells of heaven.

"I think I'll just leave you to it," I said and shuffled my way back onto dry land, far away from the chance of falling over too.

"Sav!" Dylan said in complaint. "Fine!" he added, then pointed at me as he scrambled to his feet. "But you're getting a hot cocoa with me after this."

"Deal," I said, then scooted to the bench and quickly untied my skates, and in less than a minute I had my boots on my feet and a lot less fear in my heart.

I stood at the boards and watched my new friends circling the rink, holding hands and having some much-needed fun. It was such a beautiful sight to see. If they were anything like me, it had probably been quite some time since they'd let themselves experience true joy like this.

I huffed a silent laugh as Travis pushed by Dylan, almost knocking him off his feet again, when something drew me to look to my left. The square was busy, the rink becoming close to full, but through the crowd of people, I spotted a familiar black beanie and coat. Cael was staring at the rink, a gutting expression on his handsome face.

Any happiness I had found watching my friends disappeared at the look of absolute sadness on Cael's face. He stood back away from the boards, hands in his pockets.

I blew on my hands to ward off the cold and walked to where he stood. I approached slowly so he could see me coming. When he did, his spine straightened.

"Hi," I said and stood beside him. Cael's eyes were fixed back on the ice rink.

He wanted to be on there.

I recalled what Dylan had told me. Cael was a hockey player. Was immensely talented, from what he'd divulged. But he no longer played. The way he was watching the skaters, I believed that in his heart, he still wished he did.

"You don't want to skate?" I said, testing the waters. Cael's gaze hardened, and he shook his head. A firm, unyielding no.

I huffed a laugh as Lili and Jade began to race Travis and Dylan. I wondered if those who opened up at last night's campfire felt any lighter today. Their reason for being here had been shared. They had been so brave. I wondered if it felt liberating to just place your pain in the hands of people who supported you. To pass it over to others in bite-size chunks so that your burden was lessened, and life would seem just that little bit less unkind.

"I don't know how people do it," I pushed myself to say. I didn't want Cael feeling so low. Wanted to try to make it better. "I couldn't even move my feet without slipping."

I didn't expect a response, so surprise made me turn my head to Cael when he said, "It just takes practice." He met my gaze. "I...I..." he trailed off, fighting back whatever was trying to stop him talking, and said, "I saw you." He inhaled a long, strength-giving breath. "I wanted to come and help you, but..." His words became trapped in his throat and his pallor turned ashen.

What was this moment costing him emotionally? It seemed to cost him everything to be staring at this rink, to be speaking these words.

I placed my hand on his arm. "It's okay," I said and moved before him, blocking the view that was causing him so much strife. "Do you want to grab some food?" I pointed to a cluster of food cabins nearby. He nodded and tore his eyes from the ice. It appeared as though the rink was a magnet to him, drawing him close. But he was resisting the pull. And it was hurting him to do so.

The urge to make him feel better was so strong within me that I pushed my arm through his. I was never this forward. I had never had a boyfriend in my life. I was socially awkward and had no clue how to make anyone but my family feel better when they were hurting. But I felt the same need within me to take care of Cael as I did for Ida. Like I had done for Poppy too.

I wasn't sure why. But it was an urge I couldn't ignore.

We decided on the cabin filled with sweet treats. We ordered a bunch of items—butter cookies, almond cookies, and cinnamon-type buns, all things traditionally from Norway. I handed a cookie to Cael. His troubled eyes softened when he took a bite. Color seeped back into his cheeks, and he next reached for a cinnamon bun with a hint of humor on his face. Knowing I'd made him feel just a fraction better was as heady as if I'd truly achieved something remarkable.

We had barely made it a couple of treats in, when Jade, Lili, Travis, and Dylan came running over. Dylan threw his arm over my shoulder. "Hot cocoa?" he asked.

I raised one eyebrow to Cael in question. "Let's go," he said and walked with us to the next food cabin. It felt like Christmas again here in this Norwegian square. Like a stolen scene from a movie, a slice of magic on a crisp winter's day.

It was perfect.

We all went back to our respective rooms after a couple of hours exploring the square, full and sleepy. We were only in Oslo for a single night. Norway was going to be different from the Lake District. We weren't staying in a single place. Instead, we were moving north. We didn't know what we were doing or what we were going to see, but I already liked it here. It felt different from what I was used to. That could only be a good thing these days.

In my own room for the night, I sat in the window seat and watched the square begin to quieten. Opening the notebook in my lap—the one from Poppy—I decided it was time to read another page. It only felt right to hear from my sister in the home country of the love of her life.

Savannah,

Just seeing my name in her script swelled my heart so big I thought it might burst from my chest.

I've been thinking of how to help you.

I smiled, imagining her with the end of the pen in her mouth, lost in thought.

It made me reflect on what has helped me through these past couple of years. Right up to now, when I have mere weeks left to live.

That line was a punch in my stomach. I hated thinking of Poppy in those final weeks. When she was weak and unable to walk without help. But she'd found strength to write to me. That's how much she loved me. My breathing shuddered when I took a long inhale.

Friends. People. Family. Without you and Ida. Without Mama and Daddy, the Kristiansens, Aunt DeeDee and Jorie, I wouldn't have been able to keep strong. Without the love from my Rune, I wouldn't be able to face my fate with dignity and graciousness.

With the understanding that it's my time to go home.

So that is my task to you, Savannah. To allow people in. To allow your beautifully pure heart to be seen by others outside of our family. I know you find it hard to open up. I know you find being in large crowds of people uncomfortable. But we need love, Savannah. When we are hurting and the world feels like it is caving in on us, we need people around us to hold us up.

Love, Savannah. I have realized that my biggest wish for you is love. In whatever shape that might come in. But having you all around me right now, when my days are numbered and my last breath grows near, your love gives me strength to face it. Lets me know I'm not alone.

Death is easier to face with company.

When I'm gone, I don't want you to feel alone either. You will need people to help carry you through. And if I had one dream for you, Savannah, it would be for you to find your Rune.

My stomach somersaulted in fear. Finding a love like Poppy and Rune's terrified me. Not because it wasn't welcome. But what would happen to me if I loved so hard, found my other half, my twin flame, only to have them leave in the same way Rune lost Poppy? Watching them fade, day by day, knowing that soon, their light would be snuffed out from your heart, never to be lit again.

I wouldn't be able to survive.

I choked on a watery sob when I read *I know that thought will terrify you. As you read this, you will know what my passing has done to Rune.* A tear fell from my eyes when I saw the ink penning Rune's name was smudged. And that just ripped me wide open. Because as strong as Poppy was, that thought of leaving Rune must have made her cry. Rune was her reason for lasting as long as she had. She had fought harder for more days to spend in her soulmate's arms.

I pray that he can find peace. That he can find happiness after I'm gone. That he can find meaning in my loss. And I hope that for you too, Savannah. That you don't let my death consume you. Keep your heart open and let love in when it should present itself. Because you are so lovable, my beautiful sister. I should know, because I love you so impossibly hard.

We are nothing without love. So please…just…let it in.

I adore you,
Poppy

Silent tears fell onto my chest as I shut the notebook. I closed my eyes and thought of Rune. In the aftermath of Poppy's death, he was completely broken. But gradually, day by day, he'd begun to find his way back to life again. Find meaning in why he was left behind.

Poppy had taught him that. To view the world as one big adventure. She was fearless, and embraced life with her arms wide open. Rune had honored that by taking picture after picture of the world's wonders in tribute to the girl who'd left him too soon.

My arms stayed trapped around my waist. And I realized now that that did not serve me at all. I hadn't even tried to live. I'd just allowed myself to be taken down into a back void of sadness and stripped of all hope. What would happen if I just tried to embrace life? Just for a while?

What if I allowed in love?

I opened my eyes and saw the twinkling, colored string lights that adorned the square shimmer in my periphery. I tipped my forehead to the windowpane, then looked down… Suddenly, I sat up straighter and held my breath when I saw a solitary figure walking up to the now-empty ice rink, a few scattered streetlights the only source of light.

But it was enough for me to see *everything*.

To see Cael stop at the entrance of the rink, his boots a centimeter from the edge of ice. Every inch of his body was taut, and his hands fisted at his side. Breath held, I watched, enraptured as he knelt down and removed his gloves. Tucking them in his pocket, he warred with himself for minutes and minutes, before placing his hands palms down on the ice.

And then he stayed that way. Stayed that way so long that my mind wandered, and I heard Poppy's voice in my head whisper, *"Keep your heart open and let love in when it should present itself..."*

This boy...this boy had captured something inside of me. And seeing him right now, alone at the rink that was once his place of solace, was my undoing.

Letting my heart lead me, I jumped off the window seat. I ignored the curfew set by Mia and Leo, took hold of my coat, and fled from the room. I let my courage steer me out of the hotel doors, unseen by Leo and Mia and out onto the sleepy square. Only a few people milled around at this late hour. But I didn't pay them any mind. Instead, I made my way to the boy on his knees, broken and alone, and joined him on the ground.

His head whipped to the side when I knelt beside him. Tears washed his face with pent-up pain, and, without thought, and needing to embrace the person I had opened my heart to, I wrapped my arms around him. At first, he stilled, and I worried he was mad at me for approaching him. That maybe I'd been too presumptuous and that he didn't want company in this heart-aching moment.

But I sighed in relief when Cael quickly gave in and wrapped his arms around me too...and held on like he would never let go.

His shuddering sobs were like bullets to my soul, each one penetrating farther and farther, until he had shredded me where we sat. "Sav," he murmured against the side of my neck. His tears fled down the skin of my collarbone and underneath my coat. Tears I knew he had kept trapped for too many months to count, eating away at him, day by day.

His hands were freezing from where he had been touching the ice. But I embraced the cold. If it helped Cael in this moment, helped him release himself from the heavy shackles of grief, I would plunge myself into the arctic sea just to help him heal.

I ran my hands through his hair, taking his beanie off and placing it on the ground beside us. I didn't say anything. There were no words of comfort that would help right now. Silence was soothing. And I knew what this emotional exorcism felt like. It was a torrent, a flash flood of grief so strong it destroyed anything in its path.

Cael's fingers raked at my back, like he was trying to find a way to be closer. He was raw and vulnerable, flayed open and emotionally exposed. Cael never mentioned any friends or family from home. At least I had Ida and my parents. I had Aunt DeeDee and Rune.

Who did he have to fall on in times of need? Had he pushed them away like he'd tried to keep us all at a distance?

I ran my hands soothingly through his messy waves; he continued breaking apart. He broke and broke, his salty tears endless. It felt like we were completely alone as we stayed kneeling on the cold ground, Norway continuing to exist around us.

Several minutes passed, and Cael's body began to calm. My sweatshirt and coat were drenched from his tears, but those tears seemed to be slowing too. Still, I held him. I held him until those tears had run dry and his erratic breathing had shifted to labored, heavy breaths.

The aftermath of an emotional purge.

"Sav..." he whispered, voice hoarse and deep from exertion.

"I'm here," I said and found the nerves to add, "for you." I swallowed and made myself repeat, "I'm here for you."

Cael's hands gripped tighter onto my coat, and then he slowly reared his head back. His face was red and blotched; his eyes were haunted. But, to me, he'd never looked more beautiful. Cael withdrew a hand from where it had been wrapped in my coat and stared down at his palm. It was still chill-burned from where it had been pressed against the ice.

He looked out at the ice that was spread out before us. The string lights above made the rink glisten like it was made of a million opal jewels. I wondered what Cael saw when he looked at it. Whether it looked like heaven or hell, or somewhere in between.

A stray tear escaped the corner of his eye. I instinctively reached out and brushed it from his cheek. I stilled when he turned his head, worried I had gone too far. But then Cael wrapped his hand in mine and brought my hand to his lips. He brushed a chaste kiss on the back of my hand and my heart thudded to a sudden stop.

He moved my hand north and pressed it against his cheek, skin cold and damp. And he left it there, as though the warmth from my hand was transferring much-needed heat to his frostbitten bones.

"I'm a hockey player," he said, his whispered words as loud as a scream in the quiet, sleeping square.

I squeezed his hand in my own. A small smile broke through his desolate expression. He turned to me, eyes like blue-tinged molten iron ore as he said, "You do that when I'm breaking." I held my breath, unsure if that was a good thing or not. He exhaled through his nose and squeezed my hand right back. Two firm squeezes. "It keeps me anchored," he admitted, and, although it was night, my chest filled with sunlight. "How do you know when I need it?" He searched my face, looking for an answer.

"Because I recognize the signs." The pulse in my neck fluttered as I said, "Because I often break too."

Cael wrapped his hand tighter in mine, and he stared out at the rink—I simply stared at him. This boy had me completely enamored. "I'm a hockey player," he said again, but this time with more conviction. His voice cracked when he said, "But I can't play anymore."

"Why?"

Cael's shoulders dropped. "Because it was *our* thing." Of course, I knew he meant Cillian. He seemed to think as much of Cillian as I thought of Poppy. But there was a distinct difference. His pain was much different from my own.

He'd had no closure when Cillian died.

"I was good, Peaches," he said, and I melted at the use of that nickname falling so affectionately from his lips, especially at such a troubled moment. He reached out and ran the fingertip on his free hand over the edge of the ice rink. "I was *really* good."

Cael shifted off his knees to sit on the ground. I followed suit. "Hockey isn't just something I played. It's who I am—*was*," he corrected and shook his head. "I'm so confused." His throat was thick as he pushed those words out. I squeezed his hand twice, and he gave me an echo of a thankful smile. Then he gave me two right back, and my heart raced. "I played at first because Cill…" He shifted where he sat, the topic clearly uncomfortable. "Cill played, and I just wanted to do whatever he did."

"But you loved it," I said, not a question. I could hear the joyful inflection hockey inspired in his voice.

"I love it." The use of the present tense wasn't lost on me.

"I lost them both that night," Cael said, and broke my heart again at the gutting agony lacing his voice. "I lost Cill and could never face the ice again either." He paused, and a wistful expression settled on his face. "We were so tied up together that I don't know how to exist alone. Brothers, hockey players, each other's biggest supporters. I attended his games, he attended mine. We trained at the same facility. We practiced on the frozen pond at our house all winter long and mourned it when summer rolled around. We lived for the cold. Hockey was Cill, and I am hockey. Cill was me and I was him and now it's all blown to hell."

"Cael—"

"We were meant to play together in college." He looked at me from the corner of his eye. "Harvard." Chills whispering words like "destiny" danced up my spine. I knew this, of course. But I was proud of him for opening up and telling me. I squeezed his hand. "He was in his junior year when he…" Cael couldn't finish that sentence. His head lowered. "I got in. Was meant to go this past fall. But I couldn't do it with him gone. We never got to play together for the Crimson. And now we never will." I laid my head on his shoulder in support. "I'm so fucking lost." I hugged his arm, when he asked, "What about you, Sav? Why can't you move on?"

Blood drained from my face. I didn't want to speak about Poppy, about myself. But Cael had been so open with me, and I wanted to give him something back. He clearly needed it.

"I don't know how to live without her either," I said. "Poppy died, and I became trapped in that moment, suspended in some freeze-frame I can't break free from." Cael's head dropped to lay on mine. "She died peacefully," I said, trying to chase that day from my head, but after speaking to Cael, I realized that Poppy had died in the most beautiful way. "She passed the way she wanted to go. But…I honestly don't know, Cael. I've just struggled to move on." I released a self-deprecating laugh. "If you haven't noticed, I'm a little bit…reserved." Cael huffed out a single laugh too, and for a minute I thought he might crack a joke. I wondered if he'd been humorous, *before…*

The sound of his laugh made my heart swell. "I suppose I internalize a lot. My therapist back home has tried everything to help me. This is my last-ditch effort to try to grab hold of some semblance of life after loss." I laughed again, but this one was filled with sadness; it was weak, and it made me feel silly.

"She died almost four years ago, yet here I am, suspended in time and barely living a life." I looked at a pebble on the ground just to focus on anything while I said, "I should have been able to cope by now. I know people think I should be able to move on already."

"I don't think grief works like that." I turned to face Cael, unsure what he meant. "I don't think grief sticks to any timeline, Sav." He searched my eyes, and I became lost in their depths. "If someone judges you for how long it's taking you to move past a loved one's death, be happy for them, because it means they've never experienced it."

My throat clogged with emotion. "Thank you," I said, feeling so completely understood. Just from that one sentence.

Cael shook his head. "Sometimes I wish I could rip out my heart and the part of my brain that keeps memories and just throw them away. If only for a little bit. Just to remember what fun felt like, what life was like when I was carefree. I just don't want to wake up every morning with this pit in my stomach anymore, with such boiling anger in my veins that it burns me up inside." Cael sighed, deeply, exhaustingly. "This isn't who I am, Sav. But I've forgotten how to be anything else. I wish I could just be something more than someone ruined by grief. Just for a while." He took the sentiment straight from my heart. Because I wished for that too. Often. Not to forget Poppy, but to just be done with the pain of her absence. A short reprieve.

I tracked my gaze over Cael's handsome face and tall frame. I wanted that for us *both*. A taste of freedom from grief. A reprieve to just *be*. I sat up straighter and said, "Then why don't we?"

Cael looked at me like I was crazy. It made me laugh. His eyes softened

as that foreign sound drifted into the air above us. "I love it when you laugh."
Butterflies swarmed my body, a veritable invasion.

"I mean it," I said and held Cael's hand tighter. "What if, for the time we
are here in Norway, we just push our grief aside and try to find joy?"

"I don't think it's that simple," he said, but I heard the curious note in his
voice. The silent hope that it could be done.

"Let's try anyway. Together," I said and felt overcome with emotion. The
rink went blurry in front of me. "Just for a while, let's just pretend."

"Pretend what?" Cael asked softly.

"That we're just two normal teenagers on a trip away from home.
Exploring Norway for no other reason than we *can*."

Cael stared at me for so long I became self-conscious. I was being stupid.
I *felt* stupid. My face blazed with embarrassment. What I suggested was
impossible. "It doesn't matter," I said. "I don't know what I was thinking—"

"I'm in," he said, interrupting me. My eyes widened. "I want to try," he
said, squeezing my hand and making me smile so big that it made my cheeks
ache. Cael ran a finger over my cheek. "You have dimples, Peaches."

"All of us Litchfield sisters do," I said, meaning Ida, Poppy, and me. I
froze when I realized I'd mentioned Poppy in the present tense. But if Cael
had heard it, he didn't correct me.

I ducked my head, cheeks heating, but Cael placed his free hand's finger
under my chin, like he had done that day at the Lakes, and tilted my head up
until I gave him my full attention. For a second, I imagined what it would be
like if he kissed me. If he just leaned in and pressed his lips to mine.

"It's a pact," he said and squeezed my hand twice, pulling me from
my daydream. "And if we feel the other person slipping into grief, we use
our secret signal to pull them back." He squeezed my hand twice again to
demonstrate. "Deal?" he said, and I nodded my head in agreement.

"Deal."

I was sure what we had planned was unhealthy, that Mia and Leo
wouldn't approve. I was sure pushing aside our grief was like living in a
fantasy world, reality always hovering close enough to drag us back. But I
was happy to do that.

Just to help us *breathe*.

"Cael? Savannah?" We turned to look behind us at the sound of our names. Mia was a few feet away, arms crossed in admonishment, but also wearing a look of concern on her face. "Are you okay? It's past curfew. You're meant to be in your rooms."

I panicked at being caught. In life, I never did anything against the rules. Always walked the line. Guilt instantly assuaged me. But then Cael squeezed my hand twice and I remembered why I had. Cael had needed me. I couldn't feel guilty about helping him in his time of need.

"We're sorry," I said. And I was. But I didn't regret it. Mia ran her eyes over us, double-checking we were well, and it wasn't lost on me that she noticed our joined hands.

Neither of us made a move to let go. I wasn't sure what she or Leo would think of that.

"Then let's get back inside. We leave early in the morning." We walked back to Mia, hand in hand, only releasing each other when we went to our bedrooms. Cael looked at me over his shoulder as he opened his door down the hallway and smiled.

As I tucked myself in bed and turned off the lamp, for the first time in the longest time, I looked forward to tomorrow. It was the first time in four years I had felt anything close to it.

And two simple hand squeezes had made that so.

Snow Flutters and Unburdened Laughter

Cael
Tromsø, Norway

THE VIEW THAT MET US DIDN'T SEEM REAL. I TURNED IN A CIRCLE, LOOKING at the snow-covered mountains, at the wooden houses that were scattered around us—red and brown, the colors of fall leaves, next to pinks and blues and greens: summer tones.

Tromsø.

Early this morning we had taken a short flight north to this town. For a hockey player, it was a paradise. Ice and snow and the bitter cold whipped around us. But the sky was crystal clear. Not a single cloud, the sun bright and blinding.

"Incredible," Savannah whispered beside me. I glanced down at her. Her blue eyes were wide and filled with awe as she drank in the sights. "It's like a dream," she said and held my hand tighter. My lip tugged up in a small smile as I focused on our joined hands. From the minute we'd gathered early this morning to go to the airport, I had threaded my hand through Savannah's and had barely let go.

We had made a pact. An electric, buzzing feeling was passing through my veins. I had awoken this morning with the same sense of dread I always did. But I had brought Savannah's face to my mind and managed to push it aside. We had a deal. And I wanted the break from pain that she'd suggested more than I wanted my next breath.

I had fought and fought the darkness that was trying to settle into my bones, until I saw her in the hallway and focused on the shy smile on her pretty face. I had immediately reached for her hand, ignoring the shocked silence from the rest of the group seeing us that way.

The minute our fingers had gripped on to one another, the darkness was pushed back by a strike of pure light. Without words, Savannah and I had told each other that for now, our grief wouldn't win.

That we'd award ourselves freedom from sadness, for as long as we could hold it off. We weren't naive. Holding off the pain of missing our older siblings was a temporary measure, a standoff to the invading forces that were too strong to overcome completely. But we would wear our armor and fight them off for as long as we could manage.

We would steal back some temporary joy.

The daylight was already fading; Tromsø's hours of sunlight were limited in the winter. But from what everyone had said, this city thrived in the darkness.

"We'll head to our accommodation now," Leo said and pointed behind him. A large wooden hotel was dressed from ground to top in days old snow. In fact, every part of the city was covered in the remnants of snow. The roofs of the buildings and the mountains. The only things that weren't were the fjords that dominated the view. Coming from Massachusetts, I was used to snow. But to see Savannah's reaction to this place, all wide-eyed and awestruck, made the muscles on my chest pull tight.

She'd never seen fresh falling snow.

I hoped that we'd see it before we left. I couldn't imagine never knowing what it was like to feel flakes hit your face, to feel the bites of ice snowflakes brought to your skin.

We carried our bags into the hotel, a large roaring fire in the reception. Savannah stilled, looking at a picture on the wall. It was a blown-up photograph taking up a large percentage of the decor.

"Aurora borealis," she murmured, and her hand tightened in mine. She swung her head to me. "It's always been a dream of mine to see it."

"The visibility is poor tonight," the man on the reception said, catching Savannah's wide-eyed gaze on the picture. "But you'll be able to see it in a couple of days."

The smile that graced her face nearly knocked me down. Savannah was the most beautiful person I'd ever seen in my life. Her smile and those damn dimples floored me. She'd swept into my living hell and cast me an unexpected lifeline. I'd dreaded this trip, fought it with all I had.

That was before I knew Savannah Litchfield waited on the other side.

I nudged Savannah's shoulder. "Look at you with all that knowledge." She blushed. I wanted to run my fingers over her red cheeks. So, I did. I caught her breathing hitch under my touch, and her blush deepened and appeared down the side of her neck.

"I like science," she said, as if it was a throwaway comment, not that important. I'd noticed that about her. She diminished anything unique and special about her. It was apparent she was some kind of genius but shunned and ran from any form of praise.

She'd already told me that she was going to Harvard. I didn't know what she was going to study, but just getting accepted told me how smart she was. She was always reading, silently absorbing the world around her like it was her own personal science project. I wanted to ask her what she was going to study, but I felt a pain in my chest when I tried to. It always held me off. Harvard made me think of Cill. Now, on top of that, was the fact that I wouldn't be going either.

A gutting, sharp pain twisted my gut when I realized that if Cill hadn't died, I'd have gone there as planned, and Savannah would have eventually been there too. We might have met when we weren't so broken. What would that have been like? Would we still have had this connection? Or were we only bound by grief?

Two tight squeezes hurtled me back from my inner thoughts. Savannah moved in front of me, guiding me to meet her eyes. "Okay?" she said, understanding I had slipped back into the shadows.

I pushed them aside and took a long, deep breath. "Yeah," I said and pressed my forehead to hers. "I'm here." *I'm back. I'm still wanting to keep our deal.*

"So," Dylan said, as he came to stand between us. There was humor in his face. "You two want to share anything with the group?" I shook my head. Whatever this was was ours alone. Truth was, I had no idea what Savannah and I *were* to each other. I thought of her constantly, fell asleep with her shy smile in my mind. We both held hands and held each other up.

I *wanted* us to be more. But I didn't know if she was in a place to accept that. Didn't know if I had anything left inside of me to give her. Didn't know if my darkness was fading for good or it would rise and eventually destroy what I had with her like it had done with my parents and best friend. Right now, it was my biggest fear. But with Savannah, telling her about Cillian, about hockey, opening up…it seemed to have taken away its power.

Mia came over and gave us our room keys. She gathered us around the fireplace. "Tonight is yours. But tomorrow…" She smiled widely. "I don't want to spoil things, but what you will see while we're here is…" She shrugged smugly, leaving us dangling. "You'll see."

"Shall we check out the town?" Travis said to the group. We all nodded. "Meet back here in twenty?"

I reluctantly let go of Savannah's hand and dumped my case in my room. I went back downstairs after only a few minutes. Being in my room alone would only take me back to a dark place. Dylan already sat beside the fire. He was flicking through pictures on his phone. I sat down on the seat next to him, catching a picture of him with a dark-haired guy. He quickly put it in his pocket.

"Hey," he said and pointed to the clock on the wall. "You didn't want to hang around your room either?" I shook my head. I stared at the stairs, waiting for Savannah. My leg bounced as the minutes ticked by. This place… being around so much ice and snow. It was full of triggers for me. That was the worst thing—my favorite things, since Cill, had become personal land mines.

"So, you and Savannah?" Dylan said, taking me from inside my head.

I narrowed my eyes at him. "Is that a problem for you?" I asked and heard the bite of jealousy in my tone.

Dylan held up his palms and clearly found humor in my question. "Not from me," he said, then nudged my shoulder. "I think you look good together."

I knew he and Savannah had grown close. She seemed to be able to speak to him easily. I knew how rare that was for her.

"You don't like her as more than a friend?"

Dylan quickly sobered up, and something I couldn't name haunted his amber eyes. "Trust me," he said quietly. "I'm no threat." He let that hang in the air between us, heavy and laced with meaning. His eyes implored me to understand something about him, something he didn't—or *couldn't*—say out loud. I didn't push him. Whatever he was insinuating was his truth to share, if and when he felt the need.

"Cool," I said and saw his shoulders relax, a relieved sigh falling from his lips. Just then, I heard the sound of feet on stairs, and Jade, Lili, and Travis came toward us. Savannah was only a few seconds behind them. I jumped to my feet and immediately held out my hand to hers. She didn't hesitate to take it, and instantly, I could breathe easier.

I didn't know how she did it, but her presence, her touch, her quiet nature were a damn tonic to my soul. Travis led the way from the hotel and we all stopped dead, just feet from the hotel's exit. Darkness had fallen since we'd gone inside. Tromsø, without the sun, looked like something pulled straight from a fairy tale.

"The stars…" Savannah said and looked up at the sky, which looked like a painting. I'd never seen so many stars before. Didn't know that many even existed.

Savannah tensed, and I sensed the sudden change in her mood. I looked down at her, and she dipped her head, eyes meeting the ground. Like I'd done before, I placed a finger from my free hand under her chin and guided her head up. Her blue eyes were glistening with unshed tears. I didn't know the trigger, but it obviously wasn't good. Making sure she kept my gaze, I squeezed her hand twice.

Savannah closed her eyes and quickly composed herself. When she opened her eyes again, she forced a reassuring smile on her face, and I knew she was trying her hardest to push away her sudden rush of sadness.

"Okay?" I whispered, checking in. The others turned away to walk down the street, oblivious to us trying to battle our shadows away.

"Yes," she rasped, shyly tucking her head into my chest. I dropped a kiss to the top of her pink beanie, wishing more than anything that it was her lips I was meeting. Savannah pulled back and cast me a shy glance under her eyelashes.

She was perfect.

"Cael! Sav!" Travis called from down the street. "You coming?" As Savannah and I walked hand in hand, the snow crunched under our feet. When we met up with the group at the end of the street, we came to a patch of land. Savannah crouched down and slipped off her glove. She freed her hand from mine, and I felt the instant loss. With her now bare hands, Savannah picked up the snow that must have fallen before we arrived.

A pearl of laughter sailed from her throat as her hands sank down to her elbows. I'd never heard anything so perfect. I couldn't help but smile too when she looked up at me, dimples deep, and she laughed again. My Georgia peach who was so used to the southern sun and heat was absolutely captivated by a couple of feet of snow.

She was teaching me more on this trip than anyone ever had. She was teaching me that happiness didn't have to be big gestures and life-changing moments. It could be just *this*. Witnessing someone seeing snow for the first time. Hearing someone laugh, true and honest. I didn't know something so simple could hit me so hard. Since Cillian, nothing, not one single thing, had brought me happiness.

Until her.

It was almost painful to feel it. And yet so fucking sad that it ripped me open. To go as long as I had without feeling the smallest flicker of joy, happiness, or contentment.

Looking at Savannah pressing both hands into the snow, another light laugh slipping from her lips, made me want to bottle up the sound and keep it for the days I couldn't get out of bed. This girl…she made me want to be more than the shell of a person I'd been for the past year.

"Ow!" Dylan yelled from somewhere behind us. I turned, just in time to see Travis pelt a snowball at Dylan's back.

Dylan turned his head to Travis. "You don't know what you've just started, Trav." Dylan scooped up a handful of snow and fired it back at Travis.

Joining in, Jade and Lili began gathering snow, launching it at anything and anyone in sight.

I bent down and pulled Savannah to her feet, throwing her behind me just in time for a snowball to land right on my chest. She grabbed on to the back of my coat, using me as a shield. But I caught the tinkling of her light laughter.

Dylan began to run when I saw he was the one who'd thrown it. Bending down, I grabbed snow and formed it into a tight ball. I launched it at Dylan as he ran toward Travis, hitting him in the back.

"Cael!" he shouted, only for Travis to aim for me too, a flash of protectiveness for Dylan apparent behind his thick-framed glasses. Shaking off any negative feelings, any harbored hard memories and thoughts the snow brought, I threw myself into the moment, Savannah staying behind me the entire time. Jade and Lili screamed as Travis pushed them both down in the thick snow. Dylan and Travis laughed, the united sound of us all momentarily forgetting it all to just have some fun.

The patch of snow-covered grass we were on was long and wide with a sloping hill. Dylan and Travis began running after one another, trying to tackle one another to the ground, Lili and Jade following close behind. Everyone was covered head to toe in white. I turned to find Savannah, but as I did, a snowball hit my chest again. I looked up in shock, only to see Savannah's gloves packed with snow and an air of playfulness in her stance.

"Peaches..." I warned, feeling a new kind of warmth enter my chest. She looked so carefree in this moment, so unburdened. She looked *stunning*. With a playful glint in her eye, she threw the second snowball and began to run from me.

She moved quickly—but I was faster.

The others ran after one another, over a hill and out of sight, leaving Savannah and me alone. Savannah slipped and struggled to run through the heavily packed snow. I gained on her inch by inch. She looked back, seeing me close in, and squealed in nervous anticipation at being caught. I didn't give her the chance to run any farther. Wrapping my arms around her waist, I brought us crashing down to the snow, our shared momentum rolling us over three times until we came to a stop. She lay beneath me, my body braced above hers. I edged to the side, just to stop from crushing her. But I left my hands on her waist, remaining as close as I could.

Savannah was laughing so hard she had to wrap her arms around her stomach. I was laughing too but stopped, completely mesmerized by seeing her this way. Crinkles webbed at the sides of her eyes. Tears of joy spilled down her cheeks, and her dimples caved deeply as she shook with hysterics.

My face hovered above hers, catching the white mist the freezing air created as she exhaled her warm breath. All I could see in this moment was the happiness radiating from Savannah's wide smile. All I could feel was her in my arms, her body pressed against mine.

Savannah stared back at me, and her laughter waned as the tension between us rose. I roved my gaze over every part of her face. Her peach-colored skin, the spatter of freckles that dusted over her nose. The dimples that I'd grown obsessed with, the small gold studs in her ears, and the way her long fair eyelashes hit her cheeks when she blinked. But most of all, I couldn't take my attention off her lips.

Reaching up, I brushed a long strand of her fallen hair from her face. Savannah leaned into my palm as it did, and it felt like the whole world fell away. The snow, and lights all around us, made it appear like we were in our very own snow globe, one where pain and sadness and loss couldn't break through.

Savannah swallowed, and I felt the tremor that passed through her body as my fingertip ran over the bridge of her nose and over the Cupid's bow of her lips. "You're so beautiful," I rasped, and Savannah's eyes widened at my confession. I didn't speak those things easily.

"Cael…" she murmured and inhaled a stuttered breath. I could see she was nervous. I didn't know if she'd ever been kissed. If she hadn't, I wanted to be her first. I'd never wanted anything more. She didn't know, but hockey had consumed my whole life. I'd never had time for girlfriends; between Junior Hockey and Team USA, all I'd had time for was school and sleep. This moment was as monumental to me as it was to her.

"You're beautiful too," she said, that well-known blush bursting on her cheeks. Her softly spoken, shaky words destroyed me. I knew what that must have cost her shy nature to admit.

I lifted her hand and pulled off her glove. I kissed her fingertips; I kissed down her fingers and laid kiss after kiss on her palm, the back of her hand. As I leaned down, Savannah's eyes drifted closed as I pressed my lips to her forehead. The scent of almond and cherry engulfed me. I held her tighter, my arm around her waist pulling her closer to me. My chest was laid flat against hers—I could feel her heart racing.

I ran my lips down to her temple, Savannah's hands gripped on to my hand so tightly I thought it might leave a mark. I moved my lips down to her cheek and kissed one of her dimples that I loved so much. Savannah sucked in a quick breath. I pulled back and met her eyes. I needed to know she wanted this. I needed to know she felt the same about me as I felt about her.

We wanted this time in Norway to be about seizing the moment and embracing the happiness that had been lost to us for so long. I couldn't think of anything more euphoric than having her kisses.

Savannah placed her hand on my cheek and began guiding her lips to mine—a clear invitation. I moved closer and closer still, my pulse racing as hard as hers. Then, just as my top lip brushed against hers, a million goose bumps running over my skin, the sound of our friends rushing back down the hill toward us crashed through the cocoon we'd hidden ourselves within.

I halted, my mouth ghosting over hers. Savannah's eyes closed, then opened, a huff of a laugh bursting between us. Travis and Dylan's voices sailed around us, and I dropped my forehead to hers in defeat.

"Bad timing," I said to Savannah, and she laughed again. Lifting my head, I drank in her dilated pupils and heated cheeks. I kissed her rosy cheek, holding it for as long as I could before our friends got too close. I knew Savannah would hate to be caught like this, too on display to curious eyes. Pulling away from where we lay, I held out my hand and Savannah slipped hers in mine. I was convinced that two hands had never fit together so perfectly.

I helped her stand from the snow and dusted the layer that had stuck to her clothes. She shivered, the dampness of the snow starting to freeze against her skin. Unable to resist, I cupped Savannah's cheeks and kissed her forehead, whispering, "You're the best thing to happen to me in the longest time, Peaches."

"Cael," she said, grasping on to my wrists. She could probably feel my pulse thundering under my skin. Rearing back, I went to move away, when she pulled on my wrists, stopping me mid-step. Biting her lip in nerves, she approached me slowly, then lifted to her tiptoes. I lowered down a fraction so she could place her hand on my cheek too. Then Savannah leaned in and placed a kiss on my stubbled skin.

My heart stopped.

Travis and Dylan came stampeding toward us, covered in snow from head to foot. Savannah turned to them, laughing as Jade and Lili came over too, more snow on them all than seemed to be on the ground.

But I couldn't take my eyes off Savannah.

"It's freezing!" Lili said, trembling with cold as they all came to a stop.

"Dinner by the fireplace back at the hotel?" Travis suggested to firm nods of agreement. I hung back a second as everyone began to walk back up the street. The stars were a glitter-covered blanket above, white snow vibrant against the dark night, and then there was Savannah, shining brighter than the stars and snow combined.

Feeling my absence, Savannah turned around and held out her hand. "Are you coming?"

Straightening my coat, I walked to Savannah and took hold of her offered hand. And I followed her up the street, and back to the hotel. With every step I walked beside her, I was quickly becoming aware that I'd follow this girl anywhere.

She was the miracle I never saw coming.

When we entered the hotel, Mia and Leo were in the reception. "Cael? Savannah?" Leo said, calling us from the group.

I glanced down at Savannah and saw nervousness wash over her face. Mia told the others where to get dinner, then came over to us. "We just want to have a chat with you both," Leo said, gesturing for us to follow him into a private room just off the lobby.

We followed, and Savannah's hand tightened in mine. She was nervous. There was a table in the room, four chairs around it. "Please, sit down," Leo said, and Savannah and I sat on one side. Mia and Leo took the seats on the other.

My jaw clenched in agitation. It was obvious why they had singled me and Savannah out. But it wasn't anger running through me. It was nerves. I was filled with a new emotion—fear. Fear that they were going to disapprove of us together.

I waited for Leo and Mia to speak. Savannah, clearly feeling my unease, squeezed my hand twice.

"We've asked you here," Mia said, voice gentle, "as we've noticed some developments between you both." I looked to Savannah. Her cheeks were flushed with embarrassment, but her head was held high, and it made me lose some of the discomfort I was feeling.

Leo leaned on the table. "This isn't the first trip we've done, far from it. And it isn't the first time we've had people fall for one another while away," he said.

Panic, strong and true, flooded my body, and I found myself blurting, "I'm not staying away from her." My heart beat fast as I readied for an argument.

Leo met my eyes. He didn't look pissed at my interruption. I knew I probably sounded insolent, but Savannah had been the only good thing to happen to me so long. I wasn't letting them split us up; I *couldn't*. Not when the anger had finally fallen away and I could breathe. Not when I found someone who made me feel understood.

"We're not asking you to, Cael," he said calmly. "But we need to speak to you about what we expect from you both."

"Okay," Savannah replied, placing her free hand over our joined hands. Extra support. "We understand." She nodded at me, urging me to hear them out too.

I exhaled a deep breath, releasing the panic that was running through me. "We can't stop people from developing feelings for one another," Leo said. "You are seventeen and eighteen, not small children. But we are here to help you with your grief, and what we worry about is your own progress being hindered by relying too much on one another and not on your personal journeys."

"We ask that you adhere to the lessons and teachings that we require of you—as *individuals*," Mia said. "And also," she said and straightened, more authoritative in her seat, "we *insist* that you follow the rules and boundaries of the program. No sneaking off together. No sharing rooms. It's therapy first, relationship second. Okay?"

My eyes dropped to the table. I didn't like the sound of that, but I would never voice it aloud for fear they would interfere with me and Savannah.

"If you break these rules, we will be contacting your parents and it may compromise your place on this trip," Leo added. My jaw clenched. I didn't really care for the therapy. Right now, I just wanted Savannah. Therapy hadn't helped me. She had in a matter of weeks.

"We won't break the rules," Savannah said. I said nothing.

That clearly gained Leo's attention as he said, "Do you understand, Cael?"

"Savannah's good for me," I said, meeting his gaze. Leo listened intently, calmly. I wasn't sure what he was thinking. But I wanted him to *understand*. I swallowed, looked at Savannah's wide eyes, then said, "I...I've told her about Cill." My voice was croaky with how much energy that took me to say out loud. "And me..." I trailed off. "*I'm* feeling better. My anger isn't as... controlling."

"That's *great*, Cael. We've noticed a positive change in you," Mia said, sounding like she truly meant it. "And we want you to open up to your peers. They're your biggest form of support on this trip. But we want you to confide in us too. We're not your enemies. We want more than anything to help you. *Both* of you. We are worried that you'll use each other as a crutch. It isn't healthy, and no relationship can sustain or survive that. You both need to heal yourselves first and cannot forget that as you grow closer."

"We won't," Savannah said, speaking for us both. "We'll be respectful to you both and the program. We promise." I felt her hard stare and met her blue eyes, reluctantly nodding in agreement.

"That's all we ask," Leo said after a pause. I knew he was watching me like a hawk. I knew he had caught my apprehension. But he seemed to let it rest when he tapped the tabletop and said, "Now that's settled, let's get some dinner."

"Oh my goodness," Savannah said as we watched a whale break through the surface of the water, then crash back underneath. The boat we were on rocked side to side, the air crisp and arctic around us. We were all bundled up in thermal clothes, piping-hot coffees in our hands. Our attention was glued to the water, whales cresting the water in the distance.

I'd never seen anything like this before. It all seemed so surreal. I kept blinking, feeling as though it would fade away, that we weren't actually here in this place that felt like it was make-believe.

Savannah leaned farther back into my chest. I kept hearing her breathing catch as another whale came over the surface, ever closer to our boat. The mountains surrounded us, snow-covered and still, the whales crashing into the water the only sound—that and the gasps of our group as we stayed transfixed on the incredible sight before us.

"There's another one," Lili said quietly and pointed to the side of the boat. Savannah squeezed my hand, but I knew this wasn't because she'd had a bad thought about her sister. This was because she was overwhelmed with the sights. Savannah hadn't said a word on this boat trip. Her eyes were wide, her lips parted in awe.

It was almost too much, seeing this. Surrounded by high mountains, the city of Tromsø picturesque behind us. In our grief, our worlds were reduced to only the loss of our loved one and the gutting feelings each day without them brought. Being in a place like this, seeing things in real life that I'd only ever seen on TV, reminded me just how big and vast the world was. And how tiny my life was in the grand scheme of it all. A single grain of sand on the universe's beach.

The crisp scent of the stunning fjords and the local delicacies was a long way from the smell of oak trees and the campfire smoke of my hometown. And the cherry and almond scent of Savannah brought a sense of peace to my soul that I wasn't sure I'd *ever* had—even when Cillian was alive.

Two whales came above the water, one by one, and Savannah turned her head, looking up at me with pure joy shining from her smile. My stomach flipped, and I kissed her head and held her tighter in my arms. "I can't believe I'm seeing this," she murmured, just for me to hear. She drank in the view, and a shiver seemed to cut down her spine.

When I tore my attention from Savannah and looked to everyone else on the trip, they were just as transfixed. It made me think back to this morning and the group session Mia and Leo had made us attend. Only, this session had been different from the others. There was no talk of loss or grief or the feelings that drowned us. Instead, they'd flipped the switch and asked us what brought us joy. I'd been stumped by the sudden change in tone. They wanted to know what sights and sounds or traditions we loved that brought happiness to our lives.

Fall, Jade had answered. *Hannukah,* Lili had said with a nostalgic smile. *Being around people,* Travis had said, and my stomach fell. After what'd happened to him, I wasn't sure he had many people around him anymore.

Freedom, Dylan had replied, then flicked a quick look my way. I was starting to think Dylan was hiding, and perhaps he was sick and tired of doing so. When Mia turned to Savannah, she fiddled with her hands but said, *Family.* My throat grew tight at her quiet answer. *And the world,* she added, surprising me. She kept her eyes on her busy hands as she said, *I like science. The stars. I like seeing things that take my breath away. That I don't always understand.*

I wanted to tell her that just looking at her did that to me.

When Mia asked me, I didn't have an answer. At least not one I could speak out loud. Because when Savannah held my hand and squeezed it twice, seeing me stay silent, I wanted to tell everyone it was *her.* Savannah. Right now, she was the only thing to bring any form of happiness to my life.

That was as terrifying as it was comforting.

"Are you okay?" Savannah asked now, tipping her head up to meet my eyes.

"Yeah," I said and rested my chin on the top of her head. Savannah was petite, yet she fit perfectly against me, a jigsaw piece custom—made to fit mine.

The boat kept pushing through the water, even when the whales seemed to disappear. We sailed down the fjords, seeing small villages and sweeping coastlines covered in ice and snow. They reminded me a bit of the Lake District we'd just been to. How they were isolated and alone. The perfect place to get away from it all. Like the poets Savannah had taught me about.

She hadn't known, but I'd read her paperback cover to cover, just to know what had her so transfixed. I'd wanted to understand her more, even when I was trying to keep her at arm's length.

"Look at that," Savannah said, pointing to a snow-covered beach. There was wonder on her face. It was an odd sight—to see what a sunny and golden view would usually be—covered with the white of snow. "How incredible," she murmured, more to herself than to me. I filed that away to make sure she saw it up close before we left Norway for our next destination.

The day went by quickly, and in all the hours we were outside, I never once let Savannah go. It made me cast my mind back to the ice rink in Oslo. And how I was paralyzed just seeing it. I couldn't deny the way my feet had itched to put on a pair of skates. That had surprised me more than anything. I allowed myself a few moments to remember how that felt. The rush of adrenaline I would get as I first stepped onto the ice and sailed around the rink, pushing myself to such a fast speed it felt like I was hurtling through a hurricane.

And true to our deal, I fought to separate the memory from Cillian. Focused only on the ice and how it made me feel. How I'd lined up next to my teammates for the national anthem, how I'd sunk the puck into the net. The euphoria I had felt as I'd slipped on my pads and waited in the tunnel, ready for my name and number to be announced.

It was my heart.

It was my home.

Peace suffused my muscles, bones, and mind. Just imagining soaring around the ice, stick in hand. Being in this place, surrounded by the mountains, the water, and the whales, had given me permission to *dream*. To dream and remember that I'd once had something I loved so much I wanted to dedicate my entire life to it. I had *loved* it. I had loved playing hockey with Cillian too, but in this moment, I was able to make a distinction between the two.

Hockey had also been just *mine*.

Savannah turned in my arms and searched my face. "What are you thinking of?" she asked, curled into my chest. She could read me like I could read a game.

"Hockey," I said and saw concern flash across her face. I shook my head. The others were too busy staring at the sights to notice us, so I pressed my forehead to hers. It was fast becoming my favorite place to be. "How much I loved it—maybe *still* love it. How it makes me...happy," I said and shook my head with a self-deprecating laugh. "I don't know." I pointed to the surreal-ness around us. "This place...it's making me think things I hadn't let myself entertain. Bigger things. Things I thought were out of reach."

"That makes *me* happy," she said, and I could hear that she truly meant that.

I felt a sudden rush of emotion shoot up my throat, stealing my voice. My eyes stung and I felt my hands shake. Savannah noticed. She leaned up and said, "I'm proud of you." My nose began to itch. I sniffed to chase it away, the vastness of the fjord blurring before me. She gave me a smile and I was just about undone. "I'd love to watch you play someday," she said and obliterated me where I stood.

"Yeah?" I questioned, voice thick.

She nodded. I pulled her to me, burying my face in her long hair. The boat swayed, and I tried to push the thought of hockey aside, but I just couldn't stop imagining Savannah watching me play. Her, in the stands, cheering me on. For months, I'd wanted to rid my mind of anything that could have reminded me of the past. But a spark had just been placed back in my soul. It wasn't much. It wasn't a plan to pick up my skates or to even entertain that I could somehow be the Cael from before. But there was a tiny spark that had ignited...

And I chose not to fight it.

Colored Skies and Frozen Kisses

Savannah,

You often ask me about my faith. How I just know in my soul that there is something bigger than us. Bigger than this world. And that there is a place that is filled with love and peace beyond this life. I am at peace with passing away. Because I will awake in heaven and be free from pain.

I know your heart lies with the stars. With space and science and the unexplained wonders that keep you mesmerized. Although we see things differently, they are both just as special and as meaningful. Please don't ever lose this. Don't lose yourself to grief and bitterness.

I challenge you to find magic within the world. Find wonder and hope and the beauty we have been awarded on this Earth. Lean into the everyday joys and cherish each moment with an open and pure heart. It will help pull you through the hard times.

Smile at the stars,
Poppy

Savannah

"Baby!" Mama greeted as the call connected.

"Hi, Mama," I said and instantly felt the comfort of home wrap around me. "How are y'all?"

"We're good, baby girl," she said. "Your daddy's here too. I'll put you on loudspeaker." She did, and Daddy's voice immediately rang through.

"Hi sweetheart."

"Hi Daddy! Guess what we're about to see?" I said, staring out of the reception window as we waited for the bus to arrive. The night sky and I were filled with heady anticipation.

"What?" he replied.

"The northern lights."

"Savannah…" Mama murmured, soft and gentle. "You've always dreamed of seeing them. How special for you that that dream is coming true," she said, and I smiled.

"I can't believe it," I said, unsure how to express the level of excitement bursting within me. Then I saw the headlights of the bus approach the hotel. "The bus is coming to take us to a viewing point, but I just wanted to check in with you both and to let you know I'm okay."

"Thank you, baby. You sound so strong." My heart fluttered at that. "And we miss you so much," Mama said and melted me. "Oh, try to call your sister soon. You know she can't go a day without hearing from you, and she'll be spittin' mad that she missed your call again." My heart bloomed at that. It was true. I had texted Ida nonstop since being here. I called my parents most days too, but catching Ida between our activities, her school, and her cheer practices to talk on the phone was a little tricky.

"I will," I said. I glanced at the others in the lobby. Cael held out his hand, signaling to me that it was time to go. "I'll speak to y'all tomorrow. Love y'all!"

"Love you too!" they shouted back in unison, and I hung up, feeling lighter. As I walked up to Cael, he wrapped his arm over my shoulders and pulled me to his side. We were caring less and less if the others saw us this way.

I'd also noticed that Cael never called home. Leo had told him this morning he'd spoken to his parents again to let them know he was okay. That seemed to be the case most days. Cael acknowledged Leo with a tight jerk of his chin. I hadn't broached the subject of his parents with him. He was making such good progress, but it was clear he was still in the emotional trenches, and I didn't want to pry too hard as to why. He was less angry. He was joking and smiling more these days. That was incredible to witness. I feared pushing him too hard about his parents would only see him retreat. And like Mia and Leo had said, I needed to let him explore his journey through grief himself. Even though I just wanted to make him better.

We climbed into the bus. Chills raced up and down my spine with excitement. This was a bucket list item for me. Poppy came to my mind as I thought that, but rather than letting the image disable me, I pictured how excited her face was and how pleased for me she would be. We'd often dreamed of seeing this together—her, me, and Ida. Rune's text came to mind like a warm blanket being cast around me.

She's with you…

I wanted to believe it.

Although the Aurora Borealis could be seen from Tromsø, to get the full effect we were taking a bus out of the city, away from its lights and to a place of solitude where we could see the most activity.

Cael smiled at me when I glanced out of the window, the city fading to the background and the heavily packed snow around us our only view. He placed a hand on my knee. Butterflies filled my chest, then swooped down to my stomach. It was a sensation I was becoming more than familiar with. Every day, when Cael was close, they awoke.

I let myself take a glance at his lips. Lips that had so very nearly kissed mine. I could still feel the heat of his warm, minty breath on my cold skin. Still feel how soft his lips were as they lightly brushed against mine.

I felt like everything between was going at hyperspeed, like we were in a vacuum where we felt and experienced more than we ever would back home.

Our emotions were high and we were grasping onto moments that lifted us and made us feel seen.

I felt more than seen by Cael than I had by anyone before. Being as introverted as I was, it was almost impossible for me to let people in. But he'd gently knocked on the door to my heart, and carefully stepped inside. He hadn't barged in, hadn't slammed it open. But softly, carefully, asked to be let in.

And I liked him being there. But it terrified me too.

Cael took hold of my hand and leaned against the bus seat's headrest, oblivious to my affectionate thoughts about him. He closed his eyes, and it gave me license to really study him, unobserved. He was so much more than I'd given him credit for at the beginning of the trip. I'd seen his tattoos and gauges, his stormy eyes and clenched jaw, his cutting outbursts, and assumed he was cold and brash. Someone who didn't want the company of others.

But that couldn't have been further from the truth. He was kind and pure and sensitive. I wanted him to heal from his brother's death as much as I did from Poppy's. I'd still only received breadcrumb details over his brother's death. And that was absolutely fine. Due to the nature of Cillian's death, I expected it was almost impossible to speak about without breaking.

Since we'd been in Norway, I'd sensed more of a change in Cael. I wasn't sure we could do what we'd set out to do—to forget our grief for a little while. But we were trying, and I did feel lighter. Without grief's heavy weight pressing down on my neck, I was able to look up and see the sky. See the stars, the sun, and the moon.

I was about to see the Northern Lights.

I'd had a one-to-one session with Leo yesterday. We'd talked about CBT (cognitive behavioral therapy). It wasn't the first time I'd tried it. It was a way to reframe my thoughts. Turn them on their head to find a deeper meaning within them. Back in Georgia, Rob had tried it with me too. The difference here was that *I* was willing to try. Back home, I'd been a veritable statue, soul-trapped inside of my frozen body, unable to break free from grief's ice-cold fists.

Here…my body had begun to thaw, allowing me to *try*. And I *was* trying. Here in Norway, I'd been trying more than ever. Rune had tried that approach with me too. That instead of being sad that Poppy wasn't here with me, I should experience this for her—for us both.

It wasn't simple, and it wasn't easy. And if I let my guard down for as short a time as just a few minutes, sadness tried to crash against me with the force of a tidal wave. But I was fighting back, at least for now. I was embracing the brief reprieve of peace.

As I stared at Cael, sleep taking him to safety for a while, I hoped that was true for him too. I stared back out of the window again. All that greeted me was snow. Miles and miles of snow, nothing else in sight. The bus crunched on the ice beneath its tires, and I laid my head on Cael and let the smell of sea salt and fresh air dance around me.

If someone had told me several weeks ago that I'd be here right now, with a boy I liked, in Norway, about to see the northern lights, I would have thought they were lying.

But if life had taught me anything, it's that it can change on a dime.

It was nice for the universe to show me that it wasn't always for the worse.

The sun began to lower in the distance, and I could already see lark-natured stars waking and casting their brightness into the not-yet-dark sky. It was as though they wanted front seats to the show we were all about to see.

Stars…they would always remind me of Poppy. When she passed and I was searching for a meaning to her loss, or when the urge to see her again became so overwhelming, I searched for anything to carry a sign. The stars became that for me. Space was vast and mostly unknown. It made sense to me that Poppy could have become a star after she passed. She'd shone bright enough in life that she would blaze in the heavens. For months after her death, when the wound was raw and disabling, seeing the stars had always brought me a small amount of comfort. At night, I would trick myself into believing I was seeing her again in the sky. Some nights I wouldn't let myself sleep until dawn broke and the stars had disappeared.

Just so she wouldn't have been up there, all alone.

I was younger then. Maybe it had been a silly fantasy, a way to cope. But even now, at seventeen years old and almost four years into her absence, I still stared at the stars and missed her.

I'd once read a book on the aurora borealis. Why it happened and the many myths and beliefs different cultures had given for its existence. The one that was standing out to me right now was that it was ancestors stepping through the celestial veil, showing their loved ones they were okay. Deceased souls appearing to our eyes to reassure us they were still living, in some fashion.

At that thought, a dart of sadness hit against the protective bubble I'd created around myself, trying to break in. But I held strong and pushed it away.

Then I felt two squeezes of my hand.

I tilted my chin up and saw Cael's sleepy eyes searching my face. I gave him a watery smile, and he kissed me on my head. Tucking back into the padding of his coat, I took solace in the quiet of the bus.

A while later the bus came to a stop and our guides made themselves busy creating a viewing spot for us with chairs and cameras and hot drinks. As I stepped from the bus, the bitter coldness took away my breath. The breeze sailed into my lungs, and each breath I took felt like it was scalding ice-fire.

I pulled my scarf over my mouth and reached for the hot chocolate we'd been provided. As I held Cael's hand, we took our seats—side by side— as dusk quickly fell over the land. I could see the faint flickering lights of Tromsø in the distance, but out here, we were isolated and witness to the eye-opening vastness of the sky that cities and towns often disguised.

Stars seemed to pop into the sky one by one in quickening succession. I was transfixed as constellation after constellation began to appear, looking clearer and more profound than ever before.

The entire group of us was silent, waiting for the burst of color that was expected. I gripped on to Cael's hand so tightly I worried about hurting him. But he was gripping my hand tightly in return. Unified breaths were held as a flicker of green began to descend from the sky. I stayed stock-still, like any movement would disturb the shy thread of light and scare it away.

But then it flared again, only this time it had grown in strength, like it was stretching its arms and legs after a long sleep. Green neon began to shimmer and drop across the black sky like a glittering curtain.

Before long, the entire sky was filled with green light, the flares reflecting off the white of the snow, increasing its stunning effect. Stars were sprouting in the billions, sparkling like the most expensive of diamonds. It was the greatest show the earth had ever seen.

A sense of peace so profound chased through my every cell, and I felt tears begin to fall down my cheeks. Sitting here, underneath the endless sky, I could see why people believed it was the visiting spirits of our loved ones. Because seeing this felt like seeing Poppy again. My heart swelled, my soul singing with the beauty and grace the lights gave, dancing to a song only the sky could hear.

A sob slipped from my throat, one I couldn't hold back. But it wasn't a cry of sadness or loss; it was one of breathlessness and wonder and admiration so strong it seemed to radiate from me as brilliantly as the lights before my eyes. It *was* Poppy. This was all Poppy. She had been vibrant and bright and breathtaking. She had lived for only a glimmer of time, but she had lived it boldly. She had embraced every moment life had given her...

She had outshone all the night sky.

Cael pulled me closer to him, but there were no hand squeezes or glances of concern. My heart pulled toward him even more, because he had recognized this moment as momentous and serene, not sad or heartbreaking.

It was heart-*affirming*.

As we sat under the lights, blues and reds joined the fray. It was a tapestry of light. Sitting here was being shown by the universe that it was infinite and endless. Sitting here was seeing lost loved ones dancing up high among the stars, free of pain and made whole. No fear, no more hurting.

And I cried. As the lights grew in strength, more tears fell. I prayed the myths were right and Poppy was up there, looking down on me with her dimpled smile and zest for life.

My life had been so contained, so small for the past four years. It had been reduced to a single, gutting emotion. As we sat here, the universe was screaming to me that there was more to this life than the one we lived. That when our heartbeat stopped, our soul soared northward, stardust finding its way home.

"Cael," I whispered and tore my eyes from the lights to briefly look at his face. His cheeks were wet too, his silver eyes looking like two stars had been plucked down and placed within them. I looked back up and just allowed myself to feel it. Feel everything. Admiration, amazement, magnificence, wonderment. Let the wider world invade my soul.

I even embraced the small thread of fear that frayed from the fabric of my heart, the terrifying thought of being so small and insignificant under such a mighty vista.

I felt it *all*.

I didn't move for what could have been hours or years. Stayed still on the chair, head tilted back and mesmerized by the aurora borealis and all the beauty she brought to the world, my eyes, and my heart. Then, as a ribbon of pink cut through the mostly green sky, I put my hand over my mouth to silence the cry that fought to escape. It danced even more beautifully than the others, its pale pink hue stunning against the neon greens and blues.

"Poppy…" I whispered quietly but loud enough that if it was she who had come to see me, she would hear me and know that I was here. I never stopped watching that cherry-blossom-pink beam of light as it fluttered gracefully across the stars until it faded away. But it had been there. It had ingrained itself in my mind forever. It had been temporary, it had been beauty personified, and it had burned its image onto my soul.

Then, slowly, the vibrancy of the lights began to dim, each thread fading bit by bit, until they disappeared, leaving only a diamond-washed sky.

A finger dusted down my cheek, and my eyelashes fluttered. My throat felt raw from crying, and my limbs were stiff from not moving.

"Peaches," Cael's roughened voice sounded, piercing the silence.

I turned my face toward him. "I felt she was here," I said, for once in my life not overthinking what I said and blurting out what was in my heart.

Cael's eyes closed, like that thought hit him deeply, and he placed his drink down, wrapped his strong arms around me, and pulled me to his chest. His cheek rested against the side of my head, and I felt so content I didn't ever want to leave. I'd found a heaven on earth in this place, with this boy, and I didn't want to go back to what it had been before.

A hand pressed against my back. "It's time to go," a careful, gentle voice announced. Mia. I held on to Cael for a few moments longer, then let him guide us back to the bus. Every face I passed on the way to my seat looked awestruck.

We all appeared *changed*.

The bus ride home was a blur. By the time we arrived at the hotel, it was late. But when I got to my room I was wired, electricity soaring through me. I didn't think I'd be getting sleep that night. Sitting on my bed, I found myself staring off at the wall, lost in my thoughts.

Reaching for the journal we'd been given by Mia and Leo, I opened the page and let my soul pour onto it.

Poppy, I wrote.

I think I felt you tonight. For the first time since you passed, I felt you beside me. Please say that it was you.

A lump clogged my throat.

Please say that ribbon of cherry blossom pink that broke through the green was you. Please tell me you are with me on this journey.

I sucked in a breath, desperate tears falling on my exhale.

Please say you are happy and alive, in some miraculous way. Because Poppy…I need that. I need you to be somewhere living. YOU were too big and too bright not to be living. Please tell me you were one of the stars I saw sparkling in the sky tonight, so that I can look upon you when I need you. When I want my big sister to stay with me, for as long as you can.

I can live in the darkness if you are one of the stars.

My words were scattered and pleading. But then I looked to the window, and a joyful cry soared from my lips when I saw another flicker of the northern lights trying to appear over Tromsø. And that pink…that ribbon of pink was there, weaving through the stars like the most beautiful of dancers. I held the journal to my chest like I was holding Poppy herself.

"Poppy. I see you," I whispered and watched as that pink slowly faded away but left a change in my heart. Tears streamed down my face, but they were filled with happiness. "Poppy... I miss you..." I whispered again, for once believing she might actually hear me.

I'd barely climbed into bed, still fully clothed, when a quiet knock tapped at my door. I was wide awake. It was four in the morning. I'd watched the sky like a hawk for any other sign of the lights, but they had gone. Clouds had rolled in over Tromsø, making a game of hide and seek with the stars.

The knock sounded again, and I climbed out of bed and cracked it open just a little. Cael was on the other side, eyes full of life and just as wide awake as me. "Come on," he said and held out his hand, a soft but excited expression on his face.

The rule follower within me told me to stay, that our curfew had passed and we would get into trouble if we were caught sneaking out. Mia and Leo had been insistent that we not break the rules. But then the energy that was still coursing through me told me to forget the rules and seize the moment. It had me ducking back into my room to grab my coat, boots, gloves, and hat. Quietly closing my door, I took Cael's hand and silently followed him down the stairs and out into the street.

A burst of quiet laughter pealed from my chest when he began to run down the street, pulling me behind. I had no idea where we were going, the wind whipping through my hair. The breeze slapped my face—I felt so alive.

Cael's long legs ate up the distance we were covering, trampling snow under our feet. My breath came quicker the faster we ran, my chest burning with the cold. I grew warmer and warmer, sporadic laughter still sailing freely from my heart.

Then we turned a corner, and I came to a dead stop. I clutched onto Cael's arm, as I looked out before us. "The beach," I said, taking in the sight. Snow covered what should have been a grassy verge on the approach, but the sand was untouched, and the water was flowing just as easily as on the beaches back in Georgia.

It was a dream brought to reality.

"Cael," I said, turning toward him.

"I had to show you," he said, simply, like it wasn't the most perfect gift he could have given me. The brightness of the snow made it so everything was visible in the dark, the stars up ahead like earth's very own string light decoration.

In the space of a few short hours, I'd had my eyes opened to the most glorious scenes I had ever encountered. The clouds were heavy above us and the cold breeze whipped up my hair, causing goose bumps to leave tracks on the back of my neck. But I was here, in this place.

I was lost in paradise.

"Come on," Cael said and led me over the snowy verge and onto the golden sand. We came to a stop at the water's edge. Even in the winter it looked crystal clear and inviting.

"Have you ever seen anything so beautiful?" I asked, awestruck once again.

"Just once," he said, his voice hoarse with emotion. I turned my head to him to ask what that was. But by the way he was looking at me, eyes focused on my face and adoration in his gaze, I quickly caught on to what he was implying.

I swallowed my nerves, my face heating so much I knew he'd be able to see my blush, even in the dark. Cael stepped closer, then closer still. I was frozen in place, watching his every minuscule movement. My breath came quicker, and those butterflies were back accosting my entire body. Cael didn't say a word as he stopped before me, so close I could smell his addictive scent and feel his warm breath on my face.

Freeing my hand from his—the one he no doubt felt trembling—he removed his gloves, then, with his bare hands, gently cupped my cheeks. He was so tall and broad, athletic and strong, yet handled me like I was a prized possession he didn't want to break.

His silver-blue eyes dived into mine, and he pressed his forehead to my forehead. That intimate touch brought instant calm. This was Cael Woods. The boy who had captivated me. The boy whose heart had somehow become inexplicably attached to mine. The boy who was fast becoming my safety.

I didn't speak, didn't utter his name. I just let the heat of our bodies pass between us, sharing this intimate space. Cael moved back, brushing the tip of his nose down my cheek. My breathing came quicker and my eyes fluttered closed. His fingertips ghosted over my cheeks, a soothing motion. Then his nose met mine and he reared back a fraction. I felt the intensity of his heavy stare. I opened my eyes and saw the question hovering in the static-thick air crackling between us.

I smiled, and that was all the invitation Cael needed. Closing in, he pressed a kiss on my lips—tentative, a gossamer touch. The neon lights that we had just watched dance before our eyes seemed to take root within me. Each flare moving in time with my every heartbeat as Cael's lips pressed to mine again, harder this time. I gripped on to his arms, holding tightly to this boy, giving me my first kiss.

His lips were soft and warm and filled with so much trust and affection. The northern lights and stars had rendered me speechless—this sensation was like soaring through a sunrise. It was life and death and all that rested in between. It transcended any feeling I'd ever had before and wrapped me up in beauty so tightly it was euphoric.

I kissed Cael back, shyly at first. But as he framed my face and licked along the seam of my lips, I fell into the dreamlike state his minty taste and careful touch brought to this moment. I parted my lips, giving his tongue permission to join mine in an intricate dance. One of his hands broke from my face to pass over my neck and thread into my hair. Our kiss deepened, my heart beat faster, and feelings I'd been so terrified of releasing exploded inside of me, bringing a beaming light to my nerves, showing them that there was nothing to fear.

There was *nothing* to fear...

Cael kissed me. He kissed and kissed me and joined us so close it was as if we were two stars colliding. When he pulled back, I didn't think anything else could make me feel so adored, until he whispered, "I'm falling for you, Peaches."

I drew in a stuttered, shocked breath. But as his husky voice and that softly spoken admission fell over me, there was only a sense of *rightness* inside of me. Cael wanting me and me wanting him so fiercely it occupied every one of my thoughts.

Cael's eyes betrayed his frayed nerves at his vulnerable confession. He had no reason to be scared. "I'm falling for you too," I whispered back, not wanting to disturb the peace that we had created in this magical place—standing united on this snowy beach.

The smile that lit up Cael's face was blinding.

Both of his hands wrapped into my hair, and I kissed him. Kissing him came as naturally as breathing. My chest pressed to his and I smiled against his lips as his heart drummed in sync with my own. My lips tingled under his touch, and I felt like I could have stayed here forever, kissing this boy with everything I had, giving him all of my heart and soul. Then—

I gasped against Cael's lips and drew back my head, tipping my head up to the sky. A laugh tore from my throat as a snowflake landed on the tip of my eyelash. "It's snowing."

Cael peered up at the sky too, the snowflakes turning from tiny morsels of white to thick drops in mere seconds. Snowflakes kissed our faces as thoroughly as our lips had just kissed.

Cael held me in his arms as I felt the snow on my face, and as I gazed out over the water, the snowflakes disappeared as they met the water's surface. I closed my eyes and let the snow fall all over me. Embraced the biting cold that scattered within me. "What *is* this place?" I murmured in disbelief and looked back at Cael.

He was already watching me with a gentle smile on his face. His gloveless finger traced my cupid's bow and ran over my bottom lip. He was so beautiful. The most perfect boy I had ever seen. I laughed harder when a cluster of snowflakes began to stick to his messy hair that was escaping the protection of his beanie.

"I could listen to that forever," Cael said. It occurred to me in that moment that I'd still not heard *him* laugh. Not really. Not a true free laugh.

I let my forehead fall to his and held him close, suspended under the snowfall on a beach that was dressed in winter.

Cael kissed me again. A shorter kiss this time, but it was no less sweet. He sat down on the beach, then guided me to sit against him, situating me between his spread legs, my back against his front.

And we watched the falling snow in silence. I had to blink several times to make myself believe that I was truly here. Nothing about this felt real. Not even Cael kissing me. I lifted my finger to my lips. They were warm from the many kisses we'd shared.

I'd had my first kiss.

I'd had my first kiss from a boy who was fast becoming the center of my world.

"Find your Rune..."

As Poppy's letter to me circled my mind, I noticed a familiar sight above me. "Orion's belt," I said, pointing to the three stars in the sky. A memory filtered down and I explained, "When we were younger, we—Poppy, Ida, and I—used to say that those stars were meant just for us." I shook my head, grasping on to the happiness that memory inspired and not the sadness that was trying to follow. Cael pushed back my long hair from my neck and kissed the skin just below my ear. Shivers trickled down my spine at the featherlight touch.

"You're a good person," he said and caused me to still.

"You are too," I said, after turning to meet his eyes.

He looked tortured. Clearly realizing I had noticed, he said, "He didn't tell me," and it broke my heart when I knew he was referring to Cillian. Snowflakes kissed his cheeks and eyes, clung like tiny angels to his dark, wavy hair. "He didn't tell me he'd fallen into darkness. And I didn't see the signs." I squeezed his hand, but this time it wasn't to remind him to push these feelings away. I wanted him to know that I was here for him.

Some things should never be pushed away when they are ready to be shared.

I knelt between his legs and placed my hand on his cheek. I searched his desolate gaze. "I can't speak on your brother's behalf. But sometimes we keep things to ourselves, so soul destroying that they can tear us apart inside." I kissed his cheek, the corner of his mouth, then finally his lips. "Sometimes, people don't let their loved ones know how much they are hurting because they don't want to bring them pain too."

Cael's eyes shimmered, and I caught a stray tear with my finger before it could fall. I cradled it in my hand. It was a tear of Cael's growth. "He loved you, Cael," I breathed, needing to be his strength right now. "Of that I have no doubt."

Cael's breathing was heavy, and then he said, "I've felt so alone for so long, Peaches." My heart shattered apart. Because I had too.

"You're not alone anymore," I said, voice strong and unwavering.

Cael kissed me again, then held me to his chest. I sat between his legs again, his arms wrapped around me like he would never ever let me go.

The snow fell silently around us—a heady juxtaposition to the golden beach it landed upon. Stars were full above us and plentiful between the clouds. Linking my fingers through Cael's, I said, "What did you think of the northern lights?" Cael tensed underneath me. I simply held his hand tighter.

"They were incredible," he said, "But…I think part of me that should experience joy is numb." I leaned back against him. "Sometimes I wonder if I'll ever feel anything to its entirety again. Anger was the only thing that ever made me feel something. Maybe that's why I held on to it for so long. Maybe, even though it was toxic, it was better than *nothing*." I let that sit in the air between us for a few minutes.

"Poppy believed in heaven," I said and found myself staring at Orion's Belt again. "She was never sad that she was dying," I said, trying to keep the hurt from my voice. "I could never understand how she didn't fear what she was facing. But her faith was so strong it left no room in her heart for doubt."

"What do you believe?" Cael asked, hugging me tighter.

"I honestly don't know," I admitted. "I have always loved science. Like the definitive answers it can give." I shrugged. "But there are no definites when it comes to death—except that we will all face it, one day." I lifted our joined hands and ran my free hand over Cael's fingers; they were rough but felt so perfect against mine. "After Poppy passed, I read everything I could on the scientific research around death. But the truth is, we won't ever know what happens until we get there." I pointed our joined hands up at the sky. "Stars are energy, and people are energy too. The entire universe is made of energy. Some see that as science, and some people refer to that energy as God." I shook my head. "I lean toward science. It feels most right to me." I sighed at the heaviness these questions posed. "All I know is that there's something bigger than I can ever comprehend."

I smiled as a shooting star flew across the sky. "I like to think of Poppy as a star." The sacrifice that cost me to admit was all-consuming. I hadn't told a single person that. Not even my therapist. Not my parents, not even Ida. "That probably sounds ridiculous."

"It doesn't," Cael said, his understanding tone immediately putting me at ease. "It's beautiful," he said, and in that moment, I fell for him just that little bit more.

I stared at the snow and the stars that were looking down upon us. "The sky looks more beautiful now that I know she's up there," I said and felt a walled off part of me collapse. "The stars are brighter, knowing she lives among them." I smiled to myself. "Some nights I sit for hours trying to find her. But it's impossible. Then I'm confronted with just how many stars there are in the sky. And I'm reminded of just how many millions of people have lost someone they love too. Grief makes you feel isolated and alone. But the truth is, it's the least lonely state to be in."

I turned in Cael's arms and wrapped my arms around his neck. "Is this okay?" I whispered.

"Of course," he said, and he searched every inch of my face. "You've made this trip so much better for me," he said and kissed my lips. "You're making my *life* better." I embraced him on this snowy beach, under a sky full of endless stars.

We were making each other better. And as Cael steered back my head and claimed my mouth in another kiss, I allowed myself to fall fully. No holding back, no fear in my heart. I would allow myself to become engulfed by Cael and he by me.

Because when you have lost something so precious, when something priceless comes along, you embrace it with both hands.

And you never let it go.

Melded Souls and Open Hearts

Cael
Oslo
Several days later

THE FAMILIAR RINK IN OSLO WAS EMPTY, THE LATER HOUR KEEPING EVERY-one away. It wasn't quite curfew, but the streets were mostly empty. I sat on the bench, just staring at the ice as I tied up my skates. It was muscle memory, tying these laces. The feel of the blade beneath my sole was as comforting to me as sitting before a roaring fire. White mist puffed in clouds from my mouth, and I stood. A bolt of excitement zipped through my veins, the sensation so unexpected it almost made me lose my footing.

It took seven steps for me to meet the edge of the rink. I placed my skate on the ice. I closed my eyes and, on the count of five, pushed forward. The minute the cold breeze ran through my hair, everything seemed to slot into place.

I opened my eyes and stopped in the center of the rink. Bending down, I placed my palm on the ice like I had done several days before. Only this time, I didn't let that feeling crush me. I didn't think of Cill. I just stayed in the moment, stayed in the euphoria of being back in a rink, cold seeping into my bones.

I skated to the edge of the rink, viewing the entire ice before me. And just like I had done so many thousands of times before, I pushed off and raced down the ice at such a fast speed, the bitterness of the breeze bit at the tips of my ears. My cheeks began to ache as I flew, lap after lap, circling the rink with a familiar ease. My cheeks ached again, and my footing almost faltered when I realized it was because I was smiling.

My hands clenched and I yearned for a hockey stick to hold, a puck to hit, and a net to aim for. But this…just this was enough for now. This and the happiness filling my heart as I kept gaining speed, so fast it felt like I was flying.

Then I heard a laugh—a proud and emotion-filled laugh. I came to a sharp stop, spraying the ice into the boards, only to find Savannah on the other side, bundled up in her coat, hat, and gloves, eyes shining with…pride.

"Cael, you…you…" she said but ran out of words. She didn't have to say a thing. I could feel how proud she was of me even from here.

It was an unusual feeling when I realized I was proud of myself too. And that this moment wasn't tied up in me and Cillian. This joy of skating, of hockey, belonged solely to me. I *did* love this feeling.

I *did* love this game.

Pointing to the skate hut at the side of the rink, I said, "Suit up, Peaches." I thought Savannah would say no. I thought she would insist she stay on firm ground. But she didn't do any of that. Instead, she got the skates with confidence and in minutes had them on her feet.

She was wobbly as she stood and approached the ice. I met her at the entrance and held out my hand. Savannah didn't second-guess herself. She didn't second-guess me. She just took my hand, one hundred percent trust, and let me take her into my arms. I made sure she stayed upright and guided her slowly around the rink. The look of happiness on Savannah's face melted me.

We were alone on the rink. The others were watching a movie in the hotel, resting before we left Norway tomorrow. We were only back in Oslo for one night to catch an early-morning flight. We were in the same hotel as before. Leo and Mia had given me permission to come out here. It wouldn't surprise me if they were watching us now. But I didn't care. I *needed* to be here. They understood that too.

It didn't surprise me that Savannah had found me. She had been talking to her parents and sister in her room when I saw the rink was empty and decided to come outside.

I couldn't believe she was on the ice with me now.

Stopping us in the center of the rink, I took a deep breath then brought my lips to hers. And I kissed her. I kissed Savannah with all the newfound joy I'd found on the ice. I kissed her in thanks for helping me get back here, for never pushing me but supporting me to find this missing part of me again.

"You looked amazing out here," she said and just about destroyed me.

"You ready?" I asked and began pulling her slowly, both of her hands holding mine like a vice.

"Lead the way," she said, and I let myself have it. Let myself have this one moment of pure freedom, of a life unburdened from grief. I let my soul claim its passion back. And I let it all happen with the southern girl in my arms who was changing my life for the better, day by day, hour by hour, country by new country.

And we skated. We skated under the stars that Savannah believed her sister now lived among. A flicker of peace settled within my heart when I let myself imagine that Cillian was up there shining brightly too.

Finally free.

Golden Sands and Deep Sorrows

Cael
Goa, India

THE CONTRAST BETWEEN NORWAY AND INDIA WAS MIND-BLOWING. FROM the second we stepped off the plane, we were swallowed by sticky humidity and soaring heat. Sweat dripped from my temples as we got off the bus and headed to where we were staying in Goa.

It was a paradise.

Palm trees swayed in the warm breeze, the beach sprawled out before us, white sand and crystal-blue waters glimmered like something I'd only ever seen on a postcard. When I traveled for hockey, it was mostly to cold cities and even colder arenas.

Savannah had stepped off the bus before me. I found her on the sidewalk, head tipped back and basking in the sun as it kissed her face. Her cheeks were flushed from Goa's high temperature. Her long hair was sticking to her neck, but there was happiness on her face as her eyes stayed closed and she worshipped the heat.

"It feels like Hell here," I said, only for Savannah to crack an eye open and playfully scowl at me.

"I love the heat," she said and slipped off her cardigan, revealing her peach-colored bare arms. Freckles appeared every few inches. She was perfect. She must have seen me staring, as the flush on her cheeks deepened to what I now recognized as a blush.

"It reminds me of home," she said and lifted her hair off the back of her neck. I watched a drop of sweat run down from her scalp and disappear under her white tank.

"Welcome to Goa," Mia said. "Your home for the next several days."

I still couldn't get my head around the fact that only a day ago we were wrapped in thermals and standing under never-ending falling snow. Now, the sun was burning brightly, and the smell of sunscreen permeated the air.

I slipped my arm around Savannah, not caring if the shared body heat added to my already overheated state. Savannah linked my hand that was resting over her shoulder. I was instantly at ease.

"Come this way," Leo said and led us into the resort that would be our home for a while. We were taken into a room that could be used for yoga. Calming, meditative music sailed through the room's hidden speakers. The room was painted a deep, rich red, and large plump cushions were laid out in a circle.

"Please," Leo said and gestured for us to sit down. I shucked off my hoodie, leaving me only in a sleeveless tank top. I felt Savannah's eyes burning into me. I slipped off my beanie and ran my hands through my messy hair. I smirked at her as she tracked her gaze over my arms, chest, and neck tattoos.

Realizing I had caught her staring, she said, "They're so beautiful." She traced her fingertip over the anchor that was the centerpiece on my forearm. Then over the shamrock that showed my Irish heritage. I couldn't resist it, or stand her looking at me like that, so I bent down and captured her lips with my own. I was freer with my affection now. Everyone knew about us, so we didn't feel the need to hide it. I pressed my lips to hers and immediately felt any nerves I had put at ease. I was always wary of any new activity or country we embarked on. Just as I got used to the newest place we were in, Mia and Leo unsettled us by moving us on to something completely different. It was the worst part of the trip. I used to love seeing new places. Since my brother passed, it brought me nothing but unease.

Guess it showed that I was still nowhere being healed.

A throat cleared and I pulled back from Savannah. Leo was standing, exasperated. I still wasn't sure if he approved of us. He didn't give much away. "When you're ready," he said, and chuckles ran around the rest of the group. They were waiting for us to sit before we could begin.

Savannah's face was scarlet red as she quickly ran to her cushion and sat down. She was still so shy and reserved. She wasn't with me, though, and that made me feel like the luckiest guy in the world.

"So," Leo said, "did anyone guess what we were trying to show you in Norway?"

"Nature?" Lili asked, after a few minutes of thought.

"A new culture?" Jade tacked on.

Leo smiled at their guesses, then said, "We wanted to take you to a place of awe and wonder. To see sights that were spectacular, unique, and often overwhelming to the human eye."

"More times than not, when we are consumed by grief, we feel alone, and our world reduces to just ourselves and the trauma we have experienced. Our world becomes myopic," Mia said. "By seeing such breathtaking sights in the world that can often leave us awestruck and sensorily overwhelmed, it can also shift our perspective. It can give us access to the marvels of life and the universe that maybe help open our minds and allow us to step into a new way of thinking. It can remind us we are alive, and although still fighting through grief, we still have a lot of life left to live."

The group was nodding, like it resonated with them. Even Savannah seemed to agree, to feel that way. The stars, the northern lights had made her feel more connected to Poppy than she'd been in years. I'd seen the subtle change in her. And she hadn't succumbed to her anxiety even once.

She'd seemed a fraction more settled by the time we had left. Not healed, still wrestling with the heavy grip of grief. But lighter somehow. I could see it in everything she was.

I hadn't felt it quite like everyone else. Panic rose inside of me. I'd gotten back on the ice. That was progress. At least progress with how I felt about hockey. But when it came to how I thought of my brother, not much had changed. I'd tried to picture him in the stars, but not long afterward, the doubt and dark thoughts crept in. Why couldn't I look at the northern lights and see my brother dancing among them? Why couldn't I picture him as free and at peace?

I kept my face neutral. I didn't want Savannah to see just how troubled I was.

"This leg of the trip," Leo said, "is about confronting mortality." In our one-on-one sessions, Leo had gently pushed me to open up about Cillian. But I'd given him nothing. I liked how it had felt in Norway when I'd pushed everything aside. It had become addictive. And Savannah had become my salvation. When I was with her, holding her, the pit in my stomach didn't ache; it was comfortably numbed. My anger had ebbed. It was strange. The way I used to attach myself to anger shifted to the way I attached myself to Savannah. She was the life rope that was tying me to her, keeping me from drifting away. I refused to lose that.

"What does that mean?" Dylan asked nervously.

"We will explore the natural journey that we all take—life and death and everything in between." I glanced at Savannah; she was wringing her hands together. That thought had clearly made her nervous too. I checked her breathing. So far, she was keeping it together.

"We'll be visiting three places on this leg of the trip. Goa is the first. Here, we will immerse ourselves in group sessions and one-on-ones, as well as therapy classes that can help us address some of our inner traumas."

"But this is also a chance to recoup," Leo added. "We've had two very full-on experiences in England and Norway." He gestured around us. "This place is a haven. We encourage you to relax some, swim, soak in the sun. Eat together, hang out, *talk*," he said, referring to the group.

"Get some rest, unpack, hang out by the pool. Tomorrow we'll start the sessions et cetera," Leo said and handed out our room keys.

As we grabbed our luggage, Travis said, "Should we all meet at the pool?"

I took hold of Savannah's hand. "Do you want to swim?" I kissed her again. I never wanted to stop. Life didn't feel so bleak when she was in my arms.

She smiled against my lips. "Okay."

My room was sandwiched in between Dylan's and Travis's. As we approached our doors, they were walking together, quiet whispers shared between them. I hadn't noticed how close they'd gotten in Norway. But then, outside of Savannah, I hadn't noticed much else.

Throwing on my swim shorts, I headed to Savannah's door and knocked. When she didn't answer, I went in search of her at the pool and stopped dead when I caught sight of her. She was on the edge of the pool in her pale-blue bathing suit, the warm breeze kicking up her dark blond hair around her head like a halo. Her hand rested on a palm tree trunk as she looked out onto the beach and sea.

In that moment, I couldn't believe how lucky I was that someone like Savannah had taken a chance on me. I was broken; I knew I was. The more I sat in on group sessions, and the more we all hung out, I was starting to see everyone else make gradual improvements. They were laughing more, smiling more, and some were even talking about their deceased family members more. Remembering them in good ways, sharing happy memories.

I hadn't mentioned Cillian to anyone but Savannah.

At night, Savannah would read the notebook her sister had left her. Then she would write back to her in the journal Mia and Leo had given us. Like she was having a conversation with her again.

I hadn't been given another journal. Leo and I had decided that wasn't part of my journey right now. It was too triggering for me, and we'd focus on talking therapies in our sessions instead. That wasn't exactly working either, but I wasn't writing anything in a journal and he understood that.

That seven-word note in my wallet was still there, untouched and an albatross to my life.

Despite the roasting heat, all I felt were ice-cold chills as I stood there, lost in my head. I was only wrenched from my own darkness when Savannah turned and found me across the poolside. She was like a damn mirage as her blue eyes—made only more vibrant by the swimsuit—broke out in a shy smile at my presence.

I wasn't sure I'd ever deserve that smile. But I'd take whatever she wanted to give me. I walked around the pool to where she stood. I flipped the bird when Dylan and Travis, already in the pool, splashed water at me, soaking my legs.

As I arrived beside Savannah, the scent of her sunscreen hit me first, as did her beauty. Her long, straight hair had curled into ringlets in the humidity. I decided this was how I liked her best, in the sun where she belonged.

"Hi," she said when I took hold of her hand.

"Hey, Peaches," I said back and wrapped her up in my arms. The feel of her bare skin against my own felt perfect, and as I reared back, I kissed her, slow and soft, tasting the cherry ChapStick on her lips.

"Are you okay?" I asked her. She nodded when I broke from the kiss, and I could already see her nose and cheeks turning pink in the sun.

"You?" she asked back, a slight furrow of concern on her brow.

"I am now," I said, only to feel another splash of water on my legs. I glared down at Dylan and Travis.

"Stop making out and get your asses in here," Dylan said. Without warning, I jumped into the pool, making sure to drench Travis on his floatie. Savannah's light laughter burst into the air behind me.

"Get in, Peaches," I said when I broke the surface, and watched as she slid into the pool. I caught her as she hit the water, and she wrapped her arms around my neck, holding on as I waded us through the water. We congregated in the middle of the pool, Dylan and Travis ducking off their floaties to give them to Jade and Lili, who arrived a few minutes later.

"I'll take this over rain and snow," Jade said, closing her eyes as she lay back on the float. Dylan slipped under the water, then came up underneath her and turned over the floatie. Jade screeched as she fell into the water, head going straight underneath.

"Dylan!" she shouted when she got up and gave chase.

"Don't even think it," Lili said to Travis as he dived under the water too. In only a few moments, she was thrashing in the water as Travis pushed her right off.

Savannah gripped her arms around my neck tighter as she laughed, her chest heaving as the four of them raced after each other all over the pool.

It was nice, I thought. To hear such carefree laughter. When you'd lost someone, laughter didn't come easily. For me, it never came at all. When I felt myself quietly laughing too, it felt so foreign, like my body couldn't even remember *how* to laugh.

"Cael," Savannah said, brushing her hand across my neck, right over my Adam's apple. I didn't know what had brought a sheen of happy tears to her eyes.

"What's wrong?" I asked, puzzled.

"You laughed," she said. "I haven't heard you laugh at all since we've been on the trip." Her words hit me like bullets. I used to laugh all the time. Embraced fun. I thought of Stephan, my best friend. Thought of my team back in Massachusetts. How we would always be messing around, spraying each other with ice, tripping each other up with our sticks.

We would always laugh.

I'd missed that sound. But…I had just *laughed*.

Maybe I wasn't quite as broken as I believed.

"We have to start talking soon, Cael," Leo said, but my body was rigid, and I just couldn't bring myself to do it. I *wanted* to be better. I wanted to have Leo and Mia help me, but I just didn't know how to start.

Leo sat back in his chair. We were in the red room from the first day we had arrived here. All of our group sessions had been held here. I hadn't participated. But I'd listened, which was an improvement on most of the sessions before.

"When it comes to suicide," Leo said carefully, "especially notable in men is the lack of talking." At those words my body went still. All my muscles locked, and my bones turned to stone. Leo sat forward in his chair. My eyes dropped to the ground. "Talking saves lives." Leo placed his notebook on the floor beside him. "Around eighty percent of all suicides in the United States are men. It's one of our biggest killers." I felt anger stirring inside of me. He didn't have to tell me this. I *knew* this. I had researched this. "I'm worried about you, Cael," he said, and this time, I met his eyes. "You don't talk to us. You don't even mention your brother. Not just by his name but at *all*. I know you have opened up to Savannah some, but Mia and I are here to help you through this. We are here to help you professionally. To give you tools to move on."

Leo linked his hands together. "I need you to know that there is nothing you could have done," he said. I felt a familiar flash of anger flare inside of me. Only, where it used to burst out of me through shouts and screams and fists through walls, since being with Savannah, it now instantly faded and turned to guilt and shame and sadness. It was so intense, it actually *ached* when it settled within me. Because I didn't believe Leo. He didn't know me and Cillian. He didn't know how close we were. How closely our lives were intertwined. I should have known there was something wrong with him. How had I missed it? How had I let him die?

My leg started bouncing in agitation. I opened my mouth, to try to speak, but nothing came out. It was like there was a mental block whenever I wanted to try to talk about it, to give voice to my pain and shame and fears.

Leo checked the clock on the wall. "That's our time up for today, Cael." I jumped from my seat, needing to get out of the room. Before I reached the exit, Leo said, "I know it's hard. Believe me, son, I *know*." Shivers darted down my spine at the way he had said that. Had someone close to him done what Cillian had done? If so, how had *he* moved on? "But to help you gain back your life, we have to start talking." The expression on Leo's face was earnest, beseeching. When I didn't react, he said, "I've also spoken to your parents again today." My stomach dropped. "I told them you were well. They said you're still ignoring their calls and texts." Once more, he let unspoken words hang between us.

He was right. I still hadn't called them once since I'd been away. They tried to call at the same time every day, no matter where I was. They texted every day too. My dad especially. I left them all on read.

I had nothing to say to them.

I left the room and let the sticky Indian air coat my skin. I walked aimlessly, lost to my thoughts. I just didn't know how to open up. I didn't feel that I would ever be able to do it. Savannah's face came to mind. I'd told her about Cillian. I'd told her he'd taken his own life. But I hadn't said anything else. Hadn't told her of that night, of what I'd seen…

I didn't know if I would ever be able to.

I turned the corner of the resort to see Savannah and Dylan sitting together at a café table drinking coffee. She was listening to him speak. She listened so attentively, so well. She never judged, never made me feel stupid.

Just looking at her had my muscles relaxing and my shoulders dropping. It still surprised me how another person could have such an effect on me.

Maybe one day I could tell Savannah everything about Cillian. How he'd built me up when I was low, or how he'd taught me how to take a slap shot. Or how I had found him…how the last image of my big brother was him gone, by his own doing, limp in my arms.

A wave of emotion choked me, and I ducked back into the hallway. I picked up my speed until I was running. I ran out onto a jogging trail, and I just kept going. I couldn't talk to Savannah about this. She was mourning her own sister, fought daily with not succumbing to her anxiety. She didn't need my issues weighing her down too.

So, I ran. I ran and ran until I was exhausted. Until the gutting sadness my session with Leo had brought up had faded. I ran until I couldn't think of anything anymore. Until I was so tired all I wanted to do was sleep.

Once again, I'd successfully ran away from my brother's death, as fast as my feet would take me. And I wasn't sure how that could ever change.

———

Today's lesson was out in the open air, in a secluded gazebo overlooking the turquoise sea. Miriam was our therapist for this. We'd had days of group lessons and one-on-ones. We'd had days of yoga and walking nearby routes, of meditation and music therapy.

Today was art. Painting, to be exact.

"You all have a blank canvas before you," Miriam said, and I glanced down at the paints, the brushes and the container filled with water to clean off the paint between strokes.

I wasn't much of an artist, so I wasn't hopeful of what I'd get out of this session. The past few days' activities had been okay and, with regard to facing our own mortality, had been soft and gradual. Nothing had pushed us to the brink yet. I didn't think for one second those days weren't coming.

Savannah was beside me, but none of us could see one another's canvases. I stared at that white piece of canvas and wondered what the hell she'd ask us to draw.

"For today's session, I would like you to remember the person or persons you have lost," Miriam said, and my world absolutely stopped. Invisible hands took hold of my lungs and heart and began to squeeze. I heard my heart beat slow in my ears as white noise filled in the rest of the barren space.

"You have an array of paint colors in front of you. I want you to think of who you have lost and simply paint. It can be a portrait or simply a conceptual representation of who they were to you, who they were in life. Perhaps how you feel since they have been gone.

"I want you to really pour your heart into the memories you have with this person and purge it on the canvas." Miriam walked slowly around us all, circling the silent room. The tension between all of us rose so high you could slice it with a knife.

"I want you to really delve down deep." Her voice changed sympathetically. "This can be emotionally draining. But we must face these emotions head-on. We must think of the person we have lost and not run from their memory or the pain their passing can inspire." Miriam stood in the center of the circle. She placed her hand on her chest. "*Feel* this painting. *Feel* your loved ones. Let your soul lead you on this journey and allow all the pent-up sorrow and happiness and unfairness you feel leave your body." Miriam smiled at each of us. "When you're ready, please begin."

I stared at the canvas for so long, I completely lost track of time. I didn't know what to paint. Nothing was coming forward. In my peripheral, I saw people beginning to put their brushes to their pieces. I didn't look at what colors they were using or what they might be painting. The canvas before me seemed like an impossible mountain to climb.

A familiar heat seared through me. And today, I let it. I *needed* to feel it right now. I was so *angry* at Cillian. He had taken our dreams and smashed them into pieces, so many that they could never be put back together again. He had destroyed our family. He had destroyed his friends, his team; he had destroyed so much in his path that he was like the deadliest of tornadoes.

And he hadn't told anyone. He'd hid his pain with easy smiles and loud laughs. He'd played every game of hockey like he was in the Stanley Cup final. Talked animatedly, the life of the party at family gatherings, at our family dinners. And me, I was the idiot who hadn't seen through the cracks—his fractures. I hadn't seen the sadness in his eyes. Hadn't noticed the tiredness in his voice, hadn't noticed him giving up, day by day, pretending to the world that he was fine.

But worst of all, he hadn't told anyone *why*. They'd been no obvious reason for why he'd done it. No falling out with friends, no girlfriend who had left him broken-hearted. He hadn't been in trouble. He was in the first line at Harvard, on his way to the Frozen Four, NHL shining brightly in his future. He had a mother and father and brother who adored him.

But he'd fucking left anyway.

It was only when the paintbrush snapped in my hand and the canvas blurred before me that I realized I'd been painting. That I'd thrown color onto the white canvas and poured all of what I was thinking into some kind of art piece.

I blinked my eyes and cleared the tears that had formed. And I just stared... I stared at what lay before me.

Blackness. Black swirls laced with red. Red for blood and anger. Black for the loss and the state I'd been left in. Ice trickled down my spine, picking up speed until a thought came to mind—was this painting how Cillian had been feeling that night to do what he did? Nothing inside of his heart to live for?

Death his only option.

Death, to stop the pain.

Death, to escape whatever hell life had become for him. He'd suffered in silence and died that way too.

A hand landed on my shoulder. The touch was gentle and supportive. "Beautiful," Miriam said, and her voice was shaking. I didn't look up, but I thought I heard tears in her tone. "It's so truly beautiful, Cael." I stared at the painting and saw no beauty in it. It was like a void, sucking everything bright and light into its mouth. The longer I stared at it, at the flashes of red, the swirling brushstrokes, and pitch-black opaque of the center, a deep coldness settled over the rest of me.

Goose bumps covered my skin when I truly studied the picture. It was almost like Cillian had been beside me, guiding the brush. Like he wanted me to *know* how it had felt inside his soul, giving me a glimpse of why he'd felt there was no other option. I shuffled in my seat.

I had no idea what happened after we died. But had it been possible for him to show me this? Had he somehow been in this moment with me, urging me to *see*? To *understand*. Foolishly, I searched around me for any sign that he was here. Then I shook my head at my stupidity.

What was I even *thinking*?

Yet the picture stared back at me, like it had an ominous force, a malevolent agenda, trying to swallow me into darkness too. Was Cillian's presumed depression so numbing that all his light was sucked from him into a nothingness void of despair? Was this kind of bleakness too much to live with and his reasoning for taking his own life simply to stop this level of anguish and darkness?

If it was, how could I ever hate him? How could I ever question why he didn't want to stay in this world if this was what he lived with every minute of every day?

Had this darkness stolen his voice too? Is that why he didn't tell me he was suffering? Had it robbed him of his plea for help? Had it given him no other choice but to succumb to its pull?

I tasted salt on my lips and realized it was from the tears that were tumbling from my eyes. I didn't want to feel this. I didn't want this picture to be me too. If this darkness had been in Cillian, could bring such a strong hero down, could it be in me too? Panic wrapped around me and almost brought me to my knees.

Leo appeared beside me. "Let's take a walk, son." I stood, not wanting to think and just wanting to be led away from here, from that darkness I felt was calling my name.

I felt the group's stares on my back and knew there would be one set of blue eyes hyperfocused on me. But I let Leo take me to the white sand of the beach. I didn't even feel the heat from the blazing sun bearing down upon me. Chills kept me frozen, like I was standing in a freezer, unable to escape.

Leo didn't talk at first. He just sat beside me. Until he said, "It was my father." I stopped breathing, only starting again when he said, "I was fifteen." Leo paused, and I heard him take a deep inhale. "I found him."

I closed my eyes, hearing the gentle flow of the water, trying like hell to use it to calm me down before my heart tried to lurch from my chest.

"For years it consumed me," Leo said. "So much so that I became lost to darkness too." He wrapped his arms around his legs. "I was self-destructive. I flunked out of school. Threw any possible future I had away."

He let that confession hang in the air between us, until I grabbed hold of it, reeled it in, and asked, "What changed?"

"I got sick and tired of it, Cael," he said, and I heard the honesty in his deep voice. "I'd lost my dad, but that day, I also lost myself. The boy I was died, and the one I became afterward was born." He smiled, and I frowned. "Then I met my wife." Savannah's pretty face automatically came to my mind, and I felt a spark of grace inside of me grow, and a solitary candle flame began to rise, sucking up more oxygen from the well of grief inside of me to give it more strength.

"I wanted to be better for her." Leo tapped his chest over his heart. "But I *needed* to be better for *myself.*" He finally faced me. "So I went back to school and decided that rather than running from my father's death, I would face it head-on, honor the man that was my entire world by helping those just like him…and those just like me—the grievers."

"Why did he do it?" I asked, my chest cracking open and feeling like I was bleeding out, marring the golden sand in red.

"I never knew," Leo said and ran a fistful of sand through his fingers. One by one the grains poured back onto the beach—nature's hourglass. I stared at those grains of sand. A billion tiny parts making up a whole. "Knowing what I do about depression, I imagine it was that. But I've never known." He faced me again. "And Cael, I've had to make peace with that." Emotion radiated from Leo's frame, but I could see he embraced it, wore it like a cape rather than a shroud.

Leo placed his hand on my shoulder. "I'm always ready to talk, when you are." He got up and left me on the beach. I stayed out there until the sun began to fade over the horizon, a burn-orange semicircle casting the beach in a golden glow. I only moved when darkness fell and the stars came out. I looked up at every one and thought back on what Savannah had said in Norway.

I searched each star for one that could be Cillian. But there were so many, just like the billions of grains of sand I sat upon. Lifting from the sand, I made my way back to the hotel. The lights were still open in the gazebo where we had painted.

The pull of a thread inside of my gut guided me back there, to the piece that I didn't even remember painting. When I reached the gazebo, everyone's paintings were still out, drying. I made my way around them, looking at what my friends had been thinking when they had opened their hearts. Dylan's was full of pastel colors and blues. It was affectionate, somehow. Peaceful. Like the feeling of coming home.

Travis's made my chest ache. Eleven white crosses in a vivid green field. The sun was bright and yellow shining down upon them. And there was a flash of orange and red standing to the side, hand upon one of the crosses. I understood that to be Travis, mourning his friends.

Lili's was three hands holding on to each other tightly, never letting go. Only two of the hands were lighter, almost transparent, angelic. Jade's was a riot of color, every color that could be named. It spoke of vibrant people, bright and fun and filled with life. Her mother and brother.

Then I came to a stop at Savannah's. Pale pinks made flowers of her canvas. A mason jar sat off to the side, a blossom tree in the background too. Stars hung in the sky, looking down upon the scene. It was calm and peaceful. It looked like a place I wanted to see.

"The blossom grove," a gentle voice said out of the darkness. I turned to see Savannah coming up the stone stairs from the hotel into the gazebo. She was dressed in a sage-green dress that had strap sleeves and floated around her knees. Her blond hair was down and curled with the heat. She was more beautiful than any of these paintings.

"It's a cherry blossom grove, back in Georgia. What our small town was named for." A nostalgic smile flickered on Savannah's lips. "It was Poppy's favorite place." She reached my side and ran her hand over the bottom of the tree. "It's where she's buried."

"Savannah," I said and wanted to reach out and pull her into my arms. But I felt exhausted and not myself. I didn't want to hold her the way I was feeling. Didn't want to tarnish her with my touch. Today had shaken me. Completely. I felt like I was crawling out of my skin.

"It's where she was happiest. It's only right she rested there for eternity." I was so damn proud of Savannah in that moment—and always. The girl I'd met in JFK would never have talked about her sister like this. She stood beside me, right now, strength in her stance and an outspoken love for the sister she cradled in her heart. And Savannah Litchfield, I found, had the biggest of hearts.

"What's that?" I asked, voice hoarse as I pointed to the mason jar. My throat was sore, like my soul was so tired it didn't want me to speak. But I had to. All of these feelings were bubbling inside of me, rising to the surface, begging to escape.

Savannah smiled wider. "Our Mamaw gave Poppy a jar of paper hearts before she died, one thousand of them. Each time Poppy had a kiss—an earth-shattering kiss—she was to write it down and record it. She was to collect one thousand in her lifetime." Savannah's hand slightly shook as she traced the outline of the jar. "When she was diagnosed with cancer, she didn't think she would achieve it. But she did it. With her soulmate, Rune." Savannah looked up to me. "Kiss one thousand was given on her very last breath."

My heart fired off into a fast-paced beat. I'd never heard anything like that.

"When I used to think of Poppy, I would think of loss and pain and feel her heavy, irreplaceable absence walking beside me every day, ominous and gutting. But when Miriam asked us to paint our lost loved one and who they were to us, and how they made us feel, I couldn't paint anything other than something beautiful." Savannah inhaled a trembling breath. "Though her life was short, she lived big and she lived loud and never wasted a single moment, not even when she was dying. She lived life until her very last breath. She was grace personified until the end—and even beyond."

I thought of my painting, sitting beside us in the gazebo. The blacks and reds, the void that triumphantly drank down your happiness. There was a wall behind me, and I sank down upon it, exhausted. Savannah did too, but not before running her hand through my messy hair.

I linked my hands together in my lap and stared at the cherry blossom grove, at the beauty and the uplifting colors and said, "I don't know how to talk about that night."

Savannah reached out and linked her arm through mine. "I'm here whenever you're ready."

"You have enough to deal with, Peaches. You don't need the added weight of my trauma too."

"It's not heavy," she said and squeezed my arm. "If it unburdens you, then it's the lightest weight in the world." She kissed my exposed bicep, and the shards of ice that had created an impenetrable armor around me melted in the exact place that her lips had touched.

I felt guilty for even contemplating laying all my trauma at her feet. But here I was, in Goa, at night, beside a dreamlike seaside with a painting that was haunting my every move, and I just needed to purge everything from my soul.

"*I wanted to do it for her. But I* needed *to do it for myself,*" Leo's words rang in encouragement in my mind.

"Nothing was different about that day," I said, and my vision blurred, forcing me to relive it all in my head. "I went to practice. Then Cillian had a game that night." I huffed an unamused laugh. "He got MVP. They won—a shutout. Cillian scored all the goals, a hat trick." I shook my head. "He played his heart out. Now I wonder if he played so hard because he knew he would never play again. Was that his final goodbye to the team he loved so much and the fans who had supported him since starting Harvard?"

My leg bounced in nerves. I'd never talked this much in my life. It was like slicing open my heart and letting it bleed out, willingly. "At the game, I was with my parents. But afterward, I met up with my teammates. Stephan, my best friend, had been invited to a party one of the Harvard guys was throwing, next door where my brother lived off-campus." I remembered arriving at the party, everyone celebrating. "We'd been to a hundred of them before. My brother was there, of course, but when he saw me walk in, rather than wearing the happy smile he always gave me, his eyes were stormy, and he told me to go home."

I shook my head, like I was back there living that night. "He'd never been like that to me before. It had shocked me so much. He *never* sent me home. Always stayed by my side. I just thought he must have been tired—"

My voice cut out and I choked on a sob. "There *was* a sign, Sav. And

I missed it. He'd never been like that to me, ever. He wasn't the typical big brother growing up. He was always so good to me." His face came to mind. He looked more like my dad than me; I had my mom's features. But anyone could tell we were siblings. "He was a good person and was all about family. He never treated me like I was lesser than him. Hell, he never even told me to get out of his room. He didn't send me away from the frozen pond on our property when his friends came to play hockey. He included me. *Always.*" I turned to Savannah and saw tears running down her face. Her bottom lip was trembling. "But he never told me he was hurting, Sav. He never told me that. Never told me *the* most important thing."

I sniffed back tears and just gave in to the sadness I'd held trapped inside for too long. "He'd never sent me away before that night. But he *did* then. I should have fought him, asked why he was acting that way. I think I was too stunned. He threw a twenty in my hand and told me to run to the store and grab some snacks for the house."

I glanced down at my hand and the palm that had held that money. "I didn't see it at the time, but he'd wrapped his fingers around my hand when he'd put that money in my palm. Tightly. Just a few seconds longer than normal, but I can still feel it. Like a brand." Savannah took hold of that hand and brought it to her lips, kissing me on the palm. A choked cry escaped my mouth at her touch, at her soft lips kissing that calloused, tarnished skin.

"You're doing so well," she said and laid her head on my shoulder. Her body heat seeped into mine, thawing some of the ice.

"I looked up into my big brother's eyes and he said, *"Keep safe, yeah, kid?"* In hindsight, his voice was gravelly and stacked with emotion. I thought maybe he was just getting the flu or something. I'd told him I would. I thought he was talking about Stephan's driving. But now I know he was talking about my *life. Christ,* Savannah, that was his goodbye to me, and I didn't even know it. That was the last time I would hear his voice or feel him touch my hand. That was *it.*"

Savannah wrapped her arm around my shoulders and held me as I fell apart in the crook of her neck, my tears soaking her curly hair. "I replay that moment over and over in my head, all the time, several times a day. I see the subtle hints now. Hear the slight shake in his voice. But I didn't see them at the time. His window wasn't transparent; it was thick with condensation, and I just couldn't see through it."

I looked at the cherry blossom flowers Savannah had painted, then the stars that hung like gems from the sky. "Stephan was with me. We were on our way to the store, when he realized he'd forgotten his wallet back at the house. He wanted to grab some food for himself, was hungry, and we didn't have enough cash to go through a drive-through. We turned back, only to see my brother's car roaring down the road we were on, in the opposite direction. I was so confused as to where he was going. He was meant to be at the party. But what concerned me more was the speed he was going. It was reckless. He was *never* reckless. Always calm and measured. I told Stephan to follow him. A pull in my gut was telling me something was wrong." My teeth gritted together. I wasn't sure I could do this last part. I wasn't sure I could find it in me to say what happened next out loud.

"If that's all you can say, that's okay," Savannah said, clearly reading me right. I pressed a kiss to her hair, then met her watery eyes. I wanted to tell this girl. I wanted to share this with her. "No one is pushing you to say more."

I searched her face, then thought of my painting again. I *had* to tell her. I didn't want that darkness to be my future. The truth was, I think it had already begun to take hold of me. I had come to believe that kind of darkness acted in a stealth attack. Slowly invading a soul bit by bit until it had consumed them without them even realizing. Then they were too weak to fight it off.

I sat up straighter, determined to fight the goddamn thing back. I didn't want it to consume me. "We saw Cillian's taillights up ahead and followed him. I was so worried about him. He was picking up more and more speed, swerving in the road as he fought to keep it on track." I paused, fought back the lump in my throat. I breathed and whispered, "Then I watched him purposely plow headfirst into a huge, solid tree just off the road's sharp bend." Savannah sucked in a quick breath. I was shaking, I was shaking so badly as I was thrust back to that moment whether I wanted to be there or not.

"I jumped from Stephan's car before he'd even stopped. And I ran for Cill. I ran faster than ever before. And when I got there, I wrenched the driver's side door open and saw him…" I shook my head, trying to rid myself of that image. "It was too late, Sav. He was gone." Savannah's arms wrapped around me tighter, and she crushed me to her chest. I fell apart. I drowned in my tears until my chest was raw and my lungs burned so much it hurt just to take in a breath.

"There were no drugs or alcohol in his system. We found out afterward that he'd disabled the airbag, Sav. Before he'd driven. The seat belt too. He made sure there was no coming back from what he intended to do." I tried to clear my throat, but my voice was so graveled it was almost nonexistent. "I pulled him from the car…and I held him. I held his broken body until the paramedics came and they forced me to let him go."

Racking sobs still came, refreshed and carrying just as much weight as the ones before. "I still feel him in my arms sometimes, still feel his lifeless body pulled to my chest. I tried to bring him back—CPR, pleading to God to save him—but he was gone, Savannah. He was *gone*. As quick as that… and I watched him do it."

"I'm here," Savannah said as I dropped from the wall to the floor— she followed me down too. She held me in the gazebo beneath the stars, surrounded by painted memories of the dead, and all I saw was Cillian. So, I held her tighter. I turned my back on the painting that had reduced me to *this* and fought it with all I had.

I refused to let it consume me too.

Broken Hearts and Fractured Memories

Savannah

CAEL'S LARGE, STRONG BODY TREMBLED IN MY ARMS. I PRAYED THAT I WAS enough to comfort him, to hold him through this moment. I cried too. I cried as I replayed what he had told me. I cried for Cillian, and I cried for Cael.

He'd seen it.

He'd found him.

He'd cradled his older brother in his arms... I could only imagine the trauma that had left within him. The scars that must have seared onto his broken heart. I rocked him back and forth and couldn't help but be thrust back into Poppy's bedroom, my hand in hers after she had died. How naively I had thought that if I just didn't let go, none of it would be real. That if I just stayed by her side, her eyes would open, and a miracle would have occurred. She'd believed in God so devoutly, so surely He would grant her a miracle and keep her with us all. The cancer would leave her body and she'd be healthy again. She'd get to live out her days with the people she loved most. She'd see our birthdays, weddings, and births of our future children. And we would see hers. We would see her marry Rune in the blossom grove that had become synonymous with them as a couple.

But that miracle never came. I knew now that when it came to death, they rarely do.

I curled myself over Cael and I let the floodgates open. My sternum ached as my chest racked with sadness. I didn't think I had ever cried that much in my life before. I had always held it back, controlled it. But seeing Cael break, hearing the story of Cillian, and Cael finding him—*seeing* him—wrecked me.

Cael's endless tears soaked my dress. But I saw each of those falling tears as a blessing. He had lived with this for so long. Tried to hide it through tattoos and piercings. Listened to our group sessions with forced detachment and silence. Even *I* had participated, which several weeks ago would have seemed impossible.

Cael had needed this.

I had needed to see him face this too.

I stroked my hand through his dark hair. Somewhere along this journey, my heart had reached out and melded to his. Since Poppy, I had been so terrified of falling for someone. Scared by the thought of losing them too. But minute by minute on this trip, I had felt a magnet drawing Cael and me together, so powerful, it was impossible to resist. We had shared in a pain that people outside of this experience would never understand.

And right now, with him so distraught and vulnerable in my arms and my heart cracking in his shared pain, I came to the heady realization that I was in love with him. Head over heels, completely in love with this broken boy from outside Boston. I peppered kisses along his cheek and hair. His hands and fingers that were linked through mine.

"I'm so tired, Savannah," Cael said, his depleted, softly spoken words tearing open my chest.

"Let's go and sleep then," I said and guided Cael to his feet. He was so tall and broad and physically strong. But everything in his gait screamed that he was fractured. With his arm over my shoulders and my arm around his waist, we walked back to the floor that held all our rooms. As I walked past my own, just the thought of leaving him alone made me feel nauseous. I didn't want to be alone either.

As we entered the hallway, Leo was waiting. We stopped when we saw him. "How are you doing, Cael?" he asked. I had a feeling he'd been keeping an eye on him this entire time. In fact, I was sure he was.

"Tired," Cael said, sagging beside me.

I looked up at Leo and saw the sadness on his face. "Please," I said quietly. "Please...let me stay with him."

"Savannah..." Leo said, shaking his head.

"Nothing will happen, I promise. We'll sleep above the covers. Please... I just want to stay beside him," I said, begging Leo with my eyes. I couldn't leave him alone. My heart wouldn't let me. *He's so broken,* I tried to silently convey to Leo. *He's just opened up to me and told me everything. He's too raw and vulnerable to be on his own tonight.*

Leo walked back into his own room, then came back out carrying a chair. He placed it outside Cael's room. "The door stays open, and I'll be checking on you frequently," he said. "*Don't* betray my trust."

"We won't," I whispered. The relief Leo's permission brought was consuming. I held Cael's hand tighter and walked him into his room, leaving the door open. Gratitude, so strong and blatant, shone in Cael's desolate gaze. I knew I'd done the right thing. Grief hurt worse when you were alone.

I brought him to his bed, and we lay down, fully clothed. Cael wrapped me in his arms and crushed me to his chest like it was the only thing anchoring him to hope. I held him back, just breathing in his sea salt scent. He kissed me on the top of my head and exhaled a long and defeated sigh.

"Thank you," he said, and his words filled the hotel room.

"There's nothing to be thankful for," I said and nestled in closer. It was true. This was what we did for those we loved. We held them through darkness.

"He wasn't a bad person," Cael eventually said, and that just about broke my heart.

"Of course he wasn't," I said sternly and lifted myself up until I was propped onto my elbow. I ran my fingertips over Cael's face. His eyes were bloodshot from crying, and his skin was pale yet blotchy from all his tears.

"He was just sad," he said, almost more to himself than to me. "He was just too sad to carry on." He blinked and chased fresh tears away. "And he wasn't a coward." My heart collapsed. "He was strong and brave and was the best person I ever knew."

"He couldn't be further from a coward," I echoed. "He was strong until the end. Never believe otherwise."

Cael nodded his head, like he'd desperately needed to hear that. He took hold of my hand. "What was she like? Poppy?"

Branches of love began to grow inside of me, blotting out sadness. I smiled, even though my lips shook. I just missed her so much. "She was kind," I said quietly. I gripped Cael's hand tighter. "She was beautiful. And she was so encouraging."

I swallowed back the gutting emotions that were threatening to steal my words. For the first time in such a long time, I *wanted* to talk about Poppy and how wonderful she had been. "She encouraged me more than anyone in my life. She was my anchor. She was the person who helped pull me out of the shell I so naturally hid inside." I laughed when Ida's face came to mind. "My younger sister, Ida, is like that too." My stomach fell. "But I haven't really let her in since Poppy died." Tears built in my eyes. "I haven't been the big sister to her that Poppy was to us both."

"You've been hurting," Cael said, running his finger up and down my cheek.

"So has she," I said, the truth of that fact making me fill to the brim with guilt. "It was Ida who persuaded me to come here." I met Cael's eyes. "The truth is, I haven't been myself since Poppy died."

A thought I had always kept secret screamed to be let out. Cael was searching my face, like he knew I wanted to say something too. Kissing his hand, I then ran my fingers over his tattooed knuckles and said, "Sometimes…" I took in a shallow, shaky breath. "Sometimes I think it's me who should have died." My heart kicked into a sprint as those private words became shared. "Poppy was so full of life. She had Rune. They would have married. They would have had the most beautiful life together. True soulmates."

I flicked my eyes around the dark in the room. I knew Leo was listening to our every word, but I didn't mind. Maybe it was time I shared it with him too. "Ida is like Poppy. They are so vibrant. Being around them is being smothered with happiness and hope. Me…" I trailed off. "I'm quiet, reserved." My breath stuttered. "The world would have continued without me. No great ripple of sorrow or unfairness would have occurred if I'd slipped away, as quietly as I lived. No one would have truly been affected if I had been the one to fall victim to sickness."

"I would have," Cael said. His voice was no longer weak but so bold and full of conviction that I couldn't help but look at him. He was deadly serious; I could see that in his silver-blue depths. "My world would have been affected, Savannah. I would have wandered through my life wondering why there was a sudden ache in my heart. My life would have been unfulfilled because you had never stepped into it like you were always meant to."

"Cael…" I said, choked with emotion, and he leaned in and kissed me. His hand met my cheek and his fingers threaded into my hair. I kissed him back and tried to absorb all of what he had said. My heart had swelled in my chest at his words. And I returned the sentiment. Cael had stepped into my life and spliced his soul with my own, two hearts sharing one valve. It was heady and overwhelming but joyous and almost too much of a sensation to bear.

He pulled back and joined his forehead to mine. "I would have forever felt you were missing, Peaches. And I would have searched every inch of the world and beyond, trying to find you." Cael reared back an inch. His face was serious, and searching my eyes, he whispered, "I love you, Savannah Litchfield. I'm so goddamn in love with you."

My heart fired like a cannon. Butterflies that were solely tied to Cael's voice swooped and spread their wings so wide I could feel them in my fingertips. "I love you too," I said, no doubt in my heart. It was full to the walls with Cael. He was in my marrow and blood, my every cell. The smile that spread on his face was blinding. And he kissed me again. He kissed me so softly and thoroughly that I wondered how we would ever come up for air.

Cael wrapped me up in his arms. I fit beside him perfectly, like the universe made us to match. Cael held our joined hands up between us, playing with my fingers. A deep cavern buried within me. Was this what Poppy had felt like with Rune? Is this how Rune felt about her in return? If so, how had they ever survived it? How had Rune managed to carry on with his soulmate being taking away from him?

"I tried to convince myself that it was all a big mistake," Cael said, never taking his eyes from our moving fingers. "I tried to convince myself that it was an accident and that Cillian didn't choose to leave us." He swallowed and

I waited patiently for him to continue. "But when I went home that night, I walked into my bedroom and saw an old Bruins game ticket on my desk. It was the first game we'd ever gone to together when we were kids. I'd pinned it to my wall after we'd come back. A memory I wanted to cherish forever."

My pulse raced faster and faster. "He'd written seven words on the back." Cael's voice was briefly stolen by grief before he cleared his throat and said, "*I couldn't do it anymore. I'm sorry.*"

As those words sailed into the air between us, I wanted to reach out to them and hold them within my palm. They *radiated* pain. They radiated such sadness, tears tracked down my cheeks.

I pulled Cael closer and placed our joined hands on my chest, over my heart, and cradled them there instead. "I still have that ticket, Sav. In my wallet. I keep it with me always. But I haven't looked at it since that night." Cael sounded exhausted. "When I read it, I knew what the police and paramedics were suspecting was true. What I had *seen* with my own two eyes was true. He'd taken his own life."

"I'm so sorry," I said, those words sounding more than inadequate.

"I can't bring myself to look at it again, Sav." Cael sounded so tortured.

"You once told me there was no timeline with grief. You need to give yourself that same grace," I said, kissing his cheek and brushing my nose past his.

"I love you," he said, and his eyelids began to grow laden with exhaustion.

"I love you too," I whispered, inviting in the silence of the night.

Cael kissed my forehead and a deep, tired sigh sailed from his lips. He glanced at the open door, and his shoulders lost any remaining tension. He had told Leo all of that too. He had obviously wanted him to hear it.

It was progress.

Cael faced me again, eyelids heavy. In mere minutes he was asleep. But all I could think of was Cillian and the thought of Cael finding him—seeing him pass. Then I thought of Poppy and how peacefully she had died. It hit me then. Just how special that moment was. How her death truly had been special.

I looked at Cael on the bed, sleeping. He was so handsome. So kind and beautiful. And he loved me. Cael Woods *loved me*. And I loved him too.

I curled into Cael's chest. And I fell asleep in the arms of the boy I adored.

14

Savannah
Agra District
India

"Wow," Lili murmured from beside me. The simple word echoed how I felt inside, awestruck at the magnitude of this stunning building. One that I had seen thousands of times on TV and in books. That I now stood before. It felt like a dream.

The morning sun cast the white marble under a burnt-orange glow. Cael's hand tightened on my own as the vast wonder stretched before us.

"The Taj Mahal," our guide, Fatima, said, "was built to honor a great, lost love." Goose bumps broke out along my body. "Shah Jahan built this in honor of the wife he adored. Mumtaz Mahal died in childbirth in 1631. Shah Jahan was distraught. She had been his entire world, and now she was gone. He wanted to immortalize the woman who had been a constant by his side, so he built this tomb to show the world just how much she was cherished."

Fatima turned to face us all. "The Taj Mahal has become one of the seven wonders of the world. Yes, because of its stunning architecture, but also because in life, we will all experience loss. And we will all honor our loved ones in some personal way." Fatima smiled. "The Taj Mahal is a place where beauty meets death. Where loss meets eternity. Where grief meets honor. It is truly a wonder to behold."

As we toured the famous building, Fatima told us of the domes, the history of how it was built. "White marble was specifically used so that the light changes the hue of the tomb throughout the day. Sunrise brings a visual symphony of oranges and reds; evening creates a masterpiece of the blue and silver of the moon. All the world's natural beauty encapsulated in one single day.

"If you'll follow me," Fatima said and guided us to the inside of the tomb. The decoration, the detail, the wealth that had been poured into this building were flawless. Next came the gardens. Water features and plush greenery made a garden of Eden from the landscape. All I thought as I passed through every inch of this vast memorial, was how much Shah Jahan must have loved his wife. Like our paintings in Goa, this was a tangible representation of what she had meant to him. He made the woman he adored known to the entire world.

The power of his love had done that. It was almost too much to comprehend.

We walked around this living testament to soulmates in awe, necks aching from how much there was to see. And all the time Cael held my hand. The boy I loved held me close as we toured a building where every morsel of marble and stone was pulsing with love. A feeling of contentment settled over me.

After walking for hours, we then watched the day fade to night and the Taj Mahal absorb the blue-silver hue of the moon.

It wasn't lost on me that it was the exact color of Cael's eyes.

Back at the hotel, at dinner that night, Mia said, "We brought you here—a quick pitstop on our trip to our next destination—to talk about honoring those who have died." She gave an encouraging smile. "A huge part of coping with loss is to try to find positives, though they feel few and far between. But placing your energy into remembering the person or people we lost fondly is healthy—it's progress. Lots of religions and cultures have ceremonies and festivals where they do this. But it's important to honor your loved ones personally too. In your own way."

"Does anyone want to touch on how they've honored, or maybe plan to honor, their loved ones?" Leo asked.

We were dining on local curry dishes and naan and rice, made with spices I'd never tasted before. This wasn't like our typical sessions. This was relaxed and comforting, a group of friends sharing a meal and feelings.

"We sit shiva," Lili said. She placed down her food. "It's a Jewish tradition where immediate family of the deceased sit for seven days after the person or people they lost have been buried. It is a time to try to face the initial loss, then remember them fondly, and accept the death." Lili smiled. "It did help me. I sat with my grandparents and aunts and uncles. They held me up when I was falling."

"That's beautiful," Mia said.

"We have *el Día de los Muertos,* or the Day of the Dead in English," Jade said. "I'm Mexican, and this is one of our main traditions. It's a joyful celebration of those we have lost. We remember them fondly and celebrate the life they lived. It's meant to be uplifting. And it is. It helps take the ache of grief and turn it into a celebration of the lives of the people we loved most. It's one of my favorite holidays."

"I'd love to see that one day," Lili said and embraced Jade in a hug. They were fast becoming best friends, and I hoped they held on to one another even after this trip was done. I was quickly realizing that having people to talk to, people who had traveled the same rocky road of grief as me, was immeasurable. They just understood. You didn't need to explain that a part of your soul was missing, because theirs was too.

"I headed up a fundraiser to place a memorial plaque in our town," Travis said. "A place where my friends and classmates will always be remembered. A place where we, who have lost them, can go and just feel them around us again."

"That was beautiful," Leo said.

I felt my heart beat faster. I was still not great with sharing, but I said, "I'm going to Harvard. Pre-med." Cael looked over at me and I could see the interest in his face. "My sister, Poppy. She died of Hodgkin lymphoma. She was seventeen. My dream is to become a pediatric oncologist." I met Cael's eyes when I said, "I want to help children just like her. I want to honor her memory by helping beat or treat this disease in whatever way I can." I swallowed a lump in my throat. "Or even just help those who can't be saved pass pain-free and in the most dignified way possible."

"Baby," Cael said and kissed my lips. Since the night Cael had told me about his brother, we had become even more inseparable, like that night had fused us together permanently, two halves of soulmates made whole. We carried each other through our pain. We talked about whatever was on our minds. Sometimes that was our siblings, but other times it was any number of things. He'd even spoken more about his love of hockey, which I knew was a huge step for him. It hadn't occurred to me to share what I wanted to do at college.

"That's such a noble way to honor Poppy, Savannah," Mia said and I felt my cheeks blaze at her compliment.

"Cael?" Leo said. Cael's hand went rigid in mine. He never participated in these sessions. He was doing better, spoke to Leo more in one-on-one sessions, but there was still a dark cloud that hovered over his head. I worried about him a lot. All our grief journeys were roller-coaster rides. But I felt his was more tumultuous than most.

Cael was silent as always. Leo went to move on to Dylan, when Cael said in a rasped voice, "I wanted to keep playing hockey. Like we had intended to do together. In his honor, but..." He trailed off and shook his head, a clear sign that he was done.

But he had *spoken*. He had contributed to the group and spoken of his brother to the others.

I was so proud of him I could burst.

"One day at a time, son," Leo said, and I caught the emotion lacing his voice too.

I leaned in close to Cael and said, "I'm so proud of you. I love you." Cael wrapped his arm around my shoulder and pulled me close. I felt him trembling slightly, but I wouldn't mention it. That admission had cost him dearly. But he had *done* it.

"Dylan?" Mia said, and there was silence from beside me. Dylan shook his head. I frowned at my friend. He was normally forthcoming about losing Jose. Though I thought back to what Cael had said about his brother.

Hiding his pain with loud laughs and wide smiles. I wondered if Dylan was the same.

A flare of panic sparked in my chest for my friend. Not long afterward, the table split to head to bed. Cael was walking me to my room when I caught sight of Dylan in the courtyard of our hotel, looking at a conceptual marble statue in the center of a huge water feature. He was alone. He was curled inward. And he looked like he was carrying the weight of the world on his shoulders.

I turned to Cael. "I'll say goodnight here." Cael looked over my head. He must have seen Dylan looking broken too.

"Okay," he said and kissed me. "Night, Peaches." He walked away and I followed the stone path to where Dylan sat. He looked up as I sat down. The sound of the water from the fountain was soothing, the night birds singing from the surrounding trees a heavenly soundtrack to the balmy breeze.

"Are you okay?" I asked and Dylan sat back against the bench. His gaze was focused on the water feature, but I could tell by the glazed look that he was lost to his thoughts. I placed my hand over his. Dylan's head tipped down in that direction. It was a couple of minutes later when he said, "Jose wasn't just my best friend." His voice was barely audible. But I heard him, and I heard the pain that was etched in his every word.

I stayed silent, letting him speak uninterrupted. Dylan sighed, and his exhale was shaky. He tipped his head back, and a tear trickled from the corner of his eye. "I had to see him buried, all the people at the funeral believing he was only my best friend." Dylan finally looked at me, his amber eyes haunted. "The truth is, Sav, that he was my *everything*." Dylan's lip trembled and I took his hand in mine, showing him without words that he could say anything to me. I would always keep his confidence.

"We met in elementary school," he said, and the corner of his lip tugged northward in fondness. "We were instant best friends. Inseparable. We lived on the same street. Our families became close friends too. It was perfect." He paused, and his hand tightened in mine.

"When we hit high school, I hated myself. Because somewhere along the line, or maybe from the start, I fell hopelessly in love with him." I wanted to wrap Dylan in my arms, but I also needed to give him the time to release this secret that he had buried down deep.

"I was scared to let him see it. I checked my every move around him just in case I touched him for too long. In case he saw how beautiful I thought he was." Dylan huffed out a laugh. "He called me on it, of course. Asked me why I was being so weird. That was Jose. Honest to the point of brutalness." Dylan shrugged. "I tried to avoid his incessant questioning, until I couldn't take it anymore and blurted out that I loved him."

I smiled when Dylan did. "Turned out, he loved me too. We knew our families wouldn't approve, so we kept it to ourselves. And we loved each other in secret. Made plans to leave our hometown when we were older so we could be together without shame." Dylan met my eyes. "I was never ashamed of our love, Sav. He was the best person in the world and when he died, I cursed the universe for taking him from me before we even had a chance to love freely, openly. And I had to stand at his wake and listen to everyone telling me how good of a *friend* I was to him." Dylan clenched his jaw. "I wanted to shut them all up and tell them he was my soulmate and that we loved one another so much that sometimes my heart ached when we were apart for only a few minutes."

Dylan grew even more somber. I knew whatever he was about to say was going to break him in two. "One totally normal morning, he was knocked over by a car as he crossed a road. Drunk driver. He died later that day from his injuries in the hospital. I wasn't allowed in the room because I wasn't family." His voice cracked. "But he *was* my family. He was my entire world, and I was his."

His breath hitched as he choked back his tears. "When they told me he'd gone, I had to pretend that he hadn't taken my entire heart with him. I had to tell people I missed my best friend, not my *boyfriend*. Although 'boyfriend' never seemed enough to describe what he was to me. He was my reason for breathing. And I've had to mourn him in silence ever since. In private. It's excruciating."

His tears fell then, exorcizing the secret grief that had been consuming him. Dylan turned to me. "You're the first person I've ever told that to."

"I'm honored," I said, and this time I did wrap him in my arms. He fell willingly, just waiting for someone to catch him. I couldn't imagine having to hide your grief in this way. How unfair life was sometimes, that Dylan and

Jose had had to hide their love for fear of disapproval or worse. How he had to hide who Jose truly was to him when he wanted to scream it out loud.

"I'm so sorry, Dylan," I said, and he nodded against my shoulder. The sound of the water from the water feature cocooned us.

Dylan reared back. He wiped his eyes. "When we were talking about honoring our lost loved ones tonight, I couldn't participate. How could I? No one even knew about us. And I'm terrified to say it out loud."

"You have now," I said, and Dylan's brow furrowed in confusion. "You've shared your truth with me. You've told someone that you loved him romantically. You've unburdened yourself from your secret. In turn, you've unburdened Jose too."

A glint of relief flitted across Dylan's handsome face. "I'm not ready to come out yet," he said, sadness lacing every word. "My family...they won't accept it. They won't accept me. And right now, they're all I have. I can't lose them too."

I thought about what Cael had told me about grief having no timeline. I hadn't walked in Dylan's shoes and could never understand the level of his struggle, but I thought the advice was perhaps relatable. "I don't have any experience in this, Dylan, and I'm unsure if I even have anything worth saying. But I'm sure that when you come out, if you ever choose to come out, it will be on your own terms. Whenever you're ready." Dylan squeezed my hand, and I hoped to God I was saying the right thing. "If you never tell anyone outside of me who Jose was to you, I believe that is okay too. This is your journey, Dylan. Your life. You only owe it to yourself how you live it."

"Thank you," he said and stared back at the water feature. His face crumbled like he was in physical pain. "I miss him, Sav. I miss him so much that some days I'm not sure I'll be able to survive it."

I hugged his arm to me, holding him close. "My sister Poppy," I said and steadied my nerves. "She had a childhood sweetheart when she passed. His name is Rune. They were like you and Jose, best friends turned boyfriend and girlfriend." I swallowed the lump in my throat. "When Poppy died, Rune was completely broken."

"What's he like now?" Dylan asked.

I thought of Rune visiting her grave, the tears he shed. How he would talk to my sister like she was sitting right there beside him. I thought of all the pictures he pinned on her grave, of places he'd seen, adventures they should have been on together, but now he would travel alone. *In her honor*, I realized. He was living for them both. Sharing his experiences with the girl he loved most through his treasured photographs. Photographs she adored too.

"Sav?" Dylan said, pulling me from my thoughts.

"Sorry," I said, voice thick. "He's okay, Dyl. He misses her. Every single day. But he's in college and doing what he loves with his life." Dylan was focused on every word I said. "I don't think he's found someone else. I'm…" I stopped myself from talking.

"What?" Dylan pushed.

I sighed. "I'm not sure he ever will." Dylan nodded like he understood. "I believe, like you, he feels half of his heart and soul are missing." I shook my head. "I haven't really spoken to him in depth about it." My stomach turned. "I *should* have. He's like my brother. I should've checked in with him more. I should've talked to him about what he was feeling, if he was—*is*—okay." I looked up at Dylan. "I'll be there for you, Dylan. Whenever you need me, even if it's just to talk. Or to reminisce about Jose, as you knew him. I'm here."

"Thank you," he rasped, and I sat with him for the next couple of hours in the courtyard, staring at the water feature, as Dylan slowly sat up straighter, seeming a little lighter for speaking his truth out loud.

I was so proud of him. And I prayed he was proud of himself too.

I knew Jose would have been, and hoped that whatever kind of afterlife existed, he was smiling down at his soulmate too.

Proud.

15

Pitch Darkness and Blinding Light

Cael
Varanasi, India

THERE WERE PEOPLE EVERYWHERE. EACH NARROW, WINDING ALLEY WE walked down was gradually filling with bigger crowds. The smell of spices and tea permeated the air from the vendors who were selling food and drink on the sidewalks as we passed.

Everything was out in the open here in Varanasi. It was almost overwhelming to the senses, and the city was filled with so many different things to see, to absorb, my mind spun. There were barbers cutting off people's hair for religious purposes. Pictures of brightly painted Hindu gods decorating the city. It was bustling and loud and filled with what can only be described as *life*.

Savannah held on to me tightly as we wove through the alleyways, following Mia and Leo as we approached the river that Varanasi was famous for. The river Ganges. Our guide, Kabir, had already told us of this river. In Hindu culture it was believed to have healing properties. The pilgrims who made the once-in-a-lifetime trip to the Ganges would immerse themselves into the river and let the sacred water wash away their impurities and sins.

The water flowing through a person's hands was also a way to remember their ancestors, the dead. My chest had pulled tightly when Kabir had mentioned that.

It was early morning, the sun barely in the sky, and we arrived at the Assi Ghat—a wide stretch of steps on the Ganges's riverbank. As soon as we reached the top of the ghat, I came to a stop at the scene before me. Laughter rose out of the mass of people congregated in the river. People of all ages, from old people down to infants. They scooped up the water, pouring it over them, letting it fall back into the river.

A sense of awe filled me. Just hearing their laughter, them living in this moment, believing this water was remitting their sins, was a memory I knew would never fade.

"This moment, for many of them," Kabir said, "will be one of the greatest highlights of their lives." Kabir smiled down at the children splashing, and I pulled Savannah close to me.

There was something about this place that seemed to calm me. Kabir had explained when we'd arrived that this city was known as the place where life met death. A highly spiritual place, sacred to those of the Hindu religion. And you could feel it. You could feel happiness from pilgrims and tourists alike, but you could also feel the heavy cloak of death hovering by. Like every stage of life swirled into a huge mixing pot, bubbling around you.

I looked up and turned to view the ghats at the very bottom of the eighty-something row that sat on the riverside. Those were ghats of cremation. Twenty-four hours a day, bodies of the dead were burned here. Their ashes placed into the Ganges to purify them in death. Kabir had explained to us that it was a Hindu belief that if a person died here in Varanasi, or their body was brought here to be cremated, they would break free from the cycle of reincarnation and reach nirvana.

Because of this, the city was always busy, loved ones wanting to give their deceased family members the greatest gift of all—the eternal gift of paradise.

I'd gazed up those ghats in the distance and felt a pang in my chest. I would love to have given Cillian something like this. Would love to have given him a piece of heaven after the hell he'd so secretly lived in.

The cremation gnats never stopped. Ash from their chimneys floated into the air. Kabir had told us that Varanasi was a city where death and life were intertwined stages of being. Not hidden behind doors and kept private but lived out in the public for everyone to see.

Savannah had been quiet since we got here. As had most of the group. It was a heady place to see. Could be confusing to those of us not of this faith and culture. But we were determined to learn. Leo and Mia had said this section of the trip was about facing mortality. Goa and the Agra District had slowly eased us into that notion—systematic desensitization, Mia and Leo had called it. Varanasi was us plunging straight in. And we felt it. Felt the discomfort of death shadowing our every move.

We sat down on the steps and watched the people within the river. They were elated.

"It's so beautiful to see," Savannah said, dressed in loose pink pants and a flowing white shirt. "To see people of such a steadfast faith experiencing this moment." She smiled. It was the smile I'd come to know as her Poppy smile. When she was remembering her sister fondly. It had been emerging more frequently since our time in the Agra District. She also had a desolate look I'd come to know too, when her thoughts of her sister weren't quite as easy. I was happy to see this smile becoming less frequent.

"Poppy was such a believer in a higher being." She pointed at a woman who had fully immersed herself in the river, delicately, showing the water her utmost respect. "It's like a baptism."

Savannah looked at me then. "Even when you don't share that belief, how can you watch a scene like this and not feel a sense of calm and peace? How can you not be swept away by the joy and serenity this ritual gives these people? A monumental moment in their spiritual journey. It's incredible," Savannah said.

There was an older man off to the right, alone, praying. A young couple holding hands as they immersed themselves in the water together. My heart missed a beat when they emerged and looked to each other with such love it was almost too much to witness.

"I've never seen anything like this," I said and continued watching. We watched until the sun rose higher in the sky and the ghat we were sitting at became too busy to stay.

As we made our way back toward our hotel, we stopped when a procession of people came walking through. My heart sank when I realized what I was witnessing. Kabir had told us to be prepared.

A family was carrying their deceased family member on a bed of sorts. The deceased was wrapped in white linen and being carried toward the direction of the cremation ghat. I was so shocked seeing this up close that my body locked up.

Flashbacks of holding Cillian in my arms grabbed hold of me and refused to let go. I felt my chest getting tighter and my heart beating out of sync. It was only made worse when Savannah's hand flinched in my own, and when I looked down at her, she rapidly descended into panic. Her face had blanched, and her breathing was choppy.

"Sav," I said, my voice raspy. I was trying to be there for her, but I couldn't rid my mind of Cill. I felt like if I looked down, I'd see him in my arms... gone.

Savannah stumbled, her anxiety taking full control. Her frightened face was enough to get me moving. I stepped in front of her, blocking her view. The procession faded from sight, and I cupped Savannah's cheeks and said, "Focus on me, Peaches. Look at me." She did. And in the middle of the alley-way with people pushing past, I said, "Breathe in for eight." My voice was weakened by my own thoughts, but I had to get her through this. She had been doing so well. But that was grief. One trigger, and all we had fought for seemed to dissipate to dust and we were thrust back several steps.

"Hold for four. Feel and hear your heartbeat slowing." Savannah did what I said, only for her attention to drift to the alley again. Her eyes widened, and her breathing became staccato. I turned to see what she was looking at, only to see another family procession carrying their loved one to their cremation.

A strained cry slipped from Savannah's lips. Mia quickly came beside us. She took one look at Savannah and said, "This way. We need to get her back to the hotel."

Savannah curled into me so tightly, I was almost carrying her. She seemed so small in my arms. She kept her head hidden in my chest, and I shielded her from any more triggers. We passed four more processions before we even got to our hotel.

As we gathered in the foyer, Mia and Leo quickly took us all into the conference room that we were using for our group sessions. We had one in every hotel we stayed at.

Leo shut the door behind us, and it was the first time I had even looked at the others. Everyone was shaken and shocked.

"I haven't seen a dead body before," Dylan said shakily.

Travis was white as a ghost. He had. He had seen several. Dylan threw his arm around Travis. Jade and Lili followed Leo across the room to get some tea that the hotel had left out for us.

Kabir had come back with us too. He went with Leo and the girls. I held Savannah tightly in my arms. Her eyes were bloodshot, and tears wet her cheeks. I wiped the damp away and asked, "Are you doing better, baby?"

She nodded her head but then shook it no. "It reminded me of Poppy," she said, her hands trembling in mine. She released a self-deprecating laugh. "I want to be a doctor for children with cancer and I can't even face seeing a person who has passed." She shook her head again. "Maybe I can't do it after all."

Mia appeared beside us. "It was your first time since your sister." Mia looked across the room to Leo, who was walking back toward us with a tray of tea. "Let's sit down," Mia said. "We should discuss what we've seen and how it made us feel." She then spoke to Kabir. "And it would be helpful if you could tell the group more about Varanasi and its relationship with death? It may help us all process it."

Kabir nodded. "I would be honored."

We sat down and Leo handed us all hot tea. I gulped it down immediately, trying to let the heat warm the iciness in my bones.

"How did seeing those processions make you feel?" Mia said and cast her eyes around the group.

"Sad," Lili said. "Seeing their family members walking behind them. It made me really sad. It took me back to hearing about my mom and dad."

"It made me remember that day..." Travis said. His head was bowed. "Not the good parts, the memories I had of my friends, but the bad part. Seeing them all after..."

Travis sniffed back his tears. Dylan placed his hand on his shoulder. I looked to Sav; her head was down, and her breathing was calmer but still shallow. I felt trapped in my personal hell too. The hell of seeing Cill in the car, of feeling him, unmoving, in my arms.

When no one else offered to speak, Leo said, "Knowing about death, grieving for a loved one, and even seeing them after death can be traumatic." The truth of those words was evident in all our slumped frames. "We remember that time above anything else, have it burned into our memories. When we think of the person we loved, most people conjure that image first." Leo sighed. "But the truth is, death is all around us. We see it every day, though we may not realize it. We wander through trees in the fall, the leaves dying as they turn red, yellow, and brown and drift to the ground. We see animals pass, we display flowers in our homes, and dispense of them when they die.

"We feel it harder and deeper when it's a loved one, of course. But death won't be a onetime experience for any of us. We will experience grief several times in our lifetimes. See it in nature all year round, year after year. It will never go away."

Mia nodded to Kabir. He sat forward in his seat. "It is my understanding that in the Western world, death is something that happens behind closed doors. It is more of a private affair." He wasn't judging; I could tell by his tone. "Here, especially in Varanasi, we celebrate *all* parts of life. Even death. For us, it is just another part of our journey we take as people. We live life in the open, and that means we see death in the open too."

Goose bumps broke out over my body. Savannah's head had lifted, and she was hanging on every word that Kabir said.

He pointed to Mia and Leo. "The purpose of bringing you all here, this city where life meets death, is to show you that death doesn't have to be dreaded but can be seen as a celebratory rite of passage. And it can be treasured and sacred too.

"In the space of a couple of hours, we saw pilgrims bathing joyfully in the Ganges, washing away their sins. Then we saw loved ones taking their family members to be cremated and sent to heaven. We believe dying here breaks the cycle of reincarnation and sends our loved ones' souls straight to nirvana. To us, that is something to be celebrated, not mourned."

"We all believe different things about the afterlife," Mia said. "Varanasi teaches us to embrace death in the same way we embrace life. I know that may seem like a difficult concept to accept. But this section of the trip is about facing our mortality. There is no place better to see that than this vibrant, magical city."

"If I could, I would like to show you something," Kabir said and checked with us all silently if that was okay. "It will mean going back outside."

Savannah straightened, bracing herself against her attack of grief, but then took a deep inhale and nodded. I was so proud of the strength that was building within her. I could see Savannah climbing the mountain out of grief higher and higher, day by day. She was reaching the top. She was a damn revelation. She was petite in stature, but her strength was that of a Titan.

One thing was becoming clear—she was stronger than me.

"Okay?" I said, when we rose to our feet.

"Okay," she said and squeezed my hand. Only once. "You?"

"Okay," I hushed out. I was anything but. Mia and Leo hadn't failed us yet. So, I would trust them. It had taken me many weeks so far to give over some control to them, but I could see what they were doing. And it had helped.

We followed Kabir back out into the maze of alleyways. In just ten minutes we saw another two processions. I held my breath when I saw them—I held Savannah too.

She was trembling, but she kept her chin up. And as the family passed, she bowed her head in respect and tears sprang to my eyes. I felt like I'd learned more about life from Savannah in a handful of weeks than any school in my life.

I bowed my head too. I hoped they had passed well. That it was peaceful and that nirvana truly did await them. What an image, to arrive at a place free of pain and judgment, one filled with love in all its forms. No sadness or troubles. Just peace and happiness. That thought made me feel warm with hope. Hope that it was true.

The sound of laughter came from around the corner, taking me from my thoughts. Kabir led us in that direction. When we arrived, it was to a kind of bakery/sweet shop. There were people dressed in white, laughing and eating, *celebrating*.

Kabir gestured his hand to the people. "They have just seen their loved one cremated." I frowned, unable to fathom that. I thought back to Cillian's funeral, then his wake. I barely remembered it. There was lots of crying from my mom and dad. From my other family. There were lots of strained silences, numbness, and dread.

There wasn't any laughter. And zero celebration.

"They rejoice because their loved one is now in heaven. They are free from earthly constraints. They are healed and they are in eternal bliss. The greatest wish for anyone we love is to achieve this." A lump was quick to form in my throat when Kabir spoke those words. As I looked to the family members, their smiles were wide, and they were pure.

I wondered who they had lost. I wondered who they were to them. Wondered how changed their lives would be without them in it.

"Here," Kabir said, gesturing all around us, "we celebrate death." He smiled. "Death is the best lesson in life. Death teaches us to *live*, for the short amount of time we are here. Death teaches us to live with all our heart and soul, day by day, minute by treasured minute."

A man who I assumed was the owner of the shop came out and offered us an unfamiliar sweet treat. Savannah held out her hand. "Thank you," she said and stared down at that piece of orange candy like it was a turning point in her life. She had hung on to the words Kabir had told us, eyes wide and transfixed on his explanation.

The shop owner handed me a treat too. I stared down at that orange candy, and something within me wanted to grab it and take it. But there was still a voice inside of me that didn't want me to reach out. It was irrational, I knew it. But it was like, if I did, I would have to admit that there was something good about Cillian dying. My hand balled into a fist, but I forced myself to take it. I nodded at the shop owner in thanks, who reciprocated with a wide smile.

He was celebrating with this family, with us. Death. You could see it in his bright expression that what Kabir had explained to us was firmly in this man's heart. He was providing an integral part of the celebration to a family who had just sent their loved one to nirvana.

I imagined there was no greater feeling.

I looked up at the sky. It was clear, cloudless. The sun was high, and the heat was rising. The smell of sugar and spices drifted in the breeze. I wanted Cillian to be up there too—happy.

"Varanasi teaches us to let our loved ones go," Kabir said, and the noise around me faded. As if in slow motion, I watched Kabir, the surrounding hustle and bustle turning to white noise. I felt he looked right to me, like he knew I needed this lesson most. "Here, in Varanasi, we must release the souls of our loved ones from the shackles of our hearts so they can soar. So they can go freely to nirvana without being tied to us here on Earth."

Savannah sucked in a sharp breath. When I looked to her, her eyes were fixed on me. They reflected the same fear I felt in my heart. I couldn't let Cillian go. If I did...it would mean he was truly gone.

"As difficult as it is, there's great freedom in letting go," Kabir said as he gently finished, then turned to speak to the shop owner and the celebrating family members. Savannah and I remained side by side, trapped in the shimmer of the words Kabir had just spoken.

"Let's go back to the hotel," Mia said, gathering us all together. "I think the rest of today should be one of reflection."

"We're proud of you all," Leo said and, numb, we walked behind them back to the hotel. Savannah and I held hands like it was the only anchor keeping us both from drifting away. When we arrived back, Lili and Jade took themselves into our group's private rec room. Travis and Dylan headed back out into the streets, in the direction of the river.

I turned Savannah in my arms and pulled her to my chest. I wasn't sure who needed the contact more at that moment, me or her. I felt her heart beat in sync with mine—a united rhythm of confusion. Felt her chest rise and fall. It was strange, after holding Cillian, still and unbreathing in my arms, feeling Savannah's chest rise and fall with *life*. It brought me a paramount level of comfort.

To me, there was nothing more haunting than a still chest.

"What do you want to do?" I asked. Savannah rested her cheek on my chest. When she lifted her head, eyes haunted and tired, I couldn't help but bend down and capture her lips. Every time I kissed her made me fall in love with her even more.

"Let's walk," she said. I'd come to know that when Savannah's anxiety was high, she liked to walk. She struggled to sit still for a while. Taking her hand again, we walked hand in hand back into the streets of Varanasi. We walked in silence, following no firm direction until we arrived at an unfamiliar ghat. "Do you feel comfortable sitting yet, baby?"

Savannah smiled at me, and she stole my breath right from my lungs. She nodded, and we sat down at the picturesque ghat and stared out at the river before us. At the many boats that were taking tourists on tours. We had yet to do that. Mia and Leo had told us that would come at the end of the trip.

"It's so different," I said as Savannah rested her head on my bicep. I never wanted her to leave my side. "What Kabir was telling us about how death is viewed here."

Birds landed on the steps, looking for scraps of food. Savannah lifted her head from my arm so I could see her. Her cheeks were pink from the sun, a light tan on her peach-colored skin from our time under the sun in India. "It's important," she said after a few moments of thought. That was Savannah. She never spoke until she had something meaningful to say. It made her words that much more impactful. "To see how other countries, religions, and cultures see death." She stared out over the river Ganges, at the people running their hands through the water from the side of boats, catching a brief moment of soul purification.

Savannah shook her head. "It makes you feel less alone, I suppose. To see so many mourners in one isolated place."

I folded my arms and rested them on my bent knees. I laid my cheek on my arms and stared at Savannah, hidden words from the depth of my soul craving to be freed. She turned when she felt my heavy gaze on her, clearly feeling I needed her right now.

"I *can't* let him go," I whispered, bones aching with how much that admission cost me.

Savannah's face softened and she leaned in and kissed me. It was light and gentle, just like her. She linked her arm through mine and said, "When Poppy was diagnosed, I was filled with nothing but dread. I would wake up every day with a pit in my stomach, because I knew we were one more day closer to losing her. I mourned every month that passed, because it was one more month I wouldn't get back with the sister who I could see was fading before my very eyes."

Savannah released a choked, single light laugh that was a knife to my heart. "I took out every book I could find in the library about cancer treatments. I was young but truly believed that if I could just find something we hadn't yet tried, it would save her." Savannah's accent was a fraction stronger as she said those words. Unbarred and filled with passion. I could just imagine her, staying up all night looking for a solution. "It was how I coped, I suppose. I was book smart. I was good at science. I felt I could help her. Even up until her very last days, long after Poppy had accepted her fate, I was still trying desperately to find a cure."

Savannah watched a young woman walk down the steps of the ghat and sit on a lower level. She had a picture of someone in her hand that she then raised and placed over her heart. I got the impression she had lost them too.

Another person just like us.

Savannah faced me again. Meeting my eyes, she rasped, "I used to worry about losing her. Now I'm terrified of forgetting her." Blood ran from my face. Savannah had put words to the feelings that gnawed away at me daily. I'd long wondered if I held on to this grief and anger like I had because then I wouldn't have to truly say goodbye to Cillian. Because I was holding on to him, he would never truly leave my life.

I focused on the rippling river before us and said, "Every time I try to picture a world where Cillian is gone, and I've moved on, it doesn't feel right." I shook my head. "After Cillian died, friends and relatives were around more, were engulfing us all in support—dropping off food, sitting with us while we fell apart. Then months passed, and those people went back to their lives, to their own problems and families—as they should. But we were still there, frozen in the sadness, unable to move on from grief's asphalt grip that had cemented us into the ground." I swallowed the lump in my throat. "We watched life resume around us, but still, we couldn't move."

Savannah shuffled closer to me, resting her head on my bicep, and I could breathe a little easier. "I feel like I still haven't moved. I'm still in that asphalt, watching the world exist around me, while I don't live any of it."

"What about your parents?" Savannah's voice was careful. It was obvious

I had pushed them away. A flicker of shame cut through me. Leo talked to them. Not me, and guilt assaulted me. They had lost one son. I knew they were just trying to help, but I'd just been so angry. I'd been taking it all out on them for so long.

"They've tried to move on," I said. I dropped my head to rest on the top of Savannah's. "They've returned to work. Christ, Savannah, they are *trying*." My voice stuttered when I said, "I've been a terrible son."

Savannah's head whipped up, determination in her eyes. "You have not!" she said firmly. "You are hurting, Cael. You are grieving. You are struggling. That does not make you *bad*."

I couldn't help but smile through the pain at my pint-size girl coming to my defense. And she did it with the force of a hurricane.

"What?" she asked, questioning my smile.

I cupped her cheek, heart swelling as she nuzzled into it, eyes closing at the touch. She was so soft under me yet had the tenacity of a shark. I didn't think she saw that in herself. She thought herself weak. I had never met anyone stronger.

"You're carrying me through," I said quietly, almost nonexistent.

Savannah tilted her head to me, and the love I saw in her eyes would stay with me for a lifetime. I wasn't sure anyone had ever seen me the way Savannah saw me. I'd never loved anyone like the way I was so consumed by her and everything she was and stood for.

Savannah had spent months and months searching for a miracle to save her sister. I had been given one when I'd least expected it. I had been given *her*. Maybe the universe knew we needed each other in order to survive. Maybe it knew that we had both lost and were hurting, so it sent our souls' other halves to make us somehow more whole.

I was sure Savannah would tell me it was Cillian and Poppy conspiring from their place among the stars.

"I love you," I said and kissed her again. How could I not?

Savannah kissed me back. "I love you too, Cael Woods." Savannah sat closer still. It wasn't close enough. I reached over and lifted her until she sat on my lap. She laughed and it was like hearing happiness. Then I kissed her. I kissed her until my lips felt bruised and we'd run out of breath.

When we finally broke away, a flush had coated Savannah's smooth cheeks—it was my new favorite color. Her smile faded and she stroked her finger down my jaw. "Your grief does not make you a bad person. The way you process it does not make you weak. I need you to know that."

"Okay," I said and held on tightly to her waist. Her sincerity made me want to believe that, so bad.

Savannah stared down at the woman who was still at the bottom of the stairs, her loved one's picture held tightly to her chest. She was lost in prayer. A place like Varanasi held a spirituality that was almost tangible. Magical, even.

"There is fear in grief," Savannah suddenly said. I refocused on my girl. "For me, it's a fear that Poppy didn't move on to a better place like she believed. Fear that the world is too foreign with her gone. And my biggest fear…" Savannah's voice wobbled. "My biggest fear is that I somehow become happy without her here." She turned to meet my eyes. "Because how could I ever be happy again with her gone?"

Savannah swallowed, then pressed her forehead to mine. "But I have found you and you make me so immeasurably happy." A tear fell down her cheek, passing onto mine like they shared the same track. "I have found happiness with you. Without Poppy being in my life. What I once thought was impossible. It's making me question everything I ever let myself believe." She moved back and blinked. "And the worst part is, she would have loved you, and she'll never get to meet you."

I hated seeing Savannah cry. It destroyed me. But I felt a little more pain lift in my heart when I thought of Cillian. "Cill would have loved you too," I whispered, the pain of that like a dagger to the heart.

But the smile that remark inspired in Savannah was like finally seeing the sun after an eternity of darkness.

Savannah wrapped her arms around me and laid her cheek against my chest. I held her right back, even closer when I realized she had drifted to sleep. I thought of the first time I'd met her in the airport. I had felt something for her even then, even through my heavy shield of anger. Some spark of recognition—my soul waking from a long slumbering sleep.

I kissed the top of Savannah's head as I relayed every part of our trip so far. The Lake District, the endless climbing, the group sessions, the disastrous one-on-ones, but Savannah being there for me through it all, a complete stranger. Norway, the northern lights, the beach, the kiss we'd first shared. And Savannah, day by day, merging her heart with mine. Souls melting until we were one blurred-out form. Holding one another up when the other was falling.

The scent of cherry and almond cut through the smells of sugar and spices. Savannah's soft hair pressed against my cheek as I laid my head on the top of hers. She moved in my arms and blinked as she took in the lowering sun. "I fell asleep?" she said, tired.

"Just for a while," I said, and she turned her face to me. "Shall we go back?" Truth was, I could have stayed that way with her forever. Safe in my arms. Safe from harm.

Savannah smiled and nodded.

We returned to the hotel. Night fell and I went to bed. Just as I was about to sleep, my phone lit up with a message.

DAD: Hope you're enjoying India, son. Leo said you're doing well. We love you.

My heart took off in a sprint. I thought back to the ghat this afternoon and my confession to Savannah that I was a bad son. My hands shook as I read that message over and over again until my eyes blurred. At the many unanswered messages they had sent in the numerous weeks that I had been away. They'd never stopped trying. In reality, my parents had never given up on me. I'd pushed them away, taken out my anger on them and made their lives hell. Yet they were still here, trying. Trying so hard *for* me.

Unlocking my phone, I texted back:

ME: I love you both too. Miss you.

Dad's response was immediate.

DAD: Cael. Son. Thank you for texting back. We want to speak to you more than anything. Hear your voice. But we'll wait until you're ready. We're just so happy you've responded. We miss you so much and are so proud of you. Keep going, Cael. We love you. Please keep talking to us.

ME: I will. I promise. I'm trying, Dad. I love you.

I couldn't have called them if I wanted to. My throat was thick with emotion, and my dad's message blurred as I read it repeatedly, tears filling my eyes.

They didn't hate me. The impact that had on me was total.

I put my phone down, the sprint in my heart slowing to a normal pace. I wiped my eyes, then waited for the usual ache that came with trying to sleep. Nighttimes were always the worst for me. Maybe because that was when Cillian had passed. In the dark. Maybe because nighttime gave me time to overthink. But tonight, the ache was reduced.

And, with a slightly lighter heart, I slept better than I had in a while.

Loud Colors and Louder Laughter

Savannah,

My favorite part of being your and Ida's sister was how much we laughed. How we thrived in one another's company. Although we had friends, we never needed anyone else. We were as close as close can be.

I think that's one of the things I'll miss most when I'm gone—laughing with you both. Even now, I'm thinking of the night Rune came to the door after he found out about my illness. He was there to take me on a date, and we were laughing at Daddy's horrified reaction from the doorway as Rune stood there, looking like trouble in his dark clothes and boots. I remember the punch that image gave to my chest. I'll miss every minute that I'm not laughing with my little sisters.

Laughter is the medicine that heals the soul. You have always been the most serious out of us all, Savannah. Because of that, I would strive to make you laugh. And when you did…ah, my joy would be unbridled! You have the sweetest laugh and the brightest of smiles. They must be shared more. As your big sister, I insist.

So, find joy in the world again, Savannah. Find reasons to laugh, no matter how trivial or minute. Laugh so hard tears stream down your face. And know that I'll be laughing along with you as I watch you beautiful and free.

I'll always adore you,
Poppy

Savannah

We were all dressed in white. It was early morning, and already we could hear people readying outside. Smell the burned-out bonfires that had been lit last night, and the excitement from the streets pulsed like a tidal wave of happiness through the hotel walls.

Today was the Hindu festival of Holi. A day where followers of the faith celebrated the coming of spring, eternal love and the triumph of good overcoming evil. The festival is a riot of color. Brightly colored water and powder are thrown with joyous abandon. It is filled with laughter and happiness, and for a day, everything is good and filled with positivity and light.

The people of Varanasi had been preparing for days. I was generally averse to participating in mass social settings. I often felt too intimated. But even *I* felt a fissure of excitement. I smiled at the sight of Cael dressed in all white too.

"I can see you looking at me again, Peaches," he said playfully. I decided I adored this version of him. The cheeky, playful side. He cast me a prolonged side eye.

A surprise peal of laughter left my lips and burst in the air above us. "I'm just not used to seeing you in anything but black." My heart beat faster. "You look so handsome." Cael's eyes melted. It was true. When he dressed in white, his dark hair stood out proudly, his silver-blue eyes even brighter and more alluring than normal. White clothes turned his turbulent gaze into a serene calm sea.

Cael curled his fingers into my hair, which was tied in a high ponytail. "You're going down, Peaches," he said, holding tightly to the bags of colored powder Kabir had given us all. We would be able to get more if we ran out, back here at the hotel or from vendors on the street.

I laughed again. It felt *good*. The lightness. This brief departure from grief. Celebrating the turning of spring and brightness, of evil not prevailing. I may not have shared the Hindu faith, but I was happy to embrace the ceremony and throw myself into just one day of pure fun and happiness within the most beautiful culture.

It seemed Cael was in that mindset too.

"Ooh, fighting talk," Dylan said, moving up next to us and rubbing his hands together. He nudged me in the arm. "What do you think, Sav? Me and you versus Cael and Trav?" I laughed as Travis stood beside Cael and rested his arm on Cael's shoulder. Travis was a lot shorter than Cael, and the sight of him trying to rest against Cael was comical. Travis's bright red hair stood stark against the white clothes too.

"Teams?" Lili asked, smiling in excitement as she and Jade joined the fray. We were all waiting at the door of the hotel like racehorses stomping in the stalls to be set free and run.

"Three teams," Travis said. Dylan swung his arm around my shoulders, towering over me. Since our talk, Dylan had seemed a little lighter. He'd confided in me more. Had told me story after story of him and Jose and their life together. Each time he finished a story, there was a new fleck of brightness to his amber eyes. It had become my goal to see them fill with life once more.

Some people you just click with. It was that way with Dylan. I looked to Cael. It was that way with him too.

He saw me watching and playfully pointed at me, then gave me a thumbs down. I couldn't help but laugh again. I couldn't take my eyes off him. He was smiling. The last time he'd smiled this hard was at the ice rink in Norway. Cael was a born sportsman. He clearly thrived in competition. He needed to play hockey again. It was more than what he played; it was *who* he *was*. I didn't know how to make that happen. But it was true. Sport and the thrill of competition were his happy place.

He had become mine.

The sounds of screams and laughter grew closer as the streets outside of the hotel began to fill and people raced for the ghats. Colored powder splattered on the windows, and Dylan rubbed his hands together. "I've got you, Sav," he said and kissed the top of my head.

"You better get off my girl, Dyl," Cael warned, Massachusetts accent thick but humor lacing every word.

Dylan wagged his eyebrows. Cael laughed but then pointed at Dylan in the same way he had pointed at me. I was momentarily struck. I knew I must've been witnessing a glimmer of the Cael from before Cillian passed. The one who would joke with his teammates. The free Cael, one not shackled by grief.

I couldn't take my eyes off him this way. His dark tattoos and gauges standing stark against the white of his clothes. He was tall and broad, the muscles of his arms defined through years of hockey training. I hadn't met anyone more beautiful.

Dylan whispered in my ear, "You're drooling, Sav." Embarrassment immediately blazed on my cheeks, and I nudged Dylan in the side. Dylan's laughter was light and beautiful. I nudged him in his stomach again, and he made a sound a lot more dramatic than my touch had warranted. Apparently, that was highly amusing to him too.

"Ready?" Dylan asked, when Kabir went to the door. Even Mia and Leo were with us, with their bags of colored powder too.

"Ready," I said, gaining better purchase on my bags. My pulse was racing so fast. I didn't know what to expect. But Kabir had told me it was a moment I would remember for a lifetime.

Walking over to me and Dylan, Cael dropped a kiss on my head and whispered "I love you, Peaches" into my ear; then the door burst open into what looked like the inside of a rainbow. Just before we stepped out, he added, "But I'm coming for you."

I laughed as Dylan took hold of my hand and dragged me outside into the busy street. I barely made it six feet when a ball of blue hit my chest. I coughed as the powder exploded into the air before me. I turned to see who had thrown it but was quickly hit by another ball. It was pink this time. I could barely see the street for the colors—blues, greens, pinks, and purples. People had no particular target; it was like being inside of a Jackson Pollock painting.

A ball of yellow hit my side, and I saw Cael towering over the rest of the people in the street. He was already covered in a rainbow of colors, his silver eyes as bright as the powder he wore. But I realized *he* had thrown the yellow ball at me.

"Sav, get him!" Dylan shouted from beside me. I moved on instinct and, grabbing green powder from my bag, threw it back at him. Cael's face was illuminated with happiness, and it stole my breath. My momentary pause was an advantage Cael took, and he threw purple at my arm. Then he bent down and quickly pressed a powdery kiss on my lips as if to soften the blow.

I reached into my bag, Cael backing away with his teeth gleaming in the sun, and the next few hours became a melee of color and laughter and fun. Of celebrating and experiencing a culture that had only been kind to us.

We ran through the streets, our group never straying too far from one another. Kids and adults alike threw powder and colored water at us, followed by gracious embraces. The ground became a huge piece of street art, the walls of the buildings a riot of life. And through it all, Cael remained nearby. My cheeks ached from smiling, my chest was sore from so much laughter, and my heart felt full. The constant ache of grief had momentarily slipped away, and I relished the feeling. It was freedom. It was hedonistic.

It was so incredibly *needed.*

Needing a break, I pushed myself into a small, curved-out section of a wall, just to catch my breath. My hand pressed over my racing heart, and I laughed as Dylan threw the rest of his blue powder over Lili. Her scream was deafening. Jade chased Travis through an alleyway, only for Cael to jump out and cover her head-to-toe in pink. I watched it all playing out before me like a movie. Watched Cael's hair turn, hour by hour, from black into a multi-colored neon dream.

I was so in love with this boy that it was almost too much for my heart to contain.

This was life. *This,* laughter and happiness, connection and play. The simplicity of this day had made me feel more alive than I had in years. And love. Loving Cael had been the single biggest blessing in my life. Allowing someone else into my heart was a happiness that I had chased away for too long.

Not anymore. I wanted to hold on to what we had with every morsel of strength. Now that I had him, I couldn't imagine losing him.

An older man sprayed orange water at Cael. He retaliated by throwing a blue ball of powder all over his back. Laughter and hugs were shared, and I couldn't help the smile that stretched across my face. As if it was a beacon to Cael, he lifted his head and searched the area for me. Just seeing how thoroughly he looked for me made my heart beat faster.

He was pummeled with water and powder as he stopped to find me, only relaxing when our eyes met over the crowd. The expression of relief, then love that shone from his handsome features almost made my heart burst.

Cael strode through the crowds, colored powder and water still hitting every part of him. When he ducked into the alcove that gave me shelter and a hiding place, he laughed. "You suit all these colors, Peaches. How's that possible?"

I laughed too. It felt amazing. "You suit them too." I smudged a mess of pink and red and blue on his cheek with the back of my hand.

"You okay?" he asked. Several hours had passed and the streets were slowly clearing, the city readying for the evening's calmer celebrations.

"I'm good," I said and held Cael's hand. I didn't know what had happened this morning, but the thread I felt tied us together had pulled even tighter, grown stronger. His hands ran up and down my bare arms, mixing the paint. Goose bumps spread in his wake. Butterflies invaded my stomach, and I felt breathless. There was a shift between us somehow.

"You look beautiful," he said, and I felt those words right down to my bones.

I couldn't stop touching him. I felt the lightness coming from him as powerful as the midday sun in Georgia. It was a glimpse of what we could have. Of what our future could be like. *Us*, healed and unburdened of our heavy grief. A glimpse into a future where we could laugh often and not awake in pain. Where we could remember Poppy and Cillian and not feel like we were drowning but floating instead—twin feathers drifting on calm seas.

"I love you," Cael said and ran the tip of his nose down my cheek. I knew he was feeling this strange new turn in our relationship too. Like we were soldered together, unable to be parted. My heart was beating a rhythm of his name, wanting to brand him to my soul. I wanted him closer somehow. No, needed it. Craved it. I wanted him to know every part of me. I wanted our souls to collide. I tried to pinpoint when we had reached this new turn in our relationship. It had been coming on so gradually that it had snuck up on us both silently. But it could have been the way we had both opened to each other, bearing our fears and deepest scars. It could have been how we had learned to trust one another by holding each other up in our times of need. Or it could be the laughter we had shared when we allowed ourselves to be free and temporarily unburdened by grief.

Or it could simply be that we finally understood that we were soulmates, and only sharing a lifetime could possibly make us closer than we already were.

Cael kissed me then. It was deep and all consuming, but there was an affirming touch to it too. It was a kiss that I could feel changed us. A kiss that promised a future, a partner, a bright soul to help carry us through any path of darkness we may encounter.

Cael's hand wrapped loosely around my ponytail. "I can't believe I met you," he whispered against my lips. Familiar flutters dove through my body. Butterflies that answered solely to the command of Cael's kisses and touch. "Every day I wake up, and I thank the universe that it brought you to me." Cael shook his head as in disbelief. "How have I been so lucky?" He exhaled. "I don't deserve you, Sav. And I won't ever take you for granted."

His heartfelt words made me breathless.

Cael kissed and kissed me. He kissed me until the crowds dispersed and the first part of the day was done, a spilled rainbow on the ground the only evidence of the celebration that had taken place. When Cael lifted his head, I stared into his eyes and saw my love and affection pouring right back at me.

He was my mirror in every way.

We hung, suspended in the moment, air crackling around us. In this moment, an incredible urge took hold of me. The laughter, the color, the love that had been launched in the very air around us heightened *everything*. I wanted to *seize* life. I wanted to reach out for it and never let it go, live it while I was here, happy and healthy and wrapped in gratefulness. Grateful for my health and this boy who held my heart so carefully in his cradled palms.

Cael's bright eyes spoke of the same need. I laughed again as I took in the sight of us. Cael's wide smile graced his face once more. He had a tiny dimple that appeared. I hadn't seen it before. I hadn't seen him smile so big. It was perfection, his dimple…

That seemed to match mine too.

"We're a mess," I said and tried to brush away some of the powder from our clothes and skin. It didn't help. We were caked in a smorgasbord of colors.

Cael's head tipped to the side. "You look like the Aurora Borealis," he said, and my breath caught in my chest. We did. Both of us. Another memory I would treasure for a lifetime. Especially as Cael had been there with me then too.

Cael slipped his hand into mine. "Let's go back to the hotel, Peaches." He silently led me from the secluded alcove and into the streets as this new aura danced around us. Residual laughter could still be heard in the distance from the ghats. This city, where life met death, was a marvel. It made life not feel like such a scary place. Because that's what I had been—scared of living after Poppy's passing. Terrified of my small, comfortable life changing. But life *did* change. That's what Varanasi taught loudly and out in the open.

Life changed. People changed. That was the journey of humankind. One that we had no choice but to embrace.

I went back to my room and showered, still smiling at the colors smothering the clear water as it circled the drain. When I was clean, I put on another white outfit. I left my damp hair down and in loose curls and joined the rest of the group in the rec room. Cael was talking to Travis. He was still smiling, still energized.

And I was still madly, hopelessly in love with him.

"You look at him like I looked at Jose," Dylan said quietly, suddenly appearing at my side.

"Dylan…" I said, when my heart fell. I didn't want to cause Dylan pain or discomfort through my relationship with Cael.

Dylan shook his head. "No. It's a *good* thing, Sav. It's…" He swallowed. "It's beautiful to see. It gives me hope too, you know? That maybe one day I could have it again."

I threw my arms around his waist and held him. "You will. I know you will. You're too amazing to not have it again when you're ready." Dylan kissed the top of my head.

"What have I told you about kissing my girl, Dylan," Cael said, humor in his voice. I stepped back from Dylan when Cael playfully pulled me into his arms. He immediately cocooned me and kissed me on my cheek. I was filled with instant warmth, and that static that had risen between us was still there—stronger, if possible. Dylan jokingly rolled his eyes.

"If everyone is ready, let's head down to the river," Mia said. All the group was squeaky clean after the earlier celebrations, only a few patches of faded color staining our skin, that I felt would take many more showers to dispel. Cael kept me wrapped tightly in his arms. Even the weight of that show of affection seemed easier for him today. I wanted to hold on to this side of Cael for as long as I could.

Lights flickered in the streets as dusk set in. It was peaceful, quiet, after a morning and afternoon of chaos. You could almost feel the sanctity of the festival thickening the air with every step you walked, only building when we reached a ghat and sat down upon the steps just to watch and drink in the culture. To observe a world far removed from our own.

"People will spend the evenings going to temples for *Pooja*," Kabir explained softly. I was in awe at the peace around us. At the quietness. I leaned my head on Cael's shoulder and let my body absorb the stillness, the religious significance of this city to the people who have traveled here for an array of reasons. I became lost watching people move in and out of the temples. The sound of religious music filled the air, and I watched as holy men performed rituals on the stone steps we sat on. I saw how much this festival meant to them in their hearts and souls.

The night drew on, and I held tightly to Cael, mesmerized. I didn't know if it was the high emotion of the day, the spirituality I could feel swirling in every inch of air, but I felt changed somehow. *This was how Poppy must have felt*, I thought, not for the first time. And experiencing the peace she lived with in her steadfast faith filled another part of the pit that sat in my heart. *It's why she wasn't scared.* I couldn't have been more thankful that she had that faith, to help her face death with such bravery and grace.

Cael pressed a kiss on my head, and I tipped my chin to see him. He turned his attention from the chanting holy men to me. Our gazes caught and something deeper burrowed within them. I couldn't explain it. It was just...*more*. Some soul-level blessing that he brought to my life coming alive between us. Goose bumps broke out all over my body. But not from fear. From *rightness*. Like the universe I studied and adored so much was screaming at me that he was mine, and I was his.

I knew Cael was my forever. Maybe it was Poppy sending that confirmation to me. I didn't want to live one more day where he didn't know how truly loved and cherished he was.

I wanted to give him all of me. If losing Poppy had taught me anything, it was that time is fleeting. I no longer wanted to wait a single minute to show him how loved he was. So I curled into his side and counted down the seconds until we could be alone.

Once I was back in my room, I waited impatiently for Leo and Mia to do their final checks. When they had said their goodnights and gone to their own rooms, I got to my feet. I knew I was disobeying their rules and breaking their trust with what I had planned to do, but I *needed* Cael. That was the only way I could explain it. I wanted to show him all my love, and in my heart, I felt that was worth the risk of being caught.

I had just reached the door when a soft, almost-nothing knock sounded on the other side. Confused at who that could be, I opened the door, only to find Cael on the other side. He was busy searching the hallway, clearly making sure he hadn't been seen, when he met my eyes. He swallowed, looking beautifully nervous. He opened his mouth to speak, when I took his hand and guided him inside my room. I didn't need an explanation for why he was here. I was feeling it too.

I shut the door silently, then turned to face him. When our eyes met, nerves trickled through my veins. Not bad nerves, but nerves that were set alight and pulsing with *life*. By the intensity in Cael's eyes, I could see he wanted to be with me too. I watched him swallow, his Adam's apple bobbing in his throat underneath the tattoos that tried to disguise his grief. But I saw the boy he was underneath. I had always been able to see who he truly was inside.

I took hold of Cael's hand. "Sav..." he whispered, his deep voice filling the room with an unspoken question. I kissed his palm, then each of his fingers. His were shaking slightly. "Sav," he said again, words evading him.

"I want this," I said and closed the space between us. I brought my lips to his. Cael's kiss was tentative, gentle, and so, so careful. He held me like I was fragile, a prized possession he couldn't bear to part with. I felt that way about him too.

Without breaking from his lips, I slowly guided us to my bed. As we lay down, Cael lifted above me and met my eyes. He pushed my hair back from my face. "Are you sure?" he said, checking it was what I wanted.

"Yes," I said, voice strong with conviction. But I swallowed some trepidation when I said, "I've...I've never done this before."

His forehead pressed to mine. "Neither have I." I burst with light, exhaling the last of any nervousness that lived in my heart.

"I love you," I said and slowly lifted his shirt over his head.

"I love you too," he said and reached into his jeans' back pocket for his wallet. He took out protection, and I waited for more of my nerves to hit. But they didn't come. My conviction held strong.

I was done with being scared of everything and anything, of not embracing life's moments because of fear. Instead, I wanted to embrace *love* and all that it brought—the joy, the wonder, the headiness. I wanted Cael more than breathing, and I wanted to be with him in every way.

I wanted to *live*.

With adoration in his silver-blue gaze, Cael kissed me and melted against my body, making me completely his. He held my hands, squeezing them twice. My heart bloomed as he did. And he kissed me, soft and sweet. He treasured me, respected me, and cared for me more than I believed possible.

He made me his until we were one existing soul. Nothing had ever felt so special.

Afterward, he held me to his chest and kissed my head. I ran my hand up his sternum and to the ship that was tattooed into his pale skin. Cael's fingers stroked through my hair, playing with the curls the humidity brought out. I'd never felt so at peace. So content. I closed my eyes when I realized my mind had calmed. It brought tears to my eyes.

"Sav?" Cael said, stilling when my tear hit his chest and ran down his stomach. He lifted my head toward him with a finger under my chin. Worry etched his features when I met his gaze.

"My thoughts are calm," I whispered, a watery smile pulling on my lips. Cael studied me closely, until I saw he understood what I meant. And that it was a good thing.

"Yeah?" he said in a hushed whisper and ran his fingertip down my cheek. Love shone from his every movement. I never wanted to be parted from this boy ever again.

"My anxiety..." I paused, trying to explain. "My head is always full, thoughts racing. It makes me feel out of control. Overwhelmed." I smiled and studied the tattoos on his stomach. "Now..." I trailed off and threaded my fingers through his. I looked up at him again. "With you...like this," I said, blushing. Cael's lip tugged up, showing a hint of a smile. I'd come to understand that he loved it when I blushed. "When I'm with you, it calms."

Cael cradled my cheek with his free hand. "Because your heart knows I'll protect you." He swallowed, showing vulnerability. "That I'll always keep you safe." His voice turned gravelly. "That I'll never stop loving you." My chest bloomed with warmth. "Because I couldn't love you more if I tried." Cael shifted down until we were facing one another. He kissed me, and I knew after tonight nothing between us would ever be the same. I had given him my heart to hold, and he had given me his.

But I trusted Cael to keep it safe—to keep me safe. I trusted him with everything I was.

Cael pulled me back into his chest, and I lay against him. I cherished this boy. He understood me, and I understood him. Our path to healing was still ongoing and I didn't know what lay ahead, but right now, in this moment, we were, for once, at peace. Minutes and minutes ticked by, until Cael said, "I better go back to my room, Peaches. I don't want us to get in trouble."

"Okay," I said but held him tightly just for a few more seconds. Cael's affectionate chuckle made me smile. He dressed, and leaning down, he placed his hand on my cheek and kissed me so softly my heart melted.

"See you tomorrow, baby," he said, then went to the door, looking back at me over his shoulder before he snuck back into the hallway and returned to his own room.

I lay back in my bed and felt so happy I thought I would burst. I knew I wouldn't be getting any sleep and wanted so badly to shout my love for Cael from the rooftops. I wanted everyone to know we had fallen in love, and it felt incredible. So, I reached for my phone and called the person I knew would understand the gravity of what had just happened. Ida answered on the second ring. "Savannah!" she said, her happiness radiating through my cell phone.

"Ida..." I whispered. "I have so much to tell you..."

Breaking Hearts and Letting Go

Savannah
Varanasi, India
A few days later

THE SYMPHONIC CHANTS FROM THE PRIESTS DRIFTED TO OUR BOAT ON THE Ganges. It was our final night in India, and we were attending the ceremony of Ganga Aarti, a daily religious ceremony at dusk where priests thanked the river Ganges for its purification qualities. They blew conches, rang bells, and clanged cymbals.

It was utterly majestic.

Seeing the city from this angle was breathtaking. The ghats were filled with people, candles being lit as the sun drifted down the sky, bringing in the night.

We were all silent as Kabir handed us plates made of leaves and flowers and a lit candle. I held the candle in my hand. "To offer thanks to the river," Kabir said but then added, "and to honor those you have lost."

My heart clenched tightly at that. I gasped seeing many leaf plates take to the river, people and priests setting their offerings free. Cael's head was bowed as he looked at that candle. In the single yellow flame, his eyes were shining with unshed tears.

He caught me staring and forced a flicker of a smile. He was hurting. He struggled so badly in moving past the residual anger he held for his brother. I could see he was tortured, even now. I wished so badly to take that burden from him. But it was his journey and his move to make.

"For the good memories," I said quietly, just for Cael. He blinked back tears but nodded. My heart was in my throat as he placed his candle on the plate, cast it onto the river, and it began to drift away—a symbol for why we were all here.

To try to let our loved ones go.

I held my plate a moment longer than the others, and even closer to my chest. It was the hardest lesson so far, trying to learn to release Poppy from my heart. I wanted to keep her with me forever. But holding her so close was keeping me from moving on. I thought back to what Kabir had said when we first arrived in this wonderful city. We must free our loved ones' souls too. So they are unshackled from this life.

I wanted Poppy to fly free. She deserved her place among the stars, the night sky craving her unearthly shine. I closed my eyes and silently said, *Thank you for loving me like you did. Thank you for showing me* how *to love. I miss you. So much... Be free...*

As I opened my eyes, a tear fell down my cheek. I placed the candle in the river and watched it sail away. I leaned back into Cael's awaiting arms, and he held me so tightly I almost couldn't breathe. He kept me together. I just hoped I was doing the same for him. Sometimes I thought he was progressing well. Other times, I wondered what he was thinking in that quiet mind of his.

He just had to keep trying.

As our boat bobbed on the river, I silently thanked this city for making me face death. But also for letting me see its beauty. I had never believed I could ever see it that way. But here, in Varanasi, it was impossible not to.

As I drank in the sights of Varanasi one last time, I reflected on my time here. I couldn't wait to write to Poppy in my journal of all the things I'd seen and felt. Of what I had shared with Cael. This place would always be the city that made me fall that much deeper for the boy who was fast becoming my world. Poppy had wanted that for me. She would be so happy.

And that thought made me happy too.

I wasn't healed. I was still in pain, but I was leaving this city, this country, lighter and perhaps a little more hopeful. I lay my head against Cael's broad chest, watching the holy men in their worship. Cael kissed my head, and I smiled.

If anything, I was certainly a lot deeper in love.

Heartbreaks and Kindred Spirits

Cael
The Philippines

"Here you go." Savannah handed me another nail. I took it from her and wiped the sweat from my brow. The sound of hammers slamming onto wood echoed all around us. The weather was hot and humid as the heavy sun beat down upon us.

This week we were in a rural part of the Philippines. It was a stunning place. Tropical and green, soft white sand and a crystal blue sea. It looked heavenly. Though why we were here was not so idyllic.

There was a note of sadness in the air that never left us as we rebuilt homes. At least to me and most of our group. Mia and Leo held retreats here in the Philippines, in another part of the country. A place where people could come and face their grief. That was what we would be doing soon.

But first, they had brought us to a rural village that had been destroyed by a hurricane several months ago. We were joining a charity that was rebuilding houses and giving help to the residents who had lost everything—including family members.

"Another?" Savannah asked and pulled me from casting my attention to the school that was just up the hill. Volunteers had already rebuilt the school a while back. Much of it was filled with children who had lost their parents or siblings—at least someone—and every time I saw the building, my chest nearly snapped with sadness. Most of them were younger than us. But as well as losing loved ones, they had lost their homes too. Livelihoods had been ripped away. Running water and crops had been destroyed. It was giving me a perspective of loss I hadn't seen before now.

About how truly absolute it could be.

"Exposure," Savannah said, following my line of sight to the school. I sighed hearing that word. It gave me shivers every time it was said. That was the overarching theme for this leg of the trip. We only had one more country to go after this. My blood ran cold at that thought. I didn't want to leave. I didn't want to go home, back to my life before this.

I glanced down to the dark blond who was permanently fixed at my side these days, the one I felt I couldn't breathe without. I didn't want to leave Savannah. Just thinking about it made me feel sick.

"Exposure," I echoed. Mia and Leo told us it was time to face what had happened to our loved ones. That the previous countries had been building us up to this—the hardest of the steps. Here, we would face what had happened to our loved ones head-on.

My blood ran cold just entertaining that. I had no idea what they had planned for us at the retreat. This part was obvious to see. We were helping people like us, just in another country, far away. In India, in Varanasi, we had been surrounded by people who had lost.

It was everywhere.

But I was nervous about what was going to face us on the road ahead.

"Mia and Leo want us to go up to the school after this for games," Savannah said, pulling me from my thoughts.

I nodded absently when I saw Savannah waiting for an answer. She stepped in front of me and put her hand on my bare shoulders, head tilted to the side. "Are you okay? You've been distracted since we came here." Savannah's eyes were worried. She bit her lip anxiously.

Varanasi had done something to me. Since leaving India, I hadn't felt settled. I didn't quite know why—no, I did. There, I had felt at peace. Like I had at the Lakes in England. But placing the candle in the River Ganges, that one simple act, had somehow paralyzed me. I had felt the dark cloud that often accompanied me slowly moving back overhead as that candle drifted away from me. I had tried everything to ignore it, but it was there, sticking close by.

"I'm okay," I said to Savannah, seeing light fade from her eyes. She knew I was lying. But I didn't know what to tell her. I felt down. Flat. Seeing that candle sailing away…it had shuttered something within me. I didn't know how to explain it.

Savannah placed her palm on my cheek. "I'm here for you. Always." I nodded, trying to push away the lump that immediately clogged my throat. I nodded, because I *knew* she was. I loved her so much. And better yet, I felt the love she had for me every day. "You can talk to me about anything," she added.

She cast me a watery smile, then picked up another piece of wood. She handed it to me. "Next one." I took it and subtly wiped a tear from my cheek. If Savannah saw, she didn't let me know.

The yard was full of kids playing. Travis and Dylan were in the middle of a competitive game of tag with what looked like a bunch of ten-year-olds. Savannah was reading with two girls who looked about six. Lili was drawing with a small group of eight-year-olds under a tree, and Jade was singing nursery rhymes with what looked like kindergarteners.

I stood off to the side, unsure of where I fit in. Leo spotted me across the yard and made his way to me. I was leaning against a tree, a pit in my stomach as I watched these little kids play. There was laughter and happiness. They'd lost so much, yet they seemed to have found a way to move on.

All except one. A little boy who looked about nine or ten sat off to the side on his own. He watched the other kids with what looked like envy. I felt like I was looking at a reflection of myself. He was clearly in pain and didn't know how to interact with the others.

"His big brother died," Leo said, and every muscle in my body tensed. My breathing came quicker. "He saved him. When the hurricane hit. He got Jacob—that's the boy's name—to safety, but he never made it out himself."

I felt nauseous. My blood ran cold.

Leo nudged his head in Jacob's direction. "He can speak English. They learn it in school." My feet were planted to the ground. I felt the heavy weight of Savannah's stare as she lifted her head from the book she was reading to her group of kids. I didn't turn her way. Instead, I kept my attention on Jacob. The yearning in his eyes was as clear as day—a yearning to be with the other kids. But he wasn't allowing himself.

I knew what that was like too.

My mind dragged me back to the past. It reminded me of Cillian taking me with him everywhere he went when I was about Jacob's age. I wondered if Jacob's brother had been like that too. He'd saved Jacob. My gut twisted. I couldn't imagine the guilt Jacob probably lived with because of that. That lump was back in my throat, tears springing to the back of my eyes. Because I knew, if I had been in danger, that Cillian would have saved me too. If we had been in that hurricane, I knew, deep down, that Cillian would have taken me to safety even if it meant sacrificing himself.

Before I even acknowledged it, my feet were carrying me across the yard and to the bench where Jacob sat alone. His shoulders tensed when I sat down beside him. I stared out over the yard. I smirked as a little kid trailed after Travis, trying to tag him. Travis screamed playfully when the kid got him—he was good with them.

I inhaled deeply and said to Jacob, "You don't want to play tag?"

Jacob shook his head and played with his hands. His gaze was cast down. Was this how shut off I'd been all year? Was this how I'd looked to Stephan? To my parents? How I'd looked to Savannah?

"I'm Cael," I said. Jacob flicked a look to me, then refocused on his hands. He was nervous. I got that. "You're Jacob?"

He nodded but still gave me silence. I hated it. Not that he wasn't speaking. But how this little kid had clearly lost his hero and didn't know how to move on.

My heart slammed in my chest as I pulled up a mental image of Cillian. At his smile when he'd looked down at me. *"You've got this, kid…"* I could still hear his voice, as if he were sitting down on this bench with us too, guiding me. I closed my eyes and felt the warm breeze run over my face.

"Help him," Cillian's phantom voice said. That was my brother. He was such a good person. And hell, I loved him so much.

I pictured him throwing his arm around my shoulders and taking me to watch the high school football games. *"This is my little brother, Cael,"* he would tell anyone who would listen. *"He's gonna be the next Gretzky,"* he would say. My chest would fill with so much light I could have been made of the goddamn sun. He was so proud of me. Even just weeks before he passed, he would sing my praises...

"Yo, Cael!" he shouted from the bottom of the stairs. "Let's go!"

"Where are we going?" I said as I threw on my jacket and raced down the stairs.

"Let's go get food," he said, and I followed him out to the car.

I buckled myself in and looked to Cill. He was wearing his Crimson Hockey jacket and track pants. That would be me soon, I thought. When we played together.

"Are you training well?" Cillian asked me.

I nodded. "Yeah," I said. It was true. I was on fire. Nothing could touch me lately. Everything I'd worked for seemed to be fitting into place.

"You?" I asked.

"I don't want to talk about me," Cillian said. "I want to hear all about my little brother and how he's gonna take the hockey world by storm." I laughed and he laughed too. "You know that, right?" he said. "My teammates are already on countdown to you joining the Crimson."

We pulled through the drive-through and Cillian ordered us burgers and fries. We shouldn't be eating this crap in season, but I wasn't going to argue with him.

Cillian parked, and he seemed to lose himself, just staring out of the windshield. "Cill?" I said, waving my hand in front of his face.

He blinked, shook his head, and plastered his usual happy-go-lucky smile back on his face. "Sorry, kid; spaced out there."

I laughed as he handed me the burger and fries. "Your grades are good, yeah?" he asked. I nodded. "Your coaches happy with how you've been playing?"

"Yeah," I said, taking a bite of my burger. Cillian often came home to visit, as he was only a short drive away in the grand scheme of things. But he'd been coming back more lately. Been spending more time with me. Making sure I was on track for college.

"Good." Cillian stopped eating, then put his hand on the back of my neck, turning me to face him. He seemed lost in thought again but then said, "I just know you're gonna make something of yourself," he said, and I felt ten feet tall. "Something epic."

"And you will too," I said. Because that was the plan. We would do it all together. Cill smiled, but it didn't feel real. Then he didn't say anything back. I began to frown, when he said, "Did you watch the Bruins' last game?" he laughed. "Total shutout, baby!"

And Cillian hung out with me for the next few hours, then dropped me off at home. "I'll see you at your next game," I said, and Cillian's smile faltered.

"You know it," he replied. I climbed from the car, and bent down to look through the open passenger side window. "Love ya, kid," Cillian said. "Always remember that."

"Love you, too," I said and waved goodbye. I hated it when he had to go back to college. But I'd see him again in few weeks. Then in no time at all, I'd be seeing him every day. Playing beside him at Harvard. All our dreams finally coming true...

I blinked against the bright sun that was blinding me, ripping me from that memory. I'd thought of that night over and over again. Because in hindsight, I had seen signs there was something wrong with Cill then too.

I exhaled a long breath—it was stuttered. I barely felt anger when I thought of Cillian anymore. Now, there was just a deep ache in my chest that never went away. I looked to Jacob, who was still nervously playing with his hands beside me. I couldn't believe my own ears when I found myself saying, "I had an older brother too. Cillian." My voice was rough and strained as I spoke his name aloud. But the words were coming, and that in itself was a goddamn miracle.

I caught Jacob's hands still in my periphery. "He was my best friend," I said and cast my gaze to Savannah, who was tying up a young girl's hair back into a ponytail that must have fallen out. I smiled seeing her this way. She wanted to work with kids and was worried she wasn't good enough. She was. She was perfect. Feeling my stare, she looked up. She blushed under my attention, then awarded me with a wide smile.

Some of the aching in my chest eased a little. I turned to Jacob, who met my stare. And this time he didn't look away. I cleared my throat and said, "He…" I coughed again. "He died not too long ago."

Jacob's eyes softened a fraction. In that moment, I could tell he knew we were the same. Scarred by fraternal loss. Jacob shuffled in his seat and said, "Did your brother save you too?"

Tears stung my eyes. I clenched my jaw and blinked fast to keep them from falling. His question robbed me of breath. But when I thought back to Cillian, a movie reel of old memories cycled through my head. Showing all the laughter and fun we used to share—the hours and hours spent on the frozen pond, birthdays and holidays. Vacations in Mexico, just laughing. And all the times I'd had a bad game and he would crush me to his chest, kiss my head, and tell me it would all be okay. To shrug it off and refocus.

To move on…

"Yeah," I said, barely audible. "He…he saved me too," I said, because it was true. He'd saved me in all the ways that counted. Right up until the end, he was the best big brother anyone could wish for.

Jacob turned his head to the busy yard when someone shrieked in laughter. "Do you miss him too?" Jacob asked, then turned back to me. His brown eyes were wide and sorrowful as he waited for my answer.

"Every minute of every day," I whispered.

"He was teaching me how to play football—soccer," Jacob said. "Daniel, my brother. He had started teaching me, just before…"

I saw the sports shed off to the side of the yard. "You want to play now?"

Jacob followed my line of sight. "You play football?" he asked.

I smirked. "I'm *okay* at it," I said. "Hockey is my sport."

Jacob gave a tiny smile. "On ice?"

"Yeah. That's the one."

"We don't get much ice here," he said. But then he got to his feet and beelined for the sports shed. I got up and followed him. When he opened the door, I froze. Because staring back at me were a stack of unbranded wooden hockey sticks and a bucket of practice balls.

"We had someone come here who was from Canada. He liked ice hockey too and made these from some spare wood that wasn't being used on the houses," Jacob said. He ducked his head. "He taught some people how to play a little on land. I wanted to join in, but I just…"

He couldn't make himself join in. I understood that.

The sticks practically glowed as they sat against the wall of the shed gathering dust. My hands flexed with the need to hold one. Memory after memory barreled into my mind. Of Cillian teaching me to play. Teaching me how to hold a stick…

"One hand on the top," he said. The stick felt huge in my hands, but Cill had recently started to play hockey and I wanted to play too. "Now put a hand down here," he said, placing my other hand farther down the stick. "How does it feel?" he asked, coming to stand in front of me. He placed a hand on my shoulder and squeezed. He was proud.

"Good," I said, smiling so wide my cheeks ached. "It feels wicked good."

Reaching into the shed, I pulled out a stick and blew the cobwebs from the wood. I ran my hand down the smoothed surface and gripped it in my hands. The sense of *rightness* was immediate. I closed my eyes and allowed myself to catch a moment of peace. It had been too long since I'd held a stick and not thrown it away or smashed it to pieces. I stayed in the moment, breathing in the warm air, feeling relaxed. I thought of Cillian. For a moment, I almost believed I felt his hand squeeze my shoulder again. Proud of me once more.

When I opened them again, I turned to Jacob. "You wanna know how to hold it?"

Excitement flickered in Jacob's eyes. I handed him the stick, bending down in front of him. He was a small kid, but right then I saw a hint of life flicker back into his sad eyes. "Put one hand on the top," I said, mimicking how Cillian had taught me all those years ago. "And this one here," I said, hearing emotion clogging my voice as I directed his hand. "How does that feel?" I asked, just trying to sit within this surreal moment and not let it break me.

"Good," Jacob said, and I felt the air around us shimmer. It really did feel like Cillian was right here with me. I really wanted to believe he was.

"Good," I said and ruffled Jacob's hair. I grabbed the bucket of balls and the makeshift nets that had been thrown together too. I set them up and helped Jacob learn how to maneuver the stick, how to keep control, how to sink the ball into the net. It wasn't ice hockey, didn't really resemble it in any way, but it was something.

It wasn't until Jacob scored and threw his hands up in the air that I realized everyone had stopped to watch us. Dylan went to the shed and pulled out the rest of the hockey sticks. Before he did, he met my eyes as if to silently ask, *"Is this okay?"* I nodded, feeling like it truly was, and Dylan handed out the sticks to the other kids. They waited with bated breath for my instruction. Looking to the side, I saw Savannah watching me with watery eyes.

"Peaches," I said and waved. "Get over here." Her cheeks blazed as she walked over, hating being under any kind of attention. I took a stick from Dylan. I steered Savannah in front of me and stood behind her. I showed the kids how to hold the stick, using Savannah as my example. I kept my chest to her back, moving her hands, sneaking soft kisses to her cheeks when the kids weren't looking.

When the kids were off practicing, monitored by the rest of our friends, Savannah's hand rested on my arm.

"You okay?" she asked. "That must have been hard for you."

"Yeah," I said, and I knew she could hear the rawness in my voice. "But it also felt good." I gripped the stick tighter. I opened my mouth to say something but then stopped.

"What?" Savannah said, refusing to let me close in on myself.

"It felt…" I took a deep breath. "It felt like he was with me. Just now." I kept my eyes cast down, feeling stupid. Savannah's hand landed on my cheek. She guided my face up until I met her eyes.

"Then he *was*," she said with absolute conviction. "I believe it with my whole heart. We're all part of the world, our own energies. Even when we pass, that energy remains." She shrugged. "I think that's why we feel them with us at times. Maybe their energy stays close by. It remembers us."

I drew Savannah to my chest and wrapped my arms around her, keeping her as close as possible.

A throat cleared beside us. When I released Savannah, Leo was there holding a hockey stick. "I may not have been part of Team USA's development team like some, but I know how to play a little…if you're game?" Savannah laughed, and I couldn't help the crack of a smile that tugged on my lips.

"You sure you're not too old?" I said, feeling a flare of lightness pass through my body as I cracked that joke.

Leo pointed the end of the stick at me. "For that, I won't go easy on you."

"Clear the yard!" Travis shouted, overhearing the challenge and positioning the nets at either end. He placed a ball in the center. I moved to it for the face-off. I looked over at Savannah on the sidelines, and she had a hand over her heart and tears in her eyes as she watched me.

That girl was perfect.

Leo smiled at me competitively, and then Travis blew a whistle he had found in the shed. And I was off. For the next twenty minutes, sweat dripping down my face and back, I wiped the floor with Leo, running around the yard, stick in hand and sinking the ball into the net so many times I lost count. I mourned the lack of ice and skates on my feet, the bite of coldness on my skin. But I felt more myself in that moment than I had in over a year.

Leo bent down, a wave of surrender cast in the air. But I didn't stop. Even as the kids went back into the school for class, I stayed out on that yard, practicing until I was exhausted and the sun was threatening to give me sunstroke.

Savannah and our friends stayed and watched me. I think they saw how important this moment was to me. I didn't mind the audience. I was so in my head, it felt like it was just me and the stick again.

I missed it.

I missed *this*.

Then the kids came running out when school finished. Jacob immediately approached me. He was still nervous but said, "Will you be back?"

"Tomorrow?" I said, and Jacob smiled. He ran to a woman who I assumed was his mom. She gave a small wave. It made me think of my mom. How she would travel everywhere with us for hockey. She was a great mom and I missed her. Dad too. They'd only ever wanted what was best for me. I'd been texting them every day. Opening up more. Growing closer again day by day.

A hand landed on the middle of my back. Savannah. "Are you ready to go?" she asked. I nodded, a little numb from the day. She helped me put the equipment away, then took my hand.

I didn't lead her to the cabins we were staying in. Instead, I led her to the beach. The sun was lowering, and the day had lost the harsh sting of its heat and left only a balmy breeze.

Releasing Savannah's hand, I walked straight into the sea, ducking my body and head under the calm waves. I washed the sweat from my body, out of my hair, and when I crested the water, Savannah was ankle-deep in the water at the shore.

Her head was tipped back as she basked in the setting sun, something she always did. Without her noticing, I crept closer to where she stood. Playing hockey again had brought a lightness to my chest. Remembering Cillian in a good way had chased some of the darkness from my soul.

I was mere inches from Savannah. She looked down just as I wrapped my arms around her waist and dragged her into the deeper water. I held on tight as we crashed under the surface. Then, I lifted her out of the waves, keeping tight hold of my girl.

"Cael!" she shouted, gripping my neck. She took a deep breath and wiped water from her face. I couldn't help it, but I laughed. I laughed from the very depths of my heart. Savannah laughed too, stopping only to place her hand on my cheek, a wide smile remaining on her face. And those goddamn dimples popped…

"I love it when you laugh," she said as we waded in the warm water. "And I adored watching you play today." She pushed my hair from my face. Ran her finger over my nose ring and lip ring. "You're amazing, Cael." She sobered, then said, "I hope I get to see you play on ice someday."

My laughter fell, but I wasn't upset or angry. I just didn't know how to respond. "Did I push too far?" she said, worry infusing her sweet accent, making it stronger. I could listen to her talk all day.

"You didn't," I said and kissed a falling drop of water off the side of her neck. Savannah blushed again, her freckles appearing in their thousands from being under so much sun. She ran her hands through my hair again. Her touch always made me feel better.

"I think…I think I might want to," I said. I huffed a humorless laugh. "But I don't know if it's too late. I just walked away from my junior team and I didn't even contact Harvard. I just refused to go." I met her blue eyes. They matched the color of the sea. "My parents explained it to the coach, of course. But—" I sighed. "I was unprofessional."

"You were—*are*—grieving. Anyone who doesn't understand that is not worth your time. Harvard hockey would be lucky to have you on the team next year. You're incredible."

I smirked at the fierceness in her voice. Then I sighed again. "I'm still working on the hockey thing. I need a little more time."

"Okay," she said simply, and I kissed her. I couldn't help it with how beautiful she looked right now. When I pulled back, she asked, "What was your jersey number?"

"Eighty-seven," I said. I ran my hand up and down her back. "Cillian was number thirty-three."

She smiled, probably because I'd given her another detail about my brother. I kissed her again and said, "You were great with the kids today."

Savannah sighed. "You think?"

"I *know*," I said, then asked, "Are you worried about this leg of the trip?"

"Yes," she said honestly. The sunset glittered on the water around us, reflecting in her eyes and wet hair. It made her look like an angel. "I know whatever they have planned for us is going to hurt. Badly, I imagine."

A pang of apprehension pulled in my stomach. She was right. We knew these coming weeks would be tough. But we'd gotten this far. And I wanted to keep going. I pulled Savannah tighter in my arms. "For now, we can just enjoy being here."

Savannah pressed her forehead to mine. "I'll enjoy being wherever you are."

That sentiment was shared.

19

Harrowing Stories and Doused Anger

Cael
The Retreat, The Philippines
A few weeks later

MY FEET STOPPED DEAD AS LEO LED US TO A CLOSED DOOR. MY BLOOD RAN cold when I saw the sign. We'd had days leading up to this point. One-on-one sessions. Group sessions. You name it, we had done it. It had been brutal and intense. I was already wrought and tired and at my emotional limit.

But today was where I had to face what had happened with Cillian. Today was when I faced head-on what Cillian had done.

I wasn't too proud to say that I was absolutely terrified.

Leo's hand landed on my back. "I wouldn't bring you here if I didn't think you could do it," he said. He pressed a hand to his chest. "I went through the same thing. And although it hurts, badly, it *does* help."

I trusted Leo. The longer I had spent time with him and Mia, the more I had faith in them. And Leo had walked the same path I had. This was his life's work. I had to put my trust in him if I wanted to get better.

The time we'd spent rebuilding houses was poignant. I had agreed to stay in touch with Jacob by email and letters. But doing something physical, like building houses and shelters, had been rewarding. It was the emotional side I struggled with most.

Savannah went on her exposure experience in a couple of days. She had been spending time with doctors at the retreat. Learning all about how they treated people, especially those with cancer. I could tell she had been lapping it up, absorbing it all like the perfect student she was. But I saw how much it pained her too. The strain it was taking on her grief for Poppy. In a few days' time, she went to a children's cancer ward in a hospital. True exposure. I was so worried for her. She had made such strides. I was worried it would put her back.

I worried about that for me too.

"Ready?" Leo asked.

No, I wanted to say. *I don't think I'll ever be ready.* But I nodded. I had to do this. I had to fight for my future. I'd come this far. Leo and Mia's company owned several retreats around the world. They were all places for people to go to get away from the United States and get professional help for whatever problem they were experiencing. Leo and Mia focused their time on grief, in particular, though they employed other therapists and psychologists to help their patients with an array of different issues.

We walked through the door to see a small circle of chairs, a few men sitting on them. Leo had explained to me that the people attending this section of the retreat had tried to take their own lives. For various reasons, they were still here. A few of the men looked up at me when we entered. In that second, all I saw were several Cillians looking back at me. It shook me so hard that I was finding it hard to breathe.

"Leo," a man said and greeted Leo with a handshake. He turned to me. "And you must be Cael." He shook my hand. I was robotic. Frozen in fear. "I'm Simon. I'm the therapy leader of this group." He nodded to Leo. "He's technically my boss." He tried to joke, to smile, clearly trying to put me at ease, but I couldn't move. All I saw were the men looking back at me. They had tried to end their lives. But hadn't.

Why couldn't Cillian have stayed alive too?

In a catatonic state, Leo led me to the group, and I sat down. I accepted a bottle of water but just held it in my hand. Leo sat beside me, a silent support. My throat was dry and tight, and my heart was racing too fast. My eyes darted from man to man, wondering what they had done, but more, why they had done it. Did they have family? Were any of them older brothers who'd almost left their kid brothers behind?

"Cael, I have spoken to the group and I told them you were coming." My eyes were wide and sweat beaded on my forehead. "Everyone here is willing to share their story with you. To help you understand."

My breath was choppy. So much so that Leo leaned closer. "Breathe like we taught you, Cael. You can do this." I thought of Savannah. I thought of how I breathed with her—in for eight, hold for four, out for eight. I imagined her here, counting with me too. Then the men started their stories. One by excruciating one. And I listened intently.

"...then I woke up," Richard, one of the patients, said, the room completely silent but for his voice. He wiped his hand down his face, like just talking of his experience thrust him back there, to that bad place. "I realized I wasn't gone. Instead, I was in the hospital. My parents sat on either side of the bed, gripping on to my hands like they would never let me go. I had terrified them." My lungs squeezed tight at that visual. Richard looked up at me, met my eyes straight on. "They'd had no idea how much I was hurting... I didn't tell them. I became a master at masking it." Many of the other men nodded in agreement. "I *wanted* to go. It wasn't a cry for help. At first, I was so pissed it hadn't worked. But..." He sighed and I saw some of the strife and pain flee his face. "But then I got help, and now I'm so thankful that I'm here. I mean that."

I was happy for Richard, I was. So friggin' happy that he got a second chance at life. But all I could think of was Cillian. That maybe if I'd been better at CPR, I *could* have saved him. I could have brought him back and we could have gotten him help like Richard and these other men got help.

As the group shared their testimonies, their stories were all different, but one aspect shone out that was always the same. The disabling depression they were all suffering with. The oppressive disorder that made many feel like life was not worth living and that death was the only way out.

I knew Cillian had felt this. The note that still rested in my wallet told me so. And by the stories being told to me, I knew that many had suffered alone, in silence. But to my shame, the anger I had always felt toward Cill was still there. I'd been able to conquer my outbursts and the way the rage controlled my life. But when it came to how I felt about my brother, I couldn't shake it. I was just so *pissed* at him. I stayed and listened to everyone's story, to not be disrespectful to those opening up to me, but the minute the last person had spoken, I got up from my chair and exited the room.

I needed to breathe. I needed to move. Because Cillian could have told me. *Should* have. We were so close.

Why didn't he just tell me?

"Cael?" Simon, the group leader, came to stand beside me as I paced the patch of green grass outside the retreat's therapy room. I saw Leo in the doorway, watching on.

"I can't," I said through gritted teeth. "I can't speak about it."

Simon sat down on the bench nearby and said, "Can you sit?"

I didn't want to. I felt charged with endless energy. I needed to run, to jog it off. I'd been running again every day, and my fitness was returning. It was helping. But now I wasn't sure if running a million marathons would help cool this burning inferno inside of me. I didn't want to be angry again. I couldn't go back to that person I had been before.

"Please," Simon said. Leo went back inside to the group. I didn't think even he would get through to me right now. Simon waited several more minutes for me, until I sat down beside him. My leg still bounced, but I did as he asked. When I sat, I looked up at the palm trees and the bright sun. It was scorching, but I felt like winter inside.

"I didn't share my story in there," he said. I stilled but kept my gaze straight forward. "I didn't try to take my own life." I concentrated on breathing. I respected the men back there so much for telling me about themselves, about how depression had stolen everything from them until they felt no other way out but death. But I still couldn't understand why Cillian had not told me how he was feeling. There were no two closer brothers. We'd told each other everything.

"When I was eighteen, my brother took his own life," Simon said, and I stopped moving. I felt like a hammer had been taken to my chest. Slowly, I turned to Simon. He was staring up at the clouds but then met my gaze when he felt me watching him. His eyes still held some sorrow.

"I was like you. Angry. We were close, my brother and I. Thomas." He smiled. "We did everything together. I was the youngest, just like you." Simon sat forward, elbows on his legs. "And just like you, he didn't tell me how he was feeling before he left us. I was furious. I became so angry it ate away at me like a disease. That was, until a therapist asked me a question that completely turned everything on its head."

"What was that?" I asked, voice rough but laced with desperation. I wanted to know anything that could take this anger away for good. That would help me see Cillian differently than I did. I loved him. I just needed a way to *understand*.

Simon sat back and faced me again. "We all know that depression is a nasty, destructive mood disorder. But the problem is, many people skirt over just how debilitating it can be." Guilt, swift and strong, wrapped around my heart.

Simon sighed. "Let me ask you this, Cael." I hung off his every word. "If Cillian had had a terminal illness, if he'd had a long battle with, let's say, cancer, would you be angry at him for dying?"

Just picturing Cillian dying that way made my stomach fall so low it was endless. "Of course not," I said vehemently. "Who would think that?"

"You see, Cael," Simon said softly, carefully, "depression, for some, can be so difficult to live with that it *is* a terminal illness." Something was happening to the fire inside of me as he spoke. It was growing weaker. Losing its heat.

Second by second, as I replayed Simon's words in my mind, that protective shield in my chest began to fall, exposing the mangled and sorrow-filled heart that lay beneath. *"Depression, for some, can be so difficult to live with that it is a terminal illness..."*

"Depression is a sickness that eats away at all happiness and light until there is nothing left but hopelessness and despair. Like cancer ravishes the body, depression ravishes the mind, the soul, the spirit. It's a silent killer, stealing life away gradually, moment by moment, extinguishing all light from the soul." Simon laid a hand on my back. "Understanding that can help douse the anger that you have for Cillian for leaving you. And perhaps put you on the path to forgiveness, and a chance to mourn him without judgment. To help you understand why he did what he did, and that you couldn't have done anything to stop it...and, by the end, neither could he."

Cillian... No...

I bent down and let the fire completely fade until I was raw and exposed and twisted up from guilt. And the tears came. The tears came so fast and free that I could barely breathe, could barely see. Cillian had been sick. He hadn't wanted to leave us, leave me, but his illness had taken him away. Just like Poppy had been taken from Savannah. He couldn't help it...my brother couldn't help it.

"Let's get you back to your room, son," Leo's soft voice said, cutting through my emotional collapse. When I looked up, the sun had gone from the sky and the moon was rising, stars bursting into the black sky by their hundreds. Simon was still beside me. He'd stayed with me as I had broken down.

We must have been here for hours, suspended in time, with this new perspective.

Leo put his arm through mine and guided me to my feet. I felt weak, like my legs would give out at any time. With the blame gone, it was like I had just lost Cillian all over again. "I held him in my arms," I whispered to Leo and leaned against him, gripping tightly to his arms.

"I know, son. I know."

"He's not coming back," I said, and the cries that were ripping from my chest were brutal and sore. My emotions caved in. The sadness that followed was an avalanche, building and building until it was unstoppable.

"Cael?" A voice I would recognize in any lifetime broke through the fog of my grief. I looked up through swollen eyes to see Savannah rushing over with Mia behind her.

"Savannah..." I said, and she wrapped her arms around me. Had I been calling for her? Maybe? I couldn't remember.

Too heavy for her to hold, we fell to the ground, knees hitting the grass, fully surrendering to my sadness. "It wasn't his fault," I hushed out and held her to my chest. Her cherry and almond scent wrapped around me too, keeping me safe in our bubble. "It wasn't his fault, Peaches. He was sick. He was sick and couldn't fight it..." I broke to pieces in the crook of her neck. I knew Leo and Mia were nearby, keeping watch. Just in case.

"He was sick, baby," Savannah said, running her hand up and down my spine. "He was such a good person, who loved you so much. He wouldn't have left you if he could have helped it. I didn't know him, but I know that." I gripped on to Savannah's shirt tighter and just held on as my body shed months and months of anger and guilt and shame and grief onto the ground beneath us.

Eventually, Leo and Mia helped us back to my room. I lay on the bed, exhausted and feeling so ripped open it was as painful as an open wound. Savannah sat beside me. Leo sat on a chair at my other side.

I pictured Cillian in my arms, broken and gone. It hadn't been his fault… he wasn't to blame. But *I'd* blamed him. *I* was the bad brother.

I blinked in the room, feeling like I was seeing everything differently now. Savannah moved next to me, and I curled into her lap, arms wrapped tightly around her waist. I wanted to be sure she couldn't leave me too. I heard the light sniffs of her own sorrow. I had never been more thankful for a person's love and support in my entire life than I was right then.

"I'll give you a few moments alone," Leo said, clearly speaking to Savannah. "I'll be back shortly. Call out if I'm needed."

"Thank you," she said quietly. I heard him leave the room and held on to Savannah even tighter.

Taking a breath hurt my chest, and my limbs felt like they were made from lead. I glanced up at Savannah and met her sad blue eyes. "I love you, Peaches," I rasped. "I'm…I'm so sorry…" I said, feeling nothing but guilty that I had laid all this at her feet.

Savannah shifted down the bed until she lay beside me. "I love you," she said and stroked my hair back from my face. "There is nothing to be sorry for." Concern was written all over her pretty face. Concern for me.

"He's gone, Sav," I said, and for the first time in a year, I really let that fact settle within me. It felt like being whipped with a thousand blades. But I had let it in. *Finally.* All of it. Everything. Every ounce of pain.

"I know," Savannah whispered. I felt the sorrow in her voice and touch.

"I'll never see him or speak to him again."

"I know." Savannah let tears track down her cheeks.

"What…what if he's not in a better place?" My heart squeezed at that thought. What if he never got to wherever we go?

"He's at peace," Savannah said with conviction. I could hear in her voice that she believed it.

"It hurts," I said and threaded my fingers through hers. I squeezed her hand twice. Our sign that I was falling. But I knew this time I had to. I had to feel this. I had to allow true grief in to get better.

"You're strong," Savannah said. "And I'll be here for you when you're not."

I laid my head on her stomach and held on tightly. My eyelids began to grow heavy, sleep pulling me under. But as I drifted off, I pictured Cillian's face and silently said, *I'm sorry, Cill. Sorry for not understanding…*

I miss you.

I love you.

And I wish you could have stayed…

Dark Skies and Brighter Stars

Savannah,

I think the hardest part of my illness is seeing how it has impacted all of you. I remember one particular day you and Ida came to see me in the hospital. I had just been told that my treatment plan was failing, and I only had months left to live. And Savannah, I remember meeting your eyes and knowing you understood that. That I was dying. I had made peace with it. But feeling you crumble into my embrace was one of the worst moments of my life.

There is nothing worse than seeing those you love taken down by sadness. It hurts so badly because it is out of your control. And I pray with all my heart that my last few months were beautiful. I never want to let darkness consume me, even in the most dire of circumstances.

I hope when you read this, your life is full of love and light. If it isn't, my task to you is to work to let that light in. Bathe in grace, and light and hope will spread to those around you. Infect them with joy. Cover them with a love so unyielding that they have no choice but to feel that love in the marrow of their bones.

As I sit here now, I pray that I have done that for you. For Mama and Daddy, for Ida. And for Rune, who was so hurt by my absence when he was in Norway, I didn't know if he could ever feel joy again. But I see *him smile more and more every day. He walks beside me, the soulmate I always knew him to be.*

Search for happiness, Savannah. Then spread that happiness and hope to all you meet. Especially those who need it most. You are my ray of sunshine. And always will be. I know you can be that for those who need it too.

Sending you love,
Poppy

Savannah

I tied my hair back in a French braid and put simple gold stud earrings in my ears. I smoothed the creases from my shirt and pants. I was ready. The pounding of my heart felt so strong I thought I'd be able to see it underneath my shirt. But I dug deep, worked on my breathing, and kept my spine straight.

I can do this, I told myself. I closed my eyes and silently said, *Poppy, please place your hand on my back and hold me through this.*

I opened my eyes and felt the sting of tears prick at my eyes. But I kept them away and turned to Cael, who was sitting on the bed in my room. Leo allowed him to be in here during the day as long as the door was kept open. He'd been here this morning at first light. Leo had already checked on us several times. Checked on Cael. Leo had barely left his side since his breakthrough.

Cael was watching me, sadness in his gaze. The past few days had been rough for him. And it broke my heart. After listening to the group of men a few days back, and after speaking to Simon, who had helped him reframe his thoughts, Cael had been struggling so badly.

I turned and sat beside him. Cael stretched out his hand. If possible, the last few days had brought us even closer. I watched him cry. Insomnia held him in its grip. He was racked with pain. But I held him through it all. And in those hours when he was most lost and his heart felt bruised, it occurred to me that I had moved past that stage. Since being on this journey with Mia and Leo and my new friends, with Cael, I had somehow grown stronger.

I had found ways to move on.

Warmth traveled through my veins, and I remembered Poppy's words in her journal. *"Search for happiness, Savannah. Then spread that happiness and hope to all you meet. Especially those who need it most. You are my ray of sunshine. And always will be. I know you can be that for those who need it too."*

"How are you feeling?" Cael asked, his voice raspy.

My stomach turned. "Nervous," I said and ran my lips over our joined hands. Cael reached up to place his free hand on the back of head and pulled me close. He kissed me, lightly and compassionately. I fell into his arms, and my heart swelled. As broken as he felt right now, he was still there for me, always checking that I was okay.

I stared at the sun outside of the window. "I'm scared I won't be able to cope with seeing it. Seeing the patients." I swallowed the lump in my throat. "Especially those who won't make it."

Cael held me tighter and pressed a trail of kisses over my hair. I could see Poppy in my mind. When she was sickest and frail, skin sallow. I saw her in the early days of treatment when her hair was gone and she lay on the hospital bed, what seemed like a million wires stuck into her skin. I pictured her near the end, when she lay in a coma and we thought we would never get to speak to her again, to give her our final goodbyes.

But if I was to become the doctor I wanted to be, I had to face this. I had to try. For Poppy. For children like her. For families who put their children's lives in the palms of the doctors who tried their utmost to save them.

This would be my first step to realizing that dream. The dream I was determined to fulfill in honor of my sister. In honor of my Mama and Daddy, of me and Ida and all the families that had been victims of cancer.

"I can do this," I said, wiped my tears, and sat up straighter.

I kept my eyes downcast, not as confident as I was making out, but Cael placed his hands on my face, cupping my cheeks, and brought me to his eyeline. "There is no one I know who could do this more."

"Baby…" I said and rolled my head into his touch, kissing his palm.

Cael brought me back to his lips, kissing me once for courage, then said, "I'll be here for you when you get back." I heard the subtext in his tone. Here for me, if I was broken by this exposure therapy. Destroyed by the sick children I would see today.

A knock sounded on the door and Mia poked her head into the room. "Ready, Savannah?" I nodded. Mia smiled, then looked to Cael. "Leo is waiting for you, Cael." Giving Cael one last kiss, I got to my feet and walked out the door, only glancing to Cael one more time for strength. He gave me a ghost of a smile that I knew he must have fought to wear. I then walked with Mia until we reached a car that would take us to the children's hospital.

"How are you feeling?" Mia said as we pulled from the safety of the retreat.

"Nervous," I said. "But…" I took a fortifying breath. "But ready, I think."

"You've come so far, Savannah," she said, and I heard the pride in her voice. "You have made incredible strides."

"Thank you," I said and thought of dinner last night. The group had been morose, all but me having gone on their exposure sessions. Dylan had met with those who had lost partners or best friends. His eyes were red rimmed when he returned, but there was a lightness in them too. Travis had met with some survivors of disasters where classmates had passed. Lili with teens who had lost parents. And Jade had met with those who had lost family members in vehicle accidents. And then, of course, there was Cael.

Mia and Leo had introduced me to some oncologists who they knew through their programs. I had spent days talking to them, hearing about their lives and careers. It only made me more determined to become a doctor too. When Dr. Susan Dela Cruz, one of the head oncologists in the local children's hospital, had asked if I'd like to come to the cancer ward and shadow her, I wasn't sure I could. But after talking to Mia and Leo, we decided it would be good for me.

I was racked with fear. But if this trip had taught me anything, it was that fear had to be faced to defeat it. *I* had to defeat it. I was done running away.

An hour later we arrived in the city and stopped in front of a tall white building—the children's hospital. My memories of hospitals were shrouded in darkness. But I tried to shift my thoughts and instead try to see them as a place of safety and hope for those stricken by life-threatening illnesses.

A place of healing and not loss.

As we walked through the glass doors, the smell of disinfectant gathered around me. It immediately thrust me back to Poppy lying on her bed, in a coma, pierced with wires and oxygen. But I breathed through the pain of those memories and focused on when she'd left it. When she had come home to spend her final days with those she loved most. In peace.

Susan searched my face. "How are we feeling?"

"I want to do it," I said and hoped Poppy's hand was on my back like I had asked her. I needed her to help guide me through this. I followed Susan until we reached the oncology ward.

"We have a full ward," Susan said, and my heart sank. So many children. She must have seen the sorrow in my eyes, as she reached out and placed her hand on my shoulder. "We are confident we can save many of them."

But not all...

I nodded, unable to find my voice. I was giving myself grace. My strength and conviction to do this had ebbed momentarily, but I was still here. Still trying.

Susan placed a security code into the doors, and we entered the ward. Nurses came to speak to Susan. Not knowing the language, I couldn't follow, so I let my gaze drift to the windows around the rooms. Sadness squeezed my lungs to the point of pain as I saw a young boy with no hair lying in bed, reading a book. He was pale, and thin, and beside him was a woman who I assumed was his mama, holding his hand like she would never let go. Beside him was another patient—a girl, no older than ten, asleep in her bed, only tufts of hair growing back on her smooth scalp.

An onslaught of memories rained down on me—remembering Poppy in these varying stages were like bullets piercing through my strength. Mia's hand landed on my back, and for a second, I honestly thought I'd felt Poppy. "If it's too much, we can step out for a few minutes," Mia said, and I shook my head. I was staying. I wanted to stay. To face this.

It was time.

Mia nodded, just as Susan walked back to me with a chart. "I'm about to start rounds," she said, observing my shaken state. "I know you won't under-stand the language for most of this, but we have a girl, age fourteen, whose father is English. If you want, I thought you might like to speak with her."

My pulse fluttered in my neck. Susan smiled. "She knows you're coming. She's excited to meet you."

"Okay," I rasped. Fourteen. Not much younger than Poppy was when she was diagnosed. I looked to Susan. "Is she getting better?"

I could tell immediately by Susan's pained expression that she wasn't. "She has stage four Hodgkin lymphoma. And she only has a few months left to live. She stopped responding to treatment." My vision shimmered. She had the same disease as Poppy.

And she was dying.

"We want you to face things, Savannah, but only as much as you can take," Mia said, and Susan nodded.

I pictured Poppy's smiling face. How strong and vibrant she was right until the end. "I want to do it," I rasped. "I want to talk to her."

Susan's responding smile was wide. "Let's do rounds first; then I'll take you to Tala."

Tala. Her name was so beautiful.

I followed Susan into the first room, standing back enough to give her space to do her job. I listened to her soft tone as she spoke to the children, watched her smile wide and treat them with so much kindness and respect it was awe-inspiring.

Susan told me before we entered each room where the person was in their illness. If they had just started chemo, if they were just about done. But the most painful were those who were on palliative care. I would meet their tired eyes and smile. When some would try to smile back, when their parents would shake my hand, I was hit with a moment of pure anger. It wasn't fair that they were losing their battles. It wasn't fair that their families were losing them, slowly, day by day.

Even those who were sad, crying and exhausted, to me shone bright with a warrior's inner strength.

Just like Poppy had.

We stopped at the final room. Susan turned to me. "This is Tala's room."

My heart sank, and I controlled my breathing. I didn't want her to see me upset. She was going through enough.

"I'm ready," I said, and I straightened my spine. Susan entered a private room, and I followed her inside. Tala was lying on the bed. She was frail, with short hair. Luggage was beside her bed, and she was dressed in everyday clothes. And when she saw me, her smile was blinding.

"Tala," Susan said. "How are you feeling?" She spoke in English this time.

"Good," she said, and then she turned her gaze to me again. My heart stopped when I saw she had green eyes. My bottom lip wobbled, but I took a deep breath and held myself together. "Are you Savannah?" she asked, a slight accent to her voice. It was so beautiful.

"I am," I said and moved to shake her hand. Tala gripped on tightly to my hand.

"Dr. Dela Cruz told me I would have a visitor today. From America." An excited smile spread on her lips.

"I'm so honored to meet you, Tala," I said, making sure my voice was steady.

"You want to be a doctor?" Tala asked.

"That's right."

"Why?" she asked, and I felt my blood cool.

I looked up to Susan—Dr. Dela Cruz—and she nodded in encouragement. Then she said to Mia, "Shall we leave the girls to chat for a while?"

Mia glanced at me, and I nodded. Mia and Susan left the room, and Tala patted the edge of the bed. "Please, sit," she said. "My family are coming soon." She smiled. "I'm going home today…" She trailed off, and I sat down beside her. I knew why she was going home. For the same reason Poppy had near the end.

Tala never let go of my hand. It was weak yet held so much strength.

"Why do you want to be a doctor?" she asked again. "For cancer patients?" she tacked on.

"Yes," I said. "Children's cancer, specifically." She studied me and waited for the second part of her question to be answered. "I had an older sister…"

I said and really fought to keep my voice steady and blinked away tears from my eyes. "She had cancer—Hodgkin lymphoma. Like you."

Tala's face grew serious. "Where is she now?" she asked, and my soul cried.

I stared into her forest-green eyes. "In Heaven," I said, and I let myself believe that with my entire heart.

Tala's fingers tightened in mine. She looked down at our joined hands. Then she said, "I'm dying too." Those three words caused an almighty rip in my soul.

"I know," I whispered and held her hand tighter.

A wash of tears made her green eyes shine. "I try not to be scared. But sometimes…" She swallowed, a single tear falling from her eye and drifting down her cheek. "Sometimes I can't help it."

"It's understandable," I said and shifted closer to her. "What you are facing is the hardest thing a person can face."

"Was your sister scared?" she asked, then said, "What was her name?"

"Poppy," I said. "Her name was Poppy."

"Poppy," Tala said, sounding out the name. She smiled. "I like that name."

She waited for me to answer her previous question. "Poppy wasn't scared," I said. "At least, she tried not to be." I thought of Poppy's resilience, her smiles and the innate happiness she'd radiated right up until her final breath. "She was so happy. She loved her family, and her boyfriend, fiercely. She loved *life*…right up until the end."

Tala turned her head and stared at a picture beside her bed. There was a Filipino woman in it, a Caucasian man, and a young boy and girl. And of course, there was Tala, her arms wrapped around them all. "I love my family too," she said, running a finger over their smiling faces. Turning to me again, she said, "I think I'm most scared of leaving them behind."

"Poppy was too." I wrapped both my hands around hers. "But we are okay," I said and felt something shift inside of me. I was getting better. For the first time in four years, I had hope that I was getting better. That I *would* be okay. I smiled. "And I still talk to Poppy," I said. "At her grave near where we live. And I talk to her in the stars."

"Stars?" Tala asked.

I gave her a small smile. "I like to think of her shining down upon me, living among the stars." A tear fell down my cheek. But it was a happy one. I was remembering Poppy with *happiness*. "She shone so brightly in this life, I knew she could only shine brighter in the next."

Tala was smiling, but then it faltered. "I like that," she said. "What you said about the stars."

"Then what is it?" I asked, noticing something was on her mind.

"I just feel tired a lot now. So tired." She lifted her gaze to mine. "I'm not sure I shine as brightly as your sister did. Sometimes I feel like my light is fading. That things are getting dark."

My heart skipped at her sad words. Leaning down, I squeezed her hands tighter and said, "Stars shine brightest in the dark."

The smile she gave me in return rivaled the glow of the stars, the moon, and sun itself. "My name," she said, "Tala, in Tagalog, our language, means 'bright star.' I'm named after the goddess of the stars."

I felt it then. A ripple of destiny shimmer between us. The feel of a soft hand pressed in on my back, and I knew Poppy was beside me. A sense of fate or something like it filled up the room. I knew that Tala's path and mine were meant to cross. I was meant to meet her and she me.

A knock at the door sounded and Susan popped her head in. "Tala, your family are here to take you home." The door opened wider, and a young boy and a girl entered, jumping onto Tala's bed, wrapping her into their small arms.

"You're coming home, darling!" a man said with an English accent from the doorway, blushing slightly when he saw me beside his daughter. "Oh, sorry to interrupt."

"It's no problem," I said. When I looked to him, I saw Tala's green eyes staring back at me. I smiled at him and the woman who came through next—her mama.

Rising from the bed, I released Tala's hand. She smiled at me. "Bye, Savannah."

"Bye, Tala," I said, my throat graveled. Because I knew I would never see her again.

She swallowed, then over her sister's and brother's heads, said, "I'll see you from the stars."

I gave her a watery smile. "I'll be looking for you," I managed to say back before leaving the room and walking straight into the private family room to the left. I lifted my head toward the ceiling and let the tears fall in twin rivers from my eyes. I covered my face with my hands and just let all the sorrow for Tala's situation spill forth.

Tala was so brave, so pure. She was such a beautiful soul and didn't deserve to die.

"Savannah?" Mia came into the room, followed by Susan, shutting the door behind them.

"I want to do this," I said, without a single doubt in my heart, my voice thick with emotion. "I want to be a pediatric oncologist. I want to help cure these children who do not deserve to be sick. I want to work so hard that one day, cancer won't take people away from their loved ones. I want to help so that cancer—*all cancer*—is curable. I want it. So much."

With every word spoken, my voice became stronger. *I* became stronger. I wanted this so badly that I knew I'd be going to Harvard this fall. I'd be pre-med, and I wouldn't stop until no other family had to lose a Poppy, a Tala. Lose a treasured branch of their family tree.

"I can do this," I said to Mia. "I *know* I can." I smiled and said, "Because I'll have Poppy in my heart."

Mia's eyes shone and she held me in her arms. "I'm so proud of you, my girl."

"Thank you," I whispered.

The truth was, I was proud of me too. And I was immeasurably proud of Poppy for making me see this. For her journal, pushing me and holding me through the pages when I didn't have her arms to embrace me in real life. And I was proud of Tala, for allowing me this gift—of speaking to her, of helping me find my inner strength when I thought it had been lost. I was honored I'd met her.

I left the hospital with a new determination in my step and a sense of purpose in my heart. I would take on whatever came next with gratitude in my heart. Because I had a light I could share with the world. Just like Poppy had. We shared the same blood. What ran through her ran through me.

I would do this for us both.

21

Thoughtful Gestures
and Music Reborn

Savannah
Manila, The Philippines
A few days later

It was our last night in the Philippines. This had been the most emotional and difficult country on our trip. I was still raw from my talk with Tala, but my determination had held strong. I knew I wouldn't waver from what I wanted from my life. I was going to be a doctor. I was steadfast in that ambition.

It didn't mean I wasn't emotionally rocked by meeting the children who were sick and those who were dying. From talking to Tala about her final days and what came afterward.

I'd meant what I'd said. I would look for her in the stars the same way I did Poppy. And the way I now looked for Cillian.

Tonight, we were in Manila. Tomorrow, we would fly to Japan. Mia and Leo had told us last night where our final country would be. I was breathless when they'd revealed that. Because it was the beginning of spring. And in Japan, that meant one thing—cherry blossoms would be blooming.

Poppy had always wanted to see Japan and the cherry blossoms. It wasn't lost on me that I would be ending my trip to healing among the flowers she had so loved.

"Are you ready?" I turned my head to the doorway of my hotel room. Cael stood there, in a long-sleeve button-up shirt, the top few buttons undone, and smart black pants. His hair had been styled—free of his beanie. His stubbled cheeks were cleanly shaved, and I could smell his sea-salt and fresh snow scent from where I sat. I swallowed at just how truly handsome he was.

"Cael," I said. "You look stunning." I felt my cheeks blaze. That was one thing I knew I would never shed—my easy embarrassment.

Cael's array of tattoos stood proudly off his sun-kissed skin. A small spattering of freckles decorated his nose, making his silver nose ring and lip ring stand out even more.

His arms were crossed over his torso as he leaned against the door, but his silver-blue gaze was soft as it landed upon me. I stood from the vanity seat and ran my hands down the pale-blue summer dress I wore. My hair was down in soft waves, and I had kitten-heel sandals upon my feet. Golden stud earrings were in my ears, and I'd even applied a small layer of makeup to my face.

I went to lift my head, to ask how I looked, but before I could, Cael's arms wrapped around me, pulling me into his strong embrace. With his mouth at my ear, he said, "Shit, Peaches, you look incredible." My cheeks blazed, but a wide smile pulled on my mouth.

Cael reared back and pushed my hair from my face. He searched each of my features and rasped, "I'll never understand how the hell you took a chance on me. But I'll never stop being grateful."

"Baby," I murmured as he kissed my forehead, each of my cheeks, and finally, my lips. He didn't even seem to mind the lip gloss that I had applied. He kissed me deeply, thoroughly, his gentle tongue meeting with mine. Cael's hands wrapped into my hair, and he kept me flush against his chest. He treasured me in every way possible.

If there was one thing I now knew in this world, it was how it felt to be loved. To be adored. To be held in both your weakest and strongest moments.

I knew what a soulmate truly was.

When Cael stepped back, he threaded our hands together. He studied me for so long, I grew goose bumps along the nape of my neck. "I hope you know how much I love you," he whispered. My heart bloomed like a flower in spring, but there was a hint of sadness in my soul that mirrored the sorrow that remained in Cael's raspy voice, in his gait.

His shoulders weren't as straight as usual, his wide smiles had disappeared, and his laughter had become nonexistent. He'd been working tirelessly with Leo for the past few days. But the fact of the matter was, Cael had been set back some by his exposure therapy. *No*, not set back; put on the *right* path. But it was immensely difficult for him, and I wished every day that I could take his pain away.

I breathed slightly easier now. Cael's breaths were labored. I had watched him last night when we were with our friends and felt myself panicking. He'd been so reserved, so distant that I knew the others noticed it too. He had never been very talkative, but lately, he was mostly silent and withdrawn. The past few days it felt like we were in different places with our grief. I saw that in the group too. Five of us were changing—healthier mentally, emotionally. Cael had fallen behind, and it was the hardest thing to witness.

"Are you okay?" I said, gently tracing my finger over his lip ring. I loved the feel of it against my own lips when we kissed. Cael's light gaze fell to the ground. When he looked back up at me, his eyes were racked with pain.

"I'm just sad, Peaches," he said quietly. "I'm just…" He exhaled a long breath. "I'm just really fucking sad."

"I know," I said and wrapped my arms around him. I thought I felt a tear fall on my shoulder, but when Cael lifted his head, his eyes were wiped clean. "Are you able to go to this meal tonight?" I asked. Mia and Leo had set up dinner at a local restaurant. A rare night away from the heavy counseling this leg of the trip had provided.

A chance for us all to catch our breath before our flight tomorrow.

Cael nodded, and a tug of a smirk pulled on his right lip. "I am."

"What?" I asked, suspicious at his smirk.

"I might have something planned for us later."

Butterflies accosted my stomach. "You do?"

"Yeah," he said, but I saw a flicker of concern. "I just…I just hope it's okay."

"It will be," I said and kissed the back of his hand. "I know it will be."

Cael led me out of the room, only to meet Travis and Dylan in the hallway. "Whew!" Dylan said. "Don't you two scrub up well!" I laughed, then admired Dylan and Travis. Dressed in nice button-up shirts and slacks too, they looked so handsome. It was nice to dress up a little after all these many, many weeks dressed so casually.

"Y'all look lovely," I said and kissed Dylan and Travis on their cheeks.

"Well, thank you, ma'am," Travis said and smiled widely. He looked to Cael. "You okay, man?"

Cael nodded despondently, then pressed the button for the elevator. I could see Travis and Dylan were worried for him. But they wouldn't say anything to upset him. We all wanted Cael to heal. He had all our strength behind him.

We met Mia, Leo, Lili, and Jade in reception and took the short walk under Manila's city lights to a restaurant. The air was balmy and the breeze light. It felt like the night was kissing our skin. In the restaurant, Cael sat beside me to my right, Dylan to my left. It was a circle table in a private room, and we could see everyone in our group.

Leo tapped his glass with his knife and held up his glass of water. We all followed suit. "To Japan," he said and took a drink.

"To Japan," we echoed and drank too.

When we all lowered our glasses, Mia said, "As you know, our time here in the Philippines was about exposure." She gave a proud but cautious smile. "I know how difficult this part was for all of you. It's the same with every new group we have. It's the part that truly rocks us. But it's also the one that can help us most."

Cael's hand tightened on my thigh. I reached down and wrapped my fingers around his. I felt his tight muscles relax a little at my touch.

Leo cleared his throat. "In Japan, we will reach the final stage: acceptance." Shivers ran down my spine at his announcement. The table was quiet, and when I met Dylan's eyes, Travis's, Lili's, and Jade's, I felt overcome with emotion. We had made it.

I clutched tightly to Cael and looked at him too. His eyes were staring off outside the window. I wanted to hold him tightly and take him away from all his pain. But I couldn't, so I simply laid my head on his shoulder and sighed when he dropped a soft kiss on my head.

"Japan is a stunning country, and what we have planned for you there will both inspire you and push you just that little bit farther."

Leo nodded to Mia and she said, "I'm so proud of you all. And I hope as we embark on one more country, you are proud of yourselves too." She paused, then said, "All of you." I caught her subtle glance at Cael. Because he should be proud of himself. He had shed himself of the anger toward his brother that held him captive and had opened his heart to healing.

I was prouder of him than I was myself.

The meal was delicious, and the mood around the table was light. Relief that we were leaving the hardest part of our journey behind hung in the air, and laughter was shared.

When the meal was done, Mia got to her feet. "Travis, Dylan, Lili, Jade, you guys are with me." Our friends stood and, with goodnights shared, followed Mia from the restaurant.

Leo stood too. "I'll wait for you both outside."

My eyebrows pulled down in confusion. "What—" I went to say, but then I remembered Cael said he'd had something planned. I turned to him, smiling. Worry etched his face. My smile quickly fell. "Cael—"

"I wanted to do something for you," he blurted, rushing the words from his mouth. "But I don't know if I've gone too far."

"What is it?" I said, heart beating fast in anticipation.

Cael shifted in his seat and squeezed my hand. He stared at me, as if trying to read my face for the answer to a question he hadn't yet asked. "A while ago, you told me that you could no longer listen to live orchestras or even classical music because Poppy played cello and wanted to be a professional cellist." I felt myself growing hotter, my pulse fluttering in my neck and wrists. I nodded, lost for words. He ran his tongue along his bottom lip, then said, "I found out a professional orchestra was playing just down the street—is that what you call them?" he asked, adorably nervous.

"A symphony orchestra?" I asked, breathless.

"Yeah," he said, bowing his head. "I asked Leo if I could get tickets and take you." He looked up at me again. "I'm not pushing you to see it, and if you still find it too difficult to hear that kind of music, Leo will take us to meet the others in the park that has other music playing." He inhaled, then exhaled measuredly. "I just wanted to do this for you."

His long, dark lashes kissed his cheek as he closed his eyes. "You've been there for me through so much. You've held me up these past few days when I have been cut open and in pain." My lip trembled. This boy…this boy was so kind, so thoughtful. I loved him so much.

"You've given me so much, Savannah, and I don't think you understand how much that means to me." Cael's voice cut out and I pressed my forehead to his, just feeling him, breathing him in. "I just wanted to give you something back…give you back a part of Poppy."

"Cael," I said, and my voice cracked with a small cry.

Cael's eyes flew to mine, and I saw the panic written on his face. He cradled my face. "It's fine, Savannah. I promise. We won't go." He shook his head. "I shouldn't have pushed you. I should've let you do this yourself, when you were ready. I… God, I'm so sorry—"

"No," I said and held on to his wrists. Cael's unsure gaze darted to mine. "You misunderstand," I said and smiled even through my tears. "It's beautiful." I dropped my head to meet his once more. "It's the kindest, most thoughtful gift I've ever received."

Cael's relieved exhale spoke volumes.

I sat back, never releasing him. "I would be honored to go with you."

He searched my face for any doubt. There was only truth. Poppy's biggest passion in life was music. Was her cello. I wanted to hear the music she loved playing again. I wanted to feel her memory wrap around me as the bow danced over familiar-sounding strings.

I wanted to break down this final barrier. And I wanted to do this with Cael by my side. I leaned in and kissed him. Then I rose from the table and Cael came too. "You sure?" he asked.

"I've never been surer."

Cael led us outside, and to Leo, who would be accompanying us. Leo led the way down the street, until we entered a large building. People milled about in the foyer, and Cael handed in our tickets. Leo would be seated away from us to give us this moment alone.

As we were led to the main theater, I breathed it all in. The familiarity of seeing an orchestra pit. We had never missed a performance by Poppy. We were always there, watching her play. I used to sit, mesmerized as she'd played, eyes closed and a smile upon her pretty face. She had become lost to the notes, swaying to the melodies, hand delicate as though she performed an intricate ballet with her bow.

I had loved it. Every time.

As we sat in our seats, I held tightly to the program we'd been given. There was a fissure of nerves cracking in my chest. I felt Cael watching me. "She practiced all day long," I said, and Cael's hand moved to rest on my thigh. I stayed staring at the drawn curtain that hid the orchestra from view. "I used to curl up on the window seat in our living room and read as Poppy practiced in the background." I smiled at the memory. And when I did, there was no pain. A dull ache, perhaps, but the memory no longer sliced me open. It felt... *nice*, to remember her this way.

"Of course, she played in concerts. She was amazing. She was part of many orchestras. Always first seat, because she was that talented. But my mind still takes me back to those lazy, rainy days as I read in our living room, Poppy playing beside me, Ida on the floor playing with her dolls." I could feel Cael smiling at that.

Tears sprang to my eyes. "The house has been too quiet for quite some time now." I blinked away the blurriness from my eyes. "Near the end, she could no longer play. She became too weak to hold the bow. But there was still classical music playing all the time, at home."

Cael squeezed my leg again. I looked to him, to see his eyes shining with tears too. "After she left us, the music left too." I thought about reading in my window nook again when I returned home. "Maybe when I'm home, I'll play it again. For her," I said, then smiled. "And for me."

"I think she'd like that, Peaches," Cael said, and I lay my head against him, closing my eyes as he kissed my hair. Suddenly, applause broke out and the curtain lifted, showcasing the orchestra. My eyes immediately sought out the cellists.

I watched them with rapt attention as they sat down, and the conductor took to the stage. The crowd grew silent, the air pausing around us too. The conductor gave instruction, and the orchestra broke to life.

I smiled when Vivaldi's *Four Seasons* began to fill the room. I smiled because "Spring" was one of Poppy's favorite parts. And when it began, I could see her. I could see her up on that stage once more, playing with her eyes closed, a smile on her face, white bow in her hair and swaying to the music.

I closed my eyes too. I closed my eyes and only saw Poppy. Giving me one last performance. Just her on the stage, playing to me from the beyond. None more so when her favorite piece of all time began. "The Swan" from *The Carnival of Animals*.

I let tears stream down my face as the cellist took the lead. I let the notes sink into my heart. Let the melody fill up every inch of my soul. And I let Poppy play for me in my mind. Let my sister give me this. Give me the gift of her favorite music back to me.

Cael's hand was trembling in mine as he gripped me tightly. Even he could feel the heightened beauty of this moment. A moment *he* had given me. A cherished gift he had given me back.

As the final note quivered on the string, vibrating into the body of the theater, it drifted over my head. I opened my eyes when the audience clapped in rapturous applause. I clapped too, but I struggled to stand. My eyes were wide, and my chest was raw. But it was from getting this part of me back, of my sister, my family. It wasn't in sadness. It was in love and joy and hope.

It was Poppy.

I turned to Cael as the orchestra took their bows and began leaving the stage. We stood, and I lifted to my toes and kissed him. I sank against him and whispered, "Thank you. Thank you so much."

I knew he'd heard me, even over the applause, because he brought his mouth to my ear and whispered, "I'd do anything to make you happy, Peaches."

This boy had my entire heart.

Leo hugged me as we came out of the theater to find him waiting for us. Even his eyes showed the remnants of tears, proving how moving music and the arts could be.

Cael and I walked back to the hotel hand in hand. I glanced up at the stars. Fewer were visible in the city, but there were some still shining through.

"The stars," I said, and Cael looked up too. I pressed my cheek to his bicep. "They're both up there, you know. Watching and smiling down at us."

Cael's breathing hitched, but then he said, "I really hope they are."

Leo saw us to our bedrooms, and we each went inside. I only waited ten minutes before sneaking from my room and knocking on Cael's. When he opened the door, I took my place against him, arms immediately circling his waist. And I held on. Nowhere would ever feel safer to me than in Cael's arms.

As I leaned back, he kissed me. I kissed him back, not wanting to waste a single second by his side. My stomach fell when I thought of Japan being our last country. I couldn't bear the thought of being torn away from this boy, the one I was so hopelessly in love with. But we still had time. There was still time left.

I kissed him one more time and said my reluctant goodnight. Tonight, Cael Woods had given me the greatest gift. He was so selfless and beautiful, and right now he was broken. But he was mine, and I was his.

Forever.

And ever.

And I would fight to make him whole too. In whatever way I could.

22

Broken Plates and Found Beauty

Cael
Tokyo, Japan

TOKYO WAS A RIOT OF COLORS. WE STOOD ON THE SIDEWALK, JUST LOOKING up at the city, the buildings, the neon colors that decorated this special place in digital prismed light. Even in my numb state, I could see how captivating it was.

"It's incredible," Savannah murmured beside me. Her hand smoothed over my back, and I closed my eyes under her touch. I glanced down at her. The lights reflected in her eyes, a smile stretched on her face. Noticing me looking, she said, "Have you ever seen anything like this?"

"Never," I said. Travis was on my other side, Dylan beside him; Lili and Jade were on Savannah's right side. We were all awestruck at the sights. We must have looked like the quintessential American tourists, as we all gaped at the buildings, mouth open.

"The home of manga," Travis said and rubbed his hands together. "I'm *home!*" Dylan laughed, and the two of them set off onto a conversation I couldn't follow. I hadn't read a manga in my life.

Savannah laughed at how animated they got, even more so when Lili screeched and said, "They have kitten cafes here. *Kittens!*"

"We need to go," Jade said. The two of them buried their heads in their cells, searching for the closest one. I caught Savannah looking at our new friends with such deep affection on her pretty face. She'd told me she was going to drink in every second of our time in Japan.

Because this was it. This was the end.

My heart twisted at the thought of leaving this group behind. I might not have been the most inspiring member of our mismatched group, but I'd come to care for them all—deeply. None more so than the petite blond beside me, who was leaning over and looking at a café location that Lili was showing her.

I wrapped my arm around her shoulder and held on as she talked to the girls. I hadn't known it was possible to miss someone before they'd actually left you, but that's where I was with Savannah. Each day spent here was one step closer to having to say goodbye to the girl who had become my world, my pillar holding me up. My only solace was that she was coming to New England in the fall.

How I'd cope without her until then was anyone's guess.

"Let's go," Savannah said, wrapping her arm around my waist. I raised my eyebrow. "What?" she asked playfully. "You don't want a cup of coffee while being jumped on by cats?"

A humored smirked pulled on my lip. It was so rare for me to smile lately, the act felt strange. Clearly, Savannah thought the same, as her gaze softened at my flicker of a smile.

As for Savannah, she was doing incredible. She was still introverted—that was just who she was. But there was a lightness to her now. A sense of peace radiated from her pores.

And she hadn't had an anxiety attack for weeks.

I knew Japan was special to her. She'd told me about Poppy's desire to see the cherry blossom trees here. She'd never made it.

Even I felt goose bumps break out along my skin when I realized we had arrived in Japan when most of the cherry blossoms were in bloom. Like I felt about Savannah, it felt like something bigger had conspired to have her here when the trees she associated with her sister were in full flower. We had seen some in Tokyo. But in a couple of days, we were to travel to Kyoto. That was where we would take part in the cherry blossom festivals.

I wanted to be excited. I wanted to feel at peace and feel stronger. But I didn't. I'd been talking to Leo a lot still. I knew I was behind the group now. I wouldn't be going home healed. I'd be going home *raw*. And there was a part of me that feared what I'd become without this group. Without Leo and Mia, and especially Savannah. Would I sink further into sadness, or would the anger I'd fought so hard to cast away come rushing back the minute I was faced with the triggers of home?

Leo and Mia had offered me more help. The truth was, reframing my thoughts about Cillian taking his own life was no longer my biggest issue. It was that, for a year now, I couldn't get the way he'd died from my mind. How I had witnessed it. *Saw* him. Held him and watched him die.

Every time I closed my eyes, I saw it. When I felt tired, I saw it. I heard a car horn, a screech of tires, and I was thrust back there, Cillian in my arms, broken and fucking *gone*.

I recalled the conversation I'd had with Leo only a few days ago during our one-on-one...

"Cael, Mia and I have been talking, and we think you'd benefit from further help."

I didn't even react but for a small turn of my stomach. The truth was, I knew it. I felt it. I nodded my head. I would do whatever was needed. I wasn't even going to put up a fight. What I had witnessed was traumatic, and, I knew, it would take me longer to heal. If I wanted to be better for Savannah, for my parents, for me, I had to keep going.

"After this trip, we'll find you help at home." Leo paused, then said, "We think a residential program might be best. To really dig deep and help you through." Leo waited until I met his eyes. "Is that something you'd be willing to do?"

"Yes," I said. I pictured Savannah's face again. "I'll do whatever it takes."

"Come back to me," Savannah said, breaking through that memory. Her hands were on my face, in the center of Tokyo, thousands of people milling around us like they were water running around our stationary rock. I breathed and felt like crumbling. I was getting so tired of dealing with this grief.

It was destroying me.

As I looked at Savannah, I just knew I was going to destroy her too if I couldn't get a handle on this. I hadn't told her about the extra help back home. The truth was, I didn't want her to worry.

"I'm here," I rasped. I looked around us. Our friends had gone.

Savannah must have seen my confusion. "They've gone to the café." She took my hand in hers. "Come on; we'll go somewhere else."

I stopped her from pulling me away. "No," I said, forcing a tight smile. "We'll catch up with them." I took a breath that I prayed would give me strength. Savannah didn't look convinced. "We don't have long left. We want to spend more time with our friends."

"Only if you're sure," Savannah said after searching my face.

I put my arm around her shoulders and led her across the street. "I'm sure, Peaches. I can't think of anything more exciting than being attacked by kittens while I try to eat."

Savannah's short peal of laughter was like a ray of light piercing through my overcast sky. "I note your sarcasm, Mr. Woods, but I'm gonna let it slide this time. I want nothing more than to know how you handle twenty kittens all vying for your attention."

So we went to the kitten café, and I buried my sadness for another day. It was par for the course, these days.

"I am Aika and I'll be working with you today." Aika was a five-foot slim Japanese woman with black-and-gray hair tied back in a bun. She smiled a lot and exuded a sense of peace with every breath she took. She looked to be in her sixties and had a studio in the center of Tokyo.

We were in a large, vacant space with bright white walls. There was a table before us, stacked with plates. We all lined up in front of it, and Aika stood before us.

"Before you, you will see a stack of plates. I would ask you all to take one."

We all did as she asked, then stepped back to await further instruction. Savannah looked at me and shrugged. She had no idea what this was either. Aika looked like an artist, and her studio could be for art too. Though nothing but white bare walls greeted us.

"Take a look at your plates. What do you see?" Aika asked.

"It's a plate," Travis said, clearly as confused as the rest of us.

"Yes," Aika said. "And?"

"It's smooth?" Jade said nervously.

"And?" Aika asked.

"It's a perfect circle," Lili said.

Aika nodded one quick, sharp nod. "Cracks?"

"No cracks," Dylan said, searching his plate. I did the same. There were no cracks.

"It's as perfect as a plate can be," Savannah said shyly.

"It is," Aika said. Then, "I want you all to spread out and get some space." We did as she said. Aika nodded in approval, then said, "Now, lift your plates." I did as she said, taken aback when she added, "And drop them to the floor."

We all froze, unsure whether she was joking or not. We looked to one another to see if anyone was really going to do it. Was it a test? If it was, I had no idea what it would be for.

"Drop them," she said again, gesturing with the flick of the hand to do it.

"Break them?" Lili asked, voice unsure.

"Yes," Aika said bluntly. "Drop, smash, break—into pieces."

Dylan was the first to drop his plate to the ground, the dish smashing into five pieces on the ground at his feet.

"Good," Aika said, then turned to the rest of us. "Now you."

One by one, the sound of smashing plates swarmed the room. I dropped mine, my six-foot-four height giving it some speed. Mine shattered into nine pieces on the ground. I counted.

Savannah was staring at hers. It was broken into six larger parts. Aika walked up and down the line, past the broken plates. "Now, fit them back together."

I had no idea what was happening.

"How?" Dylan asked.

"Pick them up," Aika said. "Put the plates back together."

Doing what she asked, I bent down and picked up the pieces. Kneeling on the ground, I put them in the circle shape they had once been in. Chips of ceramic or whatever it was made of had disappeared from view, leaving small chunks of the plate that couldn't be restored. I put the broken pieces in the correct place, but the plate was broken. It was that simple.

"Pick the plate up as a whole," Aika said, and only silence greeted her.

"We can't," Travis said. "It'll fall apart."

"Ah," Aika said, hands behind her back and a knowing expression on her face. "Then we shall have to fix that," she said and walked to a closed door across the room. She opened it. "Collect your broken pieces and follow me."

"What is this?" Savannah whispered to me, and I shook my head. I had no idea.

I collected my plate pieces and followed the group into the next room. I was the last to walk through, but I immediately saw why they had all come to a stop. The room was filled floor to ceiling with pottery of all kinds. Pottery that was lined with gold and silver.

Aika walked to a round table with many seats. She gestured around her. "All broken pieces that have been repaired. Can be used again."

"But even with that," Dylan said, "they're not as they were before."

"Ah, now you understand," Aika said, and it only took me a few seconds to realize what she was doing. I looked down at the broken plate in my hand. The nine broken pieces, the sections where the chips had disappeared, leaving a rough edge. My throat immediately clogged with emotion.

The plate would never be the same again. It was broken, but—

"*Now*, I teach you how to make it functional again," Aika said, just casually ripping a shred off my soul. Savannah leaned into me, and I knew she understood why Aika was teaching us this lesson too.

As I looked around the group, I saw everyone had understood. These plates had been broken into pieces, but we were going to take something irreparably damaged, and make it work again.

We were the broken plates.

"Please, sit," Aika said, and when we did, she handed out paintbrushes and a gold mixture. Once she had given us our materials, she sat down and took out a broken plate that she must have stored for this moment.

We watched her with held breaths. We knew this class was not just to learn a new skill. We all felt it was for something more. Something for us all, for our healing, hearts and souls.

Aika took the two largest pieces of the plate and coated one side with the gold liquid. "This is the Japanese art of kintsugi," she said, never taking her eyes off what she was doing. "I am using a gold lacquer like a glue to repair the plate. To put the broken pieces of the plate back together."

Aika pushed the pieces together, the two broken segments of the plate now fixed together, a stunning gold line tracking down where the break previously was. "This art form is the physical manifestation of the principle of *wabi-sabi*. *Wabi-sabi* teaches us to embrace life's imperfections, its impermanence and incompleteness."

"Like Sakura, the cherry blossom trees," Savannah whispered, emotion thickening her voice.

"Yes. Like sakura," Aika said. She then nodded to our broken plates and our tools. "Please, begin. Follow what I am doing."

My hand was shaking when I reached for my paintbrush. Savannah didn't move for a few minutes, eyes closed and breathing. I placed my hand on her thigh. Her eyes fluttered open. "You okay?" I asked quietly.

"Yes," she said. She gave me a watery smile. "I just...needed a few minutes." Savannah reached for the paintbrush and began reconstructing her plate.

There was total silence as we all worked. With every piece I glued back together, flashes of the past year came to mind. About the catatonic state I was in after Cillian died. About the anger that had taken root and spread like a plague throughout my body until it had consumed me. I recalled the first time I had shunned my parents, screaming at them to leave me alone. About when I had walked out of my teams' hockey rink and never looked back, refusing to start Harvard in the fall. When I had thrown my skates in the pond shed and slammed the door. When I had taken Cillian's hockey stick and smashed it to smithereens on the frozen pond we loved so much.

Each of them was a crack in my soul.

Crack.

Crack.

Crack.

They were the physical manifestation of my heart breaking, my soul shattering into a thousand broken pieces. I never believed that I could be put back together.

Until this trip.

Until I fell in love with the most incredible girl who made me dare to *hope* again.

Were they my gold lacquer? Was this what was happening to my broken spirit? Was this trip, these new friendships, Leo and Mia's guidance, and falling deeply in love with my girl, my kintsugi? Could I—*we all*—be somehow put back together? Or was I broken all over again since the exposure therapy? Had my pieces been refractured? Did I have to scramble to find them again? Or were they smashed into too many pieces that it was unsavable? That was my biggest fear. That it was too far gone to be healed.

"Are you struggling?" Aika asked me. My hands were suspended in the air and I realized I had been sitting still, lost in my head. Then I heard her question filter into my ears. Was I struggling?

Too much.

Swallowing, I met Aika's searching gaze. "Is it..." I shifted in my seat, uncomfortable at asking this question out loud. But I had to know. "Are there any plates that are too broken to be repaired? Any...hopeless cases?"

The room was silent as my question thickened the air. I felt Savannah's hand land on my knee in support. But I never took my eyes off Aika. My breath was held as I waited for her answer.

"No," Aika said, matter-of-fact. "The shattered pieces may take longer to find, and they certainly would take longer to fix back together. But any broken plate can be mended with time and the sheer tenacity to do it."

The relief I felt from her answer almost knocked me off my chair. I could feel Aika watching me closer. When I looked up and met her eyes again, she nodded her head once, like she could see into my soul. That curt nod was in encouragement. I knew she understood why I had really asked that question. Everyone around this table did.

"Okay, baby?" Savannah asked, her whispered voice shaking with sadness. Sadness for me.

"I'm okay," I said and gave her hand a squeeze, then carried on, ignoring everyone else's heavy focus on me.

Lost to the hours it took to fix the plate, I sat back when the final piece had been fixed back into place. As I looked down upon my lacquered plate, I lost my breath.

It was fixed. It wasn't as it was before, but it was put back together. It was something new. But it was a plate again.

"What do we see now when we look at our plates?" Aika asked, her voice softer now, gentler, like she knew we were all as fragile as the plates we'd just spent our day rebuilding. The lacquer would take time to dry. To make it as strong as it was before.

"It's beautiful," Savannah said, staring down at her plate. She blinked away tears from her eyes and met Aika's gaze. "I think it's even more beautiful than it was before."

"Ah," Aika said. "This is true." She gestured to all our plates. "A lesson then," she said and smiled. "That that which is broken, once repaired, can be more beautiful than it was before."

Chills tracked down my spine and spread out over my body. I reached out and took Savannah's hand. Her fingers were trembling, and when I looked up, tears were trickling down her cheeks, like they were her own salty tracks of lacquer. I stared, captivated by my girl. She had been beautiful when we'd met. When she was broken into thousands of pieces. But now, when this trip and therapy had gradually glued her back together with golden lacquer, she was more beautiful than ever.

I knew my own pieces were still broken. Not all lacquered back together... *yet*. But as I looked down at my plate, I knew I *could* be. Someday. I would never be the same after losing Cillian—none of us were after losing our loved ones. You couldn't lose someone you loved so much and ever return to the person you were before.

Loss changed you.

But you could *heal*. You could repair your fractured spirit with golden lacquer and hold on to *life*. That life wouldn't look the same ever again. But it didn't mean that it wouldn't be worthwhile. That it wouldn't be beautiful. Perhaps loss taught a person to love life *more*. Because you understood what it was like to lose that life. You wouldn't take it for granted anymore.

I knew I wasn't there yet. But if I kept going. If I kept *trying*, kept repairing my broken pieces, perhaps I could be.

A hand landed on my shoulder. Aika stood beside me. "I want to give you all a kit to take with you. For you to practice at home." She smiled, and her brown eyes were filled with kindness. "For when you feel life cannot be beautiful again."

"Thank you," I whispered and clutched on to that gifted kintsugi kit like it was my lifeline. Like if I just held on tight enough, my veins would run with golden lacquer, enter my arteries and repair my broken heart.

I heard Aika's voice echo in my head... *"Wabi-sabi teaches us to embrace life's imperfections, its impermanence and incompleteness."*

Nothing lasts forever. Life, happiness...even pain.

But *hope* did. If being around Savannah had taught me anything, it was that hope always hovered nearby. And if it was lost, it could be found again.

Savannah laid her head on my shoulder and just stared at her plate. I stared down at my own, the world disappearing around us. I *had* to find a way to repair my broken pieces. I kissed Savannah's hair, smelled her cherry and almond scent. I wanted a life with this girl. I wanted to find happiness with her too.

I just wanted *her*, in every way.

The golden lacquer glimmered in the overhead lights. Maybe Savannah's heart and mine had been broken by the loss of our siblings. But when we began to repair them, maybe we melded them back together to create our two hearts as one.

We were stronger that way. Beating in unison.

And I was sure they were more beautiful than they had ever been on their own.

Blossom Flowers and Old Friends

Savannah,

I know many people wonder why I love cherry blossom trees so much. I always have. We were raised among them. Their colors, their fragility were just something I was fascinated by. Most children counted down until Christmas. I counted down the days until it was cherry blossom season.

As I sit here now, they have bloomed. The blossom grove is full of pink and white petals. It is alive, so alive. The sweet floral fragrance, the stunning beauty that has bloomed, takes my breath away each time I am taken there.

I can no longer walk. I use a wheelchair now. But I don't mind. As long as I get to see my blossom grove in all its beauty, one more time, I am content. Especially with my Rune by my side. We can sit for hours there. I am safe in his arms beneath those trees. Every breath I take is cherished. Every kiss Rune gives me is a gift I didn't think I would have again.

I have taken none of it for granted.

But this year's bloom is bittersweet, as I know it will be my last on this Earth. I know that soon, when the first petal falls, my breaths will become numbered. My heartbeats will be finite. I grow tired, Savannah. Even now, simply holding the pen and writing to you *exhausts me. But I feel no fear. I want you to know that. Like the cherry blossom flower, I may have had a short life, but it has been vibrant and full, and so very sweet.*

Sweetest when I am with the ones I love. The sweetest when I am with you and Ida. With my Rune.

God knew my life would be short, Savannah. That is why He gave me my love of cherry blossoms. So that I would understand what it was to live a limited but full life. I was born in Blossom Grove to live among the trees my life was so inspired by. I believe that. Nothing is permanent in this life, Savannah. So, embrace its beauty while you can.

When you read this, know that I am in heaven, safe among cherry blossoms that no longer die. And I will be so happy to sit beneath them, thinking of my family, thriving in their lives until they return to me and, like the heavenly cherry blossom trees I wait beneath, stay forever by my side.

Until that day,
Poppy

Savannah
Kyoto, Japan

It was too much to absorb. Everywhere I turned was a blanket of pink and white. Trees lining every pathway, parks full to the brim of blossom trees. The floral scent was infusing every fraction of air, and all I saw, wherever I turned, was Poppy. I was happy that I was seeing Kyoto now, at the end of the journey. Because if I had seen this months ago, when this trip had only just begun, I wouldn't have been able to stand it.

Now, I could gaze at these trees, full of temporary life, and admire them with the respect that they deserved. And I could see Poppy at every turn and not be felled by it. But be *strengthened.* I smiled, though my chest rose up and down with soft cries as tears dropped from my eyes. They fell to the ground, leaving a piece of me forever in this place—a sister's tribute. Cael held my left hand, just drinking in this wondrous sight with me. I held out my right hand, the breeze weaving between my fingers. And, in my mind's eye, I saw Poppy beside me, holding me tight. She would be gazing upon the trees she loved so much with nothing but love and gratitude in her heart.

"Incredible," Dylan whispered behind us. I opened my eyes and saw birds circling up ahead as if they were breath taken by the sight too. "Is it like the blossom grove, Sav?" Dylan asked. I'd told him all about it.

I thought of home and felt the sharp pang of homesickness. As magnificent as this sight was, *nothing* could take the place of our small blossom grove. Especially now that my sister rested there. It was a magical place, serene and blessed.

I opened my mouth to reply when a voice beside Dylan said, "Nothing could ever replace our blossom grove."

Shock rendered me immobile for a few seconds. Because I *knew* that voice. Had *missed* that voice. I released Cael's hand and stepped around Dylan. And there was Rune Kristiansen in the flesh, beside us in this stunning Kyoto park.

"Rune…" I said, and fresh tears sprung to my eyes. I ran to him and wrapped my arms tightly around him. Rune held me close, and I felt his long, blond hair on my cheeks as he did. This was all so surreal. Being here, among so many blossom trees, now with Poppy's Rune at my side.

I pulled back and wiped my eyes. Rune was dressed as he always was—black jeans, black shirt, and biker boots. He hadn't changed a bit, except now he was a little older. And just like the Rune of old, he had a camera in his hand.

"Surprise," he said, and I shook my head, unable to speak.

He smiled. "I have been in South Korea with my mentor for a few weeks on shoots. We had a couple of days free between projects. He was meeting with some old colleagues, so I decided to hop on a plane and take a quick detour here. I'm only here for a day and night. But your mama told me you'd be here too. I contacted your group's leaders, and they told me where you'd be. I wanted to surprise you."

"You're here," I whispered, still in shock.

Rune's eyes softened and a hint of sadness flickered in their depths for a few seconds. "I never miss the cherry blossoms, Sav." He touched his camera. "I still have to show my girl."

The pictures on Poppy's grave.

Every year at the end of the cherry blossom season, near the anniversary of her death, a new picture of a cherry blossom festival somewhere in the world appeared at Poppy's headstone.

Rune and I shared a long, knowing look, and emotion clogged my throat so tightly that I couldn't speak. Rune dipped his head, and I saw him subtly wipe his eyes. When he faced me again, I saw how much he missed my sister written on his handsome face.

"Peaches?" Cael came behind me and placed his arm around my shoulder, turning me to face him. "Are you okay?" He looked to Rune, confusion in his eyes. Rune's head tipped to the side at how close Cael was to me. Heat filled my cheeks. Clearly, my family hadn't told him about Cael. Rune raised a knowing eyebrow. It broke the heaviness of the moment.

"Cael," I said and gestured to Rune. "This is Rune, Poppy's..." I trailed off, not knowing what to say anymore.

My stomach turned, until Rune said, "I'm Poppy's Rune."

Poppy's Rune... Because he had always been more than a boyfriend to my sister. He was her entire life, the beat of her heart and her soulmate. They were just separated for a little while.

Cael took his arm from around me, and his face lit with recognition. "Cael," he said and shook Rune's hand. Rune smiled and then looked at me the way any big brother would. Like I had some explaining to do.

"Rune?" Dylan said. I turned to my friend, who was looking at Rune in earnest.

"*Hei,*" Rune said to Dylan, shaking his hand, his Norwegian language sneaking through. I would remember to ask Rune to talk to Dylan at some point before he left. I believed he could help Dylan too.

"Dylan," he said, "Savannah's friend. I'm on the trip with her." Dylan gestured to everyone else as they approached us with interest. Understanding flashed in Rune's blue eyes. One by one he met all my friends. Cael placed his hand on my back, a silent support. Rune gave us all a small smile. He knew exactly where we all were emotionally. He had walked—*was walking*—this path too.

"I can't believe you're here," I said, finding my voice again.

Rune tipped his head in the direction of the park. "Do you have time to catch up?"

I looked to Mia and Leo, who were behind us. They'd clearly already met Rune, helped him plan this. Mia shooed us away with her hand. I turned to Cael. I'd wanted to see these cherry blossoms with him too. He must have seen that battle written on my face, because he pressed his forehead to mine and said, "I'll go with the group. You take all the time you need with Rune. I'll be waiting for you when you get back." Cael kissed me. It was soft and tender, and shivers ran down my spine.

"See you soon," I whispered, then went to Rune, who had moved aside to give us privacy.

Rune began walking. He put his arm around me and hugged me to his side. "I've missed you, Sav." He released me and really studied me. "You look better." He took a long, relieved breath. "You seem stronger."

"I am," I said and meant every word. "I'm getting better. I'm stronger." I lifted my hand and ran my fingers gently over a vibrant pink blossom bud, just about to bloom. "This trip..." I shook my head. "I don't even know where to begin."

We came to a patch of grass covered in low tables for picnics. Rune gestured for us to sit down. This section of the park was covered by a low canopy of cherry blossom branches—it had made a ceiling of petals. I smiled up at the thick layer of flowers, so many it blocked out most of the spring-time sun.

"I'd say we start with the boy who just kissed you," Rune said, humor lacing his voice.

My cheeks blazed with fire. But I was proud of Cael. I was proud he was mine. "You now know his name is Cael," I said, hearing how much I'd fallen for him just by my voice. Rune nudged my arm. I laughed at his playfulness but then sobered up quickly. "He lost his older brother." All humor left Rune too. "Cillian...his brother...he took his own life."

"No," Rune whispered, no doubt picturing Alton in his head.

"Cael saw it happen. Held him afterward." I inhaled deeply to stave off the pain it brought picturing Cael like that. "It's been...he's finding everything really hard."

"Of course he is," Rune said, completely supportive. It was one of the reasons Poppy loved him, I was sure. "Has this trip helped him?" Rune asked.

"It has," I said, but I had to admit the truth to myself. "But he's still in pain. The therapies we've done have brought up things that he is still grappling with."

Rune nodded, then looked up at the flowers. He closed his eyes, and the breeze danced through his hair. I liked to think it was Poppy running her hand through his long strands as she sat beside him. By the smile it pulled on Rune's mouth, he maybe thought that too.

He opened his eyes and said, "When I lost your sister..." He shook his head. "Those early days after she had gone. I didn't know how to *breathe*, Savannah." Rune's voice broke. Tears sprang to my eyes too. Because I had been exactly the same way. "Then the more time passed, the worse it got. Because I *felt* her absence. The gap between the last time I kissed her and that present moment felt like such a long time. *Too* long for me to cope."

Rune lifted his camera, and seeing something I didn't, he snapped a picture. When he lowered it, he said, "Those final months with your sister... with *Poppymin*, were everything to me." His voice was rasped and raw. I knew those months were special. I'd seen it. Seen my sister and the happiness Rune had brought back to her life for her final days. As much as she'd loved her family, only Rune could have made her passing as beautiful as it was. He had made it perfect for her. And he had come back into her life just when she'd needed him most.

Just like Cael had entered mine.

Rune put his hand on mine and squeezed. "Do you love him?"

There was no doubt in my heart when I said, "Yes. More than I ever thought possible."

Rune smiled. Smiled so big I knew it was on behalf of Poppy too. "Then you've met him," he said. "The boy you'll spend the rest of your life with."

I nudged him and said, "My Rune."

Rune choked on his laugh, and a tear spilled over the crease in his eye. "Your Rune," he echoed.

"He's a hockey player from just outside of Boston," I said.

"Boston, hey?" he said, clearly referring to my future at Harvard.

"He was meant to go to Harvard last fall. On a hockey scholarship. But he walked away from both that and the sport when his brother passed. His brother was a hockey player too, and it became too hard for Cael to keep playing...the memories...they were too difficult."

"Give him time," Rune said. "He's walked a hard path. But he might find his way back there." He turned to me. "Serendipitous, though," he said. "That Cael should've been going to Harvard too..." That's exactly what I had thought. Rune pointed up at the sky. "I'd say this has your sister's mark written all over it."

I laughed. "She did love love."

"She did love love," Rune repeated wistfully. "God, Sav. I miss her so much. Being in these places makes me feel like I miss her more but also that she's right here, beside me, too."

"I know what you mean," I said. Then I asked him what I knew I should have asked him a long time ago. "Are you okay, Rune? *Really* okay?" I saw in his face that he knew I wasn't asking about in general. I was asking about how he was without Poppy.

"I am," he said, and some tight pull in my chest settled. "Because there's no way I won't see your sister again someday. I *know* I'll be with my girl once more. I'll get to kiss her again and hold her close. I'll get to hear her laugh and hear her play the cello. I'll get to sleep beside her and just be with her. Like we always should have been. And all the years we have had to spend apart will fade to dust."

I ducked my head so he wouldn't see me break. It clearly didn't work, because he said, "For now, I see her in my dreams, Sav. I talk to her every day, and I know she hears me. I see her perfect dimpled smile. And in my soul, she reassures me she's happy and pain-free. I talk about her any chance I get. It keeps her alive to me." His voice grew hoarse, thickened with emotion. "There'll never be anyone else for me. Even from heaven, Poppy gives me more love than I could ever need." He lifted his camera. "I travel the world and take pictures for *her*. In her honor. She gives me purpose, every day. And that helps me keep going. Helps me stay away from the darkness of grief." His lip pulled up fondly at the side. "Poppy taught me that. How to cherish and love life. Even with her gone. I owe it to her to live for us both. I promised her. And would never break my promise to my girl."

"Purpose…like studying medicine will be for me," I said, thinking of Tala, of all the kids back in the Philippines, especially those who couldn't be saved.

"Like you studying medicine," he said in agreement. "We honor Poppy by keeping going, in her name. That will be enough for me until I see her again."

He was quiet for a few minutes, our conversation floating above us. "I don't regret a single moment of my life with your sister, Sav," he said. "Even the bad times. The very worst times. When she was down, in the trenches, I was there with her. She knew that. That's what made us so strong. Thrive or fail, I was beside her, holding her hand. Nothing would make me leave her… not even death."

I pictured Cael and knew that was us too. I would be with him through rain or sunshine, when he was dancing in the light or lost in the dark. I just prayed he knew he had me, one hundred percent. I knew he thought himself a burden to me. But he was far from it. He elevated me. Made me soar. I knew he hated when he broke, when he was down and sinking into darkness. But what Cael did not get was that vulnerability only made me love him more. I'd come to understand that we showed our worst to those we love best. There was no judgment. Only complete, unwavering support.

I clutched on to Rune's arm. "I'm real glad you're here," I said and laid my cheek on his bicep. "A piece of home with me halfway across the world." I smiled as the cherry blossoms swayed in the breeze again. "A piece of Poppy."

Rune kissed my hair and we sat in silence, just watching the trees my sister loved so much. Remembering her. Honoring her. Thinking of her.

Loving her.

Forever Always.

24

Goodbye

Savannah
Ōtsuchi, Japan

WE ARRIVED AT THE SMALL COASTAL TOWN OF ŌTSUCHI ON A HAZY AFTER-
noon. It was vastly different from Kyoto. A sea dominated the view. Trees
and fields. But it was remote and quiet.

I had left Kyoto feeling full but also a bit raw. Seeing that many blossom
trees in full bloom and seeing and speaking to Rune…it was beautiful but
also difficult. It was the little things, I realized, that could trigger a pang of
grief in your heart. A feeling so overwhelming and strong that, for a few
hours, it could thrust you back into the fire. But I had learned to climb out
of it, a little charred but not burned. That was progress.

Although Kyoto had been difficult at times, I had tried my hardest to
feel the beauty there too. I had visited a place Poppy had so desperately
wanted to see. And I had been there with Rune. I knew she would have been
so joyful about that. Rune had taken a picture of us both together, among the
pink and white sea of petals. And I knew when I returned to Blossom Grove,
Georgia, that picture would be leaning against my sister's grave.

Rune had come to dinner with us all on the trip. We had talked of Poppy
with wide smiles on our faces and tears in our eyes, remembering her fondly.
It had been long overdue with the boy I thought of as a brother.

And Rune being Rune took a walk that evening with Dylan. When they returned, Dylan seemed lighter in his gait. His eyes didn't seem so heavy. My heart squeezed looking at the two of them—good men who had had to part with their soulmates far too soon. I had looked at Cael then. He had wrapped his arms around me without words, as if he had read there was a little sadness on my soul. As if he had had the same dark thought as I—if anything happened to him... I didn't know how I would come back from that. It made me more in awe of Rune than I had ever been. How he had picked up his life and was actually *living* it. He was making his dream of being a photographer a reality. He had made living for Poppy his purpose.

Honor. Japan had taught that above anything. That every action should be done with honor, with purpose. That we, as people, needed to understand that nothing lasted forever. Everything was temporary, from the cherry blossoms to the seasons to the short lives of flowers or pets to both good and hard times. Everything passed; everything started anew.

Especially life.

All but love.

Life was messy. It could break you and tear you apart. But that didn't mean that life, in all its imperfection, couldn't be made and remade into something beautiful, that brokenness had to be ugly. It could be mesmerizing and breathtaking.

Simply looking at Cael reminded me of that.

And now we were here. In a new part of Japan. Small and still. Our very final stop. There was a melancholy within me. I had fought so hard against coming on this trip. Now I was desperate to stay. But I knew we had to break out of our bubble if we were to truly move on. We had to take everything we had learned back to our normal lives.

I just prayed the strength I felt within me now persevered. I felt it would. Seeing other cultures, facing the issues I had buried down deep had been liberating. I felt like a previously caged bird close to being set free.

But we had one more stop. Just one more stop before I could spread my wings and fly.

"Tomorrow," Leo said as we gathered in the hotel's rec room they had booked out just for us, "will be the culmination of all this trip has taught."

Nerves ran up and down my body like electricity. Mia and Leo hadn't told us what was going to happen. But I knew it must have been something poignant. I tried not to panic over it. But just let it come. I had become better at facing whatever life threw at me now.

I was wrapped in Cael's arms on the couch. His body was taut and his eyes haunted. I couldn't believe that, soon, I wouldn't have him walking beside me. As if he felt my heart sink at that thought, he pulled me closer. I melted into his strong embrace.

After we finished dinner, I walked hand in hand with Cael back to my room. He waited for me at the door. I needed him with me right now. Because tonight was poignant for me. I walked to the dresser, and lying on the top was Poppy's notebook.

I turned to Cael, who had been watching me with hawk eyes. His silver-blue gaze softened as I pulled the notebook to my chest. With a trembling lip and voice, I said, "I'm on the very last page."

Somehow, I had read through the tens and tens of notebook entries Poppy had left me. I had written back to her in the journal Mia and Leo had given me. It felt good to share this journey with her. Helped me to connect to her again. Through her entries, Poppy had lifted me up when I was falling down, had been the golden lacquer to my chipped shards when I had broken apart.

Throughout the pages, she had kept vigil beside me on this trip. When I had cried myself to sleep. When I had been homesick…but not as much as expected, because I had my sister talking to me every night.

But this was it.

This was the final night, the final chapter of her farewell to me. And as much as I didn't want to read it, I knew I had to. I didn't want to say goodbye to her stunning words, her uplifting prose. I hadn't wanted to say goodbye to my sister four years ago, and I certainly didn't want to say it to her now.

But I had to. Goodbyes had to be said, whether we wanted to say them or not. Like sakura, the cherry blossom tree she loved, taught—nothing lasted forever. And I—we *all*—had to accept that fact. We could believe in another life, find meaning in the universe or whatever we believed happened next.

But goodbyes, in some form, would always have to be made on this Earth.

I offered my hand to Cael. He didn't hesitate. He slipped his calloused, tattooed hand into mine. And he squeezed it twice. I cast him a watery smile. Tears already built in my eyes. My throat clogged, but I managed to say, "Will you stay with me..." I took in a deep breath. "For this final entry?"

Cael blinked against his own tears and said, "I wouldn't want to be anywhere else." His voice was hoarse, his Boston accent thick. He was enduring his own pain, but he was there for me too.

The hotel we were staying in was traditionally Japanese. Low tables and paper partitions separating sections of the room. And each hotel room had a private, secluded view of a perfectly manicured garden. Clutching on to Cael's hand, I led him to the cushioned low seating outside and sat down. He cradled me into his arms, his tall and broad body creating a protective shield around me.

I stared out at the lowering sun and to the stars that were beginning to shine. The universe was vast and imposing, so eternal that it should have felt overwhelming. But there was *something*, I thought, something comforting about all the people in the world looking up at the same stars and moon every night, no matter where they were.

I smoothed my hand over the notebook one more time. Smiled at Poppy's handwriting. This notebook had once been so terrifying to me. I had avoided it, kept it hidden in a drawer in my room. Now, it was a source of peace.

It was my personal line to a sister who loved me beyond compare.

Cael leaned in close and pressed a whisper of a kiss on my neck. He trailed his kisses up to my cheek and into my hair. I closed my eyes as he did, hearing birdsong in the dark branches of the surrounding trees. I smiled as I heard the infectious sound of Travis and Dylan laughing from another part of the garden.

Life, I thought...it really was a beautiful thing.

"I'm ready," I said quietly, recognizing the importance of this moment. It was almost sacred. To me, it was. Cael's arms circled me and held me up, and I turned to the final page.

My stomach turned when I looked at Poppy's writing. It wasn't as neat as the beginning pages had been. Throughout the notebook, I could see her growing tired. Her penmanship was weaker, but her words to me were anything but.

I remembered these days. I remembered seeing her bedbound. Her breathing so labored that she'd had to wear an oxygen line day and night. Her skin had been sallow, and her eyes had looked too big on her face. She had lost weight. But she had still been as beautiful as the petals she watched begin to fall outside her bedroom window. I inhaled a long, steadying breath, then read my sister's goodbye to me. The little sister who had adored her big sister with her entire heart.

Savannah

I'm afraid the time has come. As I write this, my hand is struggling to hold the pen. And honestly, I can feel the heavy pull of death pressing down upon me. I don't want you to worry. It doesn't feel oppressive. It doesn't feel sad or scary.

It feels like I am being called home.

People fear death. See it as dark and terrifying. But I am here, at the end, and it feels anything but. It is a heady lightness that hovers close. I can smell flowers all around me. I don't know why, but I like to think it's Mamaw taking her place by my side, to guide me through these final hours. Until she leads my soul from my broken body. And I will be revived. I will be strong once again. I will leave with the last of the cherry blossoms.

Rune is beside me now. He has fought sleep for so many days. He took me to prom, Savannah. He danced with me to my favorite song, and he hasn't let me go once. Right now, he is asleep beside me, his arm holding me close.

You have just been in and sat beside me too. You didn't say anything, but we sat next to each other and watched the petals outside of the window fall like summer rain.

That was you, Savannah. The quiet in my storm. My solace. My steady breath. The beat of my heart.

I hope when you read this, you are healed. I hope as you read this final entry, you feel stronger. And believe that I am no longer in pain. Believe that I am walking beside you through life. I pray that you are able to look up at the sky and smile, knowing that I am still alive. That I am home where I belong, patiently waiting to have you back in my arms once again.

I love you, Savannah. As I write this, tears are falling from my eyes. But they are not tears of pain or anger. They are tears of joy, because how lucky was I to have had you as a sister? How fortunate am I to have had such a beautiful soul such as you in my life?

I cannot wait to look down upon you and see you truly happy. You are living your life with purpose, and you are loved by the most perfect person. I cannot wait to see you love them back. Cannot wait to watch where life takes you.

Please, look after yourself, Savannah. Be happy. That is all I want for you. To be happy. Because happiness is everything. And love. Love so hard and so deeply that it radiates from your very soul.

Live. I am smiling now. Just imagining your beautiful face full with joy and love and life.

Savannah, being your sister has been a blessing. And even though I'm no longer on this Earth, I will always be your big sister. Talk to me often. I will hear you. I have loved every moment of growing up beside you. My sister. My best friend. You are a part of me, just as I am a part of you. That can never be extinguished.

That can never die.

I must go now. I am becoming too tired. But remember, I love you more than all the stars in the sky.

All my love forever,
Your very proud big sister,
Poppy

I couldn't see the final sentence for the tears pouring from my eyes. Cael's chest was moving up and down in fast motions, and I knew he had read it too. I turned into him and wrapped my arms around his neck. I buried my face into the crook of his shoulder, and I broke. I released four years of pent-up grief against the boy I loved more than life. Cael's hand threaded into my hair and held me to him. Cael cried with me; he cried *for* me. He cried for Poppy, and I knew he cried for Cillian, the big brother who loved him so much but left him exposed and without a true goodbye.

Maybe, I thought, Poppy's goodbye could be from Cillian too. Because I knew Cael's brother loved him just as much as Poppy loved me.

"She loved you," Cael said into my hair. "She loved you so much."

And I couldn't feel sad about that. Because it was true. To have been loved that hard changed everything. I may have lost my older sister, and I would miss her every day, but she had *loved* me. I had felt her love, and I still felt her love swirling in the very air around me. In the trees and in the earth, in the wind and especially in the stars.

Love didn't die; it was eternal. It was a tattoo on our souls. A gift that even death could not take away. If you have been loved, even if you have lost, that love will never leave. It will fill your heart and patch over the holes that grief leaves behind.

We just must hold on to it when all seems impossible.

"I love you," I said to Cael. I needed him to know that. I needed that love to patch the holes in his heart when we had to leave each other after this trip.

"I love you too," he said, and I felt the truth of that down to my bones.

"We need to make a pact." I said, and Cael studied my face. "We need to promise to always be honest with one another. To share our hopes and dreams, but also our fears and trepidations." I put my hand on his face. "If life has taught us anything, it's that there are ups and down but also joyous and precious moments." Cael's eyes dropped. I pressed my forehead to his. "We must tell each other everything...even if it hurts. That is true love, Cael. That is putting your trust onto someone completely."

Cael searched my eyes, then whispered, "Leo has offered me extra help. When I return home, he wants me to go into a residential facility that will dig deeper and aid me in coping with everything." Cael sighed—he was weary. "And I think he's right." His arms were iron-strong around me, as if I would blow away if he didn't hold on. "It was seeing it...seeing Cillian do it..." he trailed off.

"Cael," I hushed out, heartbroken for the boy I loved. "You should have told me."

His body sagged with exhaustion. "I suppose I didn't want to admit it. Didn't want to worry you. But…"

"But?" I questioned, praying I wasn't pushing him too hard.

"But he's right," he confessed, and in that moment, I was so *proud* of him. Cael had fought this trip, fought much of the talking therapies. But I realized he had given as much of himself as he could. But he needed to keep going. To be stronger, he had more of the path to walk.

"Thank you for telling me," I said and kissed his trembling lips.

"Thank you for loving me," Cael said softly against my lips, which wanted nothing more than to have him pressed to them. Cael may not have thought of himself as lovable or worthy. But in my eyes, he was exalted.

"We will get through this," I promised. Because I believed in him, and believed that, together, we could face anything.

Cael held me and I held him in the echo of Poppy's goodbye and his confession. When our tears were dry and only exhaustion remained, we looked up, watching the stars. And I smiled. Because I knew Poppy was up there. These days, that was as comforting as having her arms around me.

25

Warm Winds and Heartfelt Words

Savannah
Ōtsuchi, Japan
The next day

I STARED AT THE GARDEN WE'D BEEN BROUGHT TO AND THE PHONE BOOTH that sat within it. The sea lay over a busy road, but here we stood, in among a patch of wild greenery, looking at a simple white phone booth. It was old-fashioned English in style. There were benches scattered around, but this phone booth just stood here, rather alone and out of place.

"Years back, this town, Japan, endured a tsunami," Leo said, and my heart skipped a beat. I cast my eyes around the small town. It must have been devastated. "This coastal town, in particular, was severely impacted. Many people died. The townspeople lost many members of their families in that single disaster." Cael's hand clutched me tighter.

"This phone booth was constructed a year before." Leo walked up to it. "It is known as the Wind Phone. Inside of it is a disconnected wired phone." I saw the black phone inside. Like something you saw in an older movie, before cell phones existed.

"The man who created it lost a cousin to cancer. And he missed him. He missed him so much that he didn't know how to process it." Those words were a stab in the chest. I knew what that felt like. "He felt that he needed a place to put his feelings into words. And needed a place to express them. So the gentleman built this phone booth in his garden as a way to speak to him." I frowned in confusion. "This phone was designed to help with grief. It is a direct line to the afterworld and those who have passed over."

"To understand why this phone booth is significant, it is important to note a few things here about Japan and the beliefs that many people here carry," Mia said gently. "Japan is mostly Buddhist. And within Buddhism, people believe that the line between this life and the next is thin. They believe that everything in the world, in *life*, is connected, and that includes those who have passed away."

I liked that notion. It reminded me of what I believed about the universe and stardust and the idea that we would eventually take our place back among the stars where we all originated. About our energies surviving beyond the grave, remaining in this life just in a new form. Never leaving.

"In households across Japan, many people will have altars in their living rooms dedicated to their deceased loved ones," Mia continued. I couldn't take my eyes off her, hanging on her every word. "They are filled with photographs and mementos of those passed, and fruit and rice and other such offerings are placed before them. People believe that although dead, the loved ones are still tied to their families and must be honored."

Like the journal Leo and Mia gave us, I thought. It had kept me connected to Poppy. And I knew that even after this trip ended, I would continue to talk to her through the pages. I couldn't see myself ever stopping. I didn't know if that was healthy, but being here, hearing this about Buddhism and the Japanese culture, told me that it was okay. It was okay to stay connected to the sister I had lost. Through the journal, I had found her voice again.

"This phone booth is an extension of the home altars. It bridges that thin line between life and death in a healthy and personal way," Leo said. He pointed at the simple white phone booth. "The phone inside is not connected to anything on this earth, but rather the afterworld. The man who built this, knew there was no direct line to his lost cousin, but liked to think that his words to him, rather than being carried down a connected line, were instead being carried on the wind. It is why it's called 'The Wind Telephone.'"

My hands shook as I fixed my gaze upon that phone, and that phone booth. Shivers ran down my spine as a timely gust of wind blew around us. Cael squeezed my hand twice. I squeezed his hand twice in return—I felt him shaking too.

"Another part of the Buddhist belief system, one not too dissimilar to what we learned in Varanasi, is that because our loved ones are still connected to us, we also must let them go. Within Buddhist thought, if we cannot let go of our loved ones, cannot shed the pain of losing them, then they cannot be set free, and instead become suspended in a kind of no man's land in the afterworld," Leo said. "So one of the most common phrases used within this phone booth are, *"Don't worry about us"* and *"I'm doing my very best"*. People believe that it helps reassure those we love that we are okay, even if we are not, and helps them pass onto the afterworld and the next part of their journey."

Cael was stiff as a board beside me. It was the hardest part of everything for him, letting his brother go. Letting go of the candle representing Cillian on the Ganges truly hurt him. This, I knew, would be no different. I leaned my head against his arm just trying to offer him some comfort.

"After the tsunami," Mia picked up where Leo had left off. "Many of the townspeople began randomly turning up at this garden, to the phone booth to say the goodbyes they were robbed of. Just like so many of us are. Fatal accidents, quick illnesses...suicides..." Mia said, kindly and carefully. "There are no goodbyes. No chance to say all that we wanted to say to our loved ones."

In that moment I felt lucky. Because I had held Poppy's hand and said my farewell. I had said all I needed to say to my sister. But Cael...many of my friends here, they didn't get that goodbye. Didn't get that closure.

"Not everyone will want to do this, and that is okay. But we have found, that especially for those who haven't had their goodbye, speaking into the phone is beneficial to their healing. It can really help you say what you need to say to your lost loved ones, alone, and in total privacy," Leo said. He smiled at us all. "We have brought you here today, on our very last exercise of our trip, so you can all say whatever you need to, to those you loved most." I heard the sound of sobbing, of sniffling and gut-wrenching cries from my friends. But my gaze was locked on the phone booth. My hand gripped onto Cael like a lifeline. When I dared to look up at his face, he was ashen. His silver-blue eyes were wide and afraid.

I laid my head back upon his arm. He was cold, and his body trembled. "We will give each of you time to enter the phone booth," Mia said. "Leo and I come here often with our groups. We have been fortunate enough to secure some private time away from the public for you to do this." Mia moved to the side. "So please, if you want to and feel ready, enter the phone booth."

Leo came over to Cael and said quietly enough for only us to hear, "You don't have to do this if you aren't there yet, son." Cael nodded numbly. I honestly didn't know what he would do.

A hand clutched onto my free hand. It was Dylan. When I looked down the line, I saw we were all connected. Lili, to Jade, to Travis, to Dylan, to me, to Cael. We had gotten here. Through tears and pain and agony and opening our shattered hearts to one another, we six had gotten here to this final exercise.

"We've gotten this far," Dylan said to us all. We had. Together we had held one another up. We had done this side by side, wiping away one another's tears and comforting each other when we broke. We had a bond forged in both grief and love. I knew I would be fused to these people forever.

Lili walked forward first, releasing her hand from Jade's. I watched her, breath held, as she climbed the steps to the phone booth and walked inside. I lowered my head when she picked up the phone, knowing my friends were giving her the same grace.

The wind blew around the trees. Birds sang up ahead; the sound of slow waves hitting the shore and cars whizzing by on the busy road behind us created the ambient soundtrack. More importantly, it gave the person on the phone total privacy.

One by one my friends made their calls. Each coming out sad and drenched in tears...but seeming different somehow. Cleansed, revived—a cocktail of emotions. We retook hands to give ever-flowing support. And when Dylan returned to the line, cheeks red and eyes wet, it was my turn.

I glanced up at Cael, who tore his eyes from the phone booth to meet mine. "You can do this, Peaches," he said, voice raw and hoarse.

I nodded, then released his hand. It was a metaphor, I thought. We could hold one another up, support and dry one another's tears, but when it came down to it, our journeys with grief were our own. We were *on* our own. And we had to heal alone too.

Each step to the phone booth was a marathon. The heaviness of the door felt like it weighed ten tons. But when I was inside, the black phone staring back at me, everything grew quiet, and a sense of peace enveloped me where I stood.

With a shaking hand, I lifted the phone and brought it to my ear. Only silence met me.

But I knew she was there, waiting in the wind.

"Poppy…" I said, my voice sounding so loud in the silent space. "I know you can hear me," I said. I squeezed my eyes shut. "I read your final notebook entry last night." I hitched a breath, and my eyes filled with tears. "It was so beautiful. *You* were so beautiful. I hope you know that." I smiled through my quiet cries. "You said goodbye to me last night, so it is only right that it is my turn to say goodbye to you today." I clutched the phone tighter. "Only I don't want to. Because, if this trip and your notebook have taught me anything, it's that I believe, with my entire heart and soul, is that you are with me." I sniffed and took a deep breath. My chest felt raw and sore.

"When you died, my entire world imploded. But now I feel you around me. I see you in the stars. I see you in my dreams. And now I'm talking to you on this phone."

I wiped my cheeks and stilled as a butterfly landed on a flower outside of the phone booth. It was once a caterpillar, transformed into a butterfly. That butterfly, as beautiful as it was, would only have a short life. But its beauty would remain in the memories of all who saw it.

"I love you more than all the stars in the sky, Poppy. I will never not grieve for all the time that you are missing for my life, yet I will cherish the blessings you gave to me while you were here." My cries ebbed and my breathing steadied. "Don't worry about us," I whispered, wanting her to be free. "Take care, my beloved sister. I adore you. I love you. And I will miss you every minute of every day," I said and then placed the phone back onto the holder.

The butterfly took flight, and I watched it soar on the breeze toward the sky until it had vanished out of sight. I closed my eyes and smiled, even more so when I smelled the sweet scent of vanilla taking up the space around me.

Then I opened the door to outside, seeing my friends, and the love of my life, all waiting, holding hands, proud expressions upon their faces. And I just knew, could feel it deep in my heart...

...I was going to be okay.

26

Silent Voices and Turning Points

Cael

THE PEACE ON SAVANNAH'S FACE AS SHE EXITED THE PHONE BOOTH WAS A double-edged sword. One the one hand, I was so proud, so full to the brim with happiness for my girl, that she had been brave enough to bare her soul to the sister she missed so much. So proud of how she was now, walking with her back straight and her chin held high. But on the other hand, it made me so damn aware of how much work I still had to do. Things I didn't want to face. Pain I didn't want to endure.

Leo's hand came on my shoulder. "Again, you don't have to, son."

Savannah's grip tightened in my hand. I glanced down at her. Her blue eyes were wide and full of conflict for me. I wanted to be better for her. Hell, I wanted to be better for *myself*.

"I can do it," I rasped, and Leo studied my face. After a few seconds, he nodded, but his eyes were cautious. I knew he was worried for me.

Just before I released Savannah's hand, she pressed a kiss to the back of it and stepped away. As I walked forward, I held on to the feel of her kiss, still branded on my skin. Walking to the phone booth was like walking the green mile. To me, the phone booth didn't look enticing but rather like my biggest fears made flesh.

I stopped at the door and forced myself to open it. The silence was deafening on the inside, the lack of sound piercing my ears like it was a painful high-pitched frequency. Then I placed my hand on the phone. It felt cold and hard. My chest began moving up and down. Too quick. My breathing was too fast. Sweat beaded on my brow, but I took a deep breath and made myself pick up the receiver. It shook as I brought it to my ear.

Just imagining Cillian on the other side, waiting for me to speak, crushed me. My voice became lost in my throat, and like it did so often, that night played in my head like a movie reel. Showed Cillian crashing in surround sound and in high definition. I tried to speak, but no sound came. And despite my effort, my knees buckled and I dropped to the ground. The phone hung off the shelf, swinging back and forth. I let it go, wanting to tell Cillian how much I loved him, how I missed him and how life without him, somedays, felt like no life at all. But all I saw was him broken in my arms...gone.

Gone.

My brother was *gone!*

I broke then. Racking sobs tore through my body and I couldn't stop them. Couldn't lift myself off the cold phone booth floor. The door flew open and Leo bent down. He helped me to my feet and took me to the path. But still the sobs didn't stop. Dylan flanked my other side, helping Leo carry me down the path and to the bus that waited for us. A familiar hand landed on my back, and I knew it was Savannah. That was my girl. Always there with a supportive touch. With her love and our shared two squeezes of our hands.

The journey back was a blur, time relinquishing itself to sadness. I couldn't say goodbye. I just couldn't say goodbye.

I wasn't ready to say goodbye.

Not yet.

Leo and Dylan helped me from the bus into my room. They laid me down on the bed, and before my head even hit the pillow, Savannah was wrapped around me. I breathed some then. I always did when she was near. But the sobs still came. They came until no tears fell down my cheeks and the sun had given way to the moon. Leo stayed in the room with us the entire time, letting me purge everything from my soul.

He eventually got up from his seat and said, "I just need to speak to Mia.

I'll be back in a minute. Will you be okay?" I nodded my head. I couldn't speak. My voice was lost.

When he left, Savannah immediately sat up. Her eyes were red with sadness.

"I'm so sorry, baby," she said. "Sorry that hurt you so much."

I stared into those blue depths and knew that if we were to have any kind of future, I needed to get better. "I love you," I said, just as a knock sounded on my door. Mia came through, Leo following behind.

"Savannah," Mia said, gently, "let's go and have some dinner."

"No." Savannah shook her head. I wanted to smile at her tenacity, but I couldn't muster enough energy to do it.

"You haven't eaten," Mia said. She then looked to Leo. "Let Leo and Cael talk some."

Savannah opened her mouth to argue, but I said, "Go on, Peaches." I met Leo's eyes. The look he gave me told me he needed to speak to me about something, something I wasn't sure I was going to like. "Get something to eat."

Savannah searched my face. "Are you sure?" her gaze dropped. "I don't want to leave you."

"I know, baby," I said, sitting up and cupping her face with my hands. I kissed her forehead, her cheeks, and finally her mouth. "I'll be okay. I promise," I said, praying those words were true.

"Okay," Savannah said, full trust in me. It made me feel a little stronger. She was still in this with me.

I watched her leave with Mia, heart breaking all over again, when she turned back and gave me a watery smile. When the door shut behind them, I turned to Leo. "I need that extra help when we get home," I said. "Today made me realize just how much farther I have to go."

Leo nodded, then said, "I suggest we leave now."

Shock and panic instantly surged through me. "Now?" I said, jumping off the bed. "I don't want to leave now. I don't want to leave Savannah. I want to travel home with her and the others. See this through until the end."

Leo came over to me, a wary expression on his face. "Son, I will never make you do anything you don't want to do, but I worry if you see Savannah again, or stay until the end, you won't go." I pictured Savannah's face, remembered her arms clasped around me, how she made me feel safe and like I could just lean on her forever... I exhaled in defeat. He was right. I *knew* he was right, but I just wanted to see her, one more time. I wanted to say goodbye. Make plans for when we were apart. How we would keep moving forward.

"Cael, do you love her?" Leo's question made my head snap up and pull me from my racing thoughts.

I met his eyes. "Completely," I replied. My voice was steady. My love for Savannah was the one thing I was certain of. Everything else had shaken me to my core. My love for Savannah was concrete.

"Then you need to leave now, son. To have any kind of future with her, you must keep going with therapy. This trip isn't enough. Right now, you're in a precarious place, and I'm advising we go immediately. I've seen what happens to people when they break and delay help." My stomach churned. That was Cillian. I didn't want to be like him. "Let me help you, Cael. Take my advice and let me help."

My heart was beating too fast and I couldn't focus. I didn't know what to do for the best. I wasn't sure I could leave Savannah. "You have a real chance at happiness, the both of you," Leo said, speaking straight to my heart. "Let's make Harvard, this fall, the goal. To be with Savannah again. When you're healed and can give her your everything."

I could see that. Us both happy and healthy, dealing with our grief at college—the college we were fated to be at together. I wanted that. I wanted that so much that it was suddenly all I could see.

He knew I was teetering, then pierced me when he said, "You don't want your love for her to be lessened by sorrow. You don't want her to have to share you with residual darkness. Come with me, let us help you, and then give her your entire—*healthy*—heart. Give her *you* entirely."

Those words knocked the air right out of my lungs. Savannah deserved the world. She deserved to be loved *totally*. Leo waited patiently for my response. "Okay," I finally rasped out, my heart breaking as I did. It wasn't what I wanted. I just wanted her... but I needed to heal.

I had to do that alone.

Leo exhaled in relief. "You've made the right decision, Cael. I'll give you ten minutes to pack your things. I'll go and make the final arrangements."

Leo left the room, and I stood on the spot for a few, silent minutes. I couldn't make my feet move, like they were protesting what I was about to do. But just thinking of making it to Harvard this fall, Savannah beside me as we lived happily and pain-free and didn't just exist…it had me moving in seconds. I threw my clothes into my bag and looked back on the room, on the impression of Savannah that was still on the bed. That girl loved me, and I would prove to her that I could be in this with her. One hundred percent. That although young, we could make it.

Seeing a hotel notepad on the desk, I ran over and wrote a note to my girl. I just hoped she understood. I was breaking our pact. I was keeping something from her again, leaving her without a goodbye. But as much as it hurt, as much as my soul was screaming at me to stay safe in her arms, this was important, to us *both*.

Taking my wallet off the desk, I stared down at it, feeling the heaviness of Cillian's note to me inside. Without overthinking, I yanked it out, gasping for breath when I saw his familiar handwriting and the seven words that had destroyed me for the past year. It had haunted me, plagued me and eaten away at me until I was nothing but a mangled mess. I didn't want to live that way anymore. I was *done* with it.

Welcoming one final surge of anger, I ripped the ticket into pieces and threw it on the ground. It was an albatross to my healing, a weight that was pulling me down.

Grabbing my bag, I walked out into the hallway and found Leo in reception. I immediately looked for Savannah. Maybe I could just see her face one more time. Just a glimpse. Maybe if I just got to kiss her one final time, I *would* have the strength to leave and not fall into her arms.

But she was nowhere in sight and, deep down, I knew that it was all untrue. I'd take one look at my girl and I'd fight to stay. I'd stay and suffer and things would only get worse for me, for her, until my pain consumed us both. She deserved to be free. She'd come too far for me to hold her back.

I just needed time to catch her up.

"Mia took them to a restaurant away from the hotel," Leo said. "They won't be back until we are long gone." My heart filled with sadness.

I forced myself to leave the hotel, my heart demanding to turn around. But I fought to get on the bus and sit next to Leo. In seconds, we pulled away from the hotel, and lit up, in the distance, was the phone booth. The phone booth that exposed me and showed Leo and Mia that, for me, the journey was only just beginning.

Taking out my cell phone, I resisted dialing Savannah's number and instead made a long-overdue call.

"Cael?" Dad's voice came over the speaker, and my chest felt like it was ripping apart as his familiar sound settled over me.

"Dad..." I said, voice croaked.

"What's wrong, son?" Dad's voice was panicked. I heard my mom in the background, expressing her worry too.

"I'm coming home," I said, and Leo put his hand on my shoulder in support. "I...I need more help. And I'm coming home."

Dad's voice hitched and he said, "We're proud of you, Cael. So proud." He paused, then said. "We'll see you at the airport. Have Leo send us the flight information. We're here for you, son. We're going to get you through this."

"Okay," I said and just stayed on the line for a little longer, just taking comfort in having my parents supporting me through the phone.

A couple of hours later, when we were waiting at the flight's gate, and I felt numbed by pain, my phone rang. My heart twisted when I saw it was Savannah. I ran my hand over the picture on my phone that was assigned to her face, and fought to not splinter apart.

"Peaches," I answered, my throat thick with guilt.

"You broke our pact!" she said, her sadness slicing through the phone. "You promised me you'd tell me everything. You didn't even say goodbye!" Savannah broke into tears, and I couldn't stand the sound of her breaking, breaking because of me.

I moved to the corner of the gate's lounge for privacy and let my own tears begin to fall. "Leo was worried about me. He needed me to leave for more help." I shook my head, trying to find the words to explain. "I couldn't do it, Savannah. I couldn't say goodbye to you. I'm breaking apart, baby. I'm not healing like I should be. I had to go—"

"That's not fair," she said, interrupting me, sobs racking her chest. "I would have supported you. But you should have said goodbye to me. Held me one last time. Let me kiss you and make sure you were okay. You've hurt me. You—"

"I WOULDN'T HAVE LEFT!" I found myself shouting, louder than I'd meant to, my wrought emotions rising to the surface and taking me over. I glanced behind me and saw several faces watching me. Leo included.

I pressed my forehead to the window and stared at the lights of the planes that were readying for takeoff. I calmed and felt the beat of my heart pounding in my chest. "If I'd seen you to say goodbye, Sav," I whispered over the torturous sound of her crying, "I wouldn't have been able to leave you." I swallowed and knew then that Leo had been right. Even now I was fighting running from the airport and back to the comfort of where she was. "And I have to." A sob ripped from *my* throat as I said, "I'm…I'm broken, Peaches. So fucking broken that I have to get help before it destroys me." My voice was barely audible. I felt exhausted. I was so tired of fighting.

Savannah was crying harder and harder into the phone. It shattered me. But it had to be this way. I knew it did. Deep down, I knew she did too.

I wiped tears from my cheeks and said, "I want a life with you, Savannah. I want to meet you in Harvard in the fall, stronger and able to function. I want us to have a chance—I *need* us to. You're the one thing that is keeping me going. But saying goodbye to you… I'm not strong enough to endure that, Peaches. I can never say goodbye to the love of my life." Savannah's breathing was labored from so much crying, but she was listening to me. "I love you," I hushed out. "Please believe me. I love you so much. You're my *everything*."

"Cael," Savannah said, her voice cracking. "I love you too. I love you… so much. I'm so sorry I shouted at you. I'm just… I'm going to miss you."

"I'll miss you too," I said, still feeling broken and like my heart was being split open. "I'm going into a residential program, so I don't know how much I'll be able to talk. But I'll call and text you every chance I get. I'll need you to help get me through."

"I'm so proud of you," Savannah said quietly, and it eased some of the pain threatening to take me down. "And I'll think of you every day."

"Harvard," I said, throat tight but speaking that goal out loud. "We'll meet again at Harvard."

"Harvard," she echoed, and a sense of peace settled over me. "I'll be counting down the days."

Leo tapped me on my shoulder, and I saw the plane was boarding. "I have to go," I said. I didn't want to get off the phone.

"I love you," she said. "Let me know you land safely."

"I love you too," I said, and it took everything I had to end that call. But I kept Savannah's face in my mind and her love in my heart and knew that they were strong enough to carry me through.

After a day of traveling, I landed at JFK. It was strange to see America's skies again. All I could think of was what Savannah was doing right then. They were traveling home today. But she would be in Georgia, and I would be in therapy.

I followed Leo through the airport and out into arrivals. It only took me a few seconds to find them. Without even getting my luggage, I ran through the crowd and slammed into the arms of my mom and dad. Tears sprung to my eyes, and I whispered, "I'm sorry. I'm so sorry."

"There's nothing to be sorry for," my mom said.

"Nothing at all," my dad said, voice barely audible.

I reared back and saw their eyes were red. But there was happiness on their faces too. Their son was back, and I didn't just mean in the physical sense. I might have still been healing, but I was closer to the boy I was before than the one who had been racked with grief.

Leo greeted my parents and explained to them what would happen next. I turned on my cell phone, and a single message came through.

PEACHES: I love you so much. Always remember that. I know you can do this.

I sighed deeply. Then I texted her back one simple word.

ME: Harvard

My mom linked her arm through mine, and we headed straight to the retreat. The hard work was just beginning, but the love I had for Savannah, for my mom, my dad, for *myself*...and for Cillian. The love I had for all of them would get me through.

And I would have Savannah back in my arms if it was the last thing I would do.

Homeward Hearts and Healing Souls

Savannah

As we began our descent, I pulled out the letter Cael had left me and read it one more time. At this point, it was committed to memory. But still, I read. Because it made me feel closer to him, even though he was miles away.

Peaches,

Please don't be mad that I left. But I have to go. To be the man I need to be for you, for me, I need to go with Leo.

Please don't think this means I'm leaving you. It's the opposite. I am going so that, when we meet again, nothing will separate us. So that nothing will get in our way, and we can have the future we dreamed of. You are the love of my life.

When I came on this trip, I was shattered into a thousand broken pieces. But one by one, the closer we grew to one another, you glued me back together. I'm not fully healed yet, but I am determined to do it for us.

I love you, Peaches. Give me time, and I will run back to you as quickly as I can.

I love you,
Cael

I put the letter down and took out my cell phone. I'd been so angry at him for leaving me without saying goodbye. After everything we'd been through, I felt he owed me that much. In that moment, he had broken my heart. But when I spoke to him…I heard it. I heard how shattered he was. But I also heard the determination in his voice.

I ran my finger over the text he had sent me.

CAEL: Harvard

I smiled and my heart swelled. That was what we were aiming for. I had started this trip wanting to heal enough to attend Harvard to become a doctor. It was still the goal, only this time it offered me so much more than I could have ever imagined. It now offered me a lifetime with Cael. A lifetime of loving him, of being by his side.

When the plane touched down in Atlanta, I sighed in happiness at the heat that gusted into the plane when the flight attendant opened the exit door. I turned on my phone. A text from Cael immediately came through.

CAEL: I'm here at the retreat. They take away our phones except for a few times a week. I'll message and call when I can. I love you and miss you.

My heart fluttered. I had total faith in him. If some time away from each other was the trade-off for keeping him forever, then I could happily live with that.

I deplaned and went to collect my luggage. The doors had barely opened into arrivals when I heard, "SAVANNAH!" I looked up just in time for Ida to come crashing into my arms.

I laughed as she jumped and threw her arms around my neck. I wrapped my arms around her and squeezed. We laughed, and the sound was a symphony to my ears.

My sister.

My little sister.

Ida smacked a kiss to my cheek. "I've missed you so much!" she said and moved back. Her mouth dropped open dramatically as she surveyed me. "You look incredible, Sav!" She leaned in close. "Is this because of Cael?"

I laughed at her suggestive face. I had missed her. And not just on this trip. I had missed her for four years. I hadn't let her in. That would change from now on.

"I've missed you," I said and pulled her back to me. "Sorry for not being there for you."

Ida inched back and met my gaze. Her eyes sparkled with unshed tears. "Are you back?" she asked tentatively.

"I'm back," I said, relief and promise in every word.

"I have my sister back!" she said dramatically, then kissed my cheek.

It felt glorious.

"Honey!" My mama's arms were safe and warm as she swallowed me in a hug, and my daddy wrapped his arms around us all, Ida too.

He kissed my hair. "All my girls, back on home ground." I knew he meant Poppy too, who was waiting for us in the Blossom Grove. Months ago, those words would have broken me. Now? They were perfection.

"Let's get you home," Mama said, and Daddy went and collected my luggage. I smiled as the Georgian sun kissed my face, the warm breeze wrapping around us as it whispered, "Welcome home."

Home. There was nothing quite like it.

In the car, Ida regaled me with every bit of her life since I'd been gone. As we entered the house, a million memories swirled around me. If I closed my eyes, I could almost hear the echo of three young girls laughing, chasing one another up the stairs. It was heavenly. My heart swelled when I realized I could walk in this home and feel comforted by the memories of Poppy here and not be paralyzed. It was once again my sanctuary, not my prison.

I showered and got changed out of my travel clothes, all the time wondering how Cael was doing at the retreat. I ached for what I knew he would go through, but I begged the universe to help him through. To make him stronger on the other side.

I left my room and went to make my way into the living room. Mama was cooking dinner, the smells filling the house. But as I passed Poppy's room, rather than walk on by, like I'd done so many times before, I opened the door. It was unchanged. I went to the window and looked outside. I knew this was where she had written in her notebook to me. I ran my hand over the seat and whispered, "Thank you."

As I opened my eyes, I laughed. When I looked through the window, Alton Kristiansen was sitting in the window seat of Rune's old room.

I waved, and he waved back looking like a mini-Rune, and for a moment, I almost felt like a young Poppy, looking out at the boy she adored. I ran my hand over her desk, her bed, and whispered, "Love you, Poppy."

I shut the door behind me. Ida was waiting in the hallway. "You okay?" she asked carefully.

"I am," I said, proud to say I was. There would always be a part of me that was sad because of losing Poppy. But that was loss. That was grief. We were always a little bit scarred. But we could move on. At whatever pace we needed.

"So, now you're back and we have all the time in the world, tell me *every* detail about Cael," Ida said. I had told her all about him when we had talked on the phone and through text. It had felt good, speaking to a sister like that again.

"He left early," I said, and Mama and Daddy listened in too. We sat at the kitchen table. "He needed to return to the States for more help."

"You had to pick the boy with the tattoos, didn't you?" my daddy said, bringing a smirk to my face. Ida laughed loudly at his description of the boy who held my heart in his palms.

"He's not just a boy with tattoos, *Daddy*," Ida said. "He's the love of her life!" My face burned under my parents' attention. They knew Cael and I were together. But only Ida knew just how much I loved him.

Daddy huffed, then said, "Is that true, baby? You love this boy?"

I sobered, thinking about Cael. How I wanted nothing more than to protect him from hurt and to live in his arms. "He's…" I trailed off, trying to explain. Then, with a knowing smile, I said, "He's my Rune."

My daddy's stern face fell into softness. My mama reached out and held my hand.

"That's so romantic," Ida said wistfully. "I want my own Rune too." Daddy glared at Ida, which brought a burst of laughter to my mouth.

"Why does he need more help?" my daddy asked. So I told them. I told them why Cael was there. I'd kept most of his story private out of respect for him. But they would meet him someday, I was sure. They would be a support to him too. To be that, they needed to know everything.

"Bless that boy," Mama whispered, sadness in her voice. Daddy reached across and held my hand. Silently supportive.

"He's strong and he's so brave. So kind and patient and loves me more than life," I said.

Ida laid her head on my shoulder. "He just needs more time."

I nodded. "He's hurting, but I know he'll get through it."

My family ate together, and we laughed. When the meal was done, I walked into the blossom grove and gasped. Each year was the same, yet each year made a brand-new tapestry out of the small, secluded grove. Petals of white and pink were in full bloom. And beneath them all was a white marble headstone, shining just as brightly. As I reached Poppy's grave, I smiled, seeing the picture of me and Rune in Kyoto taped to the bottom.

I sat down, allowing the warm breeze to dance around my hair. I sighed, then with unwavering doubt, said, "Poppy... I'm going to Harvard."

Healing

Cael
Massachusetts
End of summer

WEEKS UPON ENDLESS WEEKS HAD LED ME TO THIS. I WAS FINALLY HOME. I placed my hand on Cillian's bedroom door. I closed my eyes and breathed in deeply. All of the therapies, all of the daylong sessions with Leo, Mia, and the many psychologists that had guided me through my healing… it had led me here. The unwavering support and weekly visits from my mom and dad, the single hour I got to speak with Savannah for each week drove me to this new place of peace.

I was stronger, now. I breathed easier. I stood straighter, I wasn't angry, and most of all, I understood. I understood Cillian in a way that I never had before. I understood his crippling depression. I understood why he couldn't speak to me. It was difficult, but I understood.

He was my big brother. And I missed him. Would always miss him. But I had to move on too.

I took in a deep inhale, and with my hand on the handle, I turned it and entered his room. The sun shone in through the south-facing window. His bed was made; every inch of his furniture was clean. My mom kept it nice. I breathed in the room's air and could still feel him in here. He had been so vibrant and alive when he was here. It was like he'd left his imprint on this room.

On all of us who loved him most.

His bedroom walls were a shrine to hockey. I ran my fingers over his signed Bruins jersey, framed and protected by glass. Then I came to a stop at his Harvard jersey. The one he'd received on his first start in freshman year. I'd been at that game. I remember smiling so wide my cheeks ached.

Then I stilled when I saw the wall full of pictures of me and him. Months ago, this would have gutted me. I was still sad, seeing these pictures. Of us both happy, the promise of an amazing future in our wide smiles. But the thing that had captured my attention most was the old and age-frayed Bruins ticket that was pinned to his cork board.

The one that matched the ticket on which he had written his goodbye to me.

My stomach clenched. I had ripped it up. I had been so sick of feeling sad and, in a moment of anger, had ripped it up and left it in Japan.

I wished more than anything that I had that ticket now. Months of therapy had made all the bad that I saw within Cillian's death lighter. Seeing him crash, holding him in my arms... I sighed deep when my body broke out in shivers, the memory of that night still difficult. I would always think that way.

But therapy had helped me reframe things. Made me see that I'd had the privilege of being there with him at the end. I had been there with him when he had passed. I had held him in the aftermath as his soul moved on. And that ticket...that ticket was a happy memory that had meant so much to us, and now it was only made more special by his handwritten goodbye. That ticket had been a piece of him too. One that I deeply regretted leaving behind.

In the end, I was glad I was there with him as he left this Earth. I loved him enough to have wanted him to have had me close at the end. A brother who loved him more than life, there beside him as death claimed him. It was better, I thought, to have company as you passed.

I'd held on to that thought when the image of that night had tried to destroy me. I turned away from that wall, proud that I had faced coming back in here, when I came to a stop. Leaning against the wall was the stick that I had shattered all those months ago when Mom and Dad had told me I was going on the grief trip. Only now, the stick, wrapped again in Bruins colors—Cillian's stick—was repaired and gleaming in the sunlight.

I reached out to touch it, lifting it carefully in my hand. I could see where the cracks had been. But just like the plate Aika had made us smash in Japan, and then repair, it was even more special in the aftermath. It spoke of healing and forgiveness.

It spoke of me and Cill.

"I found it by the pond." I snapped my head up in surprise. My dad was in the doorway, Mom hovering close behind. They had been so worried about me. But they were lighter these days, seeing me better too. I couldn't imagine the pain they had gone through.

Dad stepped farther into the room. His eyes glistened as he looked over the walls. Mom let her tears fall. I used to believe this room was cursed. Tainted. But being in here again now…it was all Cillian. It was filled with the brother I missed. It wasn't anything to fear. It was…it felt like coming home.

Dad put his hands in his pockets. He had just come back from work, still wearing his cop uniform. "I had it repaired." He glanced at me shyly. "I thought you'd want it…someday. Maybe. I don't know…"

I ran my hand over the wood. Too many memories had been made with Cillian holding this stick. Me beside him, my big brother, my hero… "Thank you," I whispered.

I sank down on his bed, Mom sitting beside me. She wrapped her arm around me and looked up at the wall of pictures. "You two…" she said, laughing through tears. "I was gray in my thirties thanks to you two and hockey." I laughed and wiped at my eyes. "But I loved it at the same time," she said, holding me tighter. "Taking you both all over the state, getting up at the crack of dawn for practices…watching you both playing on the pond when you didn't know I was there." Mom sobered up. "When it's hard," she said, voice shaking, "that's what I hold on to. And I find happiness there. I can be happy there, in those memories."

Savannah's face entered my mind. It was the mention of happiness that had done it. I missed Savannah like I didn't know was possible. I missed her small hand in mine, missed her flushed cheeks when she was easily embarrassed. Missed her kiss and her thick southern accent.

I just missed her, period.

"Thinking about your girl again?" Dad said, and I huffed a laugh. I'd told them all about her. How could I not? She was all I thought of. When therapy had me on my knees, it was her face and weekly call that stopped me from crumbling. Her quiet strength, the way she had walked through grief with such dignity and grace.

That was my girl.

"I miss her," I said, and my mom held me tighter.

"We can't wait to meet her," Dad said. I liked the idea of that.

We stayed in Cillian's room for another hour. Reminiscing about the times we held closest to our hearts. We smiled and we cried, but as I walked out of the front door of the house, another weight had been lifted. Day by day, the shackles that had held me down had begun to loosen, and then they'd dropped away completely.

It was one day at a time, but each day I felt stronger and stronger.

I drove my Jeep to the place that was once my second home. I knew there was no practice today. And that it would be empty. Now that I'd come home, my old coach had said I could come and practice here whenever the rink was free. He was just happy I was me again and that I'd found my way back onto the ice.

The minute I was through the door, the cold wind and fresh scent of ice invaded my senses. I followed the hallway to the familiar locker room. I threw my bag on the bench and began to put on my practice clothes, then eventually my skates.

When I reached the entrance of the rink, I let the cold breeze bite at my face. Gripping my stick in my hands, I stepped onto the ice and exhaled with ease as I did. I circled the rink faster and faster until I felt like I was flying. I may have had a year of no practice, but this was muscle memory. It was what I was born to do.

You didn't forget that.

I stared out at the seats, picturing them full again, lights shining on the ice and music blasting from the speakers. I saw me and my team lining up, hands over our hearts and singing the national anthem.

I wanted it. I wanted that back so badly.

"Woods!" I opened my eyes and came to an abrupt stop. My heart beat faster as I saw Stephan Eriksson, my best friend skating toward me. Coach had told me no one would be here today. By Stephan's wide, shocked eyes, I presumed Coach had told him the same thing. It was just like him to throw us back together this way.

"You're back on the ice?" Stephan asked, voice laced with hope.

"Yeah," I allowed myself to say and felt that response down to my bones. I was back. "I'm back," I said, and Stephen jumped on me, wrapping his arms around my neck.

He held on just a little too long. "Glad to have you here again, brother," he said, and this time the term of endearment didn't hurt. Stephan had been my best friend for years. He had been my brother—still was.

"I'm sorry," I said, when he moved back. We stood alone on center ice. It was silent but for our breaths. "I'm so sorry—"

"You've got nothing to apologize for, yeah?" Stephan said, and I saw in his face that he meant it. I went to argue. That I had treated him like shit for too long. But he stopped me with his hand on my arm. "You got *nothing* to be sorry for, Cael. *Nothing*."

I nodded, throat thick with emotion. I couldn't speak. Stephan could clearly see that and skated backward. "So, Woods," he said tauntingly, "how about a little one-on-one? I can probably take you now that you're a little rusty."

My chest lifted with lightness and filled with warmth. I smiled wide. "It wouldn't matter if I hadn't played for ten years, Steph. I could still beat your ass anytime, anywhere."

Stephan laughed and brought us back a puck. I stretched out my arms and neck and then I played against my best friend like we'd had no break. For hours we played. We laughed. I smiled. I breathed long, painless breaths.

I won every game.

And more importantly, I had a future to get back hold of. I promised my girl we would meet again.

I wasn't going to let her down.

29

Surprise Guests and Connected Hearts

Savannah
Harvard University
Fall

"MAKE SURE TO DO THE READING FOR NEXT WEEK!" THE PROFESSOR shouted over the mass of people packing away their notes and scurrying out of the door.

"I think I've bitten off more than I can chew," Cara, my new roommate, said.

"You can do this," I said, putting my bag over my shoulder and heading out of the building. College had just begun. We'd had a week of orientation, and today was the first day of classes. But better yet, I was going to see Cael again soon. Just as I had arrived, the hockey team left for an off-campus training camp. He had told me he was back today, and I was counting down the seconds until I saw him again.

We had talked every day since he left the retreat, and I could hardly breathe with how badly I wanted to see him again. To have him wrap his strong arms around me and pull me to his chest.

I was nervous too. It had been months since he had left Japan. Since we had kissed or held one another close. I'd missed him so much at times I felt like boarding a plane to see him. But I knew he needed to focus and that I'd see him again at college.

I could barely believe I would see him again in a matter of hours.

We walked to the hallway and left the building, entering the beauty that was Boston in the fall. It was so beautiful it didn't seem real. I checked my cell phone to see if he had called. There was nothing yet. I put my phone in my pocket, then looked up and stopped dead in my tracks. My heart fired off into a sprint, when, down the stairs, standing against a tree in the courtyard, was Cael. He was searching all around him, looking for someone… looking for *me*, I realized. Students muttered as they had to squeeze past my statue-like state, but I couldn't move, too shocked at seeing Cael again right before me.

"Savannah? What—" Cara said, but then her words died off into silence. Then she said, "That's Cael Woods." But my eyes were locked on the boy who had stolen my heart from the moment I had laid eyes on him. The boy who had held that heart in his hands for months, keeping it safe until I was back in his arms.

Cael was dressed in sportswear. Sweatpants and a jacket. My breathing stuttered in happiness when I saw it was a jacket that read *Crimson Hockey*. His tattoos snuck up his neck and out of the collar, his dark hair short at the sides and messy on top…then he found me and I met his eyes.

Cael's stare melted when our gazes finally collided. And like I had been a boat adrift at sea, I found an anchor in his eyes, his very presence. On shaking legs, I never broke eye contact as I began running down the steps and across the courtyard to where he stood.

Tears built in my eyes as I drank him in with my every step. He was here. Cael was really *here*. He didn't hesitate and set off to run for me too, and unable to be parted for one more second, we landed in each other's arms, chests meeting and arms wrapping around the other like we would never let go. I held on tight, my soul soaring now that I was back in his embrace.

"Peaches…" Cael murmured into my neck, and I almost broke at hearing that Boston brogue saying that word—*my* word.

"Baby," I whispered back and pulled him tighter, so impossibly tight we merged into one single form in the college courtyard.

Cael reared back and I studied him up close. It was like seeing the most glorious sunrise after too many nights of darkness. "I've missed you, Peaches," he said with his graveled voice, and I felt the truth of those words in every inch of my heart. "God, I've fucking *missed* you."

Cael dropped his forehead to mine and laced our fingers together. "I've missed you too," I said, barely able to find my voice, too overcome with happiness, his sea-salt and fresh-snow scent making him feel like home.

Cael inhaled, then kissed my cheeks, my forehead, and, seeking out my eyes for permission—which was more than given—then kissed my lips. As he did, the pain of his long absence fell away. My Cael was *kissing* me. He was *here*.

I kissed him back, sinking against him as he kissed me deeply, honestly and true. And as he kissed me, I sensed a new lightness within this boy who I loved with my very being. His kisses were searching but loving. They were optimistic, not laced in sadness and desperation.

A tear escaped the side of my eye as he pulled me even closer. I was safe in his arms once again. And he was safe in mine.

Cael broke from the kiss. "I love you, Savannah," he rasped, and I felt that love radiating from his soul.

I placed my hand on his cheek. "I love you too. I missed you so much."

Cael inched back. He studied my face like it was a Renaissance painting. Then his gaze shone with nerves. "Please will you come tonight?" he said, vulnerability in his voice.

"What's tonight?" I asked.

"An open scrimmage," he said and released one of my hands to run his fingers through my hair. My eyes closed at his touch. "I want you there." He swallowed. "It's the first event the team is doing outside of closed practice." He breathed in deeply, then exhaled slowly. I took hold of his hands and squeezed twice. Our secret sign. A smile, so blinding, lit up his face and rivaled the sun.

Lord, he was beautiful.

"I wouldn't miss it for the world," I said and laid my head against his chest. Cael exhaled, seemingly in relief. The sound of his racing heart brought butterflies to my chest.

I had him back. We were back together.

His hand kept running through my long hair, like he couldn't bear to not be touching me somehow after all this time apart.

He then cupped my face and kissed my lips. "I can't believe you're here, in front of me. It doesn't feel real," he said, and I smiled, turning my head and pressing a kiss to his palm.

"It's real," I said, threading my arms around his waist. "*We're* real."

Cael swallowed me in a hug. He towered over me, and I felt so safe in his embrace. I never wanted to break away, wanted to stay this way, always. "Harvard," he murmured, for me only, recognizing out loud that we'd reached our goal.

"Harvard," I whispered back, feeling overcome with emotion.

When Cael pulled back, he reluctantly said, "I have to go now, but…"

I didn't want to let him go. "Cael!" I looked over Cael's shoulder to see a blond boy calling him over. Cael lifted his hand, a gesture that he was on his way.

"That's Stephan, my best friend and teammate. We have a team meeting we have to get to." My heart squeezed in my chest, not that he had to leave so soon but that he had welcomed Stephan back in his life. I was so proud of him I could have burst apart.

Cael backed up, neither of us willing to tear our gazes away from the other until he was too far from sight and I had to turn away. I felt shell-shocked; my heart was racing so fast I felt lightheaded.

I was so unbelievably happy.

Cara stepped beside me. "You're dating Cael Woods?" she said, sounding more than a little starstruck. I forgot she was from around here. And was a hockey fan.

Turning to Cara, my heart feeling so full I could barely breathe, I said, "Do you want to come to an open scrimmage with me tonight? The love of my life will be on the ice."

The stadium was about half full, which Cara told me was normal for an open scrimmage. I searched the rink for Cael but couldn't find him. Just then, I saw him step out of the tunnel and hit the ice. Number eighty-seven stood proudly on his back. My heart was in my throat as I watched him skate around the rink, picking up speed with every new stride.

It was surreal seeing him like this. I knew he played hockey. We had talked about it endlessly when he got out of his therapy program and had been given his spot back on Harvard's roster for this year. He had even sent me links to some of his old games when I had expressed my desire to see them. But now that I was here, feeling the cold from the ice hit my face was different from what I ever could have imagined.

I saw Cael searching the crowd. I knew when he had seen me, as he slowed right down as he passed me. He met my eyes and I smiled at him. He smiled back. He was so perfect.

A coach blew a whistle and Cael moved into position. I was the first to admit I had no idea what was happening in the scrimmage. I was trying to learn the rules, had spent too many nights this summer trying to read up on them. I'd get there eventually. For now, I just sat in awe watching Cael in his element. Even though I didn't understand the game, anyone could tell that Cael was a step above the rest—he was faster and more dynamic, and he sank shot after shot into the net, looking as though he could go all night and never tire.

I was breathless as I watched him. None more so when he would laugh, smile, and celebrate with his teammates. He was happy here. And he had done it. He had healed. This boy on the ice was a far cry from the boy who I had last seen in Japan. If it was possible, seeing him like this made me love him even more. Like Aika had told him, he'd had the tenacity to fix himself back together, and he was even more beautiful than ever before.

As the scrimmage came to an end, the awed faces of the fans watching Cael cool down screamed to me just how talented he was and how, if he had never found himself back to this game, it would have been a travesty.

Cael came over to where I was seated. I stood and moved to the boards. "Baby..." I said, shaking my head, unable to put words to my feelings. Cael's cheeks flushed in embarrassment under my praise. It was so adorable, I wanted to kiss him and never stop.

"Meet me outside the lockers?" he asked, and I nodded. As much as I had enjoyed seeing him scrimmage, I wanted to talk to him and spend hours back by his side.

"I'll head back to the dorms," Cara said. I nodded at her and followed the signs to the locker rooms. I stood outside in the hallway and waited for Cael to come out. Some other people were waiting, greeting different players as they left the locker room.

Cael walked out with the boy I now knew was Stephan. Cael's searching eyes found me immediately. He rushed to where I stood and wrapped his arms around me. He crushed me to his chest, his damp hair from his shower sticking to my cheek. I laughed, and at the sound, Cael squeezed me just a bit tighter.

A throat cleared behind us. Cael released me, and Stephan stood there. With his blond hair and blue eyes, he reminded me of Rune. "This is the famous Savannah?" he asked, and I felt my cheeks blaze at his words. Stephan hit Cael's chest. "I love the guy, but if I have to hear about you one more time, my head might just explode."

"Dick," Cael said but laughed at his friend.

Stephan winked at me. "Anyway, it was nice to meet you, Savannah." Stephan hugged Cael. "I'll see you back at the dorm."

Cael threw his arm around my shoulders and kissed my temple. "Come with me, Peaches. We have some catching up to do."

Cael

I led Savannah out toward my car in the parking lot. I threw my bag in the Jeep, then held out my hand. Savannah took it without hesitation. "Walk with me?" I asked.

"Anywhere," she said, smiling. Fuck. I couldn't believe she was here with me. It felt like a dream. I'd focused on her for so long, all those long hard days at the retreat. Especially on the hardest days, when I didn't think I could do it anymore, it was Savannah's face and her phone calls that kept me strong.

When she shivered against the first chills of fall, I ran back and took a jacket out of the trunk of my car. It reminded me how she had struggled in the Lake District and Norway, my Georgia Peach needing her sun. I held it out, and Savannah laughed when she put it on and it drowned her petite frame.

I couldn't imagine her looking more perfect than she did with my name on her back. We cut through campus in comfortable silence and made our way to a brightly lit park. We sat on a secluded bench, only a few dog walkers milling about the pathways nearby. I squeezed her hand, bringing her fingers to my mouth. I kissed her. I couldn't stop.

She was here.

She was *actually* here.

"Cael—" She went to say something, but I spoke before she could.

"It was so hard, Sav." The adrenaline from tonight was waning, and fatigue was settling in.

Savannah inched closer, and I turned to her. She was already watching me. I couldn't take my eyes off her, like she was some mirage I had conjured up in therapy and if I looked away, she'd disappear.

"I'm here," she said. But it was like my heart needed to understand she wasn't some fever dream. My girl was in Boston; we were here together. Ready to start our lives together.

I inhaled deeply and said, "It was so hard. But I had to get better. For you, for us, I had to—"

"No," Savannah said, shaking her head. "Not better, Cael. You were *healing*. You were grieving. There is no better or worse to that. It just is. Your heart was broken, and you were mending it, day by day. And you have succeeded." She put her hand on my cheek and made me meet her tenacious blue stare. "You never needed to get better for me. You were always enough. Even when you were deep in the trenches. You were *always* enough."

Hell, had there ever been anyone who had fought for someone more than this girl had fought for me?

"I'm the luckiest guy on the planet. Do you know that?" I said and kissed Savannah's cold cheek. I closed my eyes, just feeling her against me. "I get to live my life with you, Peaches. I get to give you my heart—as patched up and as scarred as it is." Her lip wobbled, and I ran my thumb over it, blue eyes shining. "You have it, and I get to have your beautiful heart and soul in return." I pointed at myself. "Luckiest guy."

"We both are," she said and smoothed my hair back from my face. It was still damp from my post-game shower. Savannah smiled, and I knew I'd give her the entire world to make her stay that way. "We are alive, we are stronger, and we are together. That's what makes us lucky. That…" She trailed off and looked up at the stars beginning to shine.

I followed her line of sight, then asked, "That what?"

Savannah turned back to me. Her dimples popped as she smiled, and I wanted to commit how she looked right now to memory. "That we have walked a rough path to get to this happiness. And because of that, we will never take our life together for granted." My heart pounded. Because everything she said was true. Savannah kissed the back of my hand. Over my tattooed heart. She ran her hand over the black ink, then looked back at me and said, "We have lost. We know what it is to grieve and miss someone so badly we can't breathe. But because of that loss, we will love deeper, support each other further, and show up for one another harder. Loss teaches us how to cherish love. That is our future, Cael. Loving one another in the best way we know how—completely."

"I love you, Savannah. I'll never stop telling you that."

She smiled. "And I'll never stop accepting it." I laughed, and Savannah followed, the heaviness breaking apart into light pieces around us.

When our laughter fell away, she said, "I have something for you. But I don't know if it's a good or bad thing. I don't know if I've done the right thing."

The trepidation in her voice was evident. "Nothing you could do would be bad, baby," I said. Yet the worried expression on Savannah's face remained. She searched my eyes, then put her hand into her pocket. When she raised her hand, in the center of her palm, was Cillian's goodbye to me, his apology scribbled down on my treasured old Bruins ticket. The one that I had destroyed in Japan.

Only this ticket had been carefully reconstructed with golden lacquer. My breathing came heavy as I stared at this beautifully patched-up ticket lying in Savannah's gentle hand.

"I found it when you left." Her voice was quiet and filled with emotion. "When you'd gone... I went in your hotel room just because..." Savannah swallowed. "I saw your note to me, and then I saw this on the floor, ripped up. When I placed the pieces back together, I realized what they were. I immediately took it back to my room and fixed it back together with the kintsugi kit Aika had given us." She blinked then, meeting my eyes. "I'm sorry if I overstepped. I just thought—"

I crushed my mouth to Savannah's, cutting off whatever she was about to say. She had done this for me. She had taken my biggest regret and made it right. And she had made it more beautiful, because she had fixed it out of love for me. Out of love for my brother, who she had never met.

When I broke from her kiss, breathless and so fucking grateful for my girl, I whispered, "Thank you. Thank you so much, baby."

I took the ticket, which was safe inside a clear plastic envelope, and placed it in my pocket. I had it back. I had a piece of my brother back with me again. The relief was overwhelming.

"This is it," I said to Savannah.

"What?" she asked, leaning into my side, her head on my bicep. I couldn't resist dropping a kiss to her head.

"The start of our forever," I said and felt hope run through my veins. It felt so good that it was heady.

"Forever," Savannah echoed.

"We're here, at college together. I get to see you every day. I get to play hockey, get to be myself again. And you...you get to be a doctor, baby. I get to be your guy..."

"I get to be your girl," she said, happiness in her tone.

"And we get to live life together."

Life. The strangest ride of ups and downs and heartache and loss. But also, a life with the world, the stars and the sun, joy and love.

And of course, love. Love above most.

30

Honor Laps and Hopeful Stars

Savannah
Harvard College
Seven weeks later

THE STADIUM WAS PACKED. I STARED, WIDE-EYED, AT THE CROWD, ALL dressed in red. Music was blaring, and the excited shouts of students were deafening. I clutched on to Cara like my life depended on it.

This was Cael's world. The scrimmage was nothing compared to this. Being on the trip had made this part of who he was so distant, almost conceptual. But this was his arena. My nerves were high, and I had to take long breaths to settle them down. When we reached our seats, we had a perfect view of the rink. Lights danced on the ice to the rhythm of the song playing.

An announcer spoke stats as I waited with bated breath to see Cael take the ice. He was feeling anxious about this game. I'd had to meet him behind the stadium an hour ago…

"I'm nervous," Cael said and ran his hand through his hair.

"You're going to do great," I said, trying my hardest to quell his nerves.

Cael closed his eyes and tipped his head back to the sky. He was focusing on the stars, and I knew he was fighting back tears. His eyes were shining when he met my gaze again. "I just always thought he'd be here, you know. In this moment." Cael sighed. "I suppose it just hit me again that he's not."

I pointed at the stars. "He's here," I said, and his face softened.

Cael wrapped his arms around me. "I don't know what I'd do without you, Peaches," he said and kissed my lips. His team taking to the ice to warm up sounded behind him. "I have to go."

"I'll be in the stands," I said, and Cael nodded his head. He gave me a small smile, and I prayed he would get through this first game…

I blinked back to the here and now, and a million thoughts ran through my head. All about Cael. Enough so that, in what felt like no time at all, the music lowered and the announcer began to speak.

I focused on that tunnel where they came out. Then suddenly, the lights dimmed, and the announcer said, "Tonight, this game will be played in honor of Cillian Woods, our former star center who sadly passed away. Here to take a lap in remembrance, in his honor, is his younger brother and newest center for the Harvard Crimson, Cael Woods."

Everything seemed to stop in that moment—the music, my breathing, my heart. My stomach turned, and a heady mix of sorrow and pride swirled within me. The crowd got to their feet, clapping in support as Cael, without his helmet and gloves and wearing a black arm band around his bicep, took to the ice and began to skate for Cillian. For the brother he loved so much, but had lost so young, so tragically…

I gasped when Cael skated in the opposite direction, and I was given a view of his back. Because the boy I loved, who I had given my whole heart to, was no longer wearing number eighty-seven on his jersey. Now, number thirty-three was printed on his shirt.

Cillian's number.

He was skating for Cillian.

He was honoring his brother in the best way Cael knew how.

A quiet sob ripped from my throat as I watched him slowly skate around the rink, his stick held in the air, a tribute to his big brother, a man who should have been here to skate beside him. This was why Cael had been so nervous earlier. He was going to honor Cillian on the ice that they both adored so much.

I believed Cillian was here, right now, chilly wind flowing through their hair, his arm around Cael's shoulder like I'd seen him do in that picture so many months ago.

Cara had joined me at the game and put her arm around me just as the rest of the Harvard team took to the ice, skating in Cillian's honor too—a team mourning one of their own. I watched as Cael approached where I stood. My hand covered my mouth as he drew closer.

"Cael…" I whispered as he stopped in front of me. His eyes were streaming with tears, and he pressed his hand to the glass before me. I reached out and touched it too, like there wasn't glass between us, and our palms kissed. He dropped his forehead to it—I did the same. I shed tears for the man I had never met but already missed so much. And I cried for the boy I was madly in love with, who was sharing his pain with the world, to honor the brother he missed so much.

When he pulled back, I mouthed, "I love you. I'm so proud of you."

"I love you too," Cael said, then made his way to the tunnel. I kept my hand on that glass as he came out again to play. And I never looked away from him as he flew around the ice like he was born with steel blades on his feet and a stick in his hands.

He played with his whole heart.

He honored the brother he lost.

Cael scored four goals.

And Harvard won.

For Cillian.

Cael

Adrenaline was surging through my veins as I sat down at my locker in the changing room. I tipped my head back and closed my eyes, hearing the team celebrate our first win of the season. Sweat dripped down my back, and my heart thundered in my chest.

We had won. We had won for Cillian. I turned my head, like he was here beside me. I'd felt him beside me on that ice tonight. After he'd passed, I'd felt robbed of our future playing together. But he was there tonight, I *knew* it. And one thing I'd learned over this past year was that Cillian would always be with me, as he was a part of me. Not even death could take that away.

I smiled as I pictured him beside me. *You did it, little brother. You did it! We did it*, I would say. *We did it, like we always planned.*

A hand landed on my shoulder. I looked up to see my coach. The whole team was looking at me. Most I knew. They were Cillian's friends. And by the tears in most of their eyes, they felt him here with us too.

"This game puck belongs to you, son," Coach said, and I took it from him. I wasn't one for words, so I simply stood, kissed the puck, and held it up to the heavens.

This one's for you, Cill. This one's for you.

I walked out of the changing room and smiled when I saw Savannah waiting for me. She was huddled against the wall alone making herself as small as possible, her friend clearly having gone home. She would always be my highly introverted girl. The look of relief and pride on her pretty face and bright blue eyes when she saw me nearly knocked me over.

As soon as I went to her, I scooped her up in my arms. She melted against me and whispered, "I...I don't have the words for tonight, baby. I..." She tipped her head back and said, "I'm just so proud of you. And your new jersey number, how strong you were..." She shook her head when words escaped her.

"I love you too, Peaches," I said, and she cast me a shaky smile just before I kissed and kissed her, not wanting to ever stop.

"Cael?" A familiar voice cut through me kissing my girl. I laughed when I turned, and my mom and dad stood there, amusement on their faces. Savannah must have seen the family resemblance, as she instantly turned red with embarrassment.

"I take it this is the famous Savannah?" my dad said and held out his hand to Savannah.

"Yes, sir," Savannah said, melting me with her shyness and impeccable southern manners.

Dad shook her hand, but my mom stepped closer and wrapped Savannah up in a hug. I didn't miss it when she whispered "Thank you. Thank you for helping save my son," into Savannah's ear.

Savannah held my mom back, tightly, then said, "It's so nice to meet you, ma'am." She gave me a shy smile. "I love your son very much. He helped save me too."

This girl...

"We'll leave you two alone," Dad said, then hugged me, hard. "I've never been so proud of anyone in my entire life, son," he said, making my throat clog up.

Mom came to me next and said, "She's beautiful, Cael. So gorgeous and sweet." I couldn't wait for my parents to get to know Savannah. Mom stepped back and took tight hold of my dad's hand. "I'm making dinner this Sunday." She turned to Savannah. "We'd love for you to come, sweetheart."

"I'd love to. Thank you, ma'am," she said and fucking destroyed me again. I could not love this girl more if I tried. Mom and Dad had given me space while I settled into college. But I wanted them at my first game. And I really wanted them to finally meet the girl who'd saved me.

To think I'd resisted Leo and Mia's trip all those months ago. Fought it with all I was. But the universe had set me on a journey to heal. And it had brought me to my girl, to the other half of my heart, my soulmate. I would strive every day to make her happy, to make her proud. And we'd walk through life holding each other's hands, with our siblings walking beside us, their hands on our shoulders showing us the way.

And we'd be happy.

We'd be together.

And we'd forever live in honor of those we have lost.

EPILOGUE
Under Stars and Forever Skies

Savannah
The Lake District, England
Eight years later…

"IT LOOKS DIFFERENT IN THE SUMMERTIME," I SAID TO CAEL AS WE WALKED hand in hand along a familiar shoreline. Lake Windermere spread out before us, a sparkling pool of diamonds. Night was closing in, England's summer-light nights giving the lake an ethereal glow.

Cael squeezed my hand, and I peered up at him and smiled. He was so handsome. Not a day went by that I didn't thank the stars for bringing him to my life. Especially of late. In true fashion, life had thrown another loss into our path.

Rune.

Living the life he'd always dreamed, as a photographer. He had been in a war zone, capturing the conflict on film, when a stray missile had hit his hotel, taking him from us too. Cael had held me through the pain of losing another loved one. But this time, although it hurt, I didn't crumble. Because I knew Rune was back with Poppy, reunited with his soulmate in their blossom grove, happy once again. It was the biggest comfort to think of them that way. No longer separated by life but together, where they always should have been.

I cuddled into Cael's arm as he led us to a familiar-looking jetty. Only instead of a rowing boat nearby, a small boat with a motor awaited. I laughed as Cael offered his hand. "Miss Litchfield," he said, all prim and proper, which made me laugh harder. He was so playful. Humorous in his own quiet way.

"I remember this," I said, and Cael lifted me up by my waist. Before he placed me in the boat, he kissed me first. I sat down, Cael quickly climbing in behind me and turning on the engine.

"It's where it all began, Peaches," he said, a knowing glint in his eyes. It all seemed so long ago. That fated trip around the world. I had just finished med school and was moving onto my residency training. I was ever closer to becoming the doctor I always wanted to be. And I loved it. It was hard, and often emotional, but I came home to the safety of Cael, and he made everything better. On the days I would break, he was there to hold me.

Cael had stayed at Harvard only two years before entering the NHL draft. He now played for the Bruins, made the All-Stars each season, and was the standout player of Team USA. He was exceptional, and I loved nothing more than watching him play—it was like seeing true freedom.

Our life was in Boston, and I couldn't be happier. We visited Georgia often. Ida was living her own life, happy and still as gregarious as always. My family adored Cael and, of course, I had to go back to see Poppy...and now Rune, who lay beside her in their blossom grove.

"It feels strange to not have the others waiting in the hostel back on shore," I said, and Cael nodded. We had kept our promise. Our group from the trip met up once a year. They were some of our very best friends. Especially Travis and Dylan, who had found their way to one another's arms in the years that followed. Lili and Jade were married to amazing men. Lili was now pregnant with her first child.

I couldn't have been prouder of everyone.

"We'll invite them next time," Cael said, and I watched as his silver-blue eyes matched the hue of the full moon that hung above us. The years had only been kind to Cael. He was broader through hockey, and still covered with tattoos, my favorite being the peach tree that now lay over his heart.

And the kintsugi-style golden line that ran over the broken-heart tattoo on his hand—a heart that was no longer broken.

I closed my eyes and smiled as the warm breeze washed over me. This place was magical to us both. It was where we had begun to fall in love. When we were heartbroken and weak, this place had been the genesis of us and our journey to strength.

Our journey to each other.

Our journey to the healing power of love.

I couldn't help but picture Cael back then. Dressed in all black, black beanie on his head and his messy hair that I thought was perfect. Today, he was wearing navy-blue cargo shorts and a white button-up. His sleeves were rolled up to his elbows, showcasing his mass of intricate tattoos over his muscled forearms. He looked beautiful. I was in a blue summer dress. Cael loved me in blue. He said it matched my eyes.

"Peaches…" Cael said, and I opened my eyes.

My heart began to race when I was met with Cael on one knee, holding a ring in his hand. I covered my mouth in shock. Cael's eyes swam with happy tears, and I fought to breathe.

"Savannah," he said, voice hoarse. "When we came here years ago, we were both broken. We both felt there was no way back to happiness." I saw the flash of sadness those words brought up in Cael's gaze. "But we didn't know we would find each other on this trip. We didn't know we would find our soulmate and the other half of our heart outside of the States and across the world." Cael smiled as tears began to stream down my cheeks. "That trip changed my whole life. It taught me to live, to be strong, but mostly, it taught me to love, even through pain. And I have, Peaches. I have loved you more than I ever thought possible. You are my reason for breathing. You make me happier than I could have ever dreamed. You are the greatest thing in my life, and I wanted to ask…if you'd do me the honor of being my wife."

Everything stilled—the birds, the swaying branches, my heart, as he uttered the two most precious words, "Marry me."

My world filled with light as I reached out and kneeled before him. As I cupped his perfect, handsome face and pressed my lips to his. "Yes," I said, nodding, crying, overcome with so much happiness. "Yes, it's absolutely a yes." With shaking hands, Cael pushed the blue sapphire and diamond ring on my finger and it sparkled in the twilight.

"I waited so long to do this as I wanted to give you space for your studies without the pressure of a wedding. But honestly, baby, I couldn't wait one more day to have a ring on your finger and truly make you mine. Officially."

"I love you," I said. There wasn't a person on this planet who understood me more than this man.

Then he blew me away when he said, "I wasn't at a training camp last weekend." I furrowed my brows in confusion. "I was in Georgia asking your daddy for permission to marry his baby girl."

"Cael…" I said, heart melting.

"I wanted to do this right," he said and brushed my hair from my face. He pulled me to him, my back to his chest, wrapping his strong arms around me. "I want you as my wife so badly I almost can't stand it."

And I could just see it now. We would get married. I would be a doctor and Cael would continue living his dream with hockey. Then we would have a family and be so happy that there wouldn't be a single day wasted in our lives. We would love each other with our entire hearts and make the most of our brief time on this earth. Life had taught us not to take a single day for granted, and to not waste a minute.

"I love you," I said again, turning to kiss him and filled with so much happiness I almost couldn't take it. He kissed me thoroughly, deeply and with so much adoration I knew our love would never fade. Just like the stars, I thought, looking up at them now. I used to look up at Orion's Belt and think it represented Poppy, Ida, and me. Now, when I looked at it, I saw Poppy, Rune, and Cillian, looking down at us, watching us live, showering us with their celestial love too.

And then there was the north star. For Tala.

"They're celebrating up there now too, you know that, don't you?" Cael said, looking at the stars too. Because I did. Losing a loved one, no matter the circumstances, was the most heartbreaking thing a person could endure. But living for them, loving them even after loss, was healing too. Because they would always be around us, wanting us to live with all our hearts. Wanting us to love and wanting us to live a life so full, there would be no room for regrets when our time to pass arrived.

I had that with Cael. A life so sweet I could never want anything more. I was happy. Truly happy. And I was holding onto that with both hands.

And we knew Poppy and Cillian were right by our sides. So, we lived and loved in their honor. In their legacy. And love Cael I did, more than I ever thought possible. I was going to be his *wife*. He was going to be my husband. Never had two words sounded so beautiful.

And I couldn't wait for the rest of our life to begin.

The ~~End~~ Beginning

Acknowledgments

When I wrote *A Thousand Boy Kisses*, it was born from years and years of watching my closest family members suffer with cancer. That awful disease plagued my grandparents, my parents, and my father-in-law. After losing my grandparents and father-in-law, I wanted—no—*needed*, to exorcise all the pent-up pain and bitterness for the disease that had built up over the years. It had taken three much-loved people from my life. Luckily, my mam was in remission, but my father was still suffering with it. His cancer was incurable. It was a constant battle for him, but he braved it every single day.

When I began to write all my feelings about loss and living and embracing whatever hardships face us, *A Thousand Boy Kisses* was the end result.

I never planned to write a sequel. I played around with a few ideas, but nothing was calling to me like Rune and Poppy's story had called to me. The world I'd created in Blossom Grove, Georgia felt complete. I had put my heart onto those pages and shared my pain with the world. I had done what I set out to do.

And then the unthinkable happened. I lost my dad. For as long as he suffered with an incurable cancer, in the end, his death was quick and unexpected. Another form of cancer had grown within him (that we hadn't known of) and took him from our lives in the blink of an eye.

To say I was heartbroken is an understatement. Grief like I had never experienced burrowed within me and dragged me down so deeply, I felt like

I couldn't breathe. I had known loss. But I had not known parental loss. I had known pain but not the searing pain that is your dad, your *safety*, being ripped from your life.

Afterwards, months passed me by, as I was just trying to find some semblance of life again. And as a writer, as a creative, a new story began building within me. As I contemplated my "new" life without Dad, a new question began to form in my head: What happened to the people Poppy left behind? My thoughts immediately went to Savannah. The quieter sister. The one who loved softly but cared immensely.

I suffer from chronic anxiety and write as a form of therapy. And as I began to write, Savannah and Cael's story poured from my fingers. A story of loss and grief and missing a loved one so much that it makes you feel like you can never be happy again.

But you will be. My journey through grief, and what I have tried to show within this book, is that gradually, you *do* begin to live again. You begin to remember not just the sad parts of losing your loved one but the happy times you shared with them too. When I wrote this book, I wanted this so badly for Savannah and Cael because I knew my dad wanted that for me too. He wouldn't want us to fall apart. He would want us to heal as best we could and live *for* him.

A Thousand Broken Pieces was the hardest book I have ever written because it is based on the most difficult time of my life. But it also became a huge source of comfort for me too. Watching Savannah and Cael slowly rebuild, face their grief, and work through it and all its pain became inspiring to me. I hope that, for those who have loved and lost, this book has helped you in some small way too. It gave me a safe place to grieve, and for that, Savannah and Cael will always have a special place in my heart.

I bared my soul on these pages. I just hope I did my dad proud. It was truly all in his name.

To get to this point, where *A Thousand Broken Pieces* is out in the world, it took an army of people. I may have written this book to help my own grief journey, but without the support and love of all those around me, it would never have come to be.

Firstly, I want to thank my husband. The amount of tears shed writing this book was unprecedented and you were beside me every step of the way, holding me up when I was unsure I could keep going. You are my rock. I love you to pieces.

You're my Rune.

My children. You have given me a reason to keep going. When things were dark and I was broken, you lifted me up. You made me smile and laugh when I didn't think I would smile again. I love you both so much. You're my everything.

Mam. What a time it has been. As always, you have been a pillar of support through it all. And I know you have probably dreaded reading this book because of what it meant to me—to all of us. But I hope I did you proud too. I love you so much. You are the strongest person I know. The best mam, the best nanna, the best person. I hope you know that.

Samantha. You have walked through Dad's death with me hand in hand, as only a sibling can. I know you will never read ATBK or ATBP because you find them too difficult—because you lived it too—but know that I will always be immeasurably thankful I have you by my side. I can't imagine doing the past two years alone.

To my best friends, you have kept me going and your support has meant everything to me. The T-T-Teessiders, the Coven, my mams group who have become a treasured piece of my life, thank you all for helping me through.

Liz, my superstar agent. Ten years and we are still going strong. You have had my back from day one, and I cannot wait for the next ten years and all the things we have planned. What a journey. I am so lucky to have you in my corner, through the good and bad.

To Christa Heschke, Danielle and Alecia and everyone at McIntosh and Otis, thank you for working tirelessly on my behalf.

Christa Désir, the editor who changed my life. Thank you for everything you have done for me. You took *A Thousand Boy Kisses* and catapulted it to the moon. We have cried together, we have laughed, and you have held me up in the darkest of times. I can't wait for all the future projects we will do. This is just the beginning!

Dom, and all the others who work at Bloom Books, thank you for everything. I am so excited to keep writing books and working with you. You're an incredible team.

A huge thank-you to Rebecca from Penguin UK, Federica, Simona, and Alessandra from Always Publishing, Italy. My other foreign publishing teams—Brazil, Germany, Spanish-speaking territories, and all the other many publishing houses around the world who have taken *A Thousand Boy Kisses* and given it a home. I am truly grateful for you all.

Nina and the team at Valentine PR, thank you for being the most amazing team to work with. I value you more than you know. And a special shout-out to Meagan Reynoso, who has been an angel to me, especially in the hardest of times. Thank you so much.

My readers. Where do I even begin? You are the most loving and loyal group of people I could ever have asked for. You hold me up and keep me going in the times I have doubt. You support me and shout about my books from the rooftops. I love you all so much. You have no idea how much I value and adore you all.

To all of the bookstagrammers, booktokers, and reviewers who help tell the world about my books. You have changed my life. Thank you.

And to the author community. What an uplifting and supportive place to be. Thank you for always cheering me on. I want nothing but the best for you all too.

If I have missed anyone, just know that I am thankful to you too!

Finally, to Dad. You were the *biggest* reason I wrote *A Thousand Boy Kisses*, and you loved watching the journey that Poppy and Rune took. You were *the* reason I wrote *A Thousand Broken Pieces*. Like Savannah and Cael, my heart may have been slowly patched back together, but the scars from your loss will always be there. I will always be sad that you are no longer here. But like Savannah, I know you're up there, in the stars like you always wanted to be. I'll live for you, Dad. I'll keep creating in your name. And I just know you're looking down, so incredibly proud at everything that is happening to us all.

I love you.

We *all* love you.

And we will miss you forever.

Reading Group Guide

1. Both Cael and Savannah have had significant grief-filled experiences that altered their lives. How do Cael and Savannah's traumas differ from each other? How are they the same?

2. Cael has a very different reaction to his grief than Savannah. Why does Cael have a hard time expressing anything other than anger at the beginning of this story?

3. Savannah finally decides to read Poppy's journal in England. How does the beginning of the journal affect her? Why do you think Savannah finally felt ready to read it?

4. Cael and Savannah feel a connection to each other right away. Do you think this has something to do with the people they each lost?

5. Grief is a prominent part of this story. How does this book show the different facets of grief and how it is different for everyone? How do each of the people on the trip help each other through different stages and kinds of grief?

6. Dylan finally opens up to Savannah about his boyfriend, Jose. How do you think this secret has weighed on him after Jose's death? Why was Savannah's response so vital at this moment?

7. Savannah, Cael, and the other kids on this trip are able to experience many cultures. How does each culture they experience

contribute to their healing? How is grief dealt with differently in every culture?

8. What does the Kintsugi lesson in Japan teach Savannah and Cael? Why is this such a beautiful metaphor for the grief that their group has been experiencing?

9. Cael decides to leave Savannah and the trip a day early in order to start his intensive healing. Do you think this was a hard choice for him? Why did he choose to say goodbye to Savannah through a letter instead of in person?

10. Cael honors his brother at his first hockey game for Harvard. How does this show how far he's come? Why is it so meaningful to have Savannah there with him?

About the Author

Tillie Cole hails from a small town in the northeast of England. She grew up on a farm with her English mother, Scottish father, older sister, and a multitude of rescue animals. As soon as she could, Tillie left her rural roots for the bright lights of the big city. After graduating from Newcastle University with a BA Hons in religious studies, Tillie followed her professional rugby player husband around the world for a decade, becoming a teacher in between, and thoroughly enjoyed teaching high school students social studies before putting pen to paper and finishing her first novel.

After several years living in Italy, Canada, and the USA, Tillie has now settled back in her hometown in England with her husband and two children. Tillie is both an independent and traditionally published author and writes many genres, including contemporary romance, dark romance, YA, and NA. When she is not writing, Tillie enjoys nothing more than spending time with her little family, curling up on her couch watching movies, drinking far too much coffee, and convincing herself that she really doesn't need that last square of chocolate.

Follow Tillie Cole
Website: tilliecole.com
Facebook: tilliecoleauthor
Twitter: @tillie_cole
Instagram: @authortilliecole
TikTok: @authortilliecole